His eyes were the end, he'd be never could imag.... Things about him that I still wanted to discover.

"When we're free of this," he whispered. "I'll take you for a ride. Wherever you want." He leaned closer into me. He stopped just short, his mouth close to mine, close enough that I could feel his breath on my lips.

For the longest moment, he hovered there, as if he were testing me.

All I did was move my head forward an inch until my lips touched his. I couldn't help it. I'd missed him, feared him dead. I'd already kissed him before, and it felt natural now.

After my touch, Brandon did the rest.

The Academy

The Scarab Beetle Series

Fake

Book Three

Written by C. L. Stone

Published by

Arcato Publishing

Thank you for purchasing this book. Keep in touch with the author to find out about special releases and upcoming events, including spoilers, author chats and swag.

Website: http://www.clstonebooks.com/

Twitter: http://twitter.com/CLStoneX

Facebook: http://www.facebook.com/clstonex

From The Academy Series

The Ghost Bird Series

Introductions
First Days
Friends vs. Family
Forgiveness and Permission
Drop of Doubt
Push and Shove
House of Korba
The Other Side of Envy (April 2015)

The Scarab Beetle Series

Thief
Liar
Fake
Accessory (Summer 2015)

Other Books By C. L. Stone

Smoking Gun
Spice God

♠

STOLEN

*I*t's been two weeks since I've seen Wil.

I spent time during the days after returning from Florida helping Corey, Brandon and Marc clearing out the inside of a house in downtown Charleston, making it habitable for a family to move in. From dawn until well after dark, I stripped wood and removed tiles to replace it with carpet, and then spent the rest of my days in a blur, doing whatever they told me to do.

At night, I was so tired, I fell into bed.

Staying focused on work was how I didn't feel like a failure of an older sister.

I was now in Corey's room; it had become my retreat.

We'd been waiting for Mr. Blackbourne's team at the school to find my brother, to make contact, so we could start to follow him. He said we should follow him, because if he was involved with Mr. Hendricks, there could be something Wil was involved in and we needed to know what it was before we jumped in.

Word had it though that Wil had been spotted in the hallways by other students. That was good. At least he was still alive.

I rolled over as I forced out my worries, feeling my sore arms tense and strain before I relaxed.

Sometime in the night, a body materialized next to me. When my eyes opened partially, the outline seemed to be

Corey, with his broad shoulders sticking out from under the blanket. How long had he been up at the computer? What was he working on? Lately, he stayed up super late, and often got up before I woke. I'd find him at the computer then, too.

I made room for him at first. But the apartment was freezing; the sheet and thin blanket weren't enough.

When I couldn't stand it anymore, I rolled over close, pressing my front up against his back. He wasn't wearing a shirt. His skin was smooth, warm to the touch. I tried not to be too weird, but I was too out of it and too cold to be overly concerned with personal space.

He turned over, slightly, twisting to talk over his shoulder. "Cold?" The whisper was a little hoarse. I'd woken him.

"Yeah."

He moaned, throaty and deep. He flipped over and wrapped an arm around me, pulling me in until I could curl up tight to his bare chest. My cheek mashed up against his skin, right over his heart, cushioned by his muscles, but I could still feel his heartbeat.

"This going to be enough?" he asked in the same tone. "Or do we need another blanket?"

"Mmm," I said. Body heat would work. I was mildly amused. For a gay guy, he really was adorable and sweet. It was just like a cozy hug.

He didn't respond. His breathing slowed, settling again. I readjusted my face, and my eyelashes swept across his skin as I was staring blankly at nothing at all.

Some of the guilt had already faded, and I welcomed the numbness in the moment. No one complained about me being here. In fact, they all seemed relieved. It was strange to me to feel like I was wanted somewhere.

But now what was I going to do? I couldn't just mooch off of them forever. I couldn't go back to stealing wallets. I needed a real job. I kept telling myself I'd find one as soon as I found Wil, though I'd assumed we'd find Wil sooner than this. Now that it looked like it would take a while, I thought I should perhaps try again.

I tried formulating plans in my head. In the morning I would go here or there and ask about work. If I could earn something, I could pay for my own apartment instead of working for them to earn my keep. It seemed important to do that.

Corey's heavy breathing became my focus. His slow heartbeat thudded against my face.

There was a click from deeper in the apartment. I held my breath, listening. It was pretty late for one of the boys to still be up. I assumed it was Brandon.

He'd kept his space the last two weeks. All the boys had, for which I was grateful and also sorry for.

I listened as close as I could, but over my breathing and Corey's heartbeat, it became hard to focus and I started to drift back asleep again.

Until a sudden jolt woke me right up.

I'd once stuck my fingers into the back of an open stereo while it was still plugged into the wall. The shock of it had left my fingertip blackened for a year, I'd been timid around electrical devices for a long time after.

This was a hundred times worse. Wide awake, feeling every volt coursing through me, at the same time unable to move and unsure what had happened. My brain had a disconnect. My body went completely rigid.

When it was over, my only goal was trying to get my lungs to work.

"Kay--" A husky voice next to me, Corey, gasping.

My eyes opened and I was blinded by a bright white light.

And then everything went dark. A cloth fell over my face and my breathing problems from a second ago were nothing compared to this suffocation. The cloth sucked into my mouth at every attempt to breathe in, blocking out the air until all I could do was gasp and hope it was enough to keep me conscious.

A body landed on top of me. I fought, kicking. My first thought, was that this was Raven and I was going to kick his ass. I tried to curse, even though my voice and mouth weren't working after the shock and the lack of air.

I wanted to kill him.

My next thought was this was Blake Coaltar coming to get me. I'd wrecked his yacht and shot him in the leg and then wrecked his car. I guess I may have deserved it, but I would still kill him anyway.

But the bodies on top of me said absolutely nothing. There was no clue as to who this was.

I flailed, but I was weak, trying to fight off whoever it was but my body didn't want to cooperate. I was crushed and held down, helpless. My arms were tied together. My legs were tied, too. From the grunting and shifting beside me, it sounded like Corey was going through the same thing.

Tied and blinded, I was lifted. I didn't stop wriggling, though. My voice box barely managed to work; I got moans out, but being able to scream was beyond my capacity. Air was in short supply

I felt like I was being carried by someone resembling a Mack truck by the sheer size. At first, I was carried like a baby, but after my several attempts to wriggle away and claw at whatever I could, I got thrown over a shoulder. Blood rushed to my head. I was dizzy, disoriented, short of breath. The shock made it harder to fully function and I worried about passing out.

There was an elevator ride and then I was carried through the lobby, their footsteps echoing off the tile, and then we were out in the fresh air, from as much as I could tell since I had the hood on.

"Kayli," Corey's voice swept to me, weaker.

"Ugh," I cried out, which was about as much as I could muster with my gut getting a shoulder stuffed into it.

There was a thud. Corey groaned. I choked. Did they hit him? I'd kill them. Just wait until I had a hand free.

If only I could breathe. With the cloth over my face, I couldn't get enough air to gain much energy to even wiggle much. I tried scratching it off, but it was stuck to my neck somehow. In my panic, I couldn't find the way to get it to release.

Where was that stupid security guard?

I flopped over Mack Truck's shoulder. I clawed at his back, kneed him where I could, but he had a pretty good grip around my torso and thighs.

I only had a few moments before they dumped us into a river, or whatever they were doing.

So I did the most instinctive thing I could think to do. I reached down, pretending to pound at him where I could, striking at his back and butt with my tied arms. Still, my fingers were free.

I felt around for his wallet. His left pocket, from the feel when I slapped at it, was a packet of cigarettes and a lighter. The other one had something harder, square. In the dark, I couldn't tell what, but another pounding against his body and I had it in my hands. Not a wallet, but a cell phone.

I was hoisted for a moment and then landed in what felt like a trunk. There was utility carpet lined with plastic bags at the bottom.

Oh shit, someone was going to kill us. I'd seen far too many movies to know how a tied and bagged girl in the back of a car ended up. No matter what happens now, we had to get out before we got to the second location. I'd probably be the river, or the ocean... a place to kill us and dump us over.

Another body landed on top of me, forcing out what little air was in my lungs. I was on my stomach, face-planted against the floor.

The trunk door was slammed shut on my feet that had been sticking up, pushing them in at an odd angle.

"Kayli," Corey said.

"That *really* sucked."

"Don't worry," he said. "I'm going to get us out of here."

"Who are these guys?" I asked.

"I don't know," he said, "but if they ask us anything, let me do the talking."

No problem.

Corey struggled next to me. I think he was trying to

untie himself. I did the same, only my bonds were slick, and I couldn't wedge a finger between the material. I tried helping him with his, but my hands were losing feeling quickly at the odd angle. His arms were tied behind his back.

"Hang on, let me take this hood off," I said.

"With what?" he asked.

I pinched at the material, clawing. When I finally wedged a finger between the material and the hood, clawing at the edge, I managed to wedge it off my face, scraping my chin in the process.

At first, I took a moment to breathe. Even with the hood off, it was still smothering hot. I reached for Corey's mask. I nearly choked him trying to pry it off, but managed.

Corey coughed hard. He swallowed. "What's this thing?" he asked.

I felt around for what he was talking about, and found the cell phone. "Came from the guy carrying me."

He chuckled until he coughed and then said, "Kayli, you are one in a million." He shifted around. "Hang on to that thing. Give me some room."

"What are you doing?"

"I'm getting us out of here," he said. He angled himself against the back end of the car and then kicked the trunk door as hard as he could.

"When I get this open," he said, panting as he kicked, "you're going to roll out."

"What? You're crazy. I'll die."

"Don't ask me questions. Just do it."

"What about you?"

7

"I'll be right behind you," he said.

He kicked several times. I didn't think he could do it. Didn't they hear us?

He slammed both feet against the hood and suddenly it popped open.

He caught it with his feet just before it flew up too high. "Help me," he said. "Hold it down but don't close it."

I shifted over, helping him by holding the door almost closed with my feet, nearly pinching my ankle and foot to keep it down. I edged myself close to it, trying to prepare myself. "What are we doing?"

He continued to kick at the side of the trunk, just lower down. "When the car slows down enough, leap out and roll. Take the phone with you."

"What about you?"

"I'll wait until you're out, then I'll let them go for a mile or so and jump out, too. I'm kicking still in case they can hear it so they think we're still trying to get out. I want space between us jumping out."

This sounded more like he was going to let me escape and then still risk the chance they'd figure it out. "But..."

Before I could get out a word, the car slowed, and then started to turn.

Corey shoved himself at me. "Go!" He shouted at me.

I moved myself over, and before I could think, Corey shoved me with his feet.

My butt smacked down first. The rest of me followed, with my cheek scraping against the asphalt.

I shook my head, rolled over, looking after the car.

Sad eyes stared back at me from the open trunk.

Brandon.

I may as well have been struck by lightning. It was strange thinking the whole time I'd been with Corey.

I waited, watching. I held the cell phone I'd stolen between my palms. I wondered if it was broken from my jump. I didn't move, though, and didn't bother to hide yet. All I could do was watch Brandon as he stared after me from the car.

Jump, I thought. *Jump, please.* Don't get killed. Don't leave me alone here!

His eyes stayed on me, but he never moved once. He wasn't going to. He'd lied, and I didn't know why.

Before he had a chance, the car turned again, driving into a warehouse.

The heavy-duty garage door closed, trapping him. In the second location.

♠

THE CRIME
AND THE CRIMINALS

Being taken in the middle of the night, I could handle. Jumping from a moving car with my hands tied behind my back, no problem. Having my friend carted off to where he might get shot or worse, and I was really pissed.

I sat upright. My arms and elbows were scraped raw and my butt was sore. The shirt and boxers I wore were soaked from the damp concrete. My hair was in my face and I did my best to pull it away from my eyes. The air was moist, cool and thick, and I found it hard to catch my breath. Chilled, I let the dizzy feeling wash away as I sat for a moment, considering my options. I still held onto the phone. I needed to get to Brandon and see what I could do about freeing him, too. I needed to get away from the road before they came back to look for me.

I couldn't run for it tied like I was. I put the phone down and inspected the bonds at my feet. A knot bound me and I dug my fingernails in to loosen it. I kept looking up at the garage the car had disappeared into, trying to determine how much time I had before they discovered I wasn't in the car.

I was able to loosen the knot enough that I could wedge one foot free. With the rest still tied to my leg, I could still run, which was good enough for now. My hands could wait. I scooped up the cell phone, hopped up and headed to the shadows and toward the garage.

My heart stayed in my throat, pounding. I was

focused, acutely aware of sounds and movements. The breeze that picked up around me cooled my wet clothes and I shook so hard from the chill until my bones hurt. I took to grass and walked around the building, looking for an alternate entrance: a window, or anything where I could look in on what was going on.

I found a window not too far from the front garage door. I checked it slowly, peeking through it. Nothing, just an inside office and it was dark.

I circled around the back, finding more windows. They were higher on this side, and I stood on a concrete brick to look in.

The car was parked in the warehouse close to the now closed garage door. Men hovered over the open trunk.

Two of them, one particularly big in size, carried Brandon out. His legs and hands were still bound. They lifted him, bucking and hollering, which they ignored.

I caught the echo of one of them yelling back at Brandon, but the echo and everyone talking at once made it impossible to hear what anyone was saying.

The one I thought was like a Mack Truck hoisted Brandon up and carried him. I counted the people. There were four in total that I could see. It looked like there might still be one the car and I considered there might be others around in this warehouse.

They took Brandon to a ratty sofa that was on top of a wooden pallet. Mack Truck dropped him hard down on the cushions. Before Brandon could sit up, the whole place lit up with a bright white light aimed directly at Brandon, and beyond to the window.

I was blinded, the brightness burning my retinas. I could almost feel the heat from the lamps even through the window. I closed my eyes against the onslaught and then turned my head, trying to look anywhere else but directly at it. Everything else I saw was shadows, such as the outline of Brandon on the couch.

"Corey Henshaw," someone said from beyond the lights.

They thought he was Corey! I wasn't sure if that was good or bad. I tilted forward, the brick I was on teetering but I corrected my balance and focused. I kept the phone in my hands, ready to use it as a weapon, or possibly to call for the police if I needed to. I thought about calling for them now, but I didn't want to if they had guns pointed at Brandon, and I couldn't see at this point what they were holding.

I wanted to call Marc and the others, but I didn't know their individual numbers by heart. I couldn't think of who else to call.

"What do you want?" Brandon asked, keeping his head turned away.

My heart rocked against my ribs. If he was going to let them think he was Corey, if they somehow found out it wasn't true, they might kill him and then try to go after the real Corey.

"Where's your girlfriend?" one of the men asked.

Brandon shrugged. "Don't know who you're talking about. I don't have a girlfriend."

Fingers snapped somewhere beyond the bright white light. "She's probably not far. Take the car and retrace the route. See where she ended up."

"Did you want her or me?" Brandon asked. "Leave her alone and get to what you wanted."

Car doors slammed and the car started as the garage door rolled up. I caught the movement as the car inched backward. With the bright light on, it was hard to tell who left and who didn't. I was tempted to move to get a different angle, but I didn't want to miss anything and I didn't see other windows.

"Sorry it had to come to this," the accented voice said.

Was it familiar? I tried to think but couldn't place the voice. The accent was making me think I'd heard it before. "You're the only one who can help us."

"You've got a funny way of asking for help."

"We tried being nice about this," the voice said. "We asked you to come work for us."

I sucked in a breath. Some guy who spoke German had jumped from his car when I was on a walk with Corey, wanting to hire him. I was pretty sure this was the same person. Had it been the same car? In the heat of the moment, I didn't recognize it, but now I tried to recall the shape, the color.

Brandon turned his head, facing the voice. "You've got my attention now."

"We need your expertise. We've got a problem with a particular bit of code."

"That's it?" Brandon asked. "You've got a computer problem? Try tech support next time. There's usually an eight-hundred number."

"See, you're not even listening," the voice said. "Need I remind you of where you are, and that we'll have your girlfriend again, soon."

"Still don't know who you're talking about."

"Then I guess after I catch her, I can just shoot her. No need for her running to the police about this."

He wasn't going to convince them I was a nobody he was next to in bed. Not after Corey pretty much said I was his girlfriend the first time the German had approached him. Brandon shook his head. "You don't want her in the middle of this. Trust me. She's a handful."

I had to smile. I was almost proud of that.

"Enough," the German said. "You do understand my meaning."

"I'm not working with anyone I don't know," Brandon said. "Tell me who you are."

"Oh no, Mr. Henshaw. You had your chance to play fairly. Now you have to do it our way."

"Why don't you get to the point?"

I surveyed the situation. I evaluated my chances of taking on who was left or sneaking in somehow to help him. Bright lights were useful for intimidation, a scare tactic; I'd learned that much from watching too much television.

Clever, careful. That was a problem—these guys were smart. The warehouse otherwise appeared empty. If they needed a computer fixed or a code looked at, they picked a really crappy place. Either they had a laptop with them, or their equipment wasn't here, which meant this was a temporary holding place and Brandon would be moved to their headquarters. I hoped they'd stay. I didn't know where I was, but I was sure if I could find Corey's real number somehow, I'd be able to get him to track my location and get them to help. The only problem was, I didn't know his number, or anyone else's.

"We need Murdock's Core," the German said.

"Are you insane?" Brandon asked. "That's impossible."

"Since when was anything impossible for DepthCrawler? That was your signature, wasn't it? You should be able to get it, you wrote the Guard Dog security packet they utilize to keep people out. Don't you remember?"

Now they were talking over my level. What core? I could only guess it was something valuable. Maybe access to credit card information?

"Why don't you ask the guy who owns the core if you need access so bad," Brandon said. "That'd be the easiest."

"Because he died, Mr. Henshaw, or else we wouldn't be having this discussion."

"That's too bad," Brandon said. "Guess you're out of luck."

"No," the German said. "There's still you."

"I'm telling you, I can't get you access to the core. I'd need access to the building, and they're not going to let me near the place long enough to fiddle with their server. Hacking it from elsewhere would be near impossible and could take years if I'm the only one working at it. And if I could access it, what would stop me from using it? Or selling it to someone else?"

A figure stepped forward, his shadow harsh against the onslaught of light. It was the German, from the shape of him.

"You're going to figure out the key and deliver long distance to the core to me, so I can use it whenever I wish. You're going to break down the security and find a way. You can break through your own security protocols, can't you?"

"Why me?" Brandon asked. "There's a bunch of hackers who would love to give this a try."

"We're asking you," the German said, "because we're sure you can do it again."

Brandon turned his head. I could almost feel his teeth grinding and his jaw clenching from the strain on his face.

I didn't totally understand what was going on. What kind of hacking was Corey roped up in? Is that what he does?

How did these Germans find out?

"And if I do this, you'll leave us alone?" Brandon asked.

"We'll even give you a percentage."

"I don't want it," Brandon said quickly.

The German shrugged and I got hit by a beam of light as he moved. I was going to go blind tonight.

"If you say so. If you don't do what we ask, we've got

you, and we'll find your girlfriend and will make sure neither of you get back home. We're really good at that."

The car returned. A voice spoke, even though a car door didn't open. "She's not in the street from here until the Mark Clark. Either she's dead from flying off the bride on the way here because she jumped early, or she's already hitched a ride and is on her way back. Or maybe she called the police. It'll take more than two of us to find her.

"Don't worry about her. You can't use her to get to me. It won't work. This whole thing is pointless," Brandon said, his voice rising. "How am I supposed to get anywhere close to the core?"

"We emailed you before. You should know. Or did you trash it without reading it? You really should pay attention to your email," the German said.

"What do you want me to do? Sneeze on the fucking thing?" Brandon yelled at him. "I've got my hands tied, and the moment they're free, I'll be swinging. Because that's about as much as I'll do for you."

"You do realize we could kill you," the guy said.

"Don't give a shit," Brandon said. "Supposedly you need me for the core, so you're not going to kill me while I can still be useful. And I know your face and could track you down after, which means you'll more than likely kill me after I do the job anyway. So I do the job, get you what you want, and then die, or I die early without you getting what you want. Seems like I'll go with both of us not getting what we want."

"We'll find her. We could do a lot of things to her."

"I doubt it. You don't know her. She's a million miles from here by now. She knows better and doesn't give a shit about me to stick around. You won't get close to her again."

I gulped at the irony, considering I was watching the

scene from only a few feet away.

"Don't worry," the German said. "We found her once. She'll call the police and we'll find her again. She'll call your pals, and we'll find her. Any way you look at it, we'll have her soon, so you may as well assume we've already got her."

Calling the police means they've got me?

"I'm not helping you," Brandon said. "You don't have shit. And your job is impossible. Just walk away now before anyone gets hurt. Untie me."

"Thought you were smarter than that," the German said. He turned to his pals. "Let's move, gentlemen. If that girl finds his brother, it won't be long before they get here with help. She's probably on her way to that apartment. We'll get someone in the lobby to keep an eye on those friends. Maybe we'll find his brother, too." His shape against the light loomed closer to Brandon. "Think that will be enough leverage?"

Brandon struggled against his bindings, yelling and cursing. I felt the wave of his anger even from the distance.

The lights suddenly went out. The darkness swallowed them up. My eyes strained to adjust.

When they did, Brandon was gone from the couch, I could hear him yelling and fighting. They dropped him to the ground and then there was a spark from a Taser. Brandon went rigid, helpless.

They picked him up again and shoved him into the back seat of the car. No chance to jump now.

I looked for an opening, but in the shadows, I knew there were too many of them for me to fight. I had tied hands and a cell phone with no one to call. My anger made me want to shout and make them eat the cell phone and save Brandon, but I knew that I couldn't take on four of them with Brandon down for the moment. I had no backup coming.

They piled into the car. I couldn't leave Brandon. I ran as hard as I could to the street. The adrenaline running through my veins made me feel like I could outrun them, keep up and follow them to the next location.

How long would it take for them to figure out he wasn't Corey?

Brandon wasn't about to let them know they'd made a mistake. He was saving Corey from this, just like he'd saved me. Sacrificing himself. Giving me enough time to call the police after him and those goons before they came after Corey, or me.

I couldn't let that happen. They seemed to be in with the police somehow, since they said calling them would lead them to me. Was one of them a cop?

The car turned off the road before I could get too close. I caught the plate number, the make; it was similar to the German's car before. It turned, and was gone down the street within seconds.

I was alone. For a moment, I dazed out. I couldn't believe it. I'd been running without thinking, just to keep up with what was going on. But now it weighed on me so much that I sunk down to my knees, ignoring the pain as the asphalt ripped my flesh. My butt was still sore, my skin scraped. None of it mattered, but I still felt every little cut and bruise. They were throbbing reminders of what had just happened.

Brandon. My heart ached so much. He'd made sure I'd escaped. He should have jumped with me. He should have jumped first. We could have made it.

Why didn't I hear them coming?

How was I going to find him?

♠

INTRODUCING
THE MAGICIAN

Panic filled in my heart, threatening to take over. Instinct told me to steal a car and go after them.

But my hands were still bound, and I wasn't sure where I'd find a car in this broken-down district. Still, I needed to act fast if I was going to help myself or Brandon. Rage bubbled inside me, but I smothered it as best as I could to focus and try to formulate a plan.

I touched the cell phone, holding it close to my chest. I was tempted to try and call their bluff about the police. I could tell them the make, the plate, and say they were swerving all over the road, and get them picked up by the cops. The cops would find Brandon in the trunk. The only problem was, even if they were bluffing, if I called the police and they swarmed the area, these bad guys might take it out on Brandon before the police got to him.

Right now, I had a slight advantage. It wasn't much of one, considering I was still tied up and lost. Being where they didn't expect, though, maybe was enough. I knew it was the German, and I knew a bit about their plans. Whatever Murdock's Core was, Corey would know about it, and then we could find them. Somehow.

I waited by the street for a while, trying to figure out my next move and working to undo the knot on my wrists.

But as I struggled, I couldn't twist my hands around far enough and needed both hands to undo the knot. I knelt on the grass and twisted the bindings on my ankles until I could get them off, keeping the rope. I didn't have a weapon, so hanging on to anything I could seemed like a good idea.

I stepped up to the open garage doorway. From what I could tell, besides the lamps and the couch, which looked like it'd been picked up by the side of the road, the whole place was empty. Maybe it wasn't even theirs. I was surprised the electricity still worked, until I circled the inside of the place and nearly tripped over the generator behind the couch.

A cop could probably try to trace the generator and the lights, but I suspected they'd turn up stolen or untraceable. I would cover my tracks, if I were a kidnapper and had planned this. There was nothing here to go on. Fingerprints, maybe, but if they had a cop on their team... And it would take time to search a database. I wasn't sure how much time I had.

I padded back outside. The road was clear. The other buildings surrounding it looked dilapidated. I checked my phone, three in the morning.

I couldn't read anything else on the phone other than numbers. It was all in what I assumed was German.

I had a limited amount of time before Mack Truck figured out I had his phone and found a way to trace it back. If Corey could do it, I knew these guys could.

I jogged to the end of the street, checking the signs. I didn't recognize either of the streets I was on. There was no way to tell how close I was to anything remotely populated. This abandoned warehouse district was probably crawling with hobos.

I checked the phone again, staring at it, then thought of the settings. I found the language, and changed it to English.

The phone wouldn't translate the text messages, but I at least could use the GPS and internet to get a location.

And I stared in horror when it told me I was smack in the middle of a very abandoned, very dangerous part of North Charleston.

I stopped walking, checking out the neighborhood. North Charleston wasn't a place to mess around. One wrong move and I wouldn't have to worry about the German anymore. The locals—gang members or hobos—would be happy to murder me.

I hurried along the street, sticking to the shadows. I wouldn't stand a chance with even a drunk old man right now with my arms tied together. I needed to keep walking.

I watched behind me as I picked a direction and started out. I couldn't spot anyone tailing me, but I didn't know the area and I didn't want to risk it in case the German left one of his pals nearby just in case.

I needed a place to go that was safe. I used the phone as I walked and checked the GPS and surrounding areas. I searched for a Wal-Mart, a 24-hour gas station, anything that would be better than the street and abandoned buildings.

I picked a direction that seemed likely to run into something open. While I was walking, I tried to figure out how to contact the boys. I was miles from the Sergeant Jasper and the German was ahead of me. If he got his goons to watch the building, I'd get kidnapped again. I needed help. Outside help.

As soon as I was at a building that I could identify, I called for a cab.

Cab companies are one of the best non-official security teams you will ever have on your side. Ever worry about someone following you late at night? Call a cab. They not only show up right on time, but they're usually faster and the drivers are fearless.

I didn't have any money, but I hoped the driver would be sympathetic to my cause. I'd need whoever it was to fetch Marc for me. If the German was watching the building, I couldn't go inside. But if the cab driver wanted to get paid, he would have to take a short walk upstairs.

Waiting was hard. I bounced from foot to foot to keep warm. The chill was getting to me now that the shock was wearing off. I forced back thoughts of Brandon, telling myself he was fine right now. From the sound of it, they needed to get into some building for him to access whatever it was they needed him to do. They needed him, and as long as they thought he was Corey, he was safe. Hopefully he kept his attitude in check long enough that they didn't shoot him before we got to him. I just needed to hurry. These Academy guys were like the CIA: smart, efficient and all that spy stuff. They'd tracked me down with a math formula. Corey could find the German. I just needed to find *them*.

My feet became sore the longer I scraped my bare feet against the concrete. Wearing nothing but the boxers Corey let me borrow for going to bed, along with a thin T-shirt, I knew I'd appear to be a mess for a cab.

Down the road, a cab turned onto the empty road and headed my way. I was surprised to find the vehicle was nothing more than an old red town car with a sign on top like a pizza delivery vehicle, except this had the cab company's phone number. Apparently I called the cut-rate cabs. Really, it was a red boat of a car. I couldn't believe it still moved.

The driver leaned out the open window. He had a wide face with a thin line of dark hair along the jaw and chin trimmed into a stylish beard. He was young, my age or somewhere close. He had dark eyes, a short crop of brown hair. I could peer into the window opening. He was a little on the lean side, and from around a Hawaiian shirt and tank underneath that, there was a tattoo peeking out at the chest. It took me a moment to identify it was *I Am*

What I Am in a fancy font. His wide eyes stared at me, blank, most likely stoned. Still, had to respect a man that respected Popeye.

"You pick up?" he asked.

I nodded, and felt like an idiot opening my own door. I had to put the phone in my mouth to do it. Was he new to town? Didn't he know he had to open doors for girls? But then he was a cab driver and I was a barefoot girl in an abandoned warehouse district out in the middle of nowhere. He probably thought I was high or a hooker. He probably didn't want an ambush.

Plus, I had bound hands. That probably didn't do much to impress him.

I fell into the back seat, feeling my bones switch from vibrate to sudden stop since I'd been on edge for so long. I breathed in the musty old car and coughed.

The guy twisted around, looking back at me. He did a visual sweep. "What's wrong with your wrists?"

"Tied up," I said. "I was kidnapped. I escaped."

His eyes widened more. "No shit?" He shook his head. "You okay?"

"Fine. Just don't want to stick around."

He checked the outside of the car, leaning over, suddenly alert. "Are they still here? Let's get going." He started turning the car around.

He seemed to be handling it pretty well. Most people would have called the cops right off. Good thing about a stoned driver, he didn't want to call the cops, either. It wouldn't look good to the taxi company if he got arrested for driving while stoned. "Do you have a knife or something?" I asked.

He stared quietly for a moment, like the question didn't register with him. Then he leaned forward and presented his bare palm. I was confused, until he flicked his hand and suddenly there was a pocket knife there. "Like this?"

A magic trick. I appreciated the gesture, maybe he meant it as a way to cheer me up. I could appreciate a magician with talented sleight of hand tricks. As a thief, I understood the work and practice it took to achieve the skill. "Open it up for me?" I wasn't sure I would be able to open it without cutting myself.

He braked and stopped the car in the middle of the street long enough that he could open the knife. There was no one around to block traffic, anyway. He turned and offered it, but then stopped. "Uh, want me to do it?"

I held out my wrists. "Sure. Hurry up. It's cutting off circulation."

"Who kidnapped you?" he asked.

"Long story."

"This one of those trafficking things?" he asked. "That's fucked up." He sawed at the bindings. He managed to snap two and that was enough that I could unwind the rest. He pulled back. "Did you need to go somewhere? The hospital? Isn't that where people go when they've been kidnapped?"

I rubbed at my wrists, working out the deep creases in my skin. It felt so good to have the rope off. I hurried and turned off Mack Truck's cell phone. I didn't want it tracing me back now that I was on the way to find the guys. "No, actually, can you drive over to the Sergeant Jasper?"

"The apartment building?"

"Is there another one?" I asked.

"There's another one?" Through the rearview, I caught the slight slope of his mouth as he grinned. He was toying with me. He caught himself. "Sorry. Long night. Uh... sorry."

"It's fine," I said, trying not to be too annoyed at his joke, considering it was a very awkward situation. "We need to hurry, though."

"Why?"

"I want to catch the guys that did this."

"Are they at that apartment building? Shouldn't we make an anonymous call to the police or something?"

I leaned forward, putting a hand on his shoulder. He turned his head but kept his eyes on the road as he drove. "Listen," I said. "I don't need the cops on this right now. Don't say anything."

"Dude," he said. "This is big shit."

"They have a friend of mine," I said.

"Where?"

"I don't know. They took him. They'll kill him if I call the cops, I think. But if I get to my friends, they'll be able to find him."

"Him? They're stealing boys, too, now?"

"Can you just drive, please? You don't have to get involved."

"Don't worry. We're on the way." He pointed to street signs. "We'll be there in a few. We'll stop these traffickers. I've heard of them on the news. Maybe we should be calling the FBI. Isn't that their job?"

I clamped my mouth shut, trying to bite back the edge in my voice. I shouldn't snap at him. He was the one helping.

But I considered the FBI option. Wouldn't the FBI call in the local police and defeat the purpose? If a policeman was involved, would the FBI keep things on the down low? It was a risk. I needed Marc or someone else to help me figure out what to do.

He set out on the road. For a while he was quiet, but he kept looking at me in the back. About the fifth time he diverted his eyes when I caught him staring, I'd finally had enough.

"What?" I snapped. I really wasn't in the mood.

"What's your name?" he asked.

"Mary," I said, dropping the lie off so quickly, I even surprised myself. Why did he need to know?

"Oh," he said. "Sorry. You just look like this girl I knew once."

"Who?"

"Kayli," he said. "Girl I went to high school with."

My mouth opened and I found myself staring hard back at him now, checking the outline. I didn't recognize him at all. "She wasn't a close friend, was she?" He had to be mistaken. Maybe this was a coincidence.

"I sat behind her in math class two years straight. Never noticed me, though."

I was barely awake in math class. I hardly remembered anyone from school. I couldn't even tell you my teachers' names. "That was a few years ago, wasn't it?"

He lifted his eyes, checking me out in the rearview mirror. "She was real cute. Had this button nose, like yours."

Without thought, I moved my hand over my face, covering my nose. It looked like a button?

He squinted at me, and then slightly turned like he wanted to look at me full on instead of through the mirror but didn't want to take his eyes off the road. "Are you sure you're..."

"What's your name?" I asked.

"Avery," he said. He took his right hand off the steering wheel and held it out, offering a sideways handshake.

I took his hand and studied him, but I still didn't recognize him. It struck me funny that anyone would remember me, and not just as that girl that slept through math class. Avery knew my name, even these few years since I'd been out of school. Guilt weighed on me since I'd lied when he'd been so compliant and nailed who I really was. At first, I wasn't going to admit to anything, but something changed inside me. Maybe I was tired and weak after the night and needed some stability in a truth rather than lies. "I lied," I said, squeezing his hand. "I'm Kayli."

"I thought it was you," he said, the sloped smile returning to his face. "I was pretty sure. Took me a few minutes, though. It's been a while." He released my hand and reclaimed the wheel. "Whatever happened to you, anyway? Didn't see you around after that."

"Got my GED and quit."

"Funny. So you got out at sixteen or so? I was a year and a half behind you there." He slapped his palm against the wheel. "They always told us to go to college or you'll end up working hard jobs. No one ever tells you the hard jobs aren't so bad."

"You like driving a cab?"

"Are you kidding?" he asked. "I know this town better than most people, and work when I want. I could work anywhere, really. I meet interesting people. All I have to do is drive."

I had to smile at that. It left a little hope for me. Maybe after I got Brandon back, I could drive a cab. It sounded interesting.

I was going to comment, but then I noticed through the windshield when the Sergeant Jasper came into view. I didn't have time to reminisce any more. "Okay, I need to ask you a real favor, Avery."

"Sure," he said. "What's that?"

"Park outside the building, and I need you to go in and get someone for me."

27

"Who?"

"Anyone in apartment 737."

He turned on the road that would get us to the parking lot. "Isn't there a security guard?"

"She won't even notice. Just smile and walk to the elevator like you belong there. Anyway, go up to 737, and then whoever answers, tell them Bambi is outside."

"What?"

"They'll know who it is. If they don't believe you, tell them the first time I ever met them, Marc was working at the pretzel stand."

Avery scratched at his scalp through his thick dark hair. "Geez. A lot to remember."

"Can you do it?"

"Yeah, I can do it." He pulled up to the curb in front of the building and parked, leaving the car running.

I slid down, not wanting to be spotted in case the place was being watched. "I'll wait here."

"Hang on," he said. "I don't like you out here alone. You got kidnapped once already."

"Where's your knife?"

He pulled it out of his pocket and passed it off. I took it, testing how it opened.

He scanned the parking lot. "I still don't like it."

"Just hurry. If anyone can help, those guys upstairs can. Get them and then we need to get away from here."

"So we have to kidnap one of them because someone stole you? Should probably call the police," he said. "Or the FBI." He opened his door. From my angle on the floor, I caught his angled chin and what I thought was a sharpness in his eyes. He was sober now, and on the alert. His lean body was hard, too. He looked like a slacker, but underneath that stoner exterior was a hardworking guy. "Leaving my keys. Drive off if you have to." He made sure to lock the doors and left.

My heart soared for a minute as he closed the door. Avery was awesome. Why didn't I pay attention to him in high school? I picked up my head to watch him walk into the building. He was wearing cargo shorts and a loose-fitting Hawaiian shirt, partially open. I tried to imagine him at fifteen or so, about the age I would have been in tenth grade. Maybe he had grown taller. Or I didn't recognize him with the beard on his chin.

I shrugged it off. If a guy didn't plant himself in front of me, I usually didn't notice him. That was probably my problem in high school. I never noticed the quiet ones. To be honest, I barely remembered names and faces from any of my classes. I could probably pass by a teacher on the street and not recognize him.

I counted off minutes, hoping someone was home. Please, please, someone. Brandon was out there all tied up. He'd gotten zapped again. Would they keep doing that? Would they beat him up? Use torture?

Brandon said he'd die before helping them. I was worried he might be enough of an idiot to do just that before I had a chance to get to him.

The moment of quiet waiting was hard. With Avery there, I had things to distract me that were immediate. Now all I could see was Brandon's face as he'd pleaded with me to escape. Emotions welled up, and my throat thickened as I held back tears. Every blink, all I saw was his sad blue eyes. Brandon saved me, and lied and stayed with the German to give me time to escape.

Stupid Brandon. If he ended up dead, I'd never forgive myself for not staying with him.

The sky was cloudy, with the moon playing peekaboo between clouds. The streets were quiet, the streetlamps lit up, and casting yellow light, letting me see shadows in the car. On other nights, I might have felt safe being back at the Sergeant Jasper. Tonight, it was uncomfortable. Who knew who was watching? I sniffed, wiping at my face to make sure the tears were gone. I could suffer and feel guilty later. Focus was what I needed now. Save Brandon. Find him and save him.

Voices outside startled me. I popped my head up, checking to make sure they weren't here to kidnap me again. I had the knife ready. I clutched the cell phone.

The sound of a key in the lock made me hesitate. The door opened and Marc filled the space, staring in after me. His dark hair was messed up, like he'd just rolled out of bed. He had on a black tank shirt and jeans. His mismatched eyes, one blue, one green, stared hard, like he needed a good look before he believed it was me. At first he appeared confused, with his eyebrows scrunched. That morphed into recognizing me and then a barrel of silent questions spilled out between us. I imagined he was trying to figure out what I was up to, like I'd planned this.

God, he was beautiful.

I finally thought I'd be okay, which was something I hadn't been sure about until that moment. Marc would know what to do. We could save Brandon.

He leaned back, looking at Avery behind him. "You gave her a knife?" he asked.

"Marc!" I cried out, jumping into action. I closed the knife and dropped it into the driver's seat and then grabbed his arm, tugging. "Get in. Hurry."

"What?"

"Come on, get in! We have to go. We can't stay here."

Marc's mouth hung open, his eyes sweeping over me. He reached out and traced a finger across my chin, causing pain from a scrape I'd forgotten about. "What happened to you?"

Avery hurried around the car, opening his door. He grabbed his knife, put it into his pocket, and then sat down. "Dude, she said we have to go."

Marc twisted his lips and got in, slamming the door closed. He turned his body, and his shoulders rounded out and it was like he filled the whole space. His hard stare made me feel safe and I feared his anger at the same time, even if that anger wasn't directed at me. I sensed he was fully aware there was danger and he didn't like not knowing. I'd seen that look on him before, when he'd discovered a bruise on my face and had then proclaimed he'd save me from ever getting hurt by my father again. As he spoke now, his voice rose in volume, and deepened at the end of every comment. "Are you in boxers? Where's your shoes? Are you drunk? What the hell is going on?"

"Avery," I said. I leaned over and nudged his shoulder. "Drive off. Anywhere. Circle the city."

"Bambi," Marc snapped. He snagged my arm that had reached for Avery and held it in a firm grip. "Talk to me. Don't just tell him to drive without thinking. What's going on? Someone's chasing you?"

Avery took off from the curb. "It's like I was trying to tell you on the way down. She was kidnapped, man. They kidnapped the other dude. They might be coming back for her. So we had to kidnap you. It's complicated."

Marc's eyebrows squished together, causing a wrinkle between them. "Back up a minute. What? Who do they have?"

I began explaining, starting from when I was asleep and Brandon and I were attacked, all the way to where they disappeared down the road with Brandon in the back seat. "But they still think he's Corey."

"Holy shit," Marc said, his mouth slack for a moment. Then his entire composure changed. "Adrien," he barked.

"Avery," Avery barked back.

"Sorry. Avery. Drive to..." Marc took out his cell phone. He started typing into it. "You know the fountain downtown?"

"The pineapple? Who doesn't?"

"Head there."

"If you say so."

Marc typed at his cell phone. He looked up at me, his mismatched eyes darkened, studying me. His hand went out, touching my chin.

His touch stung as he brushed his finger along the scrape. I pulled back, smacking his hand. "Don't worry about me. We have to go get Brandon."

"Do you need a doctor? Anything else hurt?"

I felt scraped everywhere, and bruises, and I was sure to be sore later. It didn't matter to me right now. I'd take some Tylenol later and call it a day. Brandon first. "I said don't worry about me. Brandon might get killed. They're after this...core thing. They called it Murdock's Core. They wanted Corey to get access to it. They'll probably kill him or use him to get Corey to do what they want if they find out he's not the real Corey. We've got to get him away before they find out they've got the wrong one."

"On it," he said, showing me his phone. He'd sent a text to Axel. The texts were innocent enough. *Let's all eat pineapple salad. Bring enough for a girl who loves to eat. She needs new summer clothes, too. We should take her shopping.*

I'm guessing this was code for meeting at the pineapple and that I needed clothes. I was wondering why he was using code at all. Did he suspect these guys were listening in?

"What supplies? What can we do? Can you find what this guy wants? This core? If we can get Corey to get them access to it..."

"We need to evaluate these guys and see just how dangerous they are."

"I know, but maybe we can make a trade and then..."

Marc brushed a fingertip along his eyebrow. "They said the owner of the core was dead. It could be they killed him. If that's the case, we're going to have to be careful. This isn't like we give them what they want and expect them to behave. And we don't know if what they want is going to lead to more deaths, or worse."

The German didn't specify why he wanted this core. I still didn't even know what it was. I imagined it was some sort of hacker thing that made money or was valuable and they could sell it. I mean, why go through the trouble without it being worth a lot of money? Still, it seemed like they went through a lot of trouble to get to us when there had to be easier ways of getting what they wanted. Brandon said they could get hackers to get what they want. But the German wanted Corey specifically. I wondered why.

"If they are willing to threaten lives to get it," I said, "then they want it soon. They could have waited with a couple of good hackers willing to cooperate. Either they have a limited access window or there's something else. What do we do?"

"If that means they think Corey is their best bet, we might have a bit of time. They won't kill Brandon if they think he's their ticket into this core. They're going to look for ways to make him cooperate. That means they'll be looking for 'Brandon' or you, or one of us. We'll have to work quickly and catch up. He said Corey already had the information." He tapped at his phone, and then started focusing on it. "I'm checking his email."

"You know his password?" I asked.

He smirked and rolled his eyes. "I know everyone's password."

"You don't know my password."

"It's your mom's name and your birthday."

I planted my foot on his leg, pushing him in the seat. Angry impulse.

He gripped my ankle and used it as leverage to tug me, sending me sliding onto my back in the seat. "Stop it. I'm trying to type."

I grunted, and corrected myself. I wanted to hit him, but had a feeling he'd do the same thing and it'd be pointless "How'd you know?"

"Corey figured it out when we were looking for you the last time."

Jerk faces. They were snooping in my emails? I was going to say that was wrong, but not too long ago, I read his criminal history, via Blake Coaltar, who showed it to me. I hadn't sought out the records, but I did read them and I felt like I was setting a double standard if I complained out loud.

"Dude," Avery said. "You read her emails? That's bullshit."

I didn't need his help, but I was floating at his reaction. I smirked at Marc, silently gloating that someone else knew snooping was wrong.

Marc swung his phone in a motion toward him, but looked at me. "Who is this guy?"

"Friend from high school," I said.

The moment I said it, Avery looked up through the rearview mirror, meeting my eyes. I guess he expected me to say he was just the cab driver. Avery smiled at me. I guess I scored a few points.

Marc chuckled. "You have friends?"

Couldn't blame him for thinking that. I didn't expect it, either. "Surprised me, too." I leaned over, getting in Marc's way on purpose and trying to look at his phone. "Is there an email from this guy?"

"Looks like he must have deleted whatever email he was talking about. Hopefully it's still in the trash bin." He put a hand on my head, pushing it over. "Will you sit back and let me take care of this?"

"Am I supposed to sit still with Brandon kidnapped? No way. Find out where this guy lives. I'll take care of him. Just point."

"What are you going to do?"

"We're going to find a set of Tasers and then do the same thing. We'll bring him back to that warehouse and then..."

"No," he said, although he was smirking as he said it, like he didn't wholly want to tell me no.

"Why not? Call Raven. He'll do it with me if you don't want to."

"The first thing we need is to connect with Axel. We don't need these guys to find the real Corey and we don't need anyone getting heroic. First step is information gathering. We need to find out where Murdock's Core is."

My mouth fell open. "We're going to give this guy what he wants? You just said--"

"We need to get to it before they do. At the very least, we'll know where they'll be, even if we don't know when. And we know they're wanting it and will head there, so we can at least monitor and capture them that way if we don't locate them before that point." He showed me his phone, where Axel had replied already about meeting us. "We need to prepare, though. We don't know what we're up against. Or who. It'll be better if we find that information before we confront them."

"Will Corey help us?"

C. L. Stone

"No," he said. He squinted at me and shook his head slightly. "Because he's not going to know about this. Limited liabilities."

Limited? I understood he didn't want anyone else kidnapped or killed, but Corey should know about his brother. "But we need Corey to get to the core."

"We are, he's just not going to do it knowing his brother's life is on the line and risk him being exposed. If they find out they've got the wrong guy, they'll be after him next. So he needs to lay low. But Corey won't like that once he hears his brother is being held against his will. We'll have to feed Corey information carefully and give him space to work. So don't tell him about Brandon. Don't worry. I've got Raven with him now."

Did I agree with this? I'd be pissed at them all if my brother was in real danger and they were keeping that info from me. Maybe he was right, though, in a way. Maybe Corey knowing his brother was in trouble would make it worse right now. "They'll be okay?"

"Maybe." He sat back, and planted his hand against my calf, slowly sliding his palm up and down along my skin in a soothing motion. "Are you okay?"

I furrowed my eyebrows at him. "Yeah?" I didn't mean to make it a question, but I wasn't sure why he was asking. I'd already told him I wasn't worried about the scratches.

"You're pretty calm for someone who just got kidnapped."

"You're pretty calm," I said in an accusing tone. The truth was, now that Marc was here, and the others were starting to get into action and help, my hate managed to roll back into a simmer, still bubbling but waiting to strike out at the right person. It was amazing how my confidence lifted around the boys. Fear didn't work into the equation, only anger and revenge. I wanted to help, I had a desire to pay the boys back for everything they'd done for me and this was a big way to do it. I was focusing on controlling myself until I could get to Brandon and get him out. The goal of saving someone changed my fear into something else: drive, perhaps, or controlled determination.

Marc continued to stare at me, massaging my leg. He was waiting me out. He wanted a real answer.

"You're not going to make me run off to South America while you solve all this yourself, are you?" I asked. Deflecting was better than what I was really thinking.

"I probably should. I'm keeping you with me because if we split up, this guy will have an easier time kidnapping you a second time. We need to stick together. And because you'd probably run off and try to hunt this guy down on your own."

I grunted. True.

Marc went back to checking emails. I leaned back, giving him space to work. I caught Avery looking back at us. Our eyes met. At first, he averted his eyes, looking out the window. When he looked back, he was silently asking me if I was okay really. I nodded, trying to smile and reassure him. He probably had no idea what to make of Marc, and why this was all happening. He couldn't have been expecting this when he picked me up as a simple fare earlier. Maybe he didn't agree with the strategy and didn't feel he could voice his opinion. He pursed his lips, staying quiet.

I wanted to reassure him more, but the truth was, the less he knew was probably better.

"I've got a name," Marc said suddenly. "Randall Jones. That's it. Came in an anonymous email with a German IP. Tried to trace the source of the IP address further for a specific location, but I can't do this on the phone very well. Corey could do better."

"Randall Jones? There's got to be a hundred of them."

"It's going to be someone who died recently." He did a search on the phone again. "They said the owner was killed, right? There's a Randall Jones in the news that died. He was a wealthy landlord in Mt. Pleasant and he was killed three weeks ago in a burglary. Not a lot of details. I think he's our best bet. I don't know his connection to this core they're talking about, but he may have been involved somehow. We can get Corey looking up information the police have about what happened and we can check out his residence for now." He released me. "The first thing we need are some clothes for you and to catch up with Axel. We'll meet up at the fountain and figure out our next move."

"Almost there," Avery said.

"Hey man," Marc said. He reached over, touching him on the shoulder. "Thanks for driving us and helping her out. Seriously. Really cool of you."

Avery slid another glance at me. I got it. He was thrown into this, and Marc, in his own way, was basically dismissing him after the ride was over. I understood Marc was getting him out of this mess before he got in any further.

Marc had the right idea. Avery didn't need to be here. I didn't know how dangerous these German people were, but this was our mess, not his. "Can we pay him?" I asked. "What do we owe?"

Avery shook his head. "Naw, I turned that off when I recognized you. Kidnapped girls don't pay fare. My momma'd shoot me."

"Your momma's a good woman," Marc said. He shifted in the seat, tugging his wallet from his pants and then pulled out a thick wad of twenties. I was surprised to see it. He must have grabbed it on his way out. "But you still get the biggest tip ever."

Avery shook his head, like he didn't want it, but Marc shoved it at him. Avery made a face, but held out a palm, taking the cash. I knew all too well how hard it is, when you're poor, to turn away money. "Coming up on the fountain," he said.

Marc and I hopped out. Cool concrete touching my toes was soothing and chilling at the same time. I turned to wave at Avery. "Thanks," I said.

He started to wave and then stopped. "Hang on, Kayli."

I paused. "What?"

He curled his fingers at me and I approached. He reached into the console of his cab and pulled out a card and passed it to me. "In case you get kidnapped again or something."

I checked out the card, which had his name, cell phone number and email address. It didn't say taxi driver, and it didn't advertise the company he worked for. I wondered if he picked his clients up 'off the books' of the cab company. I clung to it. "Okay," I said. I wasn't sure I'd ever see him again, but it was sweet.

He nodded, his lips tightening. "Call if you need anything," he said. He waved and started rolling the car forward.

I watched him disappear, feeling oddly disconnected now. I suspected the only reason he was leaving was because both I and Marc basically said he should. He'd been involved so far, heard the story. The reality was, he was risking his life, too, for someone he barely knew from high school. Hopefully he went home, and had a beer or something on Marc's cash for a job well done. He deserved it.

That he could escape and live a normal life was something I was envious of.

♠

THE PINEAPPLE FOUNTAIN

Several parks in downtown Charleston have fountains, but only one in the shape of a pineapple. Pineapples are common decorations in Charleston, which was always strange to me because South Carolina didn't *grow* pineapples, at least as far as I knew. It was supposed to be a symbol of welcome, or something like that. Nothing like giving someone a pineapple to visitors when they arrive. Maybe the locals enjoyed the look of confusion from new folks. I don't know. Small amusements.

Marc and I waited together inside the row of hedges circling the fountain. The fountain's edge was on the same level as the sidewalk, so you basically could step into it if you weren't watching where you were going. The top was split into three tiers, like a pineapple sliced into thirds widthwise. It wasn't running, so I imagined they turn it off at night. The three tiers and the base held pools of water, dark and ominous in the predawn.

I scanned the area. The park was mostly safe, but it was very early in the morning, and hooligans didn't always stay in North Charleston. Sometimes they ventured out, waiting for one of the rich on the peninsula to be in the wrong place at the completely wrong time.

The sky was still hazy and overcast. Marc sat on a bench nearby while I walked around the pineapple fountain, getting as close as I dared to the edge without jumping in completely. I was more stomping around to burn off steam than anything. When I got close to Marc, I'd kick out, trying to fling water over on him. Wasn't sure if I was hitting him, but I gave it my best shot.

"Will you sit down?" Marc said after my umpteenth attempt to splash him. He was sitting on the bench with his elbows on his knees, well out of the way. He was bent over, with his head bowed and his hands covering his face.

"I'm trying to stay awake," I said. Four hours sleep and a kidnapping should make anyone tired.

"We'll get some coffee in a bit."

"Until then, if I don't keep moving, I'm going to pass out."

Marc sat up sharply. "I wouldn't be opposed to that."

I kicked water at him, and he dodged by leaning over a little, even though the spray didn't reach. "You think I'm going to sleep now? After all that—"

"Kayli," called a severe, smoky voice. I turned, spotting Axel coming toward us.

I gave one more kick in Marc's direction before I left the fountain. Axel was coming around from the far side, tailed by Kevin. I did a double-take. I hadn't seen Kevin for a week or so and it felt like a lifetime, and even before then, I hadn't seen much of him. His girlfriend usually called and he disappeared shortly after.

He was tall and dark-skinned. His dark eyes were critical but he was there when his teammates needed him. And he watched out for my brother when I couldn't. For that, if nothing else, I had to give him some respect.

Axel was wearing a black leather jacket and jeans. His hair was loose around his jaw, and he wore glasses. His dark eyes and the strict look on his face told me his was in business mode.

I stiffened at the sight of him, doing my best not to stare. We'd gotten really close a couple of weeks ago, but since then, I'd avoided him, and he'd given me space, but I still felt on edge around him.

Mostly because I often caught myself staring at him, attracted to him in a way that almost frightened me. Maybe it was his dark Mediterranean features, or the way that when he caught me staring, he met my eyes and held them, not allowing me the opportunity to look away.

As he stood there, he challenged me silently to come talk to him, but I resisted, keeping my mouth shut, letting Marc take the lead, not needing the distraction of Axel while I was in kick-ass mode.

I kept expecting Raven and Corey to come, but they didn't, a fact that made me nervous. Like not seeing Corey meant he could get kidnapped like we'd been. "Where's the others?" I asked.

"Don't worry about them," Marc said. He turned to Axel. "What are we doing here?"

"Getting Kayli clothes for one," Axel said. "You didn't offer her your shoes?"

"She didn't need them. She was too busy playing in the fountain."

"Did you touch her?" Axel asked.

The question surprised me, like he was accusing Marc in a jealous way, but the idea didn't fit the situation. Well, not at this moment, at least. I stared between them, trying to figure it out.

Marc shook his head. "Just her skin."

"What's the plan?" Kevin asked. "What do you want me to do?"

Axel pointed at him. "I need you at the hospital. Find Dr. Roberts. Don't spend too much time alone. Pick up someone if you need to. Victor Morgan is in the area. He might be able to help with what we need." He turned to us. "Where's that phone?"

I handed it over.

"Corey and Raven are going to meet you there, Kevin," he said. He passed the phone on to him. "Stay with them at the hospital. I want this phone analyzed there. I want twenty-four hour surveillance on Corey. I want everything on this phone, and I want to know everything about these guys. Shoe size, what they had for breakfast this morning, their mothers' favorite flowers, everything. Take turns with Raven sleeping, and one of you two will be running errands if Corey needs anything, or as a go between him and us. No one leaves him at any point."

Marc opened his mouth again in protest but then promptly closed it again. He swallowed and then relaxed his shoulders. Axel really was in charge. Not even Marc questioned this.

"But first," Axel said, "she needs clothes. She can't run if she can't keep up. And we need to clean her."

Kevin put down the backpack that I hadn't noticed until now. He dropped it in front of his feet and started digging through it. "I don't know your size, Kayli," he said. "I had to make a guess. You're about the same size as my girlfriend, though, so hopefully close enough." He pulled out a pair of loose-fit crop cotton pants and a T-shirt, along with a sports bra and a pair of underwear. They were all new with the tags still on, Wal-Mart brands. They must have made a stop. He pulled out a pair of flip-flops with them and passed them over to me.

I understood I probably should put something on, but I wondered why they didn't bring me clothes from the apartment. Had they been there? Or were they avoiding the place because it could be watched, since it had been compromised once already. "Where do you want me to change?" I asked.

"Here," Axel said. "We need to do a sweep."

I waited him out for an explanation and when he never offered, I had to ask. "What?"

"If these guys might have a tracker on you, we need to find out now." He pulled out a comb from his back pocket and showed it to me. "I need you to undress here, and I should check for any bugs. Just in case."

I snorted. "Are you serious?"

"We don't know how sophisticated these guys are. We need to check you out." His face was unreadable. He meant business.

"What do I have to do?"

"Get undressed. I'll brush out your hair and check any crevices for anything unusual. Then get dressed in the new clothes. Marc should be checked out. That cab will probably have to be swept. We don't need that guy hunted and killed because of you. But we'll send another team to deal with that. And we need to do it here, because we don't know how close these guys are, and taking you to a shop or gas station to change means more time spent with them possibly able to track us, and getting others involved in case they decide to come in and attack. We could be cornered. Do this here quickly. We need to get going, so hurry up."

I wanted to make some protest about him being around while I was naked. It was the natural girl-modesty response. I stared at him, considering my options. He knew more than I did about this spy thing. I'd seen movies where there were bugs planted on people as small as a fly. Was that true? Could one be on me right now? I still had the boxers on and the T-shirt. In the struggle, Mack Truck could have put anything on me and I wouldn't have noticed. It was something I hadn't thought of. Suddenly my body was itchy, like a live bug with a tracer device had been planted on me and crawled all over my skin.

I needed to hurry. Axel was right, we didn't have much time and we needed to get to Brandon. If this was what I needed to do, it didn't help to just stand here.

I still put the fountain between me and the other boys until I couldn't even see them anymore and I was sure none of them could see me. I was wondering why we were doing this out in the open, not that there appeared to be anyone around. There could be a lot of reasons, I supposed, but if we were quick, no one might notice us here anyway.

Axel followed. When I challenged him with a glare, he was completely unreadable. Either he was trying to keep things professional, or there was something else on his mind. Maybe he simply didn't care about nudity when lives were on the line.

I put the new clothes aside and then started to strip. I was going to try to be coy, but he was the one who had to check for bugs in places I wouldn't be able to check alone. I had to let him inspect me so there was no point in trying to be delicate.

Axel's eyes never wavered. At first his face was blank, and stayed on my face.

I lifted the T-shirt and ripped it off, facing him full on and bare and his eyes stayed with mine. I challenged him, daring. I don't know why I needed to, but it was like I was waiting for some reaction from him. Not getting one made me uncomfortable, like I wasn't attractive enough to warrant some sort of approval.

Crazy girl stuff. Resistant to being naked in front of guys, but if you have to be, you want a compliment.

And my heart was wild because he'd once seen me nearly naked before. We'd even kissed, and fooled around a bit. Now it was like I was testing him to see if he'd lost interest. If maybe I wasn't his type. I realized it must be hard for him to deal with someone like me, hot and cold like I'd been with the guys. Did I think they'd simply wait while I made up my mind?

And here I was, testing him. I wanted to poke his buttons until he caved. I wanted to prove to him, and to myself, that he was still interested.

I slipped out of the boxers, kicking them toward the fountain. At first he stood completely still, like he was waiting for me to do something. Give him permission?

"Do you have to comb my hair?" I asked.

He blinked, his head shaking slightly as if I'd disturbed some deep thinking.

And then there it was: His eyes did the sweep. He dropped his gaze quickly to my feet, as if trying to avoid looking directly, but once he looked at my feet, his eyes slid up slowly. He angled his head, taking in my calves, thighs, over my hips and stomach, to my chest. Very slow, very deliberate. He'd done the same to me with my clothes on, but now it was all in front of him.

Fair was fair: I'd seen him naked.

He met my eyes again. His expression was so hard to read, but I could tell he was struggling. That made me happy. Axel at least felt something when he saw me naked.

He moved forward with a comb he pulled from his pocket and did a finger twirl. "Turn around."

This was familiar, too. He'd done this once before, with a brush, trying to collect my own secrets from me.

I turned where he wanted me, and he gathered my hair in his big hands. He started at the roots and worked the comb through. He circled me as he worked, trying to make sure he brushed everything down and got rid of every tangle. Locks covered my face. His fingers followed the comb, touching every strand.

I covered parts of me with my arms from the cold, and partially in preparation if anyone did come by. It was super early still, and the only light we were getting was from dim lamps still lit up and down the park and further out there was some ambient light from streetlamps and homes. Someone would have had to get really close to notice I was naked, and the park was deserted except for us. "Is this even necessary?" I asked, considering what was more awkward, being naked in public or Axel combing my hair for bugs.

I also wanted to avoid talking about us.

He was quiet for a moment, and then held out a palm.

Inside his palm were three dark specks. At first, I just assumed it was dirt or something. When I looked closer, they appeared to be little microchips.

"Are those them?" I asked. I couldn't believe he found three already. "It's not just dirt or something? I did jump from a moving car."

"Trackers," he said. "I've seen these before."

"Are they working now? Are they GPS trackers?" I was wondering how they put these on. It must have happened while we'd struggled in bed or on the way to the car trunk. Tracking us from the start meant they were assured we couldn't have jumped up and run off at some point.

"They aren't really designed for GPS. They just send out a frequency," he said. "There's a local scanner out there somewhere that can pick it up. It wouldn't have enough energy for a satellite transmission but it can make it easier to follow you if they wanted to tail you. If they're searching for you now, this is what they're looking for."

"How come they didn't find me before? They were looking for me while I was keeping an eye on Brandon and they were talking to him."

"You may have been close enough to Brandon that they were picking up the same frequency from him. These wouldn't have that far of a range and they're not very precise, but if they picked it up, they'd know they were close. It's like playing Hot or Cold."

48

"What if they're following us now?"

"We want them to follow if they are, but we want them closer. We don't want to make this easy for them. If you want to get to know your stalkers, you need to get them as close as possible and draw them out into the open, into the public areas." He tossed the three units into the fountain and continued to comb my hair. "With these, they could stay at a distance and keep an eye on you. That's not what we want."

Sophisticated. This German and his pals were even smarter than I thought. Could I have ever survived this without Axel and the guys? Probably, but at least with them, it'd be easier. I'd not thought about bugs, and probably would have been picked up pretty quickly if they came across that signal.

I sucked in a slow, long breath and exhaled. I was fooling myself. These guys didn't even need me.

Axel took his time, going through every lock of hair. The teeth bit into my scalp when he got close, but it was necessary, because the little trackers were really small. He checked behind my ears, in my ears, angled my chin around to look underneath my jaw. He wanted to make sure nothing else fell out and attached to my skin. I'd never caught lice going to school, but I thought the process to clean out those real bugs must be similar. Checking for metal bugs was like catching lice, but way more dangerous. That was a crazy thought.

Again a silence fell between us, and I stared at the dead fountain, almost falling asleep where I stood as he inspected me.

"Are you so worried about your brother that you're avoiding me?" he asked quietly.

There it was. The question I'd been thinking he'd ask sooner or later. "No," I said. I wasn't in the mood to elaborate because if I said what I was really thinking out loud, he'd ask more questions. It was something some of the other Academy boys asked quietly, or sometimes in odd, roundabout ways and I distracted them with something else.

They wanted to know how I felt, and the truth was more complicated than they wanted to really know. I thought over time, I'd eventually get over how I was feeling, but that wasn't the case. My feelings only grew stronger.

After I responded, and I didn't know what else to say, I remained quiet, hoping he'd take a hint.

"You can tell me if you're not interested," he said. "Not trying to be passive-aggressive about it. I'm interested in you. I just want to know where I stand."

I grunted.

"What was that?" he asked a little louder.

What an ass. He waited until I was vulnerable, naked and couldn't run and he was going to corner me with something like that? Did he really need to know that badly? I had to remind myself not to let him brush my hair from now on. That seemed to be his way of saying we need to talk.

It was difficult now, though, to not simply give in. Wouldn't it be nice to be able to lean into him? To feel like I'd been missed and worried about, and just be held for a while? I'd felt so vulnerable since I'd been kidnapped, and while I wanted to hug Marc and the others, I didn't, because hugging wasn't what I did. I wanted to appear brave, to look like I was unshakable.

But on the inside, I wasn't. I needed something from someone else. I needed to feel grounded somehow. It was hard to describe and telling the others what I needed felt impossible.

And yet I had the feeling if I told one of them I simply needed a hug, or a kiss, they'd do it in a heartbeat.

Why was that so? It felt like a selfish thing, what I wanted from them. I wanted them to feel things for me, even though I had no right to. But I wanted all of them in different ways. In some cases, in very close, intense ways. But if they knew what I was feeling—that I couldn't decide between them—they'd call me out on it.

"I don't want to talk about this right now," I said sharply, trying to make it clear that I hated this. "I want to find Brandon and then..."

"How long do you think I'll wait?" he asked.

My hands clenched into fists and I stared through my hair at the fountain. My first instinct was to tell him to not wait, and yet I was biting my tongue hard to stop myself. Again, selfish. I didn't want him to hate me, but I didn't want him too close to me when I was so conflicted with the others. I couldn't tell him about it, because he wouldn't understand.

He stepped around until he was in front of me and I got an up close look at his chest in the dark jacket. "It's the others," he said. "You're trying to avoid a sticky situation by keeping us all at a distance."

I made a face and then shook my head. It was like he could read my mind. "How do you know?" I asked.

"We've had this discussion, about the others getting close to you. At first I thought the last couple of weeks was about separating yourself from the other guys. I know a few of the others have a crush on you, or more than that. Corey's someone you feel safe with for some reason, because he's too much of a nice guy to make a move. I understood you wanted time to try to sort it out, but I think you're making it worse. And I don't like waiting."

My jaw dropped and I accidentally sucked in air at the same time, catching some hair into my mouth. I spit to get it back out again and clawed it away from my face.

"Stop," he said. "I'm almost done."

"Stop talking like you know everything."

"I didn't know for sure until now."

I groaned. He did that to me before, too. He knew just how to push my buttons to get the answers he wanted. He might have picked up some hints from the other guys, and I'd given away that the other guys were getting close, but he wasn't sure how close before until just now when he bluffed me out. Was it obvious that I avoided the other guys except for Corey?

Did he know Corey was gay? I couldn't remember if Brandon mentioned if the other guys knew for sure. He did feel safe, because I could talk to him and hang out with him, and sleep in his bed without feeling weird.

Except last night, when Brandon took his place. Had he done that before and I didn't realize it because it was dark and I couldn't tell the difference if I couldn't see their eyes? Brandon was simply there. I'd snuggled into him, assuming it was Corey. I wasn't sure if Brandon was being deceptive before, or if he just assumed he could and didn't realize I hadn't picked out it was him.

Either way, they didn't need to know about this. "Don't tell the other guys."

"You can't hide forever. We've talked about this."

I didn't know how to react to this, because I didn't know the answer to the problem now any more than I did the last time he brought it up. Marc, Brandon, Raven and Axel were single, and they were interested in me, and there was only one of me. There were several reasons not to pick at all. Part of that was because if I picked wrong, and it didn't work out, I'd lose out on all of them. Not to be selfish about it, but they were all I had left.

On top of that, I couldn't choose between them. Getting close to them made it difficult. They each were incredible in their own way, and choosing one felt too much like I was hurting the others, so avoiding the issue was my way of dealing with it. In a small way, I was hoping they'd lose interest and leave me with only one option so I didn't have to choose between them. "Maybe I shouldn't do...I mean, maybe I need to not do this with anyone. Not from the group."

Axel stopped combing, dropping his hands and standing still in front of me. "Because you're afraid we'll fight and it'll break up our group or for other reasons? Like you can't decide?"

Damn. I rolled my eyes, avoiding looking at him, hoping I could get away with some other lie, but another one didn't wouldn't come to mind. What other reason could there be? "Maybe it isn't the right time to talk about this." Or like we should probably never talk about it.

He parted my hair, caught my chin and lifted my face until I met his dark eyes. The swell of a storm rose behind his gaze. "Not even something like this would be enough to break us," he said. "And they're not stupid. They'll know. If you want to stay with us, we've all got to come out with how we feel about each other. There's no way around it."

Panic seared me as much as the cold was seeping into my body, making me shake uncontrollably. Was he suggesting we should confront them all? I envisioned Raven lashing out, Brandon accusing me of being selfish, of the pain in Marc's eyes. Or maybe if Axel turned them all off by telling them I couldn't choose, and they didn't want me after that, he could claim me for himself. Maybe that was the answer. If I couldn't choose, the boys would choose for me.

Did I want that? I never before had been unable to make a decision. I normally just bulldozed my way through relationships and then ended them on my terms.

"I don't know," I said. I locked gazes with him. I was afraid to admit that I couldn't make this decision, and I didn't want him to think it was because he wasn't good enough to single out. I just didn't have an answer.

The corner of his mouth dipped down. His eyes shifted from mine to move over my face, my hair, my cheeks, my lips, my ears. Was he scanning for another bug?

"We need to figure this out," he said. "Because I'm not going to avoid pursuing you for much longer. I want you."

My heart raced and tripped and raced again. I just stared back, naked, daring. My knees shook, maybe from the cold, but I was also on fire from head to foot at the gaze he leveled on me. I had resisted this long, but now I realized I was feeding the flames by avoiding him. My resistance was weakening, but I didn't want him to know. I didn't dare. I was scared he was wrong and the boys would feel betrayed.

He was quiet for a while, but then his eyes narrowed. "I have to check the rest of your body," he said. "Every part of you. I found three so far but I need to make sure there aren't any more. These things can get into weird places. Do you trust me?"

I swallowed and nodded. A rush of heat washed across me. His being able to change my thoughts and feelings so quickly left me so conflicted.

He started from my neck, brushing the back of his hand down my body, along every crevice. Something told me this was more than an inspection. This was an examination. He would root out any more scars he thought were interesting. He'd check any tan line, any bump. He already admitted he was attracted to me and would learn every inch of my body.

I was aroused that he was studying me.

The back of his hand slid down between my breasts, and then he lifted each one, checking the undersides. He knelt lower, poking at my belly button.

And then he was facing my crotch and I closed my eyes. His hands slid between my thighs and he parted them a little. His hands brushed in the corner where my thighs met my groin and followed back toward my butt.

When his hands slid down to check my knees and feet, I stared again at the fountain. Somehow, I wasn't annoyed or angry that he'd gotten so close to parts of me. I trusted him. His hands were smooth, the warmth of his touch welcome when I felt so cold now.

I wanted him to continue touching, but this wasn't the place, and we didn't have the time.

When he was finished, he stood up. "Seems like we got it all, but to be safe, you should rinse off in the fountain a little in these little crevices. I'm not sure if the devices are waterproof, but it might wash away any we've missed. Then get those clothes on."

It was over. He turned his back on me, allowing me some privacy once again by maintaining a vigilant watch on the surroundings.

Why did I still hope for him to say something? He was the one trying to make this as doctor-patient as possible, and I was the one needing something more. I was simply greedy, needing of his attention and for him to give some to me, even if I resisted and bit my tongue and seemed to be indifferent.

I swallowed my needs and fears and without another word, did as he told me to do.

♠

RANDALL JONES

I did a quick, cold splash in the fountain and tried to dress quickly. Crop pants weren't my thing. I think it was because they were in fashion lately and I wasn't about to succumb to fashion trends. The sports bra squeezed my chest until I had a uni-boob, but given Kevin probably didn't know my bra size, I couldn't blame him for that. The underwear was a little big, the pants were a little tight around the butt, but the T-shirt I wore covered my hips. The flip-flops were the closest thing to my own size so I had that going.

When I was done, Axel had already tossed my old clothes into the fountain. We were making a mess, but maybe some hobos could use some new clothes. I felt bad since they were Corey's. I kept Avery's business card, tucking it into my pocket. I still wanted to hang onto that.

Marc looked at me when we'd returned to the group, quietly asking if I was okay. I guess he knew what I'd been through. I waved him off, trying to tell him it didn't matter. We had to get out of there.

The fact that there had been bugs at all left me feeling creepy-crawlies all over even now. I was scratching behind my ears and around my neck, thinking there was one left.

The boys lead the way to a black car. Did it belong to them? I didn't recognize it from the weeks I'd known them. Axel held the front passenger door open and looked at me pointedly, silently telling me where to sit.

Marc never said a word the entire time. He avoided my gaze, impossible to read.

We took off in silence with Axel driving and Marc in the back seat.

Kevin had split up from us, walking in the other direction. Had he parked further down the road? He was supposed to go to some hospital. I wondered why they were going there instead of some Academy bunker. Didn't the Academy have a safe house or something? Some sort of fortress so kidnappers couldn't just grab Corey?

Or was it that the hospital was a public place with security and internet and Corey could do his thing in relative safety? Maybe it was good protocol thing. I'd have to figure it out later.

It was only four in the morning, and only a fraction of the homes around us had lights on in the windows as Axel drove through downtown Charleston. Some people were getting up for the morning jog, the morning coffee, the morning commute. We were on our way to find Dead Randall, the only link we had to this core, whatever it was.

"Where are we going?" I asked from the front seat, tugging at my pants. They were too tight and kept sliding down over the underwear. "Are we going to check out Randall's house?"

"We're going to look in for a little while," Axel said. "We'll figure out where he worked. Maybe he had this core in a warehouse or somewhere else. First, we need to figure out what a core is. When we find the core, we'll keep an eye on it. We find these guys getting close to it, and we'll jump them."

"That's our plan?" I asked, smirking. "Jump them?"

"We've got to find it first," Axel said. "Then we'll figure it out from there. For all we know, this core could be a nuke. Or a code that breaks into National Security. We'll have to be careful."

"I've got Corey figuring it out," Marc said. He sat in the back with his head bowed, staring at his cell phone. He typed into it. "I told him this was Murdock's Core and it has his Guard Dog security packet. He's going to fill me in when they figure it out what it might be."

"If it's Murdock's Core, why aren't we chasing a Murdock?" I asked.

Axel shrugged. "The email said Randall, didn't it?"

"Yeah," Marc said. "Randall Jones. The only thing in the email. No Murdock."

That was kind of odd. Why call it Murdock at all? "How is Corey involved anyway?" I asked. "They said something about he wrote the security packet... doohickey thing?"

"He's got some security software he wrote," Marc said. "But it's freeware. Free software. It's a pretty sophisticated cryptic thing. Apparently whoever has this Murdock's Core, they used his software for the security. So they assume Corey could hack it."

"They said Corey could figure out the password, too," I said. "They thought Corey could do it quickly. Can he really break into it if they'd gotten the real Corey?"

"Give Corey a few minutes," Marc said, his eyes lit up and he lifted his head. "All I gave him was a name, and he's already on the trail for what this thing is. He'll be able to find out more. He might even be able to give us some good info about that cell phone once Kevin gets there with it."

Axel took state road 17 out of downtown, crossed the bridge and headed north toward Mt. Pleasant. Old Historical Charleston neighborhoods cleared and we got into the suburban sprawl on the other side of the bridge.

Before we got too far, Axel's phone on the dash lit up and he touched the surface to answer. "What's up, Corey?"

"Hey guys," Corey's voice came through on speaker. "Looks like this Murdock's Core is a burner phone service. Sort of."

I sat up. He'd figured it out so quickly? I wanted to ask how he did it, but didn't want to interrupt. I turned back to look at Marc, who only grinned proudly and mouthed something that I thought was, "Better than I thought."

"What do you mean, *sort of*?" Axel asked.

"More sophisticated. It's a service not even on the Feds' radar. Includes an eight-hundred number you dial into that keeps track of your phone numbers and voice mails at a central server. Technically, you can use any cell phone you'd like. If you want to be super careful, you can switch out SIM cards and it keeps track of your business contacts and lets you keep the same number, it just changes your ID number on your phone regularly. Better for business if customers don't have to keep up with new numbers all the time. There's more to it, but that's all I can get without looking either at one of their cell phones they use, or figuring out where the core is. But the core is a central server that keeps the usernames and passwords required for accounts and manages the service."

"So it's an illegal cell service they want access to?" Marc asked. "This is illegal, right?"

"All cell phones are required to be regulated and tracked, at least in the States. Whoever this Randall is, he might be the owner or something. Someone has to run it. But yeah, one-hundred percent illegal operation if the government can't regulate it. What I'm not sure about is how exactly they're hitting cell phone towers for service and getting away with it without being traced by the FCC or the NSA. I mean, I had to hack into some deep networks to even figure out this much."

"Thanks Corey," Marc said.

"Is Kayli there?" Corey asked.

"I'm here," I said. Hearing Corey was good for me. He was safe. Had they told him what had happened to me? Or to Brandon?

"Just wanted to say hello," he said. "You okay?"

Corey was being cute. "Yeah," I said, my heart lifting at his concern, even if I wasn't sure exactly how much they'd told him.

"We've got her," Marc said. "Don't worry."

"Okay. Going to work on the cell phone when Kevin brings it. I'm tracking the messages I've gotten from them. Their emails are hard to trace because they're from a different burner cell. Seems like they were all sent from the same phone, and it was bought here with cash, and these IPs don't have any other activity. Their GPS signals that were stored are public places and random. They're very careful."

"Do your best. Call with updates," Axel said before he hung up. "Let's find this Randall Jones. That'll get us closer to finding out where this core is." He sighed and shook his head. "I don't like that we're looking for something illegal."

"Maybe we should give these kidnappers access," Marc said. "And then let them all go down with the Feds."

"Maybe," Axel said. "We need to get ourselves out of this mess, first. We may need to check out who is involved with this service. Anyone who needs an underground cell phone might be someone we're interested in checking out."

Marc smirked. "It'll be like an Academy payday."

My eyes widened, and I looked over at Axel, who was unreadable at first, but his eyes were shifting from the road, to the dash, to the mirrors and then over to me. When he met my gaze, he held it for a long time. There was a slight shake of his head. "It's not what you're thinking."

"What am I thinking?" I asked, because I hadn't made the connection yet. I only heard Academy payday and I was wondering how uncovering a core would be that. I thought they didn't get paid.

"The Academy won't use the cell phone service," he said. "But imagine who would use such a service? Someone who wouldn't want to be overheard enough to risk possible jail time for a conversation over the phone."

I hated to play Devil's advocate, but I had to. "We don't know why they would need one," I said.

"So it'll be better if the Academy investigates, wouldn't it?" he asked.

I wanted to say it wasn't our business what they were doing, but at the same time, maybe I was wrong. Simply having an illegal cell phone line, and buying into it, was a good indicator of corruption. I wondered if the Academy would keep such a service for themselves though. Or was it too great a risk to be discovered that way. I mean, right now there were bad guys looking to get access to this core they discovered. The Academy seemed, from what I understood, to operate in plain sight using everyday items that blended in. Anything sophisticated attracted attention.

The car was quiet as Axel drove on. Mt. Pleasant didn't have a mountain on it at all, as far as I knew. The highest point in Charleston was any of the buildings downtown. Still, Mt. Pleasant was a collection point for the high-end middle class and wealthy who preferred suburbs over islands and couldn't get one of the limited homes downtown. Mt. Pleasant homes and shops were newer, the roads well maintained and without need of historical permits.

After what seemed like an eon of staring out the windshield, Axel pulled into one of the ritzier subdivisions. These homes had garages at ground level, and the homes were built on top of the garages. Being close to the water, it served as protection against hurricanes and flooding.

He slowed through the neighborhood, gliding through the streets. A few blocks later, he made a circle, selected a house and parked in the driveway.

Was he insane? "Someone's going to see us," I said.

"This house is for sale. There's a sign in the front yard."

Oh. "The neighbors will see us."

"The neighbors are asleep. It's four a.m. Let's go."

Marc hopped out and opened my door before I got to it. I got out, clutching at my pants to keep them on my hips correctly. He closed the door quietly and turned, following Axel without saying anything. He even avoided my eyes.

Oh god. I paused in the driveway, watching them walk to the street and turn. I started off slowly, creating distance between us. Was he mad at me? Why wasn't he talking? It wasn't that he hadn't talked before, it was that something was suddenly on his mind and he seemed to be avoiding only me. Or was I being paranoid? No. His lips were tight, face grim.

I tramped after Axel, too afraid to address Marc and start a scene. Maybe he was feeling the edge because Brandon was missing. Had I ever seen Marc truly upset before? What was he like?

Did he blame me for all of this?

"Where are we going?" I asked. "Is this his house?" I didn't understand why we parked somewhere and left the car.

"No," Axel said. "We're just borrowing it."

"I thought we were going after Randall. Which house is his? And what are we looking for?"

"If we find out who he is, how he died, it might lead us to these German guys. Maybe they killed him and left clues. Crime scenes usually are riddled with them. And if we find this core in the meantime, hopefully we can do the right thing by it. First thing, though, is to make sure Brandon is safe."

I followed the guys to a greenhouse in the next cul-de-sac over from where we'd parked. The house was similar to all the others, stacked on top of a garage. There were low hedges, and a brick mailbox and an American flag hanging from a pole in the front lawn. If Randall Jones had been hosting an illegal cell phone service, you wouldn't have been able to tell from his front lawn.

"This it?" I asked. It didn't look very expensive, not compared to some other properties I'd seen elsewhere in Mt. Pleasant. I don't know why, but when the German asked to find this core and get it, I expected it was from someone rich. Really rich. Why get something if not to sell it for money?

Axel and Marc stood close to a palm tree planted on the corner of a property a block down the street from where we'd parked. Their heads moved in opposite directions, checking out the neighborhood, the layout. I imagined they were doing spy calculations to figure out the best move. The lights were off in the Jones's home. The garage doors were closed. The property looked still, uninhabited.

"Is there a Mrs. Jones?" I asked.

"I don't know yet," Axel said. "I think so, or else this property would be up for sale after he died."

"Are there little Jones children?"

"Don't know."

"What *do* we know?"

Axel turned his head toward me. His dark eyes met mine, and he challenged me that way. "I know we should be quiet and take a look around." He headed to the garage.

"We can't just barge in," I said.

"We don't have time to do this the right way," he said. "We have to do it the quick way." He hunched a little, sneaking up toward the house and trying to be discreet about it.

Marc followed him close, a shadow. He still hadn't said a word, not even a breath about the mission we were on. Was he being quiet because he had to be or because he was angry at me? Why wouldn't he look at me? This was going to drive me crazy. I'd have asked flat out but it really wasn't the time to get into a fight. I swallowed back my bubbling fear and tried to stick close to them.

The Jones's front porch was on a second story balcony with staircases leading up. The garage doors had a single normal door between them, making a lower level entryway. It was tucked behind the staircase that lead to the porch. Stupidest design ever. Someone could hide underneath the staircase and break into the garage.

Guess where Axel headed?

"There could be a security alarm," I whispered to him as I followed.

"Quiet," Marc said, surprising me by responding at all. "And stay close. Go where I do."

Axel walked up to the door, jiggled the handle and waited. He did it again and then waited again. He examined the door closer, pulling out a keychain with a flashlight attached. He aimed it at the door, examining the lock.

I turned around, scouting the area. We were shadowed by the staircase, and there weren't any front lights on. I angled to keep myself between his light and any neighbors that might be snooping.

Breaking and entering was worse than getting caught pickpocketing. I was on edge, waiting for an alarm. I turned, trying to look the other way when Marc materialized in front of my face, closer than he'd been before. My heart leapt.

"Ugh," I whispered. "You scared the sh—"

"Shh," he said.

"Come on," Axel whispered.

I turned, and Axel had the door open. He was holding it and gesturing I should enter. He was going to play courteous Southern gentleman now? I smothered a groan and walked in. Maybe he wanted me to get shot first if the widow got spooked and came down with a loaded gun.

The garage was wider than I thought with two cars parked on either side, one was a minivan. Yup. Family. There were kids. Shit.

"We can't be here," I whispered. I wasn't going to spook some mom when her husband just died and with kids here.

Axel moved forward, close enough that his chest pressed against my back. His hand slipped over my mouth, covering it.

His breath fell against my ear. "Listen," he whispered. "We're going to get some information and slip out again, but I can't do it if you're talking. I need you as quiet as possible. Please." He wasn't fooling any more. He was begging.

I nodded against the hand pressed against my mouth. When he released me, he moved to the lead. I looked behind us. Marc was at the door, holding it open, keeping an eye on the street and the neighborhood, being a lookout.

There were boxes stacked together on shelving near the back. Trash bins were against the wall. There was old workout equipment in the corner. The cars were newer models, the inside of the minivan was spotless but there was a car seat. There were a couple of bicycles, one with training wheels, and a tricycle.

Axel tucked his head around the other car, a smaller SUV. He tried the handle, no luck: it was locked. He was lucky the alarm wasn't set to super sensitive.

He was so quiet, he could have been floating. He went over to the boxes, examining the different ones. He pointed to me, and then pointed to the trash cans.

I shook my head. No way was I digging through trash.

He pointed again, more insistent this time and I scowled. Kayli Winchester went from pickpocket to trash diving. Not exactly a promotion.

The trash bins were big, blue, and there was a recycling bin next to it. I tried the recycling first, old cans, newspapers, glass wine bottles...a lot of them. Poor lady. Her husband was dead. Couldn't blame her. For that reason, though, I had to leave the recycle bin alone. The cans and bottles made it impossible to move much around without them clanging against each other.

The blue bins held black trash bags. I gazed in at them, trying to figure out the contents just by looking at the outside. What was I supposed to do with these?

I glanced back at Axel, he pulled a box down, opened it and examined the contents. He closed it again, pulled another down and then opened that one.

I groaned. He was making noise. I listened, not hearing anything coming from the house, but not trusting my ears. Kids were a problem. They wake up easily. They move quietly and could spot us and alert their mom.

Taking too long would get us caught. I ripped open the trash bag on top, examining. This one was filled with typical kitchen garbage, the second one had a collection of smaller, transparent bags. If I had a home office, I'd have those clear small trash bags in my trash bin. This was probably a winner. I lifted the entire thing out and closed the bin again. They weren't going to miss it. Job done.

I started back between the two cars. I meant to wait on Axel since he was opening boxes still, trying to figure out which one he wanted to take.

Marc turned his head when I got close, his mismatched eyes focusing on me. He glanced at the trash bag, seemed a little confused but then redirected his attention to my face and held. A stern frown and a wrinkle between his eyebrows told me so many things, none of them good.

I stared back, narrowing my eyes, trying to relay how I hated this silence and dared him to say something right here. Want to stare me down like that? I'd send us all to jail just to knock that look off his face.

At the same time, my heart was cracking badly. His look made me not care about dying by the Germans. It'd save me the heartache.

Maybe he was upset because it was Brandon and I who were kidnapped, which meant we were sleeping in the same bed. Maybe he finally made that connection. Even if I hadn't initially thought it was Brandon, maybe he thought...

This was the problem with dancing between different guys trying to make a decision. The growing paranoia made every look appear to have a suspicious glint. Still, I couldn't shake that something was wrong with Marc. He knew something and couldn't tell me about it now.

Axel found two boxes he wanted and then hurried back between the cars toward the door. He took one look at the bag in my hands, cocked an eyebrow, shrugged and then nudged me out.

I followed him and Marc back to the abandoned house. This time, Marc opened the back door. He took my trash bag and stuffed it into the back. Axel dropped his findings into the back and got in to drive. Marc directed me to sit beside him in the back seat, with the stuff between us. Axel started up the car and we were off. We were quiet until we left the cul-de-sac and on the road again.

"Boxes first," Marc said. "Probably more important if they kept it."

I took one of the boxes and started sifting through it. It was tax records, over five years old. How long were you supposed to hang on to these? Apparently Mr. Jones made just over thirty five thousand dollars that year, and owned a small vacation house in Florida. He had retirement accounts in 401Ks, a few million dollars in various funds. That may or may not have increased over the last couple of years.

I scratched a fingernail over my eyebrow, looking at the paperwork. Maybe it was my criminal intuition talking, but this made absolutely no sense at all. He was no different than any of the other people on this street, with nothing noteworthy. He had money, sure. Apparently he had an office in town and owned several rental properties. Vacation rentals. Business hadn't been booming the last few years, but he was in the black.

But his money was inside bank accounts and 401ks. Secured. Even if Corey could hack this account, why would the German go after this one and not someone who had even more money? If he owned the core, how was it his accounts seemed so average? How valuable could this core be?

"What's Murdock's Core?" I asked quietly. I was still nervous since we were still in the neighborhood, as if someone could hear us. "What are we looking for? Tell me what that is? I mean, Corey kind of figured it out, but explain it to me." I knew the answer, but I thought someone else spelling it out would help clear up what I was thinking. Technically, cell phone signals come from towers, but how would an illegal cell phone network operate?

"Sounds like there's an underground communication network," Marc said. He was using his cell phone as a light in one hand and thumbed through files in the box.

"Like in the sewers?" I asked, scrunching my nose and making a dumb face.

"An underground cell service."

I stared at him blankly, waiting for him to explain the details because that totally wasn't helpful.

He only took a moment to notice I was staring and caught my eyes. "You do know what a cell phone is, right?"

"Maybe," I said in a sarcastic tone.

He made a face, sticking his tongue out at me. "Where have you been living?" he asked, matching my tone.

"I was living under a rock," I said flatly. "Humor me. Pretend I don't know anything about how cell phones work. Let's pretend I'm an evil mastermind and wanted to create an underground cell phone service. Tell me what you'd need to run one."

He sighed, stuffing folders back into the box and leaning back. "Cell phone towers are built to not only keep you communicating, but also to keep track of you. So there's signals flying through the air constantly. It's not just cell phones out there though. There's radio waves, satellite signals, wireless internet connections. The thing is, if it's traveling through the air, it can be caught. Like picking up a radio signal by dialing into the right frequency."

"So if you have a cell phone, someone else can be listening. I figured. So how does this illegal one work?"

"I'm having to guess," Marc said. "What I figure is this works on a completely different frequency, or a deceptive frequency. This core keeps it all in line. But that means it should operate on completely separate towers, or operates on corporate-owned towers. The only trick is, if it is connected to corporate towers, it's more likely to get caught."

"Okay, say I wanted to be completely anonymous. I'd need my own cell phone towers and this core to operate everything. How does the cell phone know not to connect to the corporate towers? And how do they keep others from picking up these open air signals?"

"Every cell phone throws out a signal, looking for an ID number, cell phone towers throw back an ID number and if they match, the phone will make calls. It also can track where your cell phone is. The government can easily keep an eye on you this way. An illegal cell phone...maybe if it's in a different frequency, those cell towers don't know to pick it up?" Marc looked to Axel. "I'm talking out of my ass. I don't know how it would work."

"The point is," Axel said. "Corporations in this country are required to keep cell phone records for up to two years and the FCC is supposed to know about any communication system going on within the borders. It prevents terrorist activity from happening. They monitor for suspicious activity."

I raised eyebrows. "Like how you guys can track bad guys and keep an eye on people. Like we're not supposed to."

"When does anyone do anything they're supposed to?" Marc asked. "The government requires all cell phone services to keep tabs of your location, calls, text messages, everything. We don't monitor individual cell phones. We look for unusual activity and then investigate in person to figure out what's going on. And usually we're only focused on family, or things that seem really odd, like with Coaltar. That's how we trace people. Encrypted, invisible cell phone signals that the government doesn't know about is something a whole lot more dangerous." He shrugged. "I mean, I could be wrong. There could be reasons for keeping your phone service underground. Some people are just paranoid and don't want any government access. That's going to be the problem. Sparing people who maybe were just that paranoid and aren't doing anything illegal."

I scratched absently at my eyebrow. As a thief, it was hard for me to consider anyone listening in on my phone calls. I couldn't imagine normal people simply being okay with this, but then if you didn't have anything to hide, you didn't have much to worry about. I guess if I didn't like it, I'd not use a cell phone.

I also knew if people like in the Academy could listen in on cell phones, others could, too. Some of them might be like these German guys who discovered an even more secret cell phone service. What would they do with it if they had access? "So is this core worth money?"

"The core is the data in the system," Axel said. He focused on the road as he talked. "It's all the data cell phone services normally keep, but they don't distribute it to governments or anyone who asks. Or maybe they completely delete it after sending out the signals. Some gang trying to get their hands on it probably means they want to access the information. Either they want the list of names using the service, or they want the service to run and try to capture information on these people. If people want to be anonymous, those secret phone calls probably have to do with money and crime. Whatever it is, this gang is willing to threaten lives for it. This Mr. Jones may have already been a victim."

"How do you steal it?" I asked. "I mean, they'd need to access the core long enough that Corey could find a way to break in. But then what?"

Axel sighed. "Imagine if you had even a minute of all the activity on cell phones throughout the city. How many passwords and access codes to bank accounts could you pick up? If you could listen quietly to cell phones, you technically have a key to thousands of passwords when people call their banks and so forth. Then they wait and use those passcodes to steal what's in those accounts."

That made sense. That was still a lot of information to go through. There had to be millions of calls made throughout the day. For an elite and secret cell phone service, it'd narrow down the list to those with disposable cash. "So they only need to access this core for a minute. They don't really need to take it."

"For as long as they could get away with," Axel said. He turned his head, looking at me. "They either need access to the core directly, or they need access to the proper signals, pulling them out of the air, and then they can try to decode it as it flows. Apparently Corey wrote the code they can't break through. Corey could probably give us more information on which would be the most likely way they'd approach it. I imagine gaining access to the core would be better...or rather, more profitable. Catching signals in the air limits the data. The core is where all the data flows." He refocused on the road. "I mean, if I were going to steal this information, I'd prefer the core."

"But how is Mr. Jones related to all of this?" I asked. I pointed to the tax documents. "This family is upper middle class at worst, barely rich at best. If he made a secret underground cell phone service, wouldn't he be really rich?"

Marc shrugged. "The cash may be in an offshore bank somewhere. And if it's only a local cell phone service, then it'd be a limited market."

It still didn't add up for me. It was early in the morning and I was hungry. My brain wasn't working. Or something about this didn't make sense and I couldn't put my finger on it. "Help me out here. He's got some secret underground cell phone service and he never even spends the money he earns from it? That's really far out there."

Axel let out a slow breath between his lips. "Whatever it is, we don't need to worry about that just yet. We just need to find this core, and if that fails, we're at least giving time for the others to work on our alternate plan."

"To do what?"

Marc smirked. "You're not as smart as I thought you were."

"Shut up, I'm still new to this." I stopped a moment, thinking. "So the bad guys are looking for leverage to make Corey do the work they want. So they'll be looking for me...so you've got me out there looking at stuff out in public."

Marc nodded. "Yup."

I thought about what an alternate plan could be and just started making it up. "So if you guys cart me around while we look for this core, some of your other people will watch to see who is tailing us?"

"Bingo," Marc said, his grin broadening. This was a good change. At least he was distracted from being mad. "Corey goes into a secure location so they can't access him. So even if they think they're looking for Brandon, they can't get to him. So they're left with you if they think you're the girlfriend. If we can't find this core, we're hoping someone will still look for you and we might be able to figure out who they are and where they're hiding out at."

I twisted my head, looking out the windows, trying to look for cars following. The sun wouldn't be up for a couple of hours yet, but I didn't see any headlights. "But Kevin and Raven are with Corey. So who's following us? More Academy people?"

"You don't need to know anything about them," Marc said.

"How am I supposed to know who are the bad guys and who are the good guys if they catch up with us? If you don't tell me, I'll guess."

"Go ahead and guess," Marc said. He crossed his arms, his eyes challenging.

Despite the sparring between us, this was something of a relief. I was starting to wonder if my previous assumption of him being mad might have been a mistake. I admired a lot about him, even though at times he was chauvinistic. He was a street smart, ex-thug, now working for the good guys. His hair brushed to the front, the glint in his eyes; he looked like a rock star to me. Badass and smug, but despite my pushing him away at times, he was always right there.

A random car rolled out from a side street, turning right a block ahead of us and driving on. "Is that them?" I asked. I wasn't really guessing. I was just going to point out every car until he said who was who.

"Let's try to not talk about that so openly," Axel said. "It doesn't matter who is on our tail. Our job is to pretend they don't exist. We shouldn't be pointing them out. Talk about something else."

"Like the Academy?" I asked.

"No," Marc said.

"Sure," Axel said at the same time.

Marc frowned and shook his head. "Not right now. Not yet."

"She's ready for it," Axel said. "If she's asking, we should tell her."

"Why can't you tell me?" I asked.

Marc shifted in his seat, stretching and fiddling with the box. "It's not that I don't trust you," he said. "It's that you don't trust us. If I tell you certain secrets and you get pissed off at me, there's nothing to stop you from going to someone like Blake or your brother and telling them everything."

I was going to say I wouldn't do that, but the truth was, I'd already told Blake things because I was uncomfortable with them. Trust was hard to earn if someone kept secrets all the time. I folded my arms, sitting back, staring out the window.

Marc returned to the paperwork, flipping through some of the files. "Maybe we should find a way to ask the wife. Maybe she knows about the cell phone service and hasn't told anyone. She'd know where it was."

"Maybe he didn't tell her about it," I said quietly. "If there was a secret money account with a possibly illegal underground cell phone service, would you tell your wife? It didn't look like she got control of a bunch of money even though he died. She's still in the same house. If I got a billion dollars in a Swiss account because my husband died and left me an illegal cell phone service, I'd move at least to Isle of Palms, maybe Kiawah—probably out of the country."

Marc sighed. He pressed a palm to his face, rubbing. "Okay, I was just thinking maybe we should have a team keep an eye on her. Just in case they turn to her next. She's got kids and all."

I wanted to kiss Marc right then for being so sweet, protecting a family he didn't even know. He was right.

This team might target the family, if they hadn't already. "Can you get more Academy people to watch the house?"

"We could do that," Axel said.

Marc started sending a text from his phone.

"But now what?" I asked. "Isn't he a landlord or something? Maybe he keeps this core at one of his properties. Or at least at work."

Marc nodded, but kept his eyes on his phone. "The most obvious is probably the most likely."

"So we break in and check out the place?" I asked.

"Maybe. We need to scope it out, first. Go through that trash."

"Do we have to?"

"Cover our bases," he said.

I dug through the trash, avoiding clear plastic bags that looked like they were for bathrooms and bedrooms. Two were stuffed with paper. I opened one, and noticed little Jones got a D on his spelling test.

The other must have been from an office. Gum wrappers, old mail. I flipped through the mail, mostly ads, some for high-end credit card applications. Among the envelopes, there were invitations to parties, some thank you notes. "Should we check out his friends? Wouldn't one of them might know what he was up to?

Marc lifted his head, read the address on one of the envelopes I held up and nodded. "First, let's scope out the office. If we don't get any leads from that, we'll check out his friends."

We fell into a silence. I pretended to read documents, but my eyes were hurting trying to read in the car, so I opted for staring out the window and when that didn't ease the headache, I sat back with my eyes closed. Marc quietly thumbed his way through the documents, learning what he could.

After a few moments, I started passing out. I caught myself and sat up quickly, moving to stay awake.

Marc pulled his attention from a file. "What's wrong?"

"Nothing."

"If you're sleepy, go to sleep."

"I don't want to sleep." I didn't. I wanted to be awake. Last time I fell asleep, bad things happened.

"Liar," he said. He dropped the file and shoved the box to the floor. He snagged my elbow, and tugged. A few locks of his brown hair fell forward into his eyes as he looked at me. "Come on, Bambi. Relax a little."

I didn't know what he was doing at first, and thought he just wanted me to sit back a certain way. Then he tugged again harder and I nearly face planted into his lap. I caught myself just before my nose knocked into his thigh.

"What are you doing?" I asked.

"Shush," he said. He pressed his fingertips over my eyes so they would close. "Sleep."

"I'm going to get kidnapped by jerks and you want me to sleep?"

"You're not getting kidnapped," he said. "Now shut up and get some rest while you can."

"But..."

"We're going to check out this office, but it isn't open. We're not going to break into it right now. We'll wait until someone comes and opens up and check out the place. That's probably a good thing. We'll lay low and let these guys chasing you catch up with us. We're executing both plans at once this way." He dropped his hand onto my head, urging me to relax against his leg. "Sleep and I'll wake you up if anything interesting happens."

"It's a good idea," Axel said. "Do it now, while you can."

I grunted, but I really was tired. Stress was weighing heavy. I wanted to stay awake for Brandon. He was more than likely terrified in some trunk, or held at gunpoint to break into a core that he had no idea how to begin. How long could he fake being Corey? I felt like I should stay awake for his sake.

I also knew that if I was too tired to kick someone's butt, I'd be no help at all.

As I started to pass out, Marc kept his hand by my face, and a gentle thumb traced a soft spot right behind my ear. When I split my eyes open just enough to peek up at him, he was staring out the window, his head propped up in his other hand. Something was bugging him.

As I drifted off to sleep, I knew he was worrying about Brandon.

♠

HEAT

*W*hen I woke up again, the sun was up. The car was parked and my face was buried in Marc's thigh. I was tempted to remain. Numbness was welcome when I was sure chaos would follow. One more moment lost in the fog of sleep was tempting.

Marc's hand was pressed against my face and at first, I thought he was trying to wake me. But as I stretched and got up, he moved quickly, breathing in sharply and turning his head. There was a red mark on his cheek. He'd been asleep, too.

"Some lookout you are," I croaked, and then swallowed thickly.

"Your hair's a mess," he said. He stuffed his fingers into my hair and shook it around to tangle it more.

I slapped his arm away and wiped the sleep out of my eyes. The driver's seat was empty. We were alone in the back of the car. We were in a parking lot, with other cars on either side, making it harder for me to figure out where we were and what was going on. "Where's Axel?"

Marc sat up more, scanning the area. He pointed. "Over there."

It took me a minute to figure out what he was pointing at. We were surrounded by a strip mall I hadn't been to before. Different sections of the Charleston area had different styles and feelings. By the look of the brightly painted architecture and the ritzy signs and all the palm and palmetto trees and sand in spots, it felt like Isle of Palms.

I could see through a big window that Axel was inside the rental office we'd been on the hunt for. The sign overhead read "New Palm Realty" and displayed pictures of fancy beach homes in the front window. The office was lodged between a Chinese restaurant and a designer handbag store.

Inside New Palm Realty was a plump woman sitting behind the desk. Axel was standing in front of her, talking and motioning with his hands. He was wearing a black jacket and jeans that showed off his butt. We were dozens of feet away, but I could tell the woman's line of sight was currently fixated on Axel's crotch.

"What's he doing?" I asked.

"Scouting," Marc said. He slumped back. "Must have spotted an opportunity. We'll have to wait here until he's done."

The woman's eyes lifted from Axel's waist to his face and her face became animated as she spoke to him. There was no way to figure out what they were talking about from this distance.

My flip-flops had fallen off. My body was sore. I tried to find a comfortable position without lying down again. I stared out the window, watching Axel continue his conversation. The woman he was talking to was in her mid-forties, looking none the worse that her boss wasn't there. Business continued without Mr. Jones. I wondered if his wife owned it now.

I swallowed hard and stretched again, blew out a breath and sat back. I didn't like waiting. I was hungry, and needed coffee to wake up. I wondered where Brandon and Corey were. I was paranoid that Brandon was already dead. Maybe the German figured out they'd made a mistake. Maybe he had them both and was torturing them.

Marc leaned against the far edge of the seat, looking out the window, avoiding me.

I may have rested and gotten some energy back, but I could tell something was still bothering him. I was ready to get this part over with. "I give up," I said. "What's going on?"

Marc turned his head and did that wrinkle between the brows look. "What?"

"You're mad about something."

He cocked his head. His mismatched eyes confused. "I'm not mad."

"Yes, you are."

He grunted, scrubbing a palm over his face. "If you mean having to sit in a car while someone has Brandon over a barrel? No, I'm not happy."

"Is that all?" I asked, staring him down. I was willing to believe that was all it was, but I wanted to be sure.

He faced me full on, his eyes searching me, like he wasn't sure how much to tell me. His lips tightened.

"You're angry about something. You've been glaring since...I don't know. Since the fountain," I said.

Marc's face froze then, like he wasn't sure. "I don't need to fight with you."

"About what?"

"Nothing."

I made a loose fist and then punched him in the chest. "Tell me."

His mouth tightened. He acted like the punch didn't do anything to him. "Bambi..."

"Don't call me that."

He smirked and then when I tried to punch him again he captured my wrist. "Stop that."

"Tell me or I'll do it until you tell me." I wasn't going to let him hang something over my head, dangling it just out of reach. Something was off and I wanted to find out what or I wasn't going to be able to concentrate.

He groaned. "You are a pain until you eat." He held onto my wrist and then flattened my palm against his, holding on to it while interlacing our fingers. "I'd been out all night when your friend showed up. I'd just gotten into bed."

"What were you guys doing?"

"Looking for Wil," he said. He pressed his palms together against my hand he was holding, warming me. His mismatched eyes darkened as he looked at me. "Corey and I went out scouting some of his classmates' homes. We didn't bug anyone. We were trying to figure out the most likely people he could be staying with, narrowing the list."

My mouth fell open and my heart fluttered for him, and Corey, too. "I thought we were waiting until...." I wasn't sure what we were waiting for. My brain was foggy. We had visual confirmation that Wil was in school, even if he wasn't attending his classes. Our next step was to figure out the best way to establish contact without scaring him or getting him into trouble.

Part of me hesitated, too, because the longer my brother went without contacting me, the more I stressed that he didn't want to talk to me. Wouldn't he have found a way, even if he was in trouble for some reason?

Marc rolled his eyes and smirked. "I'm not very good at waiting. Corey felt the same. He wanted to go." He sighed and then lifted my hand up, kissing my palm. Before I could comment on that, he shook his head. "Then while we were out, Corey was texting with Raven. Corey said Raven was telling him that you and Raven are going out. But that Corey wasn't supposed to tell anyone. Corey checked with me to see if it was true or not. I told him Raven was being an ass, but it still kind of pissed me off."

My eyes widened, my heart stopped. I swallowed. I didn't know what I was most surprised to hear. Raven confessed to Corey. Marc dismissed it so easily. Was Raven kidding with Corey? And why was Corey concerned?

Marc took a look at me and then smirked wider. "Yeah," he said. "I thought the same thing. Corey was all worried, so I told him there was no way. Raven must have been fucking with him. I was angry with Raven. The next thing I know, I'm waking up to the doorbell and now I'm here. And Raven keeps trying to check in with me about where you are now. I can't tell him to fuck off because I know it's Corey asking about you, too. I want to talk to him about screwing with Corey, but it isn't the time."

My confused look must have been throwing him off on what I was thinking, because I was mostly concerned he was jealous of Raven. But he was dismissing it as impossible. That seemed more dangerous.

If he got mad at the thought of Raven fooling around and saying he and I were a thing, what would happen if Raven said it was true? Or Axel says he was interested? Or possibly Brandon?

Despite what Axel believed, none of them were going to be happy about hearing the truth. I'd gone pretty far with all of them, without the intention of letting it get that way. I needed to make a choice, but it was impossible right now. We were in the middle of a serious situation and this wasn't the time to talk about relationships and get everyone pissed off at each other. "So you were glaring at me about it?"

He shook his head, took a slow breath out. "I was just mad. I'm still mad but it's all just bad timing and circumstances and Raven fucking around."

"So you're not mad at me?"

83

"No." He turned his head, looking at me quietly for a moment. He leaned in, his face moving close to mine. "You've been really distant since you found out Wil could be in trouble. I've been kind of a mess since then. I can't really focus on anything when there's a problem I want to fix."

"It's not yours to fix," I said. I stared back at him, my eyes unable to focus on his while he was so close. My thoughts were all over the place, thinking of Corey and what Raven had said and also about what Axel had said and how I could put off my decision until later.

More important was the issue of my brother. "At first I wanted to just find him and ask Wil directly, but now...I don't know. Now Brandon's gone and we can't keep an eye on Wil. Even when we get Brandon back, I don't know what I'm going to do."

It felt strange to confess like this with my thoughts so jumbled. But the determination in Marc's eyes drove me to answer him and I understood his desire to fix stuff. I usually felt the same way about problems. But I was a complicated mess, and I wasn't his problem.

"You don't need to worry about me," I said. "Wil isn't dead. He's just lost. We just need to make sure he's not in trouble. Once he's found, I'll get a normal job so you guys don't have to keep me working with you. I'll keep an eye on Wil and hopefully he'll come back when he's ready."

He moved his hand and thunked me in the shoulder. "Stop that. It's not like you're a mooch. You've done more than your fair share of work around here. I've seen you scrape old wallpaper out in a few hours and move on to sand a floor. You're wearing yourself out. And I don't need you running off thinking you've got to stand on your own. Trust me, it won't work like you think it will."

I swallowed hard. Out of all the guys, he seemed to understand more than anyone that I couldn't just stand still, and I didn't know how to completely leave. But also that I had to prove I could, that I wasn't mooching off of their kindness. "I can go," I said firmly. "I mean it. If I'm sure Wil is okay, I'll go and get out of your hair."

"No," he said. He lifted my hand again, putting it against his face and kissing the palm. Then he spoke into my hand. "Don't. Please. Or if you do, I'll go with you. You're not mooching. If it'll make you feel better, you can work with me on something other than house refurbishing. You wouldn't feel so bad then if we're working together. It makes a difference when you can see who you're helping."

"What do you mean? What kind of work?"

"Call me crazy, but unless you get that excited look in your eyes, you're not happy," he said, smirking against my hand. "I remember that glow you had after you did the bounty hunting thing in Florida. And you've got that excitement again now. I mean, outside of Brandon being in danger, you seem to need something more than a normal job. You're a thrill-seeker and an adrenaline junkie. You're as fucked up as we are. We need something like the Academy to keep us busy, or we go insane."

I wanted to pretend that wasn't the case, but it would have been a lie. I was worried about Wil, but I wasn't the depressed type. I thought about Florida, and helping to find a little girl and her father and reunite them, and nothing has been the same since. Maybe it wasn't just Wil disappearing that had changed me.

In a way, I was afraid to examine it too closely. I liked the guys, and perhaps even needed them right now, but I was hesitant to make too strong a connection. I felt they'd back away if I got too close. Alone was better for me.

He looked up over my shoulder and I turned to check out what he was looking at. The only thing I could see was Axel still talking to the lady.

Marc released my hand, and a moment later he grabbed me by the hips, tugging me hard toward him. I choked on a surprised cry and landed flat on my back in the seat.

The back of my shirt caught on the seat, and the hem started to ride up, right up to the sports bra, exposing all of my stomach as Marc crawled over me. I twisted to keep him off and to adjust my clothes, nearly falling off the seat as I did.

Marc corrected me quickly and then hovered over me. One of his knees worked up between my thighs and his other foot planted firmly on the floor. He bent over, and captured one of my hands, holding it.

"I'll show you I'm not mad anymore," he said. His eyes lowered from my face to my exposed stomach. His hand drifted down.

His fingers traced over the soft skin between my belly button and my ribs. My insides shook at his touch. He lowered down, kissed me quickly on the lips and before I had a chance to kiss him back, his head lowered, and he kissed at a spot right above my belly button.

A tremor worked through my body. I grasped at his shoulders, holding my breath. Really wasn't expecting that. Wasn't expecting a kiss, either, and yet I didn't stop it. So messed up. How could I feel this strongly when I was around Marc, like I need him to cover me all over and hear those promises he made?

Disaster loomed. Axel could be back any second and Marc was on top of me. I desired the affection, but every bit of me was wound up tight with worry. If I told him the truth now, there really would be a fight. I was trying to work out a delicate way to fend him off, and yet I was having a hard time thinking with him so close, touching me.

He flattened his tongue against my skin, licking upward toward my ribs. He moved up my body, his hands planting on either side of my head and then lowered his mouth against mine again. His lips were gentle at first, and then firmed when I started to respond. I couldn't help it. He lured me out and then chased me down.

When his lips left mine, he trailed kisses down to my neck. He suckled at my skin and his stomach lowered to my belly, his weight pressing me into the seat. He traced along my side with his hand, up until his fingertips traced the bra's edge.

That tripped my brain into panic mode. Kissing was one thing, but I didn't want to go that far. Not here and now in the back of the vehicle. "Marc," I breathed. "Axel could..."

He got up quickly, checking through the windshield. He lowered again, pressing his mouth to mine for a moment. "I'll watch for him. He's still busy."

"I don't want to do this here," I said. I wasn't going to tell him the other truth. I didn't want the first time with Marc rushed in the parking lot with the German possibly watching and the threat of Axel interrupting looming over us.

Then I realized I was thinking of a *first time* with Marc. It was enough to cause a rush of desire through my body. It couldn't be helped; I did want him. I felt the ache inside me growing.

He breathed slowly and then kissed me again, slowly, longer. He was promising me he wasn't going to go that far. His lips clung to me, telling me he'd do whatever I wanted. I moaned. He was unbelievable. How could I read him so easily? When other boyfriends would have called me a tease, and told me off or would have kept going until

I had to push them off, Marc simply understood and was patient. It didn't matter what we were doing. He'd go where I wanted him, but he still wanted to kiss me.

Did I just think of him as my boyfriend?

His hand at my side slowed, too. The edge of his palm rubbed the outside of my breast slowly, and when I didn't protest, he slowly edged his whole hand until he was cupping one breast. He squeezed gently.

I moaned against his mouth again, responding to his kisses. My own hands had been against his chest, immobile as I was enjoying him doing things to me, being selfish and letting him touch. Taking it all in. But now as he kissed me, my hands drifted up until I was cupping the back of his head. My fingers moved down over his neck, feeling his soft hair. I started working my hands over his shoulders, exploring, feeling the muscles and how his shoulders were shaped, wide. As I continued down his arms, I felt his biceps flexing. All the things I'd admired before on his body, I wanted to feel out and get to know.

A tiny part of my brain knew I should have pushed him off. Initially, it was what I had meant to do, but damn, he could kiss.

His hand on my breast stopped and then his whole body lowered until he was closer to me with his stomach pressed against mine, his chest was against mine.

His kiss became deeper, more urgent. He suckled at my lower lip, dove for another kiss and his tongue darted out into my mouth, seeking out mine.

If someone could win me over with a kiss, he was going to try. It was working, too.

He pulled back a bit, his lips still hovering over mine. "Don't run away again," he said, begging in such a soft voice that it almost didn't seem like him. "I'll chase you if you do."

"I don't know what I'm doing," I whispered.

"Don't make it complicated," he said. He backed his head away until the green-blue eyes met mine. He studied me. "We could make this a thing. Start simple. Do you have feelings for me?"

I did something that was almost a snort. What a stupid question.

"Don't get all indignant," he said. "Just tell me simple. Do you hate me?"

"No."

"So you do like me." He wriggled an eyebrow at me. "You'd have gone on a date with me if we'd met under normal circumstances."

"Maybe." Couldn't help it. I didn't do easy commitments. Never had been able to. Whenever I got asked out in high school, I always turned down the first request and waited until the guy asked again before I'd agree to it.

He smirked. He shifted and I moved over a little until he could relax on his side, propped up on his hand and looked down at me. His other hand moved up, tugging a strand of my hair away from my face. "I've got those wiggle sparks for you," he said quietly. "You don't want to rush anything. I get that, but I swear, I haven't felt it like this before. Stop thinking about what we should be doing. I wouldn't ask just any girl to move in with me right after I met her. If you really feel strongly about it, you can still sleep on the couch, or we'll figure something out." His hand trailed down, and his palm met my belly again. "But if you feel any spark in there, if you're not repulsed by the idea of us together, just stay. You can contribute if you want, but you don't have to. I'll won't ask. You're not costing us anything extra."

My insides trembled again. This was everything I needed to hear, and the worst thing he could have told me. It was exactly what I needed: him, a place to stay, someone who understood I was starting from nothing was afraid I would eventually get kicked out. He was looking for my brother. Without my knowing about it, he'd been on the hunt and helping me. Trying to fix things.

Marc was here right now, with me, helping me again. It wasn't enough to help me with Wil. He was giving me a foothold, and at the same time, telling me to stay.

But I couldn't answer him, because my situation with Brandon niggled at the back of my mind. Axel's kiss was etched in me. Raven's hard stares, his touch, his brisk attachments made me crave him. They each tugged at me in different ways. I closed my eyes tight, unable to look at him anymore, because I was sure once he learned the truth, he'd take it all back. He couldn't feel that way about me if he knew his other friends were that into me and that I shared those feelings.

And with that thought, I swallowed hard to push the pain back. I couldn't be lured in by daydreams of him and his promises and then later get thrown out. I started pushing him off, pulling myself up.

Marc resisted, capturing my hand and trying to draw it in. "Don't..."

But I couldn't answer him. I couldn't risk hurting any of them and getting kicked out of this group I'd been growing attached to.

It might just kill me if they did.

As if answering my silent pleas, the driver's door opened. Marc sat up quickly and I did, too, putting space between us.

"Get a nice nap, you two?" Axel asked. He sat behind the wheel and then turned to look at me right behind him and then eased, looking at Marc. If he saw anything, he wasn't going to say so.

"What'd she say?" Marc asked. He moved, jumping into the front seat of the car and settling in. He glanced once at me, a bit of the pleading still in his eyes but it started to fade. I wondered if he thought I'd heard Axel coming and that's why I moved away from him. It was like he understood, but was hurt that I felt the need to hide 'us' from Axel.

While they weren't watching me, I fixed myself, and rubbed my hands across my face, trying to get out from under the spell Marc had cast.

Axel pulled the glasses off of his face and rubbed at his eyes. "Randall died here. Random robbery homicide. No suspects. No witnesses except a few people working late at the Chinese restaurant who heard the shots fired."

"Happened here?" Marc asked, and then scanned the place, as if it was happening in front of him now.

Axel shrugged. "He left the office late that night. He'd been walking to his car, caught a couple of bullets in the chest and someone took his wallet and phone. They found the wallet a few blocks later with everything taken out except a couple of ID cards. His cell was turned off, so they couldn't follow it. The police are still looking for information, but they don't have any leads. They think it's connected to several other attacks that have happened in the area. Though those have all been robberies, but no homicides. Until now. The police are saying he must have resisted and so they shot him."

My eyes kept darting to Marc, but I shook off the overwhelming thoughts about him and what we'd done and focused on Axel and what he was saying, getting back to business. I curled up a bit and stared out the window. I was looking for Mr. Jones's ghost. "Robberies in Isle of Palms?" It was a ritzy place to get mugged.

"Yeah. What's the world coming to?" Axel rocked his head toward the rental agency. "But as far as I can tell, this lady doesn't know a thing about a communication core." Axel shifted in his seat, and he scanned the area again. He took out his cell phone and started typing into it.

"What's wrong?" Marc asked.

"I don't like this," Axel said. "Kayli's right, this guy doesn't seem to have any connection to a secret communication service. There's no sign of a profit of any sort. This guy doesn't seem all that intelligent, either. I mean, he had an okay business going..."

"He still worked," I said, catching on. I snapped my fingers, suddenly getting it and pointing at them. "Because he's not the owner. He's just a user."

The boys looked at each other and then turned, looking over their shoulders at me.

I kept going. "This guy owned vacation homes, right? And he's been in the black, even with the recent dead zone of a tourist season there's been lately. I bet he uses a secret phone to appeal to people who are looking for indiscreet services. You know, like guys trying to find a secret spot to take their mistresses. Look at his office," I said, pointing to the corner of the strip mall it was nestled in. "These are million dollar vacation homes he was renting out, right? Simple business. But he was here, doing business as usual. I mean he was working when he got knocked off. If I had extra cash stashed away, like the million I'd earn running a secret communication thing, I'd be travelling and letting other people run my business. You don't make a bunch of money like that and not spend it. I don't think he owns this core. I think he's just a lead. He was a target because he had one of their phones."

Marc furrowed his eyebrows, sitting back. "His phone's on the underground system. That's why it was stolen."

I nodded. "We find out where he bought it from, we'll figure out where this core is, who owns it..."

"He wouldn't have a bill," Axel said. "It's anonymous."

"We need a cell phone," I said. "Couldn't Corey track down this core if we give him a cell phone that worked with the network? That must be how they found it. We could make a couple of calls and track where the signal goes."

Axel rocked his head in a nod. "We could do that. We'd have to find someone else who owned a cell phone on the network. And then we have to hope they'd let us borrow it long enough to run..." Suddenly, his own cell phone started going off. He pulled it out and checked it. He put it on speaker and held it out. "Corey, tell me some good news."

"Not this time," he said. "The phone Kayli stole just got wiped."

"Come again?"

"I was rooting around when the entire data set blanked out. Must have been done remotely while I had it on."

"What could do that?"

"I don't know. Something sophisticated."

"If it's sophisticated, it's traceable. Make sure it's dead, or let Kevin or someone get rid of it." Axel hung up. He sat back a little, staring out the windshield, silent. Suddenly, he punched at the steering wheel. "Damn."

"We'll find him," Marc said. "He's not going to get himself killed."

Axel glared out the windshield. "We don't have time to trace a bugged cell phone. I really don't like not knowing what's going on."

Marc sat back, rolling his head along the headrest. "Let's think for a moment. This underground cell service. It's still cellular. We could set up something to listen for unusual signals. Then we can source a cell phone or tower."

"We don't have the time to set that up, and then wait for a chance something has come in. I don't know if we've got anyone trained on this side of the globe. I mean, it's Charleston, for Christ's sake. This shit happens in New York or Washington."

"You want to call in the Feds on this?" Marc asked. "Or CIA? Or local police? I mean, this is usually beyond what... what we do."

Axel sighed, shook his head. "Believe me, I want to. I'm considering it, but I've got some reservations. By the time they caught up with what we know, they'll still be ten steps behind." He shoved a finger across his brow, gliding back and forth. "They're not going to pull a civilian like Brandon out in a swoop and destroy evidence to possibly one of the biggest assets they'll come across in this area. They'll see this cell phone service as a way to identify local crooks. 'Corey' currently looks like he's involved with it, and given his record, he might be facing a trial at the least. And we run the risk they'll start a full investigation that will take months before they act just to catch bad guys who need a secret cell phone service."

I piped in. "Do we know anyone local that listens? Tracks signals?"

"The Academy just links into NSA and FCC networks," Marc said. "I think the FCC looks for illegal signals, if they know about them. But only if they know there's something to listen for. Maybe the NSA."

A particular smoking Irish guy came to mind. I'd met him briefly, but he could be our best shot. "Doyle does it," I said flatly. "He might know."

Both of their heads shook, like they thought I was joking. They stopped, turned and faced me.

I widened my eyes at them. "What?"

"Who's Doyle?" Marc asked.

"That friend of Blake Coaltar. Didn't I tell you guys about him?"

"The one that hacked our video cameras?" Marc asked.

"No," Axel said, shaking his head. "No, we're not seeing him."

"Why not?" I asked. "You need someone who does that stuff. He does it."

"That guy sounds like he's just asking for the FCC and the FBI to visit. And he's friends with Coaltar."

"So?"

"So you aren't going."

I grunted, and sat back with my arms folded. "Or we could wait for you guys to get lucky. Maybe Corey could rig up enough satellite dishes, computer systems and so forth that this guy already has set up."

Axel twisted his lips, shaking his head. "It's a bad idea."

Marc shrugged. "Have a better one?

He glanced around the parking lot and swiveled his head around. "Let's grab some breakfast first. I've got a few things I want to try before we resort to talking to this Doyle."

"Gotta love her brain, though, right?" Marc grinned. "If we were really trying to get into this core, or even solve these murders..."

Axel sliced his hand across the space between himself and Marc. "Let's focus. This guy the German said died because he owned the core, it has to be someone else if it isn't this Randall guy. This means they've killed multiple people. If we can connect the two deaths, and then point the police to any leads, or even get the FBI involved if we have to, we'll be good to go. Right as soon as we find Brandon, we can send the police after them. Our goal now, though, is to get Brandon out as soon as possible. We can sort out this underground network later."

Tension mounted in the car. Axel didn't seem to be in the best of moods. I glanced at Marc, who appeared sympathetic. The longer we went trying to find where these guys were, the chances were greater they'd find out that Brandon wasn't their guy, and he could get killed.

We were running out of time.

♠

TURTLES

*A*xel veered into a McDonald's. Three egg sandwiches later, splitting one with Marc, stealing his hash brown, and downing my own coffee and half of Axel's, I was finally feeling awake and ready. The only reason why we stopped at all was because Marc insisted we couldn't continue to work like this on an empty stomach, and Axel could drive and eat at the same time. Marc bitched about the coffee, but downed his own as quickly as possible.

I didn't want to eat anything. I wanted to stay angry, but after I started, I felt better, still angry, but better.

"She really is a pit," Axel said as he drove toward downtown Charleston again.

"I think she eats more than I do," Marc said.

"I'm right here," I said. I wasn't really perturbed they were talking about me like that. It was kind of amusing, but I'd been starving so I would have eaten anything. Did I really eat that much?

They both chuckled. Axel in a grumbly, stoic way. Marc's laugh was light, proud. He kept smiling back at me like he'd won something.

It was the edge of disaster staring me in the face. I pushed that thought away. "Where are we going now, anyway?" I asked.

"We're going to drive around for a little bit, and try to lead these guys out into the open. If not, we need to find another phone on this network," Axel said. He weaved his way into downtown traffic, taking roads that were heavily congested. "I don't want to take plan B, though. It'll take too long."

"I still say we could go check out Doyle. Can't we just tell him to be on the lookout now while we deal with plan A? Save us some time in case we have to do plan B?"

Axel shook his head, and a lock of his dark hair fell against his face, almost in the way of his glasses. "My problem is still timing. The longer we're waiting, the more likely Brandon is discovered. It would be different if they weren't killing people over this, but now it looks like they are. How long will it take us to even convince this Doyle guy to do us a favor when we don't know anything about him? He may not be that easy to convince to help us."

I sighed. Maybe he did have a point. Doyle was more than likely our best bet at finding a secret underground cell phone network, but who was to say he would help?

Marc pushed his head back against the headrest and closed his eyes. "I hate being chased."

"Do we have anyone following us?" I asked. I looked behind us, trying to pick out cars.

"Uh huh," Axel said. "Two of them. Team A is three cars behind us, Team B is in the other lane, behind Team A."

I tried studying our surroundings, but I couldn't see anything beyond the car right behind us. I was too close. I tried checking the mirrors. "Are you sure it's them? How did they know where to find us?" I asked.

Marc redirected his pointer finger, aiming it at my face. "We sent someone who looked like you to our apartment. And made sure her team could get her back out and take them for a ride around Charleston. But now they've lead them back to us."

I dropped my mouth open. "Where's our team?"

"Following the bad guys," Axel said. "Now that

they've been able to identify which cars are the ones scouting for you, we're basically leading them where we want while they are looking for an opening. It's not easy when there's two cars with several people inside. We want to take one out and question them without alerting the others."

I studied the cars, as if I could see through them and figure out who was following us, trying to remember the German's face and pick him out. "How did you get them to switch and follow us? What girl? How do you know?"

Axel held up his cell phone. He eased the car forward as space became available through traffic. "We're not just sitting on our asses. I've been getting updates. When one of our own is in danger, we call it in. We've got a lot of people out there now scouting for Brandon. More than you might think."

I was impressed. I didn't know the Academy that well, but it seemed they were working this as best as they could. "Can't we do something to hurry it along? They want me, don't they? They're looking for an opening? Let's lead them somewhere."

"They may not do anything during the day and in public," Axel said. "And this is the best way for us to stay safe while we're figuring out an opening. We can't risk our necks and all get caught by these guys."

I breathed in, sitting back. Axel was making circles around downtown, and then looped onto the Mark Clark Expressway. There would only be so many times he could make circles before he'd need gas, or the people following us figured out we were leading them on a goose chase because we knew we were being followed. "What happens at night?"

"Hopefully, this will be over before then."

"What if it isn't?"

Axel shrugged. "I might drop you off at the hospital

with the others."

"Why the hospital? What's up with that? How is a hospital keeping Corey safe?"

"Who is going to try to kidnap any of us in the middle of something like a hospital? There's security and video and people being monitored continuously. It's second best outside of being inside a police station."

As crazy as his idea was, it did make sense. Still, I kept looking out the back window. "So we'll drive around all day." That didn't sit well with me. Being chased all day? No. I was too used to being the hunter, not the hunted. I didn't like it. "Can't we do something else? Shouldn't we speed this up somehow?"

He adjusted his rearview mirror. His eyes were intense, a storm brewing behind the otherwise calm exterior. "Would you like to go somewhere?" he asked. "We've got one team behind us. I'd rather have two or three, just in case. They're headed this way."

"How can we trip these guys up? Let's just ram this car into theirs and get this over with."

"We're doing this as fast as we can. The best thing we can do right now is keep them busy. Eventually, this team is going to need to take a break, and they might head back to where Brandon is. As long as they don't know we're looking at them, we've got some advantage. It's what we need right now."

"We could go check out the neighborhoods around Wil's school," Marc said. "If we have to drive around anyway, it may be worthwhile to do something useful if we're being bait. Kill two birds at once, right?"

"I don't want to go where Wil is if there's German killer hackers following us," I said.

"And it's all the way out in Goose Creek and Summerville," Axel said. "And some of those neighborhoods have secluded spots and stretches of road without anyone around." Axel pulled forward out of traffic, getting off the Mark Clark, and checking street signs. He turned on his cell phone again and started tapping at it.

"If you need to text, should I drive?" I asked in a warning tone.

Axel scrunched his eyebrows and looked at me in the rearview mirror. "Do you have your license?"

Was he being serious? You needed a car to get your license. "I can drive," I said.

"She doesn't have a license," Marc said.

I made a face at him. "I know enough to not use a cell phone while you're driving."

"She really hates that," Marc said. He glanced back at me and I shot him a look, trying to tell him to stop interpreting like I didn't have a voice. He squinted his face back at me and smirked.

"I can tell," Axel said, though he ignored my request and continued to use his cell phone anyway. After a moment, he placed it back into his pocket. "How about a nice visit to the aquarium?"

I wasn't sure if he was joking or if he was talking about just driving in that direction. I'd never seen the aquarium.

The advertising on the way down the block closest to the aquarium featured sharks and turtles. The aquarium was adjacent to a port for tours of a fort and a park.

Axel parked along the street at a park. The streets were filled with mostly locals, but some tourists were lingering along the sidewalks, huddled together and looking at their phones, making me think they were looking at GPS or lists of tourist attractions. It was late in the season for tourists but I guess some people wait until the off season for their vacations.

I got out of the car, scanning and trying to figure out

where the people following us would park and try to
follow. "How are we doing this?"

"Going on foot will help us, actually," Axel said. "I
informed the teams following us to stay back but keep an
eye on who follows us inside." He came around and
hooked an arm around my neck, drawing me toward the
building. "Come on. I'll give you the tour."

"You come here often?" I asked.

"He practically lives here," Marc said. He started
walking behind us and then next to me on my other side.

I recalled Axel's glowing fish, and figured maybe he
got his fish at this aquarium. Maybe he borrowed the labs
here for his experiments. Did he work here somehow?

While we were walking, Axel didn't let go of my neck
and Marc gave me a confused look. I ignored it and stared
ahead, afraid to focus on either of them.

We had to cross a wide open expanse of sidewalks and
gardens to get to the entrance of the aquarium. I kept
wanting to look over my shoulder to check out who was
behind us, scope out every face, try to find people that
looked shady.

Axel anchored the crook of his elbow into the back of
my neck, and forced me to look forward. "Stop," he said.

"Why?" I asked.

"You're way too obvious," he said.

"Shouldn't I be obvious?" I asked. "I mean, I was just
kidnapped and now I'm heading to an aquarium. We know
Brandon isn't here. Isn't this going to be like confusing as
all hell to anyone else?"

"Confusing is good," Marc said. His hands were
stuffed into his jeans and his shoulders were hunched. He
gazed around at every face nearby. "Makes them more
curious. But she's right. She should be looking over her
shoulder. If we're making it obvious we're with her, then
we should make it obvious, too. Make us appear like idiots

that don't know what we're doing."

Axel pressed his lips together and then nodded. Slowly, he slid his arm out from around my neck and looked behind himself, stiffly, like it was going against his instincts and training.

"Besides," I said, "they assume I'm Corey's girlfriend. I should look all upset."

"Don't start crying and blubbering, please," Marc said. "I don't know if I can take that."

"Ugh," I said. I pressed my palms to my face and rubbed hard at my eyes and cheeks. I made sure my cheeks were pinched hard enough that I looked like a wreck. I moved my hands away and glared at Marc. "See?"

Marc stopped walking, his face changing from smirk to full concern. His hands reached out, palms open. "Bambi..."

I made a face and smacked at his hand. "Stop," I said. "I'm supposed to..."

Marc straightened and then made a face back, with his tongue out, shaking his head. "Don't look like that. All crying and shit. You look different; I don't like it."

"Are they following us or what?"

"They haven't gotten out of the car yet," Axel said. He showed me the cell phone he was looking at shielded by his chest. "Just try to look normal. If we can't get them to follow us inside, then we're no worse off. We've got people following them. Eventually someone will need to inform a boss about this. Someone following them is paying attention."

Spy stuff. I tried to relax. We'd find Brandon. I had a part to play until then. It was hard to be bait, but I tolerated it for now.

We entered the aquarium and Axel only needed to look at security and wave at the front desk attendant to get us in. Several workers said hello to him. He smiled politely, but only replied with a good morning, keeping anyone from engaging in conversation with him.

The air was cold inside the building and I covered my stomach with my arms to keep in some heat.

I tried not to, but I couldn't help but be distracted by the gigantic walls of glass, displaying various fish, sharks, and turtles. Every time I tried to focus on people, I'd see something colorful out of the corner of my eye, and then was staring at a bright orange or yellow fish.

My instincts told me to find a seat somewhere and be on the lookout to observe the crowds of people. Most places had a certain flow. Malls were busy with eyeballs on items in windows and at store signs, always up, always scanning. My advantage before was I could keep my hands down and out of the line of sight, to sit near uninteresting walls and wait until people were focused on items, so I could determine what was in their pockets.

The aquarium had a different vibe, because the walls of glass extended down to the floor, and fish could be even further down swimming along the bottom of the tanks, or at waist level or pop up above heads. With their constant movement, eyeballs were everywhere. They did keep people' attention, though. There was also an echo from the glass, so it was loud and hard to focus.

So I used it to my advantage. I changed from checking faces, until I was looking for eyes who weren't focus on the fish. In the crowds, it was more difficult, but I started to get the hang of it.

Axel stood beside me, and it only took him a few minutes before his hand clamped down on the back of my head and forced me to look back at the fish. He leaned in and whispered to me, "Stop looking."

I shifted uncomfortably, walking out of my flip-flops and then putting them back on. "Let's capture one of them."

"We need to let them make a mistake. And we need our other teams to watch them. All you have to do is stand still for a while. Just enjoy the view."

I breathed out slowly, resisting his hold by pushing back. "I don't want to wait."

"If we don't, if they know we're onto them, we could die. Or Brandon could."

I stilled my head. "What if he's already dead?"

"If he was," he said quietly, "they wouldn't still be chasing you. He must still be refusing to work with them if they're still bothering to chase you."

That made some sense. I gulped, trying to reclaim some control. I didn't like a plan that involved me standing still. "I need to do something," I said. I looked to the side, where Marc had separated from us a little, but still within talking distance. "Let me do something. Like, let's give them an opportunity too good to pass up.

Axel mumbled something and then grunted. "You'll be bait. If you can sit still for a minute, we'll see who comes in after you and will give them a jump. But you have to trust me, and you have to be willing to sit still."

I didn't like that idea, either, but if it would get us to Brandon sooner, I'd tolerate it. The German's urgency, the dead Randall investigation, the other dead owner of the core, the kidnapping, it was all overwhelming. Right now, I just wanted to get Brandon and bail on it all. Let the German do what he wanted. Marc was right: Let's get Brandon, get out and let the police deal with the investigation. "I'll do whatever it takes."

Axel nodded. He shared a silent conversation across the room with Marc. It took only a few minutes, but as I was studying the both of them, I understood it. Axel silently told Marc about the change of plans, and Marc wasn't happy with it, but he was going to let it happen.

Marc made a circle like he was giving us space and Axel guided me through a public area and then toward a door marked for employees only.

The hall smelled strongly of disinfectant and fish and salt. It was tiled and there were rows of doors. Axel moved quickly through another door, into another similar hallway. A short walk and another door later, I was in a lab.

The room was white, with the tiles having a few dull spots. Counters held containers of unidentifiable liquids. Smaller glass aquariums filled the room, with small fish and one that was filled with water but appeared empty of any fish. Deeper inside the lab, there was a large aquarium built in the center like a huge hot tub, and inside were two large sea turtles. One had a bandage around a back leg.

"What's wrong with the turtles?" I asked.

Axel gazed over at them and then shook his head. "Rescues. Injured and brought here from the beach. The aquarium hosts a turtle hospital. These two are new. Not stable enough to join the others in the bigger aquarium."

I pouted, feeling sorry for the things. "This is the best spot for getting a jump on these guys?"

"We need a secure location with a limited amount of exits and a place where we aren't likely to be interrupted. If we're going to lure them into trying to capture you, we need to give them a temptation they can't refuse." He showed me a computer terminal near a counter. He pulled out a stool and smacked his hand on the seat. "Now sit and do what you promised."

"There's no one else in here," I said. "How do you know no one will come in?"

"Because it's my office," he said. "I'll be in the next room."

I glanced around the room again, looking at the turtles, the fancy tanks and chemicals. I had a lot of questions by only one came out. "The sick turtles stay in your office?"

"The ones I rescued, yeah," he said.

I sought out his eyes and locked in on his gaze. My heart, despite the anger welling there at the people chasing us, found a small spot of warmth just for Axel. During the time we'd been back from Florida and I'd been diving head first into my own misery and working for the other boys, Axel had been saving turtles and working here in his lab. Somehow, that meant something to me. It was something I hadn't know, but now that I did, I adored him for it. It spoke about him in ways he simply couldn't have told me. Seeing was better.

I looked at the turtles, who seemed so big in the tank. They floated, fins down, looking unhealthy. Axel rescued them. I wondered if the others knew.

He motioned again for me to sit, and I did. He leaned in and whispered in my ear. "Once we've got Brandon, once we're out of this mess, maybe you'll come by and help me out once in a while. Unless you really do like construction work."

"I can?" I asked.

"Soon," he said. "First things first. Be bait."

I turned, looking at his face. He was his usual stoic self, but there was a hint of a spark in his eyes, something deeper. I'd read enough faces to tell me there was a plan already in place, and Marc was already well aware. I was to sit still. He wasn't going to tell me anything else.

Because they didn't want me to override their plan and ruin it from the start.

Because I wouldn't like it.

I sat on the stool, staring at the screen, trying to put together their plan while pretending to do as he told me.

I listened as Axel left the room. And then I checked over my shoulder, studying my surroundings, my exits, of which there were only two doors, and one closet. No windows. No place to go, except maybe up in the ceiling. I didn't like my options if something went wrong.

I didn't like not knowing the whole plan.

I waited, swinging my legs and purposefully flicking the flip-flops to make sounds against my heels to fill the space.

If they separated from me, these criminals would try to come after me. They'd send in a team to zap me again. Only this time Axel and Marc were waiting in the wings, ready to rush in.

But is that what the German would do in a public place? Maybe this office was secluded but then they'd still have to carry me out, and they'd have to go through security. Maybe they were willing to follow us and keep an eye on what we were up to, but would they be stupid enough to come in after me like this?

I wouldn't. I'd recognize something was going on if we split up in a strange location.

The problem I had with the whole situation was still gnawing at me from the inside. It wasn't just this set-up. It was something that had been bothering me since the beginning. One was what Brandon had said right from the start: Why had this German team bothered to drag in Corey? Why were they interested in someone who wasn't willing to participate, when there were plenty of criminal minds and hackers out there ready and willing and able to break into Corey's security thing, even if it did take time? I mean, a couple of extra weeks or more wasn't worth the risk of kidnapping and murder, was it?

Before they had asked Corey for help. Now they'd kidnapped him and were following me to kidnap me again to force him to work. They were taking a lot of chances.

No, something still wasn't working for me in this entire situation. The urgency didn't sit with me. It had been weeks since they'd contacted Corey, even before I talked to him since they'd been looking for him.

I tried to remember that day with Corey. I'd been frustrated, and Corey had offered to go on a walk. Outside, in a public place with plenty of witnesses and traffic around Colonial Lake in downtown Charleston, this German man stopped his car in the middle of it all and ran over to talk to Corey. He'd insisted Corey come talk with him in private, despite Corey refusing. He hadn't kidnapped him then. No urgency. He wanted Corey, and he was willing to negotiate, and then when Corey refused, he had walked away.

Now the story was different. He'd kidnapped Corey. He'd threatened his life and then mine.

The question that came to mind over and over again rushed through me: Why now? What was different? Why did they wait until weeks later to kidnap him? What would make *me* rush in and do something so risky?

As I sat looking around in Axel's office, at the turtles, and everything else, I considered that. Why was I here now? Because someone was threatening my life.

Which...could mean *their* lives were being threatened? Could that be why they were doing this?

Maybe someone else was on the hunt. They'd discovered an enemy, and if they didn't act quickly their plans would fall apart. They had come for Corey now to secure him and to make sure they would win.

I sat up quickly. It suddenly made sense to me. The German and his gang of thugs might have been okay with going slow before, but since their game changed, they had to move up the timeline. Their only option was to get Corey to the core to give them access. It was something they were willing to kill someone over.

Which meant they were afraid of their enemy.

I turned my head to look at the computer screen. My skin prickled, like back when I used to steal wallets at the mall, and I got the feeling security or a cop was watching me.

There were a lot of questions I didn't have the answers to yet, but one thing I was sure of: we were all in danger, because there was more than one group eyeing the prize, and at least one group was willing to murder to get what they wanted. The question was which one was chasing us right now.

Both?

Axel said they'd spotted two cars following us. Could both be the German's teammates or was one car a different team? Did the German know who was hunting him?

While I was trying to figure out if I should chase down Axel, or continue to wait like he said, a door opened. I twisted, expecting Axel to come back. Maybe he had realized the same thing.

In the doorway stood a woman. She had a white lab coat on over a pair of slimming black slacks and a light cream sweater. Her deep red hair was pulled back into a bun near her neck. She was slender, with pale skin. Her vivid blue eyes and the small curve of her lips as she entered told me she was proud of something. She spotted me. In an instant, her face changed to mild surprise.

"Oh," she said in a quiet but very precise tone. "Are you the new intern?"

I thought Axel said he wasn't disturbed in his office.

Something was off about her eyes. But instead of trying to figure out what, I was trying to think of a logical reason for me to be in Axel's office and to get her to go away because she was putting herself in the middle of mortal danger. Her question gave me the perfect out. "Yes," I said, quickly. "Do you work for Axel? Are you who he's been expecting? He's in the...turtle hospital. You should go see him."

"He's not in the hospital room," she said simply. She

walked in a circle around me, her heels clacking sharply against the tiles. "And he didn't ask for me to join him. The question is, who are you? And what are you doing here?"

"I'm waiting for Axel," I said.

"It'll be a long wait," she said.

I hopped off my chair, sliding slightly against the tile in my flip-flops. "Who are you?" I asked.

She clicked her tongue against the roof of her mouth a few times. "No, no. That would ruin the game, and we've just gotten started."

My heart dropped in my chest, and the smug look of satisfaction once again locked into her blue eyes as she stared back.

I knew I was in trouble.

♠

ALICE

What do you want with me?" I asked the woman.
"Oh, nothing," she said. "Although you seem
to have a very interesting set of friends. Way
more useful than the Germans I've been watching. And
way more attractive, I might add."

I clenched my fists. How long exactly had she been
following us around? How much did she really know?
"Leave them alone."

"Thanks for the opportunity to talk to them in person,"
she said. She reached into the tank with the turtles,
flicking the water with her fingers. She brought her hand
back out and sliding her wet fingertips together. "Warm
water for sick turtles. I hope someone will check on them
while your Axel is busy."

Anger swept through me in a wave and I lurched
forward, raising a fist at her face. Something about her,
maybe her cool exterior and her superior way of looking
and talking at me, made me furious. Curses exploded out
of my mouth, threats and name calling alike. I was tired
and on the edge. I would rip her eyes out to make sure
Axel and everyone else got out of this untouched.

"Don't," she said sharply, stepping aside to keep the
turtle tank between us. When I moved one way, she
dodged the opposite, staying out of reach. "Stop your
flailing and listen for a moment."

"So was it you who killed this Randall guy?" I asked.
"Or was it the Germans?"

"The Germans wouldn't have the guts to commit
murder. They're a bunch of computer nerds who stumbled

across a toy they don't understand." The corner of her mouth lifted. "And do I look like I'm capable of killing anyone?"

Yes. Instead of answering though, I glared at her, waiting her out. On the surface, perhaps she appeared innocent, but her eyes were cold, proud and devilish. Perhaps men would look at her pretty face and not suspect her, but there was something completely wrong inside her, sociopathic maybe. It was hard to put my finger on it. I simply knew evil when I saw it.

Her smirk deepened and then she leaned forward, using the edge of the turtle tank for support. "I've got a secret for you."

"Don't want to know, and I don't care," I said. "If you want your core, I don't care about that either."

She took on a sorrowful look and made a pout with her small mouth. "Shouldn't we be friends? After all, there's a killer out there. You want your precious boyfriend back. All I want is something you've already said you don't want. We could work together. Can't we compromise?"

I pulled back, standing up straight, and tried not to grit my teeth. "What do you want from me?"

"Get your fake boyfriend back," she said. "The one the Germans have. Convince him to break this code on the core, and I'll return Axel to you. And the other one. The cute one. Although I do kind of like him. He's really pretty."

I didn't believe for a moment that she'd simply let Axel and Marc go if I got her access to the core. "So you can just kill us all in the end?"

"I would never," she said, putting her palm to her chest and feigning a look of disappointment. "But these Germans are very sloppy, and the FBI will be here as quickly as they can to try to save them...that is if you cooperate with me. How well you work will be how quickly I make that call."

"You'll call them on yourself?"

"Not quite," she said. "But someone has to take the blame."

I narrowed my eyes at her. "You're going to throw the Germans under the bus?"

"They'll go down for two murders, and you and your friends can go back to saving turtles and...well...whatever it is you do," she said. "Although I'd tell Corey to stop trying to build security codes. Every code you try to build stronger, someone else will do anything to break through. It's a dangerous and futile effort."

"What are you going to do with the core?" I asked.

She shook her head and held up a slender finger to her lips. "Shh...A good girl never tells," she said.

"What's going to stop me from taking you out right now and then just calling the police on whoever you've got working for you?"

She backed up a step away from the turtle tank and reached into her pocket. She lifted out a small vial and held it up. "Because your precious boys have already been injected with a poison, and unless you get me what I want, this sweet little liquid will eat away at their insides, until their organs melt and all you have left is soup."

My mouth popped open, my eyes widened. In a flash, I was lunging around the turtle tank to get at her. I'd stuff it down her throat and make whoever worked with her bring back Axel and Marc.

She held out her hand in a stop motion, warding me off and holding out the vial. "I don't have a cure on me. The cure is rare, and no hospital within a hundred miles of here will carry it. Not to mention, it would require an autopsy to discover exactly what the poison was."

She said it in a past tense, like it already happened.

Had she done it before? I stopped again, fighting against my instinct to take that chance. There was a possibility she was lying. She almost... sort of... admitted to murder. She was telling me now she could murder Axel and Marc if I didn't act quickly. "Who are you?" I asked.

"My name is Alice," she said. She bowed her head slightly, lowering her hand and putting the vial back into her pocket. "And I understand your name is Kayli. You don't look it, but I've been told you're intelligent. Let's hope you prove that to be true."

I was willing to ignore the obvious insult for now. She could have called me whatever she wanted, but I was only looking for a way around her poison, trying to shake out the lies from the truth and how far her and the team she had was willing to go to get this core. "You promise if I can get this stupid phone thing for you, you'll let Axel and Marc go?"

"As healthy as possible. The poison is slow, but after about twenty four hours, it's very effective." She winked and started to walk backward. Without looking, her back was already at the door, like she was well aware of the layout and knew precisely where she was. "Your Corey should know what to do."

"How am I supposed to find you to make the exchange?"

"Oh you won't have to find me," she said, her contemptuous smile broadening. "Simply get the core to stop using the Guard Dog security protocols. I'll know when it's free. The moment I do, Axel and Marc can be yours again. Hopefully in time." She winked and pushed back on the door before disappearing behind it.

♠

RELEASED

I listened for Alice walking away from the door, and the silence that followed. For a moment, I wondered if I had passed out and then dreamed it all, because it seemed completely ridiculous. Axel hadn't been gone long. Could she really have taken him and Marc by now? I took a few steps toward the door she disappeared behind, trying to figure out if I should follow her or not. I decided it was better to go looking for Axel instead.

I pushed through the opposite door, finding a hallway: dingy tile, closed doors with frosted windows. Administration. There was some office-like activity behind some of them clicking on keyboards, the small murmur of telephone conversations, a low radio playing soft pop.

No Axel. I wanted to find him and prove to myself it was all a lie. Without seeing him and Marc, there was no way to know if Alice had been telling me the truth. Shouldn't she have given me some proof? Like a photo of Axel holding up today's paper?

I got an idea and started walking up the hallway. This was a public place with security, which more than likely meant cameras everywhere and a security office with video screens. I could use that to find them, find out who Alice was working with, and at least see which direction they went.

I followed the hallway and a couple of corridors that seemed to still be administrative offices before I spotted a door marked "Security".

Bingo. I combed my hair with my fingers and forced a quick smile, trying not to betray how scared I really was. I took in a long breath and held it as I opened the door and walked in.

The security room was a wall of TV screens, each one showing entrances, registers at the gift shop, doors to the bathrooms, and certain hallways. I studied them, searching for identifiable faces.

"Excuse me," a male voice said.

My head snapped toward the voice, spotting a pudgy male sitting behind a desk. His security uniform's shirt was tight and gaping between the buttons around his middle, making me wonder if he ever lost any and had to sew them back on. He stared at me with bored eyes, his cell phone planted in front of him on the desk, the screen filled with a game.

"You shouldn't be in here," he said.

"Oh, sorry," I said, trying to use a high- pitched, friendly voice. I touched my cheek with a fingertip. "I was told you could help me with an announcement. I need to find my little brothers. They ran off and now they're missing."

"What's their names?" he asked, still appearing bored.

"Axel and Marc," I said. "They're..." I wasn't sure this was a good idea but I was going for it. "Twelve. They should know better. I thought they might try to stick their hands in the turtle tanks again but..."

He held up his hand and then pressed a button on the desk, and then another and leaned forward. "Axel and Marc, your sister is waiting for you at the security office. Axel and Marc, your sister is at the security office."

"Thank you," I said once he'd stopped pressing the button. My eyes went the TV screens again. "So I should just wait here?"

"Yeah," he said. "Attendants should be looking for

117

them now, too. They'll direct them here."

I nodded, not caring what he'd think if Axel or Marc did happen to show up and they weren't exactly kids.

Time passed, with me looking at the screens. One by one, I scanned them, waiting to see their faces, or anyone I might recognize. I spotted a few people at first who appeared to look like them, but then was disappointed when they turned and weren't them.

Alice had said she had them, but I wondered what would happen if security was on the lookout, and would it stall Alice and her team, or the Germans. I hoped I wasn't wasting time, but I didn't want to run into trouble if Alice or anyone else was waiting to ambush me. At the very least, I needed to get out of here without getting kidnapped again.

I focused on the exits, including any windows I could spot. I checked hallways, and even some cameras that were focused on the parking lots.

Nothing. Tourists came and went, but no one looked like Axel or Marc. If Alice got rid of them, she did it while she was talking to me.

My heart pounded as I started to panic. I checked the screens again and again. I was anxious to leave, but worried if I did, I would miss a clue, or seeing Axel and Marc somewhere. As time passed, standing still became too much. If Alice was telling the truth, I had a day to get her access to the core in exchange for the guys. I was willing to sacrifice the German group to go to jail. Maybe it was wrong, but they dragged us into the middle of this in the first place.

I studied the exits, trying to figure out the best way to leave without getting caught. Would a quiet employee exit be better? Or should I leave through the public way? Public might be the better choice. If I was grabbed, I could scream bloody murder and get other people's attention. I needed to get to Corey and Raven. They were the only ones left now. They were the only ones I really trusted to help, and yet I wasn't even sure how to get to them without Alice or the others following. What happened to those Academy teams chasing us? Were they in trouble, too? Did they spot Alice? I didn't have a way to contact them.

This was my fault. I told Axel to hurry along with a new plan to chase the Germans out, not realizing there was another team ready to swoop in. He had said we weren't really sure what to expect, and we needed to be careful. Why didn't I listen?

I stood for as long as I could to be sure I wasn't going to miss Axel or Marc by leaving. "Oh," I told the security guard, pointing at a random screen. "I see them. By the turtle tanks. Just like I thought. Thanks!"

The man coughed and nodded, but he was still focused on his phone. Not caring and having no idea that two grown men could have been kidnapped under his nose.

And he'd never know.

I rushed out of the security office and stopped, checking the hallway and trying to figure out my plan. Even if I got outside, I didn't have keys to the car.

I reached into my pocket and felt for Avery's business card. I didn't know anyone else's number anyway. I wasn't even sure if I should call him. It was risky. There was a lot of danger out there and I was calling him back into it.

It was either this, or I took my chances alone at this point. As tempting as it was, walking the streets of downtown Charleston was making me a target, considering there were two teams keeping an eye on me. I needed a quick getaway for now.

I found an office that was empty, and helped myself to the telephone. I pulled out Avery's business card and dialed.

A mumbled yawn greeted me at first. "Yo."

I hesitated. Hearing his voice made me second guess calling him in. "Avery?"

There was a pause and fumbling and a crash on his end of the line. Heavy breaths muffled the phone. "Kayli?"

Did he fall out of bed? "Are...you okay?"

"Fine! Fine. What's up? Need a ride?"

Good question. Where was I going? I had to forget the hospital. If they found the real Corey, then Brandon would be in trouble.

While I was considering, he continued, "Is this about your kidnapping? You know, I've been thinking. Maybe you really should call the police."

"Not really an option right now," I said. "If you aren't busy, could you give me a ride?"

He shuffled on his end of the phone. "In trouble?"

Yes. "Maybe."

"Where are you?"

"The aquarium."

He laughed and then stopped. "Oh wait, you weren't kidding?"

I bit my tongue, wanting to get him to hurry up, but not wanting to make him panic bad enough to call the police himself. Every minute I wasted, I wasn't getting this core, and Axel and Marc could be dying. "Avery... I don't have a lot of time."

"Okay, I get you. Let me get there."

There was movement and shuffling, and I heard the clank of keys. I thought I was supposed to hang up.

"You still with me?" he asked.

"You don't have to keep me on the line."

"Probably better if you are," he said. "If I hang up, I might not be able to call you back if something goes wrong. And if you get kidnapped, I probably want to hear for clues, right?"

True enough. "Just hurry."

"Got you, got you, okay."

I was quiet as I heard him walking, getting in the car, shuffling, starting the car, grunting, sneezing, driving, cursing at other drivers.

I shifted my weight from one foot to another, trying to settle my heart. Every moment lost, and Axel and Marc might be dying from poison. I was considering my options as to how I would get Axel and Marc back, and I still didn't know where Brandon was. Getting to the core meant using Corey. All roads seemed impossible.

There was a gentle knock at the door. I jumped, and considered if it was another employee. Getting caught by security and thrown out for invading someone's office would suck. I pulled the phone away from my ear, and ducked under the desk. I held the phone to my chest and waited.

There was a long silence, outside of Avery on the phone calling my name.

I smothered the phone deeper between my breasts, trying to drown him out and listen.

There was an outline of more light as the door opened. Then the door closed again. It was quiet. I waited, listening.

But I still felt it. A presence. It was like when my father would sneak into the hotel room, right before he started beating on my brother and I. Was it someone who owned this office? Or that security guard? Or...

I didn't have much of a weapon outside of the phone in my hand, but I'd use it if I needed to. I prepped myself, getting up on my hands and knees, ready to dive and bite to get out of here.

Pant-covered legs appeared. Male, for sure, just from

the style and shape and the shoes. I held my breath.

Whoever it was started to bend over.

Panic seized me. If it was Alice or her goons, I was cornered and only had one shot. I put the phone down quietly and then lashed out, ready to take down whoever it was and then run for the door.

I connected with knees. A dead weight dropped on top of me, crushing me underneath. A hand reached around my mouth, grabbing before I could call bloody murder.

Still I fought, I bit at the hand, I bashed at a hip with the end of the phone. Like hell I was going to be kidnapped again.

Up until I realized whoever it was wasn't really fighting back. He wasn't doing anything except trying to still me.

I dared a look back, trying to figure out my attacker, and finding a pair of cerulean eyes.

For a moment, my heart lifted. Corey? He was here? How...

But I was wrong, because there was a bit of light and the eyes were ones I'd seen a thousand times behind my eyelids since the night before, haunting me because I wasn't sure I'd ever see them again. There was that constant gaze, an underlying sadness and depth of emotion that threatened to swallow everything around him up.

Unmistakable.

Brandon.

♠

ESCAPE

The moment I stilled, Brandon lifted me off the ground until I was standing.

"Bran..." I started to say.

He grunted, grabbed my wrist and yanked me until I fell into him. His fingers snarled into my hair, grabbing the back of my head while his other hand went around my waist.

His lips crushed against mine, cutting off any words.

Instinct took over at first. When his lips parted, my eyes closed. I was still out of breath and he broke the kiss enough that I could suck down air, and then he met my lips again harder than before, not giving me enough time to think or breathe.

His hands moved over me constantly. At first he cupped my head, massaging it through the tangle of my hair, tracing his thumbs across my cheeks. His fingertips slid down toward my neck, tracing, sending warm waves through me even as I shivered from his touch.

At first his lips were strong, deliberate. Like he had done it to shut me up initially. When I responded, he relaxed. His head tilted and he deepened the kiss. His body closed the space between us. His chest and stomach pressed up against mine.

In a crazy way, I needed to feel him, connect with him. *What happened to you? Are you really here? We were kidnapped! How crazy was that?*

No one seemed to understand that there had been a

moment when everything was normal and suddenly I was dragged into a nightmare and without a way to get out.

Brandon understood. He told me with his kiss. He'd been there. He was here now. They might even still be following us, but we still had this, each other. We had a moment where we were alone and alive, knowing the other was okay and breathing.

It felt good and damn if we were going to give up now.

When he eased his kisses some and I'd caught my breath enough, the questions began swirling in my head. I didn't want to stop kissing, but I still needed to know. "Bran—"

He smashed his lips against me and kissed me until I almost forgot the question. He finally stilled and then released me. "Shh," he whispered against my lips, staying close and covering my cheeks with his palms. "Sorry. I couldn't help it. Don't say anything."

"But...you?" I couldn't believe he was here. I touched him, like somehow touching him would erase all the fears I'd had about losing him. "When? How?"

"What are you talking about?"

"I mean, where's...the kidnappers...?"

"They're outside. They're waiting on me. I told them I could come in and get you."

"Why? How could you? They let you go to get me?"

"They're in trouble," he said. "We all are. They aren't murderers. They're just desperate. I said I wouldn't move an inch to help them."

"I know," I said. "I met the other team. One of them anyway..."

"God, you..." he whispered against me. He kissed me hard, closed mouth, his jaw clenched. His fingers twisted into my scalp, grabbing gently at my hair. "I never thought I'd see you again for a while there."

Through all the panic in trying to find him, I couldn't imagine what he'd gone through, willing to sacrifice himself just to stop bad guys from chasing after me. "Why didn't you jump with me?"

"I needed to save Corey," he said. "And you. They would have hunted us down quickly if they didn't have who they thought they wanted. Better to be a decoy for a while."

"Do they still think you're Corey?"

He nodded. "They found something he's been working on that had the same DepthCrawler ID. He should have known better than to leave a signature they could trace back to him." He kissed me again and then stopped and backed up a few feet. I could see, even in the low light, that he wore a tank shirt and dark slacks. The shirt was tight, showing off his chest and his defined muscles. Even his Adonis belt appeared deeper. The effect in the dim room was striking.

"It wasn't Corey's fault," I said. "He told the guy no before."

He pointing a finger at me. "He said he'd seen you before. The leader. Eddie. How do you know him?"

"I saw him. When I was with Corey..."

"When?" he asked. "I mean, what time? I don't remember."

"That day you guys first brought me to the apartment. Corey took a walk with me around the lake next to the apartment building. The German..."

"German?" he asked.

I guessed Corey hadn't said anything about this. "Sorry. Eddie, I think. He said something to Corey in German and then Corey told him to go away. I didn't know his name."

"Shit," Brandon took a few steps and then roughed his fingers through his hair. "Why didn't he tell me?"

"He turned them down," I said. "And then there was Coaltar and my brother."

He grunted and started walking. "We need to go."

"Wait," I said. I picked up the phone. "Avery?"

"Still here," he said. "In traffic but I'm getting there."

"Who the hell is that?" Brandon asked.

"A cab's on the way," I said. "I needed to escape."

Brandon scowled. "Why did you..."

"We don't have time," I blurted out. Now that the initial shock of him being back was over, I needed to bring him up to speed quickly. "Marc and Axel were taken by Alice."

"Alice?" he asked.

"She's on the other team," I said. "She's...she poisoned the guys."

Brandon lifted a suspicious eyebrow.

It did sound crazy. I mean, who uses poison? "She said we had twenty-four hours to get the core or it's going to kill Axel and Marc."

He grabbed my arms, making me drop the phone on the floor. "What do you mean? Axel was here?"

"Yeah," I said. "Who do you think brought me here?"

Brandon pressed his palm to his eye and shook his head. "I don't know what's going on. I keep getting shoved into trunks. I guess Eddie didn't want...Alice to know they had me."

"Alice already knows. They're using me to get to you, and for us to go get this core. Axel and Marc were here with me, trying to get your kidnappers to chase us and bring you in."

"I heard they were following you when you got to downtown Charleston. I didn't know who was with you. Why aren't you all at the hospital? I thought Axel would bring everyone there."

"We went looking for this Randall Jones."

Brandon pursed his lips. "They told me about him. Someone killed him and stole his phone. They don't know who. They think it is the same people who are hunting them now. Their team keeps getting killed off..." He turned and then faced the wall. "They could be lying, too," he said. "I don't really trust them."

"Avery's on the way," I said. "He's bringing his cab. We should go with him."

Brandon's head jerked back and he started barking at me, "A cab driver? I thought for some reason he was someone in the Academy. You're saying he's not?"

"He can help!" I cried. "We need to get away and get this core. We give them the core, we get Axel and Marc back. We can sort it out after, once everyone is safe. That was Axel's plan. We'll follow it, just now we've got to save Axel and Marc."

"God, you're so...crazy. You shouldn't have...you..." He turned and rushed me, kissing my cheek before I realized what was happening, and then slid his mouth to my ear. "This is all fucked up. We need to get out of here." He picked up the phone and talked into it. "Avery? No, this is Brandon. Never mind, listen... No, I was kidnapped, too. Hang on, just pick us up at the south service entrance. You know the one? Yeah."

"Where are we going?" I asked.

"You'll see," he said. He hung up the phone and tugged me toward the door.

Out in the hallway, Brandon hurried, pulling me along with him. I had to jog to keep up with his longer strides. I didn't have a chance to look back, but I sensed we were running from someone chasing us.

Once we were out in the public area, we melted in with the crowd. There was a group of school kids mixed in with a few tourists. Brandon weaved his way through the space like he'd been in this building a lot. I supposed if

Axel worked here, they got a chance to visit.

Brandon stopped in front of a doorway marked employees only. He checked around and then bolted through the door. I chased after him.

"Why are we running?" I asked. "They can't do anything if we're in public, right?"

"Hurry," he said. "I thought I saw..."

There were footsteps behind us, heavy ones.

When I tried to stop and turn around to see who it was, Brandon grabbed my arm and tugged me along. He could probably run faster than I could, but he seemed to want to keep himself close to me.

There was a thunder of footsteps behind us. Brandon barreled down the hallway and pushed through an emergency exit.

Despite it being emergency doors, an alarm never sounded. So much for security coming to maybe ward them off.

Avery's beat up taxi was stopped at the end of the sidewalk, doors open, with Avery, wearing dirty jeans and a Hawaiian shirt and standing ready. He held onto the back door like he was holding it open for us.

Brandon waved wildly at him. "Let's go!"

Avery must have picked up on the urgency, because he jumped behind the wheel before we were even at the car.

Brandon pushed me in front of him, into the back seat. He landed on top of me just as the back window fractured with a loud crack.

It took me a moment to realize it was a gunshot.

"Go!" Brandon shouted from on top of me, covering my body.

There was a sharp bang in the air, and then thuds and clunks against metal, but the car was already lunging forward.

I was dizzy as the car moved, turned, zoomed forward. I caught Avery in the driver's seat, ducking down, and yet trying to look behind us. I had a moment of worry, more scared of him not looking at where he was driving over getting shot at.

"Haha! Can't stop this tank," Avery cried out. He pounded his fist on the dash. "Whooohoo! American steel for the win!"

I smacked the back of his seat. "No bragging. Just drive."

"Head to North Charleston," Brandon said. "We need to..."

"Are you kidding?" Avery asked. "We need to head to the police station!"

"What's in North Charleston?" I asked, trying to overpower Avery by being louder.

Brandon started to sit up, looking out the back and then sitting up more. The back window had a hole in it. He felt around, sweeping for broken bits of glass or searching for the bullet that had caused it. The rear window was in pieces, but tempered to hold together. "They've seen this car. They know this plate now. We need to change vehicles."

"I can't give up my car," Avery said. He turned in the street, weaving through traffic. "Why don't we go to the police?"

Brandon looked at me, his cerulean eyes asking me what he should tell this guy. We were mixed up in something deadly. He didn't like bringing in more people, but what choice did we have?

We needed to ditch Avery, and at the same time, needed to make sure he was safe.

Who knew who would get kidnapped next?

♠

THE PLEDGE

Brandon told Avery to take a long, winding route to avoid the possibility of being tracked, so he weaved a path through downtown Charleston, taking run-down streets and business sections instead of taking the highway.

I tried to catch Brandon up on what had gone on since his kidnapping: Randall's house, the discovery of what Murdock's Core was, to Axel's decision to go to the aquarium to try to catch who was following us. I wanted to hear Brandon's side, but he insisted I tell mine first.

Brandon directed us to a large gray garage in downtown North Charleston. It was close to an abandoned warehouse district, one of many in that area. There wasn't a sign on the building, and it was next to a restaurant supply store and a fairly large, empty parking lot.

Being in the area made me nervous. This was North Charleston, after all. Why were we here?

"Listen to me," he told Avery once he stopped in the lot. "Don't drive this car anymore."

"I need to," Avery said. "And the back window is broken. I'll at least have to drive it to a repair shop. And I'll need to drive some fares to pay for the work."

"Do you have a piece of paper?" Brandon asked. Avery handed him one, along with a pen. Brandon scratched an address out. "Go here and don't stop until you get there. I'll tell him you're on the way. You want to talk to North Taylor. He'll set you up with a car."

"What about my baby?" Avery asked, making a face and then pressing his palm to his car's steering wheel. "I can't leave her."

"I'll tell him to fix her up," Brandon said. "But you can't drive this again until we solve this."

"You really should call the police," Avery said. He tilted his head in my direction. "Mind if I talk to her for a minute?" he asked.

I looked at Brandon, who shrugged and got out of the car and started off toward the building.

Avery and I both got out and stood beside his car. He watched Brandon but talked to me. "Are you sure about this?" he asked.

"What?"

"Look, you don't know me that well," he said. "But despite what you might think, calling a cop or a Fed in on this wouldn't be that bad. I mean, if they're killing people, you know?"

"They're not going to understand what's going on and sending them in would..."

Avery's look turned serious, his eyes wide and his lips taut. "This isn't a game," he said. "And the FBI isn't stupid. They might have more information on these guys than you even know about."

Normally, that would probably be the case. I lowered my voice. "Avery," I said. "Please. If they see a cop coming, they might take it out on Axel and Marc. I don't want to take that chance. Once I get them back, the FBI or the CIA or whoever can jump in and do whatever they want."

Avery's gaze drifted from watching Brandon, who was kicking a rock around near the corner of the building, to my face. "So all I need to do is get Axel and Marc back?"

It was a sweet offer, but Avery had probably heard too

much during my conversations with both Marc and Brandon. "It's dangerous," I said. "You should go home before they think you're with us."

Avery lifted a hand, rumpling the Hawaiian shirt. His hand was empty, and then he turned it over to reveal the back, when he turned it again, his hand had another one of his business cards.

More of his sleight of hand. Impressive.

"Kayli, I can do more than just drive a cab. Keep my number. If you're going to be chasing these guys, you'll need it." He opened his car door and wedged in behind the wheel. "But I'll be holding you to your word. The moment your friends are out of harm's way, the authorities get to fly in."

"Sure."

He grumbled a bit more but then drove away, leaving Brandon and me behind.

I sidled up next to Brandon. "Who's North?" I asked, watching Avery's car disappear down the road.

"An Academy friend," Brandon said, offering nothing more.

I was sad, again, to see Avery leaving. He had helped, and then had been dismissed quickly. He was right about calling the police, no doubt, but he didn't understand all that was going on, and he was going to get killed if he stuck around. Sending him out with a new car was the best thing this Academy could do, and I, for once, was grateful that there was someone to take care of his car while we were busy dealing with things. I owed Avery a lot after this, myself.

After Avery was out of sight, I turned, looking at the large building, waiting for Brandon to tell us why we were here. I assumed we were at a secret Academy place to pick up a car, or weapons, or the spy planes, *something* to help us get Axel and Marc back. And hopefully set Alice on fire.

Brandon walked right up to a side door of the garage. There was a window that was chest height. The window was on the small side. He felt around the edge, trying to pop the screen off.

I ran over, scoping out the neighborhood to see if anyone was watching us from other buildings. The area seemed deserted. "What are you doing?" I hissed. "You're breaking in..."

"It's my place," he said. "I'm not going to call the cops on myself."

"You own this?" I asked.

"There's a lot of things you don't know about me." He wedged the screen off the window, then slid the window over to one side. "I may not be a fancy hacker, all smart and everything, you know, but I can do a few things."

He compares himself to Corey? "You leave your window open to your garage? You do realize it's in North Charleston, right?"

"Shut up and get over here." He bent over, presenting his hands to boost me up.

I stepped into the cradle of his hands and heaved myself over. This was an office space and I found myself on one of the desks as I slipped in. It was dark but there was enough light coming in from the window that I got the general layout. There were two doors, one leading, I guessed, deeper into the garage. The other was narrow, like a closet.

There was a thunk at the window, distracting me from my snooping. "Unlock the door," he said.

I went over, released a couple of bolt locks and then opened it. There was a ding almost immediately, and a security panel on the wall lit up. I wondered why there wasn't an alarm on the window. Or perhaps he left it that way just in case...he needed to break into his own garage?

Brandon pushed me out of the way and went for the panel, typing in a code. The panel beeped a couple of times and then silenced. Guess he really did own the place.

He flipped a switch, and overhead fluorescent lighting illuminated the office. There were a couple of desks with computers and a few tall file towers. There were schematics hanging on the wall, designs for machinery parts that I didn't recognize.

Brandon shut the window and then went to one of the desks. He started up the computer and then bent to open a drawer. He fished out a cell phone, checked it over, and turned it on.

I studied him. His messy hair, the rough start of a beard on his chin, the cerulean eyes that were focused on the screen. On top of the ever-present sadness was something more. A drive. Determination.

Anger.

I recognized that all too well. It echoed inside of me. They'd pushed us around enough. Pushed us into a war that wasn't ours to start with. Our lives were at risk, and all we wanted was our people back and to go home.

"Do you guys just keep cell phones everywhere?" I asked.

"Comes in handy, doesn't it?" He pushed a button on it and started thumbing in a text message.

"Can we talk now?" I asked.

"Yeah," he said, looking up at me. I caught the bruises around his shoulders then, the one under his chin.

I sucked in a breath at the sight. Amid the chaos, I'd been completely oblivious to it. Before, all I saw was that Brandon was back and was too excited to see him.

I reached out slowly, touching a purpling spot on his arm. "What happened after you left the warehouse?" I asked.

He tilted his head down, looking at the phone,

frowning. "They tried to beat me until I agreed to help them. And when that didn't work, they told me why they were trying so hard. They thought Corey was friends with this other team. That's why they did what they did. They'd had enough of their own team killed and were willing to do almost anything to save themselves."

"Who... I mean this other team. Who are they? I only met Alice, but there has to be more of them."

"We don't know," he said. He looked up at my face with those determined, angry eyes again. "I almost felt sorry for them, but they brought this on themselves. They were originally going to exploit these secret phone lines, listen in on passwords and things like that. Now they're being hunted, told they'll live only if they pass over access to this core. Every time they fail to get the core, one of their members dies. There's only three left on the team now, I think. That's all I've seen."

"Alice may have Axel," I said. "And Marc. Or someone does. I don't know for sure, because I didn't see them with her. She just said she had them. She also said she poisoned them."

"If they aren't with her, they're laying low for a reason," he said. "Something tells me, though, that if Axel was still standing on his own, he wouldn't have left you for that long, and he wouldn't let us run off like that. I was with Eddie and his team, but I only ever saw Eddie. The others on his team were usually in the dark or gone doing something. They kept themselves at a distance. Didn't want to take too many risks so they limited who talked to me."

"They didn't trust you?"

"They thought I was Corey. They thought "I" could have been working for the other team, until they realized I really did have no idea what they were talking about."

"What are we going to do?" I asked. I sat on the desk.

135

I drew my feet up and curled up with my knees against my chest. The crop pants started to slide off my butt, but I had given up trying to look presentable. I was surprised I still had the flip-flops on. "How are we going to find Axel and Marc? Even if she was lying about a poison, we already know her team will kill to get what they want. We've only got a day. We'll need Corey to get it and he doesn't even know what's going on right now. And Raven and Kevin..."

"On it," he said, showing me the phone. He'd sent a text to a phone number with some message about a hockey game and the score last night.

"Uh..." I lifted a brow, looking back at Brandon. "Did you hit your head?"

"Code. Corey will understand," he said.

My heart lifted in the moment he said something about Corey.

Sure enough, a moment later, the phone buzzed.

Corey: "Yeah, great game. That girl in front row was pretty hot, wasn't she?"

Brandon smirked at the phone.

"What?" I asked. "What does that mean?"

"He's asking about you," he said. He typed in a message.

Brandon: "She had a nice ass, yeah, but remind me how much you owe me for that bet? That big guy took out two of our players. Adam and McCarthy didn't stand a chance."

Corey: "Randy was pissed. He's going to be hitting hard in the follow up game."

I didn't understand any of this, except who A and M and possibly who R was, because something told me those weren't who they were really talking about. It must have been some twin brother code.

I stared at Brandon as he focused on the phone and continued to type messages to his brother. "Should we find this core, then? Give them what they want?"

"We need to get Axel and Marc back, or at least confirm where they are. We may need to make contact."

"How..."

"I was going to work with Eddie to figure out what was going on and possibly help them, but we need to work faster than they were. I was willing to play along before, but Eddie and his team have absolutely no clue. And we're dealing with real murderers now."

"What do we do?"

He tapped at the phone, staring hard, and his jaw clenched. "If needed, I'm going to offer myself up," he said.

My feet slipped off the desk from my curled-up position. "You can't."

"I'm who they want," he said. He turned and looked at me. "Or who they think they want. They need someone to get access to this core. That's the only playing card we have in our hand right now. They think I'm the key."

"So you're going to offer them yourself instead of the core? Can't we just give them access for now?"

"We may not be able to. If I offer myself up, we can make a trade. That's how we find them."

He had to be crazy. He'd just escaped and now he wanted to dive back in again. This time with murderers. "Am I supposed to sit here while someone's got a timer on your life? Do you think we can just walk up to her with you and she'll just as easily pass over Axel and Marc? No way. Find out where this Alice lives. Find the German."

"What are you going to do?"

"We're going to find a set of Tasers, first off," I said,

going with my original plan. "But this time, we offer up the team to these new guys and walk away. This isn't our business. They're fighting over who steals this stupid core thing. Well let's either give them the team, or the core, and we trade them for Axel."

"No," he said, "they'll kill us on top of it all."

"Who are they? That's what we need to know."

He grunted, sitting back in the chair and kicking at the desk. "Corey sounds like he's been searching for this core, but he's not having much luck. The Academy will want to pull us both back out of harm's way. I don't want to go in if I can help at least figure out where Axel and Marc are. The fastest way is to call them out to get me."

I understood his impatience. I wanted this to be over, too, and he might have been willing to sacrifice himself to get to the end, but I wasn't willing to take that risk. Not now. Not when I'd already made a huge mistake letting Axel and Marc go when they'd told me before to be careful.

"What would the Academy do next?" I asked quietly.

"The Academy can't even help if we don't know where these guys are." He sighed, closed his tired eyes and pressed his palm to his face rubbing at his jaw. "I don't know. I guess they'd go back to the aquarium. They'd look for... this Alice girl. Find out who she is."

"How do we find out by going back?"

"Security footage," he said. He sat up and then started typing into the phone. "I can get Kevin to direct some people there to grab copies. Corey and Raven can search through the footage."

It was a start. I liked this plan. He was right; I didn't want to sit around in some hospital waiting, either. "What can we do? I don't know if Alice and her team might follow us. And Eddie might be looking for us now, too. We have to avoid them, but we should probably at least find where this core is. Axel said locating it would mean we might find them breaking into it later and catch them at it."

"We need a backup just in case we can't find it." He showed me his phone where a text message had come in. Corey was sending some code I didn't understand, but I was guessing it meant he was getting Kevin to go pick up security footage. "We need to do it alone, too. We can't risk anyone else, not even from other Academy teams. We don't want anyone else getting picked up."

"Are we not telling anyone else?" Were we going to let Corey know?

He squinted up at me. "Limited liabilities."

Protective brother. Marc had said the same thing. Why get Corey involved if the two of us are only going to get killed as a result? Or for that matter, if we limit what even the Academy knew, they wouldn't send out a fleet and get us all killed. "But we can't get the core and break into it without Corey..."

"The first thing this other team is going to want is information. They want to know who Axel and Marc are and if they'll be useful. I don't know about this poison or her threats. I've got Corey doing what he can from where he's at. I can still trade myself in later, I guess. So we've got a little time to go after this core. We just don't have a way of guaranteeing that they won't just kill us all after we deliver. That's why we need to be ready for minimal sacrifices. If they only have one, that's better than two."

"Don't be an idiot," I said, wanting to say more, because it was a ridiculous thought.

But if anyone had to be the sacrifice, it probably should have been me. Who was I? A thief without a family. My own brother didn't even want to talk to me. Brandon had a brother and friends and so much more potential. The only thing was, I wasn't valuable enough to be even considered a trade. Alice had a chance and she sent me back. They wanted Corey.

Brandon grunted and then focused on the phone. "I just need a starting point." He rubbed his face again and yawned. "And a whole lot of coffee."

"And an army."

"I don't need an army when you have secrets and resources neither team knows about."

"Like a secret garage in North Charleston?" I asked. "Are there cars in here?"

"Bikes," he said. He leaned over, grabbing a business card out of a holder and passing it to me.

Henshaw Customs.
Unique motorcycles and supplies.

Brandon's name was on it, along with an email and phone number.

He never told me. I'd been with the guys for a couple of weeks, and even while I travelled in my own little world for a while, I still had daily conversations with the guys. Not once did Brandon mention he had a garage where he worked on bikes. And for having a business, he wasn't at it often. One of the other guys once said he goes to the shop, but for some reason, I didn't picture this. "You started all this yourself?"

"Yep."

"You live in a tiny apartment."

"It's not that small. And so what?"

"This might sound like a weird question... but do you make much money at it?" It sounded rude, but if I had cash from a business, I thought I'd live somewhere nicer. Maybe that's why he kept his shop in North Charleston. It wasn't making much money.

"I like spending my money on better things than

where I sleep."

"Like what?"

"Like nosy girls who ask me too many questions."

I kicked him.

"I like travelling," he said.

"Where?"

"Wherever there's a nice place to surf. Or wherever I'm sent by the Academy when on assignment. It's up in the air."

He returned his attention to the phone, talking with Corey about plans in a secret code. I leaned over, keeping my foot on his chair for balance, trying to read what he was typing. After a text, he switched windows and dug through an email box and the trash bin inside it.

"There were thousands piled up in the bin," he said. "He never cleaned it out."

Corey's trash bin was filled with thousands of messages. "You're going to check all those? For what?"

"I just need to find a way to communicate with Eddie without him getting our location. I want to try to get info on this Alice if he has any. I'm also hoping Eddie maybe sent another email to Corey that we've missed. If you've already investigated Randall, maybe there's someone else with a phone that can lead us to the core. Like someone with a live, working phone from this network. Corey's been trying to find this signal, but there's thousands of signals and it could take weeks to track down." He sat back, and planted his hand against my calf, slowly sliding his palm up and down along my skin soothingly. "Are you okay?"

I wasn't sure how to answer. He'd had his life threatened, been beaten, never thought he'd make it out. Suddenly he'd made a daring escape. I'd been wildly trying to save him and then suddenly he was back.

And then he'd kissed me, and I felt completely

reckless. If I was going to die, I was going to fight and do whatever and to hell with the consequences. Brandon was beautiful, the protective older brother and he owned his own business. The angry smoldering behind his eyes told me he was going to do whatever it took to make sure we got out of this. I was willing, but I didn't want to sacrifice him. Knowing that it might be the only way to get Axel and Marc back if we didn't find this core on our own wasn't the solution I wanted, and in that moment, there wasn't anything I could do to change it. I hated that idea. It drove me to want to do something, anything, but I was powerless.

He continued to stare up at me, massaging my leg, waiting me out. He wanted a real answer.

"You're not going to make me run off to South America while you solve all this yourself, are you?" I asked. Deflecting was better than what I was really thinking.

His face tightened. "I...can't do this alone. I want to. I don't want you in danger, but you and I are here right now. We're so close and letting anyone else in, like the FBI or someone else, that would mean we'd lose time, and we don't have that luxury. Not with a poison on Marc and Axel. Not when they'll continue to hunt for my brother even if we disappear. We won't be safe until we get our team back and we're locked away." He bit his lip, his mouth twitching like he wished to say more, but couldn't.

I was quiet for a long moment, waiting him out.

Finally, he sighed. "If I told Raven and Kevin how bad things are right now, they'd insist we go back. You're the only one who understands how deep we're in. You'll work with me, won't you? You'll help stop this?" His eyes shimmered, showing me the depths of despair he was feeling, well beyond what I'd been feeling up until that point. I'd been scared, angry, but sorrow wasn't among those feelings.

For Brandon, he was already worried we'd lost. If all of this ended badly, he'd consider it his own fault.

It killed me. I wanted to do anything to stop that look. I nodded, promising to go with what he wanted. I spilled what I knew, wanting to resolve it all as quickly as I could. "We need to go see Doyle," I said. "You remember him? He works for Blake, I think. I was telling Axel we should go... and he was into it before he got kidnapped." It was a lie, but that was the only other lead I could think of. Maybe if he was convinced that Axel was into it, he'd actually go. "Doyle listens in on phone signals. He might have noticed this underground system."

Brandon's intense eyes studied me. "Maybe. Give me a minute. Just in case Doyle doesn't have anything, maybe I can at least get another name as a lead. And Corey can do some research. We need anything right now."

He went back to checking messages. I'd let him have his minute, and explore a bit. I needed to do something besides sit around or I was going to pass out somewhere. I got up and went to the other door that had to lead to the rest of the garage.

"Don't touch anything," he said as I opened it.

"I'm touching the floor," I said.

"You can touch the floor."

The inside of the garage was dark. "I need to touch the light switch."

"You can touch the light switch. It's on the right."

I flicked on the lights.

The vastness of the garage struck me first. It expanded back further than I originally thought it did. There was a long wall of tools, toolboxes and tables lined up in the back. There were motorcycles in a row on the far side, parked diagonally like the outside of a biker bar. Each bike looked complete and ready to go, parked just far enough apart so he could pull one out. Tall shelves broke up the interior space and blocked off part of my view of one corner, but seemed to hold various parts too big to put on the shelves. There were large wood crates, too, with parts and some looked big enough to hold entire bikes inside.

Then I found the bikes he wanted me not to touch for real. There were a few display cases around the garage, each one holding a shiny bike with a paint job that blew my mind. Flames, ice and snow, beautiful women, dragons. Some details were molded from metal, and then painted.

I looked up.

More bikes were suspended from the ceiling. More 3D designs he was showing off. I cringed underneath them, worried one would fall, but they were so still. An Ace of Spades, a bike featuring Wizard of Oz characters, one had aliens. He was an artist and bikes were the canvas.

There was one bike up on a table in the middle of the shop, unassembled. So he didn't just design the art, he built the motorcycles from the wheels on up.

I shuffled forward in my flip-flops to one of the display cases to check out the bike in detail. It was designed to look like it was on fire, and I was trying to imagine what it would be like to ride it.

As I leaned in, a light flickered inside the box, and the floor of the display case lit up, and then the bike itself lit up. The LEDs were positioned so the glow of flames looked almost real, flowing back and flickering in a continuous wave.

"You should see how she rides," Brandon said from behind me, making me turn. He was standing near the door, his hands on a panel against the wall. He released it and then motioned to the fire motorcycle. "I don't take her out as often as I used to."

He caught me off guard, and then did it again just by standing there in his black pants and the white tank shirt. He really was incredible, with a long, sculpted torso, long legs and strong shoulders. His dirty blond hair was a mess, and that start of a beard was sexy. The deeper angles of his face and those blue eyes were overwhelming. His body was attractive, but his eyes were killer. The depth, the volume of pure, raw feelings, would make any girl do anything he asked just to have all that attention and affection on her. If he could feel that deeply, who wouldn't want to be by his side to be the person he felt so deeply about?

"Kind of hard to do that when you keep it in a display case," I said. I was looking for anything to distract my heart from getting too excited. It wasn't just his looks, either. It was now knowing about the bikes and the art, that he owned his own business. He was a secret spy that tried to do good for other people when called upon. So many surprising talents in one person.

What could I do? Steal a wallet? Big deal. He was super-hot and could make a bike look like it's on fire.

I tried to find something else to talk about. "So what are we waiting on?"

"We need to sit still a minute," Brandon said. "I need a confirmation from Corey about what we're doing." He smirked and then strolled forward. He stood beside me, examining his work on the fire bike. "This one took a month. The light effect was the hardest."

"Why?"

"The wiring was a complication," he said. "And to make it look real without looking stupid. Everyone wants a bike like Ghost Rider." He turned his gaze to me, focusing on my face. I met his eyes and then regretted it because I was hooked. They swallowed me up, unrelenting.

"I don't think it turned out too bad," he said, his voice quieter

"No," I said. I was fumbling for some compliment to let him know how amazing it really was, but my twisted brain didn't give out compliments very well. "Not bad."

The corner of his mouth lifted higher. He inched closer, putting an arm around my shoulders casually. The edges of his nails teased my skin as he held on tight. He turned to the bike, staring at the flickering lights. As he did, his fingertips traced along the edge of my collarbone, dragging his fingernails across in a gentle scratch. "Next time I get a chance, We'll take it out. Want to light up Charleston with me?"

My insides lit up, feeling as hot as the bike looked. Telling myself to get it together, that I didn't need this complication now didn't do any good. Now that I'd let him in, he was chipping away at my heart. When he said things like that, it made me forget why I had pushed him away in the first place. "Why wait? Might be our last chance," I said.

His arm around my shoulder drew me in closer, and his other hand came up, the palm pressed to my cheek until I was forced to focus on his face. Those eyes darkened. He spoke in a low voice, with the hint of a growl under the surface. "I keep my promises, you know. All of them. I'll get us out of this mess."

I stared back at him. In my way, I was pleading with him to continue, even as my brain was telling me we shouldn't. So much was at stake; we could die. Axel and Marc were poisoned and we needed to hurry.

I couldn't stop the swell in my heart, the hope at what he'd said out loud, and all the promises he hadn't. His eyes were telling me we'd get through this, and in the end, he'd be there and he wanted to show me things I never could imagine. Things about him that I still wanted to discover.

"When we're free of this," he whispered. "I'll take you for a ride. Wherever you want." He leaned closer into me. He stopped just short, his mouth close to mine, close enough that I could feel his breath on my lips.

For the longest moment, he hovered there, as if he were testing me.

All I did was move my head forward an inch until my lips touched his. I couldn't help it. I'd missed him, feared him dead. I'd already kissed him before, and it felt natural now.

After my touch, Brandon did the rest.

He kissed hard, like he had before at the aquarium. I knew then that his kiss would never be soft, tender. He couldn't be. He was too passionate. Like the depth of his eyes, his kiss would go deeper and seek out your soul. He would go as far as he needed to make sure you felt as strongly as he did. He wanted to make sure I was ready to go that far.

I wanted to. Even through the chaos of not thinking I'd ever see him again, I'd thought about how he'd kissed me before, and thought myself the worst jerk in the world for not being able to choose between him and Axel and Marc. He was a good guy, and deserved better.

And then that thought struck me. I was getting in deep with Brandon and with all of them, and I was going to tear them all apart if I kept going. I did need Axel after all. If we all lived through this, I needed to let them all know the truth. That I was a mess of feelings and I cared about them and if it meant I needed to sacrifice myself and leave to save their friendship, I'd do it. I couldn't hurt Brandon and the others anymore. It was the first time, outside of my brother, that I cared about anyone. I saw their little group and suddenly craved belonging in it. Knowing someone else had my back, who would be patient with me, even when I was distant and feeling alone. I admired them. They knew things I wanted to know. They did things I wanted to participate in. It was hard not to fall for guys who were so good-looking and talented. The fact that I was surrounded by them daily, even though I'd kept my distance, was time with them, and I was slowly losing my ability to simply walk away and never come back.

When he kissed me then, I clung to him, desperate to hold onto him, afraid of losing him again.

He slowed his kiss then. He held my face in his hands and then pulled back, half opening his eyes. "Kayli," he breathed.

"Brandon..." I whispered, fighting back the emotion building in my throat. We were alive. We'd been running since the night before, when we were in the trunk of a car together, sure we were going to die. We'd been given another chance, and while we could run away, we were heading into battle again soon, and didn't want to waste a moment.

I swallowed hard, but stared at him, unable to stop the pain from creeping in again at the thought of Axel and Marc captured by a team that was possibly torturing them to get out information.

"I know," he said. He traced his thumbs across my cheek and massaged gently. "I know you're going through a lot of shit. And now we're in the middle of this. And it's all my fault."

"We don't have time for that," I said. I wanted to take the blame, too, but we could argue that point later. "This is the German—Eddie—who put us in the middle of it. We can take care of him later. Let's get this core."

He sucked in a breath, breaking away from me to turn and stare at the fire bike. I was suddenly cold and wanted him back but bit my tongue. We'd had our moment, and now we needed to focus.

"I don't want to just hand over this core, that's the thing. I also don't want anyone else killed, Eddie or not, this is way too deep. We should have the FBI in on this, but I'm worried they'll be too late by the time they catch up."

I didn't really want to get close to the police but if we could shirk these guys by getting authorities after them, that'd be great. I saw his point, though. Trying to explain our story to them, they might not be able to save them, and we wouldn't be able to trade a core, or anything else, after that point.

I swallowed and took a step back. I covered myself with my arms, leaning back against the work table, trying to push back my messed up feelings for now. These people won't be that easy to get. They knew a lot more about Corey and us than we knew about them. But they didn't know the difference between Corey and Brandon. I guess we had that going.

And they didn't know about the Academy.

"What do we do?" I asked. "Shall we go talk to Doyle?"

He raked his fingers through his messy hair. "You said you checked out Randall and his phone got stolen. Eddie was pretty sure this other group got that. They were looking into Randall, and trying to trace that phone number, but it was shut down before we got a chance to even try. I didn't know what I was doing, but I could pretend. Our next step, for them, was to find you, because I wasn't going to do anything if I thought another team was going after you. I said I wouldn't help them at all unless you were safe."

"Was that true?" I asked.

He looked at me, his eyes and the sun-kissed touches to his blond hair were colored with the lights from the bike shining in them. "What?"

"Were you not going to work without me, or did you use that as an excuse to escape?"

He stared at me for the longest time, quiet, his eyes intense on mine.

Before I could react with a retort, he closed the space between us and kissed my lips briefly, holding onto my cheek. He kept his head close as he pulled back a fraction and held my gaze.

"Both," he said. "I thought if I could find you, Axel would see us coming and could hunt them, and we would finally end this. They followed you to the aquarium, and then let me out of the trunk to get me to lure you out."

"But Alice already had Axel and Marc by the time you found me. They were already gone when you showed up."

"We were too late," he said.

"How did you know I was in that room?"

"That was what was taking so long. They had their guys watching the exits so I had to get to you and find another exit they weren't covering. At some point they must have followed me inside to make sure I didn't try to run off with you. Not that it worked."

I pulled away. I breathed in slowly, taking in the situation. Alice had intervened even without this Eddie noticing. "You might be bugged," I said. "Axel found some on me. We thought they were from the Germans...Eddie."

Brandon sighed. "Wherever they're from, we don't need either team finding us again. Let me change clothes."

I followed him back into the office, and from a standing shelf, he pulled down a T-shirt and a sweatshirt, both saying Henshaw Customs over the pocket. He passed the sweatshirt to me and put on the T-shirt. From the same shelf, he took down a pair of work boots and a pair of jeans. He changed quickly, turning his back on me when he changed his pants and I averted my eyes to give him privacy.

"Don't we need to take a shower to wash out the bugs?" I asked.

"They had you do that?" he asked.

"I took a bath at the pineapple fountain downtown," I said.

Brandon smirked. He plucked a comb from a desk and then filled a cup of water from a water cooler in the corner and started to comb through his hair and behind his ears. "Water alone will usually take care of bugs like this. I don't exactly have a shower here."

"You change here often enough that you keep clothes on tap?"

"If I'm neck-deep building a bike, I usually lose track of time. This is for when I need to get going."

"Do you have a pair of boots around?" I asked. I showed him my flip-flops. "These aren't my style."

He grinned and then found me another pair of boots. They were too big for my feet, but I could clomp around in them with the laces tied tight enough. I skipped on trying to wear a pair of his jeans, but put on the sweatshirt.

Once he was done, he headed back into the garage, looking at the range of motorcycles. I followed.

"I think we should..." he said. "I don't know..."

"Let's go talk to Doyle."

"Doyle?" he asked. "Are you sure we're not asking for trouble? He is friends with Blake Coaltar after all."

"Doyle's got access to phones," I said. "I was trying to tell Axel and Marc we should... it was Axel's next move after the aquarium." Again, a lie, but couldn't be helped now.

"I don't have another idea right now," he said. "I don't like it, but if Axel thought it was okay."

I smothered the urge to grimace. "Yup. That was our next move, all right."

"Think you can find him again?" he asked. "Do you remember the way?"

I nodded. I didn't exactly recall the address, but I remembered the directions. I'd recognize it driving up, especially since it was still daylight. I pointed to his bike in the case. "Why not take the flame one?" I asked.

"We need something quieter. We're doing the spy thing, remember?"

"You just said the spy word," I quipped. "We're not supposed to say it."

He smirked. "You're the worst spy ever."

"You just said it again."

He selected a black bike, a newer model with very clean lines. It looked like a toy compared to the more Harley-looking motorcycles nearby.

He passed me a full face helmet from one of the shelves. It was brand new, and still had the plastic on it. He grabbed another one hanging on a hook. Must have been his as it was worn and had different etched drawings on it like tattoos in a mish-mash.

Within minutes he had the bike ready to go. I climbed onto the back and he took off.

The bike was quieter than any motorcycle I'd ever heard before. Spy bike.

When we were on the road, I instantly regretted not taking a pair of jeans. My legs froze. The only heat I had was from the bike, or Brandon, and I couldn't put my legs as close as I wanted to his.

My arms wrapped around his stomach, hanging on.

When he had to stop at a red light, he let go of the handlebar and cover my hand with his. He'd squeeze it, reassuring.

And I knew that the moment we'd solved this thing and our lives weren't being threatened, he'd be on me about a relationship update. He would be eager to figure this out as soon as possible.

And the only thing that scared me was that I didn't have an answer for him.

♠

LISTENER

*P*icking our way through Hannahan on the back of his bike was more complicated than I had thought it would be. It was hard to see around him and the scenery kept flying by at the speed he was going. He kept having to stop when we got to the old country roads and I was trying to remember the directions.

"We could just call Coaltar," Brandon said.

"Do we really want him to know what's going on?" I asked. "Besides, after I wrecked his car, he's probably pissed. He hasn't talked to me since then."

"I can't believe I even suggested it. I don't know anymore," he said and then yawned. The circles under his eyes told me he was dragging as much as I was. "Tell me Doyle drinks coffee."

It took another half hour of riding on the bike, stopping to check where we were, before I found the street that would lead us to Doyle's place.

Once we were there, it was unmistakably his place. There were satellite dishes in the yard, although it seemed there were a few new ones added. I wondered how no one noticed this. From the main road, it was hard to find, but I was sure if a helicopter or plane went over it, they'd see it.

Did planes go over this bit of Hannahan?

Brandon parked the bike a distance from the front door. He fixed his Henshaw Customs T-shirt as it was stuck into his body. I got off the bike, ripping off the helmet. It was stuffy. My hair fell around my shoulders and I combed my fingers through it, finding windblown tangles at the ends.

Brandon's hair was stiff against his head when he took his helmet off. One stroke of his hand through his hair, and it was fixed. I was jealous. I wasn't really concerned about my looks, but I knew tackling my hair with a brush later would be a painful experience. Maybe I needed to chop it off.

We started slowly up the path to the house. I was eyeballing the satellites, trying to count them. Brandon inspected our surroundings, looking awestruck at the museum of satellite dishes. Before we could make it to the front door, a loud gunshot cracked through the air.

Brandon immediately jumped on me, pushing me down to the ground. I got a mouthful of grass. I fought against him to spit it back out.

"If you know what's best for you, you'll get off my fucking lawn," shouted a voice, a hint of Irish behind the bellowing.

"Doyle!" I cried out. "It's Kayli!"

"I don't know a Kayli!"

I pushed Brandon off of me, crawling up on my knees. Doyle was on the porch, with a shotgun pointed up and out toward a tree. I imagined that was what he'd shot at as warning to go away.

Doyle's thin face looked almost white under the natural light. His dimpled chin jutted out and his eyes were buggy under his mop of unruly hair. "Go away," he said. He wore rumpled jeans and a wrinkled T-shirt, the white writing on it faded so much it was unreadable. "Get!" he cried out at us, like chasing off a cat.

"I'm the friend of Blake's. Remember?"

He squinted at me. "Blake who? I don't know a Blake. I don't know anything. I don't know words, even. What are words?"

155

"This is useless," Brandon said. "Let's get out of here before we get shot."

I put my hands out and stood up slowly. Doyle pointed the gun toward me, without really aiming it at me. He made a face. "Whatever you want, I don't have it," he said.

"I just need help," I said. "I need to know..."

"Nope!" he said. He took one hand off the gun and stuck a finger in his ear. "I don't care. I don't want to know. The only thing you could possibly need me for is something I don't need to know. When I helped Blake last week, I got more than I bargained for."

What did Blake do last week? "You don't have to look up anything," I said, lying. I wanted him to hear me out. I came closer, taking it one step at a time. I had a feeling he was all bluff. He was too lazy to bury two bodies so he wouldn't bother to shoot us.

"Kayli," Brandon hissed behind me.

Doyle fumbled with his gun. "Don't you do it," he said.

"Do you know about Murdock's Core?" I spit out quickly.

Doyle made a face and twisted his features. "God...damn...shit..." He snarled and twisted away, pulling the gun around and holding it in his arms sideways. "Why the hell did you have to ask about that?"

"What do you know?" I asked.

"Oh nothing," he said. He waved his hand in the air and shook it. "Just everything. I mean for Christ's sake, they only made themselves completely obvious by over-complicating their security. If you want to get away with anything, don't make things so obvious."

Brandon stepped forward, up beside me then. "Can you tell us where the core is located?"

"Oh no," Doyle said. He cradled the gun in one arm

and pointed a finger at Brandon. "Listen here, junior. If you knew anything about this core, you'd stay away from it. I mean, it is a shitty piece of work. The only thing that made it at all difficult was the security dog packet thingie. But then you don't really have to bust through the security when members blab their own password in person when they talk on their regular cell phone lines. The thing about security is it could be the best in the world, but a person with a password is the weakest link."

"Doyle!" I snapped my fingers at him. I was trying to remember how Blake negotiated with him. "What do you want for information about where the core is? We need to find it. I'm not asking for you to get involved. I wasn't even here. I just want an address."

Doyle tightened his mouth. His hair fell into his face and he raked it back. "I need some cigarettes. I'm out. I'm a mess when I'm out."

"Why didn't you go get some?"

"Do I have to do everything around here?" he asked. "And I think I need a new microwave. This one is busted."

"Do you want cigarettes or a microwave?" Brandon asked. "I've got a motorcycle. I can't carry both."

"What are you? An ape? Use your brain." Doyle pointed at his own head. "I'm not even asking enough. This is shit I could die from if you hint at who told them..."

"Don't make me tell NSA you're listening in," I said.

"Tell the fuckers," he said. "It's their line I'm borrowing. They'll just put another shitty protocol up that I'll have to work around. And there's no proof here that I'm listening to them." He pointed again at us. "One of you go fetch what I want and I'll give the other the info. I prefer the female, but I'm only saying that because I'm not gay."

If I didn't know he could get the information we

wanted, I'd have wrestled him to the ground and get Brandon to teabag him for good measure. I eyeballed Brandon, asking him quietly to go get a microwave and cigarettes. It wasn't like I'd be able to buy anything myself.

Brandon sighed heavily, lifting up his hands in a gesture of defeat.

"You're lucky I grabbed some cash out of the till at my shop before I left."

♠

COMPANY PROPERTY

Doyle had the location of the core before Brandon got back with a microwave strapped to the back seat of the bike with bungee cords and a couple of cartons of cigarettes tucked under his arms.

With a few more curses, Doyle took his payment and we were on our way.

An hour later, Brandon and I were stopped in front of the gate blocking off access to Kiawah Island. My legs were icicles, but my chest was sweating underneath the heavy sweatshirt and from being pressed up against Brandon. I imagined my hair was looking like an 80's teased style and could effectively have worked as its own helmet.

The guard at the gate greeted us with a smile. "Good morning," she said.

I was tense. I'd never been to Kiawah, but then, I never would have gone willingly. I didn't like even the thought of the place. The whole island was basically owned by the rich. Security blocked off everyone except people who lived here and who worked for the people who lived there. It wasn't exactly my social circle. But then, even if I was rich, I wouldn't live here. It felt too much like cutting out the real world, and normal people weren't good enough to come check it out.

"Hi," Brandon said. He took off his helmet and presented a smile. "Is the gift shop open?"

"Sure is," she said. "You know where it is?"

"Yeah," Brandon said.

The woman nodded and then moved the lever that lifted the barrier.

That was how easy it is to get on the island? If I'd known...probably wouldn't have made a difference. I was still thinking like a thief. It just seemed silly anyone could enter the island to access the gift shop.

After a few more minutes on the bike, Brandon parked in a lot facing a hot tub and swimming pool that overlooked a beach.

"Oh my god," I said, stripping off the helmet and blowing hot air toward the scene. There was the gift shop nestled into a quiet corner of the parking lot. Even with the few cars parked, there was no one around. I felt safe venting about how flabbergasted I was at this scene. "You've got a whole ocean right there, and they build an open pool and hot tub in front of it?"

"I know, right?" he said. He took our helmets and plopped them onto the back of the bike. "I can't blame them though. It isn't even that great of a beach. I mean, see those waves?"

I squinted, checking the water, which seemed really still, serene. When waves washed up, they were low and gentle. "Yeah."

"That's how it is. Like all the time. Unless there's a hurricane or something. No wave action at all."

I blinked for a moment, taking a second to figure out what he was getting at. "You mean no chance to surf?"

"Folly is better. North Shore."

"North shore?" I asked. Marc had mentioned it once, but I'd been in a funny state of mind. Now I recalled it wasn't possible. You couldn't go in the water at North Shore. There were strong undercurrents. "You can't surf there."

"Not at the point," he said. "Not near the lighthouse,

but there's a spot nearby..." He waved his hand through the air. "Forget it for now. Let's get going."

Still, I had to agree with him. Why would the rich want a beach that never saw any wave action? But then, perhaps tall waves were too noisy for Kiawah residents.

We took to the beach. He made a point of holding my hand, claiming we needed to look like visitors enjoying the beach. I didn't fight him on this issue. I didn't think it was totally necessary, but I'd already lost three boys within twenty four hours on my watch, and I didn't want to lose him again. Holding on to him made me feel like he couldn't disappear again.

We were on the lookout for a house on the beach with an L-shaped pool in the back. We got a satellite picture view of the place from Doyle, and then an old real estate photo he dug up from the Internet. He checked for who owned the house currently, but it was actually a real estate company, and the owner of the real estate company was a corporation. Doyle said it was probably so they could write off the home as some sort of business expense. He didn't have time to hack into the mail system to check whose name was getting put on mail delivered to the house. Brandon sent the info to Corey who confirmed the information, but said that someone in the Academy knew someone in the post office and would ask.

The walk along the beach was better, because driving up, there was a row of trees in front of every house, essentially cutting off our view. Besides, if we walked the beach, we could pretend to sit and enjoy the ocean while we were really checking out the house.

The house itself appeared to be three stories, and a multimillion dollar place, according to the real estate websites. Like I'd told Axel and Marc, if I owned a fancy core everyone wanted, I'd have a million dollars...and a private island was a more likely location for someone that rich. Kiawah Island seemed the type of resort island getaway most people around Charleston would live in. Charleston peninsula was where the rich lived to be seen. Kiawah Island was where the rich went to escape public view.

We were quiet as we walked. It was hard to enjoy the serene surroundings when we were on the hunt, but the breeze caught in our faces and my senses were filled with salt and sand and I had the urge to go walk in the water. I was having a hard time walking on the sand without tripping in the boots that were too big for me, so I stopped to take them off and walk barefoot.

Brandon kept his boots on. We walked on the damp sand just beyond the tide rolling. The sand was cool to the touch, and while my feet were cold, it was actually helping to keep me awake. The sand, the warmer sun, and the sound of the ocean made me want to plant myself down on the dry sand and take a nap.

I studied each house as we came up to it, looking for similarities to the photo I'd seen.

"Almost there," Brandon said. He squeezed my hand, like he'd done every few steps since we started. I wondered if he used holding my hand as his own method to stay awake. "I think it was like ten houses down from the gift shop."

"Wouldn't it have satellite dishes and an antenna all around it? I mean, to send out a signal and act as a core for a cell phone service?"

Brandon did an eye roll, smirking. "Did you see an antenna in the picture? No, because it's a secret phone service," he said. "The core might just be a computer server inside. And an antenna could look like anything. It doesn't have to have prongs sticking out all over. It could just be metal, reaching outward. Besides, we're not one hundred percent sure it is here. I mean, this is a normal house. I'm not sure I'd keep a core in my home."

"You don't think Doyle could pinpoint the signal location?"

"I don't exactly trust Doyle not to lie to us for free cigarettes and a microwave."

I made a face at him. He squeezed my hand and stuck out his tongue, mocking.

He did have a point. I didn't think I'd keep an illegal underground cell phone service at my house. Then again, a house on the beach would keep it from looking suspicious, but would it have enough range for locals in Charleston to use it? I didn't understand how cell phone towers worked very well, but even I knew about cell phone bars, and the ranges from towers, and once you got too far away from one, you didn't have a signal at all. "How close do you have to be to a tower to have it give you a signal?"

"Not sure," he said. He used his free hand to rub a couple of fingers at his temple. "Corey would know. I wish he was here."

I studied Brandon's face then. His cerulean eyes had a particular depth to them now. The determination was there, the anger, but they were subdued by that sadness again. "What's wrong?" I asked.

He stopped rubbing, and turned his head to look at me. The sadness subsided, but only a little. It was replaced by something unreadable and I wondered what he was really thinking. "I'm tired," he said. "And sore. And we've only got so much time..."

"There's something else," I said. If it was important enough to think about now, he had time to tell me.

Brandon sighed and again tightened his hand around mine. "I honestly didn't think I was going to make it out alive," he said. "If it wasn't by the team I was with, with Eddie and the other Germans, it would be with this new team, who seemed to be killing anyone standing in their way. I was sure Eddie would have sacrificed me to save his team by giving me up next. I would have never seen you again. Or my brother. Or any of the guys. And now that two of them are gone, and I haven't seen my brother or Raven or Kevin or anyone, it's like I don't know for sure if I will ever." He lifted my hand slowly, bringing it to his lips, and kissed the knuckle. "But I've got you, though. I'll be hanging onto you for a while. I'm glad you seem to be out of your slump. I've not seen you look so alive. Angry, maybe, but alive."

I bit my tongue, wanting to give a retort of some kind, but it was just an angry impulse to defend myself, even if there wasn't much to defend myself from. I couldn't blame him for saying that. I just didn't like being looked at so closely that people could tell what I was thinking.

Funny how now I felt awake for the first time in weeks, and it was because I was busy saving people from getting killed.

Distracted in my own thoughts, I walked quietly beside Brandon. It'd been too long to actually answer anything he'd said. Brandon appeared to be back into his own thoughts, too.

I refocused on what we were there for. I expected this house to be covered with security and guards, even though from the real estate photos, it looked normal.

I mean, if it were easy to waltz in and get access to this core, Alice would have done it by now and wouldn't need Corey to do it for her.

That meant it would be harder than it appeared to get to this core. Eddie'd had weeks to get access to this thing and failed. What made us think we could do it in a day? The house probably had radioactive laser security ready to hit a fly if it crossed into his yard.

I tried to put that thought out of my head. People at the mall didn't allow me to take their wallets either. I found a way, though. Doyle had been right. People were the weak link. It was a morbid expression in a way. People aren't generally stupid. They're just vulnerable. Wasn't I, after all, weak in a way? We were weak and doing what we were told to save our friends. We were putting other people's security, people we didn't know, at risk.

That didn't sit well with me, either. I didn't want anyone to have this core. I didn't really want it to exist, either.

A few houses later, we found an L-shaped pool and the house that matched the real estate photos, just in a different paint color. The house was three stories, a Cape Cod style, bluish gray slate walls and white trim, with a balcony on the second floor, overlooking a small garden and pool and the beach. It all looked plain, like the other homes, except for the third floor, which was completely glass, gleaming in the sun. A third floor greenhouse? I couldn't see in from the reflection. It must have been a hot box in the summer.

The extravagance of it seemed to even outdo the neighbors' ostentatious homes. I imagined the owner could view far out into the ocean and around the island from all angles. That probably meant if anyone was up there, they could see us.

We stood on the beach together, looking at the house. I was trying to identify something that might be the antenna, but nothing stood out to me. It was just a big, fancy house. There wasn't even a tiny satellite dish or weathervane. The sand from the beach was cut off by a low hedge from the garden and yard. The pool looked clean, with an unrestricted view of the ocean from it. I wondered how they kept local kids from getting in his pool. I guessed local kids probably had their own pools.

In fact, not a lot of the homes had fences at all. I could look right at the back porch. Most homes had hedges to block of sweeping sands, but that was it. Back doors were exposed. Did they really trust the one security guard in the front to be all the protection they needed? I suspected there were security alarms everywhere. I looked for cameras, not spotting any, but that didn't mean they weren't hidden somewhere.

There was a van parked on the driveway, near a side door. It had rolled up backward, facing the road, and the rear doors were open. The back of the van was empty now, so I couldn't tell what was being delivered.

Brandon whistled, a low one meant just for me to hear. "That's a big fancy house. Seems bigger than even Coaltar's."

"It is bigger than Blake's," I said, and then shut the idea of Blake Coaltar out of my mind.

"If this is the house, and there is a core here," Brandon said, "then we should get inside and look for it. Maybe we can poke around and ask a few questions."

"Ask questions?" I blinked at him, and took my hand away so I could rub at my tired eyes. "Sure. Let's just walk in and ask the kids where the secret illegal core is."

"I meant more like, 'hey kids, which rooms are you not allowed to go in?' or 'which room does daddy yell at you if he finds you in it?'" he said, and smirked. "There's ways to learn stuff without asking directly."

"They teach you this in spy school?" I asked.

"You just said the spy word," he said. He refocused onto the house. I did, too. Maybe Academy spy training taught him how to ask things without asking directly. Wasn't my thing. I was more for waiting until people weren't home and then breaking in a window and snooping around.

And exactly how were we supposed to deliver the core anyway? It's not like we could walk out with it and it'd still be operational. She said she wanted access. It seemed like she needed to give us more direction. But then, she assumed Corey would be able to do it. We needed a Corey.

"We can't stay too long," Brandon said. "They might not notice us now, but they will notice if we're standing here, staring at their house from the beach. We'll have to move on and come back."

How were we going to learn anything and get this core if we were going to sneak around? I was about to point this out when a couple of men came out of the side door, returning to the van.

Brandon immediately encircled my waist, turning enough to make it look like we were embracing on the sand, rather than staring like we were. He ducked his head close to mine, his cheek pressed against my face.

I was the one left looking at the house over his shoulder.

"Tell me what you see," he said quietly into my ear, his lips brushing at my skin.

I swallowed, trying to focus, and checked out the van. The men were in black jeans and long-sleeved black button up shirts, clearly dressed up to deliver to opulent homes rather than common ones.

They shut the doors and headed for the front of the van, keys in hand and ready to go. The sign on the back of the van read: A1 Party Supplies.

"They're hosting a party," I said quietly. "Or they just hosted one. It's a party supply company. Could we sneak in that way if they're having a party tonight?"

Brandon groaned, and buried his head into my shoulder. "It isn't the best of circumstances, but we don't have time to do this another way. More eyes means more chances we'll get caught where we're not supposed to be, but we don't have much of a choice, and it might be our only opening." He backed up, pulling away from me and then captured my hand. "We'll need to get ready. And we'll have to do some research. We still don't know for sure if this is the right house."

"This house is owned by a company," I said. "That probably means it isn't like a normal house, and it might just be used for company events, right? Maybe no one really lives here. It's just a party house. So if it's a company party, we can check the company newsletter or something for information."

Brandon caught my chin, and then squeezed my face, giving me fish lips. "Look at you. All this thinking smart. Someone's getting the hang of this."

I talked through my squished lips. "I'll cut you if you call me cute."

Brandon tugged at my arm, dragging me across the sand. I held onto my boots and hurried along, about to curse at him for pulling, but he cut me off.

"We don't have a whole lot of time," he said. "We're not totally sure this core is here. We'll have to work out our plan B, and try to get details on the owners before we crash the party."

I stomped to keep up with him as we headed back. "If this is the core, Alice is watching from somewhere. Did Eddie know about a house on Kiawah?"

"I don't know," he said. "He was more focused on me tracing numbers connected to the core, and trying to work out how to break the security code while the information streamed. He didn't seem to want to break into where the core was to access it after our first conversation. I think something changed his mind from that way of thinking."

"Was it Alice?"

"Who knows," he said. "Maybe. I don't know anything about her and he didn't talk about an Alice." He checked his phone, reading text messages. "Corey has the videotapes and wants a description of her. If you recognize her face, he can run that image through some data scanners and find out a lot about her. Her real name, for one. If she has a driver's license, a police record, or if she walks into any major airport, we can track her via facial recognition. It'll take time, but the sooner Corey can start working with her image, the better. That's our next step right now."

"She had red hair," I said, feeling a swell of hope at this realization that computers could eventually help us track her down. I wanted to get to work right away, to relay information that might be relevant to Corey finding the right person. "Blue eyes. Bitchy personality."

Brandon shook his head, then motioned to the bike and further to the road. "We should get out of here, and get to a safe location to talk it over. And maybe grab some coffee."

♠

PLANNING A DATE

Brandon and I ended up in a small cafe on the road just outside of Kiawah, next door to a local grocery store on John's Island. The café was tiny and the area was surrounded by trees, with a good view of the lot and the road so no one could sneak up on us. There was one old man server, and no customers.

I'd ordered an iced mocha, which was more burned coffee than mocha. I swallowed as much as I could quickly, before taking a bite of a sugar doughnut from a box we shared. The doughnut only just covered the bitter coffee taste.

Brandon had downed a hot coffee and was working on a second, all the while texting his brother, typing in my descriptions, asking me detailed questions about Alice and exactly what she had said.

Corey eventually came back with a few photos. They were still shots of the aquarium from various angles. The photos were focused on crowds, particularly women with longer hair like I'd described.

I thought at first we'd never find them, but just when I was about to complain that we were wasting time, Alice appeared in one of the pictures. She wasn't wearing the coat, but just the pair of slacks and a loose blouse on her thin frame as she entered through the main doors. Corey followed up with photos of her journey through the aquarium before she disappeared behind an employee door. She walked in alone, with that smug smile on her face but the camera didn't reveal the sheer contempt and malice in her cool eyes.

"That's her," I said, sitting up quickly and nearly spilling my mocha. I stilled just long enough for my cup to stop shaking. I reached over, pointing my finger at the phone Brandon held up. "That's Alice. She was wearing a lab coat when she came in. Like she was trying to trick me that she worked there somehow. She seemed to know a lot, like my name and Axel's."

Brandon nodded, then studied the picture and sent a message on to Corey. "Since Eddie was trying to save his life and his crew, he might have given her a lot of information. It didn't bug him to tell her about us. We were no one to him."

"We're doing the same thing, you know," I said. "We're giving up this core to Alice, and might be giving her the lives and livelihoods of...well rich snobs. But we don't know who this might affect in the long run. And she said she'd blame Eddie for the murders that have already happened."

"We'll have to worry about it after we get Axel and Marc back," he said. "The goal right now is to prevent any more deaths. Eddie and his team have been trying for a year to get at this core. We have to figure out how we're going to get access to someone else in less than a day."

"I don't know what she expects even Corey to do for her. For us to unlock the doors and let them in? It's not like we could steal the hard drive...or whatever it is the core works from. Wouldn't that defeat the purpose if we shut it down by trying to move it?"

"I get the feeling we're supposed to break in, shut down the security, and let the system keep flowing. But then anyone could read it." Brandon picked up his coffee, took a couple of long sips, and put it back down again. He puckered his lips, and grimaced. "Why did it have to be Marc that got kidnapped? I've been spoiled by his coffee."

"Not like he could make you one now, even if he were free," I said. "He'd be with us chasing after Axel."

"And chastising the people here about their coffees, giving them the lecture about beans and brewing." He sighed, and stretched himself out a bit, his bones cracking in different spots. Long, lean arms and legs flexed out made him appear to be super tall. He relaxed again, a frown at the corner of his mouth. "The Academy won't be happy about this, you know. I'm avoiding them to save Axel, but they won't like being in the dark. As far as Corey knows, we're laying low just to seek out information."

"I figured they didn't like it when their people get kidnapped and would want us to do whatever it took to get them back," I said. I may not know that much about it, but I couldn't imagine the group would like two of their guys getting tortured and possibly killed over an illegal cell phone scheme.

"They won't like this business about Corey's security packet, either. They're not going to like that he's got software out there that people are interested in and can trace back to him. Or that he resurfaced his old hacker name for something new he'd been working on. He's made himself a target."

I wondered if it was the new game Corey was working on. "How?" I asked. "I mean, what did he do? How did these bad guys find him? So he left his name in the code? That's a thing?"

"He learned it when he was younger." Brandon pursed his lips and then bent his head down. He rubbed at the blond bits of hair at his temples and then across his eyebrows. "He's way too smart. With the way our parents are, they wanted us to be on athletic teams and it was his way of rebelling. If he could be exceptionally good at something else, maybe our dad would give up demanding we participate in sports all the time."

I bit my lip, sitting back, and crossing my arms across my chest. I'd not heard about any of their parents or any other relatives. They all knew about mine. "So your father was mean?"

"He wasn't abusive. He was going to turn us into sport stars," he said. "The Henshaw Twins. The trouble was neither one of us cared. We didn't want to be recognized as a pair. We wanted to be individuals and we didn't like him telling us what to do and what to participate in. Corey didn't like sports. I didn't like the sports my father picked out as money-makers. I prefer surfing over basketball or football or hockey. And you can't really succeed at a game unless you really want to be there."

I couldn't imagine Corey playing basketball for a living. Not that he wasn't athletic in his own way. He was really strong. I'd watched him lift hundreds of pounds of metal, roofing material, and wood in the couple of weeks we'd spent fixing up old homes in the North Charleston area. For a nerdling, he had an admirable body. "So how did he end up with this security packet thing? Why did he even make it?"

"It probably happened a while back," he said. "During high school, we spent nearly all of our time in athletic departments, playing different sports. He didn't have time for normal classes he wanted to take that required extra computer hours and homework. He focused on what he could learn on the Internet when he got a chance, staying up all hours and sleeping through class. He ended up in chat rooms with hackers who taught him tricks. At first, he did small kiddie hacks, like taking down a website, or discovering access to private corporate emails. Once he started, he said he was hooked. He said it was like figuring out a puzzle, but each one had a surprise inside. Sometimes the result harmed, or it could help. He choose to help...most of the time."

I pressed my lips harder together, biting my tongue to stop myself before I admitted knowing what I knew. They'd been criminals once. Maybe they weren't now, but they'd all been arrested, in one way or another. Did their arrest record say something about wire fraud? "And the rest of the time?" I asked.

"Well, he was with hackers," he said. He looked up, frowning. "I didn't even know anything about it at first. I just thought he was playing computer games so I didn't bug him about it. Then one day, I found him with some really odd computer supplies. He'd kept a number of gadgets out in the garage, where I'd stored some motorcycle parts. I asked him about the equipment, and about what he needed them for. He told me about writing security code, and then asked if I'd help him with a project. He said it would help other people. I believed him."

"He lied?" I asked. It seemed ludicrous, and I didn't believe for a moment Corey would ever intently harm anyone else.

"He didn't lie," Brandon said, his voice a little deeper with the resolve behind it. "He simply didn't realize it could be illegal. I didn't either. The police department called it fraud, but they were pressed to define what it was we were actually doing to the judge."

"What *were* you doing?"

"We were finding money that didn't exist," he said. "He found a way to access accounts in banks that were of companies that didn't exist, I should say. So they weren't really supposed to be there. Small accounts with no name, no address, no identifiable source. They were old, with no owners. Some were just numbers. I don't really understand the logistics now, but he told me they were forgotten, dormant accounts. Pockets of money lost in the system of banks. Some, he said, were criminal accounts. Criminals funneling money through places to get the money clean sometimes left these 'chump change' accounts open with a few hundred dollars leftover. And criminals would never report their stolen money to the police. So we could take it, and keep it, or use it to give to charities or whatever. The biggest part was, the accounts were super old, and so it was even less likely these people even knew the money was there. Corey said it was wasted money collecting mild interest automatically over the years in the banking system. We were simply taking care of it."

Stealing. He was trying to make it sound like money found on the street that you couldn't find the owner for, but really, it was money in a bank. They were stealing from a bank. "And someone reported the stolen money?" I asked.

"Some hacker got nosy, found Corey's signature and traced him," he said. "That's the thing. Most hackers leave a signature, their trademark. Corey developed his own trademark and used it in every single piece of hacking and software he'd ever written. It's like using spray paint to tag your name on a train or wall. I don't really understand it but that's how he explained it. Anyway, this hacker left a little anonymous tip, and the FBI tracked him down, found out what we were up to, and then tried to charge us with everything they could throw at us. Mostly they didn't want us being able to hack into bank accounts. They were going to lock us away for life, if they could."

This story sounded familiar. Axel had once told me his own, about how he had caused an accident, and his father had him locked away. That was mostly understandable. Now Brandon was telling me they were picking up forgotten dollar bills on the street, essentially, and trying to play it off like the FBI were the bad guys. I made a face, sat up and shook my head. "Seriously," I said. "You were taking money without working for it. You had to know it was stealing. If you kept the money for yourself, that's wrong. It might have been money without an owner, but it was money that didn't belong to you. You didn't earn it."

Brandon's face twisted into a scowl. "No, you don't understand. We didn't use the money for ourselves. We knew keeping it was wrong, but we didn't see the harm if we were just putting the money to some use. It was tempting to keep it, but we always put the money into charities. Specifically, though we didn't know it at the time, the Academy's local charities."

This was an interesting twist. "The Academy has charities?" I asked.

He nodded. "A few. They're mostly for redeveloping neighborhoods, like you were participating in. Or sometimes school programs. It's really open. Whatever the city happens to need. Anyway, the majority of the money went to those. It's how the Academy found us, really. When it came out in court about what we were doing with the money, Academy lawyers stepped in. It was a good thing. Our father had hired us a lawyer, but he wasn't any good. He kept kowtowing to the prosecution. We were almost sentenced to prison. Instead, we got community service...for the Academy." He blinked, and looked down at his phone as it lit up. "Corey's got the photo of Alice circling. It'll take time to track her, if she's anywhere traceable. We'll find her." He picked up his phone, and his coffee and I picked up my cup and the now empty plate of doughnuts. "We need to get ready."

"What are we doing?" I asked.

176

"Reliving our first date, apparently," he said with a smirk. "Corey found access to that company, and there is a party tonight. An electronic invitation went out. Guess who it's for?"

"Who?"

"A *Mr. Murdock*," he said.

I jumped up, nearly knocking back my chair. "Coincidence?"

"Corey thinks he might live at that house. He's trying to dig up details, but he's not exactly the most notable of the CEOs. I mean, he's on the board, but he's not in news reports where the company is mentioned. In fact, he can't find out that much about him or his family at all."

"And he's alive? I thought the owner of the core was dead. That's what…didn't Eddie say that?"

"Maybe there was a second owner. We'll have to find out. Anyway, we need to go shopping for clothes."

I had a mental freeze as to what he was talking about, but when I thought about it, I realized our first date had been a party, where I was supposed to steal a wallet, and then replace it.

I cringed. I'd have to wear a dress.

♠

MISTAKEN IDENTITY

*H*ours later, at twilight, we approached Kiawah Island inside the back of a town car. The driver was part of the Academy. I only caught the name, North Taylor, apparently the same one who was supposed to give Avery a car. I hadn't said a word to him nor had I gotten a good look at him, but he picked us up outside of a strip mall, and his brother drove Brandon's bike back to his garage for him. Brandon said he called in a few favors, and some Academy people would be helping us out from this point.

I was in the back seat with Brandon. The plan was to get dropped off for the party giving us the appearance of being guests. North would have to drive off, preserving his safety. When we were finished, we would meet another driver in a different car by walking the beach and heading to the gift shop parking lot.

Corey, in the meantime, had himself and a security team at the hospital working to scour the city for this Alice and anyone associated with her. We weren't sure if it was her real name, or who she was, but they were searching local driver's license photos, and then extending those to national databases when that was unsuccessful. It would take a few more hours.

Our only goal was to confirm the core was here, and to possibly learn as much as we could about Mr. Murdock. Brandon and I needed to figure out who really owned the core and gather as much information as possible. It would be just in case we couldn't find Alice and her goons before time was up. We would have to negotiate. Brandon said the Academy would have us put a tracker on anything we handed over to Alice, if we did exchange for Axel and Marc, and that proper negotiators would be in place to make the trade with us.

"Corey says if this core is anywhere, it's probably in a room with the highest security. So look for doorways with control panels in the wall next to them." Brandon fiddled with his suit jacket buttons, buttoning and then unbuttoning the coat. "This thing doesn't fit very well. If it's undone, it feels like it'll slide off my shoulders, but then when I've got it buttoned, it's too tight around my chest."

"Try wearing a dress," I said. I had on a short red dress with spaghetti straps. It was a cold night, too, and I didn't have a jacket to wear. It was hard enough finding a dress I'd actually wear. It was the last one I looked at, and had rejected offhand before Brandon yelled at me that we were wasting time, and who damn well cared what I wore, and that the last twelve dresses I tried on had looked fine, and to just pick one.

"You look good in your dress," he said in a monotone. "I know you don't like them, but you really can wear a dress, you know. You've got the body."

I ground my teeth to bite back a retort. It wasn't that I didn't appreciate the compliment, but I was completely uncomfortable. I knew he was trying to be nice, and I didn't need to overthink his comment. "You look pretty good in a suit," I said. "But I think I like it when you dress down better."

Brandon didn't reply, but I caught the edge of his smile in the darkness, and his arm threaded around my shoulders, holding onto me.

North pulled the car up to the gate, said two words to security, and then the gate opened and the car rolled forward.

Moments later, we were at the front of the house we'd spied on earlier. The house was lit up, the yard was full of guests. Cars were dropping off people by the driveway and then moving on into the night.

"We're lucky this wasn't some sort of small family event," Brandon said. "Or some quiet affair."

"What kind of party is it?" I asked, eyeing the guests as they walked up to the front door. North pulled up behind another driver dropping off guests, stopped the car, and ran around to open the door on my side first.

"A wedding reception," Brandon said as he slid out behind me. "We can pretend to be on the husband's side. The employees at his company were invited to attend."

Mr. Murdock was getting married? I guess he didn't realize two teams were trying to break into his precious illegal cell phone service. It seemed pretty ballsy to have hordes of guests at the same location where your core was.

Standing outside, the chill prickled my skin. I glanced once at North, who remained quiet, but studied me in my dress once and then looked away.

He didn't look like a driver. He was barely our age, maybe younger. It was hard to tell. He had such a serious expression.

Get out while you still can. It was the only thing I could really think to say to him, but couldn't say out loud. He didn't need to be in the middle of this.

Brandon took my hand, guiding me up the sidewalk. North moved quickly back into the driver's seat, and the car followed the line and turned around to leave. Brandon focused ahead. I tried to do the same, ignoring the desire to slide back into the car and run off and not go into the lion's den. *Think of Axel. Think of Marc. Do this for them.*

The wedding reception was mostly inside the house. This made me nervous. We did need to be inside, but this meant more eyeballs and the increased chance we might be noticed trying to sneak around.

Fortunately, the party itself was packed. There was a formal parlor that had been cleared of furniture and in the corner, a string quartet played instrumental versions of popular songs. People held onto tiny plates of finger food and flutes of champagne. There was a pile of wedding gifts stacked up on one large table in the front entryway. Attendants all wore black suits and white gloves.

"Blake didn't have a quartet," Brandon said to me as we dove into the thickest part of the crowd.

"He had a band," I said. I used our cover to study people and look around the house, searching for doors that had security panels. "I think that's more than a quartet."

"He didn't have an ice sculpture," Brandon said.

"Yes, he did," I said, although I couldn't really remember. I just wanted to contradict him. Why were we comparing parties?

"This house is bigger," he said.

I looked around the house. "Yes," I said, noting the rooms were large and open compared to Blake's old-fashioned house. "But Blake's house is an antique built two hundred years ago. This one is new. And why do you care whose house is bigger? Is this a guy thing?"

Brandon grunted as he scanned the room. His hand covering mine tightened. "I don't know," he said. "Just ignore me."

What was it about parties that made him agitated? I tried to forget about it. I focused, trying to figure out where I'd hide a core in my own home. I didn't even know who Murdock was. Corey had said he had dark hair but I hadn't seen a picture.

My first goal was to identify security. Most obvious were the attendants wearing dark suits and standing along the sidelines. Their eyes surveyed lazily. Occasionally they leaned in and commented to a passerby, but otherwise, they looked bored.

Two were positioned at the foot of the stairwell. Brandon and I circled most of the downstairs rooms, but it seemed, aside from the busy kitchen, all the rooms were open to party guests as spill over rooms since it was so crowded. The core couldn't be downstairs.

"We need to get upstairs," I said to Brandon. "If they're guarding the stairwell, it's probably up there somewhere."

"I know," he said. "There has to be another way up. Even if I distract security guards, you'll be exposed going up, and the ones on the other side of the room are watching."

I studied the space. The majority of people were eating from the buffet that was set up in the dining room. If there were a back stairwell, then maybe it was beyond the kitchen. "Do you think there's two stairs?"

Brandon bit his lip. He pulled out his cell phone and typed into it. He got an immediate reply from Corey and showed it to me. "Yeah," he said.

Corey: Beyond the kitchen, behind door number two on the right.

"Ask him if there's a bathroom that way."

Brandon typed in a message and Corey confirmed there was.

"Good," I said. I went to the buffet table and took a champagne glass. "I'm going to go pretend the downstairs restrooms are full."

Brandon eyeballed the glass. "We shouldn't separate."

"You need to keep an eye on the guards. If they come after me, try to stall them. Or stay behind if somehow I get kicked out."

Brandon pursed his lips and looked around. "Kayli...I really don't want you going alone."

I didn't want to, either, but I was a girl sneaking upstairs, and I could pull off looking like I was tipsy and had gotten curious. If Brandon came along, it might be harder to explain.

To ease his mind, and to quell my own nerves, I got up on my toes and kissed his cheek.

"I'll be back," I said. "I'll just find the 'kids should stay out' room. I won't go in."

He frowned but then kissed my mouth quickly. His eyes held my gaze after, and he squeezed my hand. "Ten minutes," he said, "or I'm coming after you."

"Fifteen," I said. "And no heroics if the guards kick me out."

"No getting kicked out," he said.

I left him, turning a couple times to look back. He picked up his own champagne, and while he tried not to be obvious, his eyes kept watching me.

I dove through a small group of people chatting, smiling and saying excuse me. Everyone was dressed up and laughing, gossiping and drinking and eating. I wondered how many of them were in on the illegal phone service.

The kitchen was organized chaos, with a kitchen manager in a white suit barking directions to chefs and attendants dropping off empty plates and champagne glasses, only to pick up trays of food and clean dishes and get sent back out again.

I was trying to slip in behind an attendant when the kitchen manager pointed at me. "Miss!" he cried out. "You're not supposed to be back here."

"Sorry!" I clamored. "There's a restroom back here, isn't there? The other ones are occupied...and I need to change my pad." Want to ensure men got out of your way

183

and gave you access to the bathroom? Talk about your period.

The kitchen manager's face stiffened. "Uh, sure," he pointed to the door at the far end. "There's one back there."

I thanked him, and smiled pleasantly at others nearby. After I got to the door, they resumed their jobs.

In the back hallway, there were several doors. I followed Corey's instructions, finding a hallway behind a door and heading up.

The second floor carried an echo from downstairs, which made me paranoid, as I couldn't hear if anyone else occupied the floor. It also meant I couldn't hear someone sneaking up behind me, like a security guard, or the owner.

Still, I tiptoed my way through the hall, taking a long detour to avoid the main staircase, and avoid being seen. The hallway had a thick carpet. That was good for me. It kept me from clomping about in my low heels. It was also cluttered, with potted plants and framed pictures. It might have been a party house, but it sure looked like someone lived here. The pictures were of the same family, the more recent looking ones with a lot of adult siblings with a few smaller kids and a stern looking elder man in the center. I wondered if that was Mr. Murdock. Maybe the wedding wasn't for him, but for one of the grown kids.

Most of the doors along the hallway were closed, save for a couple of bathrooms. A big set of doors at the end of the hallway looked suspicious at first, but when I peeked inside, I spotted a large bed: the master bedroom.

Most other rooms were bedrooms, and one was an upstairs office. Even inside it, there was a plain-looking computer. I shook the mouse, and it instantly opened up to reveal a browser on today's news. The history was email boxes, bank websites, the stock market, news, and

YouTube videos of cats and dogs.

The desk drawers were surprisingly clean. The bills had the real estate name on the front. I looked for Murdock's first name from all the envelopes, and I got a variety: Trisha, Ethan, Gregory, Harold. I wasn't sure which one was the Grandpa Murdock in the photos.

I was going to steal some of the mail, but I didn't exactly have a place to stuff it, and wasn't sure how helpful it would be. I did find a cell phone bill, which was interesting and ironic. I guess you couldn't own an underground cell phone service and fake having a normal cell phone. I grabbed the bill, hiked up my dress, and stuck it in the waistband of my underwear. Maybe tracking that phone number would help. I'd have to get it to Corey somehow.

The rest of the floor didn't hold anything interesting. The core wasn't on this floor.

I pursed my lips, glancing back toward the main stairs. They were they only way up to the third floor. I'd have to use them without alerting the guards. Sneaking around wasn't my area of expertise. Plus, I wasn't sure how much time I had left, and worried Brandon might do something stupid and chase after me. I should have told him twenty minutes.

I slipped the heels off my feet.

I couldn't imagine what Brandon was doing. It unnerved me that he was out of sight. It was how I had lost Axel and Marc. Still, he was in the middle of a crowd. It's not like Alice could get her thugs to knock him out and cart him off. Not even Eddie would risk it.

Alice did manage to get Axel and Marc out of the aquarium, though.

I already didn't like not knowing what I was hunting for. It made it more difficult to steal. Or break into.

I did my own version of tiptoeing down the hall,

crouching when I got close to the stairs to avoid being seen. I contemplated how I would sneak up the stairs, but then, I decided it was probably best to not make it look like I'm sneaking around. Best to just move as quickly and quietly as normal.

I peered over the line of sight where the guards were downstairs. I waited until I was sure they weren't looking and started heading up.

I was on the start of the third stair, turned and then just when I made it to the third step I heard a male voice.

"Hey!"

I started to dash upward a couple more steps. Whoever it was, maybe he wasn't talking to me.

"You! Hang on a second!"

I stilled. Curses escaped my mouth. I should have been better. I could have gone faster. I was going to get kicked out. Brandon will have to find a way. At least I was pretty sure the core was upstairs.

I turned, ready to face a guard, holding the flute of champagne to my lips, ready to pretend I was drunk and lost.

I focused on the first set of stairs, but the guards had their backs turned, looking bored. Had they said something to someone else?

From down the hallway on the second floor came a man. He was in his thirties, with dark hair, a lighthearted grin, and wearing a dark suit, but different from the attendants. It was much more formal. A partygoer?

He looked at me inquisitively. I supposed he must have been the one to ask me to stop. Instead of answering at all, I stared back.

He approached the stair, stopping at the first step. "You're Janet's daughter, aren't you? Little Angela? God, I haven't seen you in years. When did you grow up?"

My lips parted. He was mistaking me for someone

else? It was a better excuse than I could come up with. "Oh," I said slowly, and then forced a smile. "You remember me?"

"You don't think your Cousin Ethan would forget about you?" His smile broadened and he opened his arms wide. "Come give me a hug."

My spine rippled. Ethan Murdock. One of the kids. This was way deeper into the lie than I wanted to go, but it was way too late now. Angela must have been a good enough likeness that I could get away with playing that role, but it wouldn't take too many questions from him to prove I wasn't her.

I faked a smile and slowly moved down the steps, spreading my arms a bit.

Cousin Ethan hugged me tightly around the middle. I tried to return the hug but it was awkward I gave him a little pat.

He released me, looking at my face. "Were you exploring? You always did run off to poke around the house when you were younger, too."

"I..." It was on the tip of my tongue to say something else, but I changed my mind and nodded. "Sorry," I said. "I didn't mean to be nosy."

"No need to be shy," he said, coming up the steps ahead of me now. He gestured to the top of the stairs. "Have you seen the observatory? I think it's my favorite."

Did he live here? This could be extremely dangerous if he did own this core.

Might as well...

I hopped up the steps beside him, forcing my eyes wide and trying to look curious. "I saw all the windows," I said. "Can you see far?"

Ethan nodded. "I hate to say, you can peek into the neighborhood. Just be careful where you look. You'll get way more than an eyeful." He made a gross face and then

187

laughed. "Did you graduate from high school yet? How's Aunt Janet?"

"She's fine," I said, going with the flow, and also feeling a sink in my heart. I realized now that if the owner was Ethan, and if Ethan was willing to let little cousin Angela into this observatory, then it probably wasn't where this core was either. I was wasting time. "I shouldn't take too long, or take you away from the party."

He waved his hand. "What? Like they can't handle themselves?"

Or they might try to sneak in and steal your stuff. I shrugged and followed. If Brandon came to look for me now, then maybe it wouldn't be so bad. Ethan seemed friendly.

We cleared the stairs to a third-story landing. This one was just a small foyer-like space, with walls all around and a single door.

The door had a security pad next to it.

Bingo! It did have security. The core must be here! He'd let me in? Wouldn't he want to keep the core a secret?

Ethan went to the security pad and then typed in a number. I watched, memorizing the sequence in my head, repeating it again and again to remember it.

Ethan opened the door and stepped in and then to the side to allow me space to enter.

The observatory was big. I didn't know what an observatory was supposed to be. I could only picture a Clue game board and I wondered where the candlestick was.

The foyer area we left was the only walled off section of the third floor. The rest of the space was an open floor. The room was designed to give ample viewing of the large windows surrounding us. The room itself was mostly seating arrangements overlooking every possible angle.

Low sofas, and coffee tables were clustered together. The air was cooler up here, reflecting the temperature outside. The light was minimal, and across the floor in low lamps.

The view was impressive. While I'd seen higher up over Charleston at the apartment, the house overlooked the ocean, some of the neighbors' homes, and over the trees to look out toward John's Island.

I surveyed the area. There were telescopes positioned near different windows. Among the clutter of furniture, I looked for a computer, a server, a locked safe. Anything.

Ethan moved ahead of me to one of the telescopes. He pointed the eyepiece and then gestured for me to come closer. "Come take a look," he said.

I couldn't get out of it. If I got the dime tour done with quickly, he'd have to go back to his party. Or maybe if I stayed up here long enough, and acted interested, he'd give me a chance to snoop around on my own. Nothing in the room looked like a core. No electronic doodad computer that Corey could fiddle with. Wouldn't a core need a huge server to store data? Or to operate at all? Alice presumed Corey knew more about this, but I wasn't sure even Corey would have been able to figure out exactly where this thing was. I was starting to wonder if it was even up here at all.

Then why have a security panel on the door?

I moved to the telescope and looked through it. It was pointed at the ocean. There was a ship out in the distance, and a couple of stars off the shoreline. The moon peeked out from behind a cloud.

"So what are you doing these days?" he asked while I was looking. "Going to work for your cousin, aren't you? Come work for me?"

"I don't know what I could do," I said. I stood, finding Ethan standing nearby with a light smile. I felt a pang of guilt since I was lying to him, plus here to steal his core if

C. L. Stone

I could. I didn't know him. I didn't know why he started the core, or why it had to be illegal and underground. He was showing his little cousin the observatory during a wedding reception he was hosting. Despite what I might have been thinking, he didn't seem that bad. He didn't look like a bad guy or a killer. Maybe I didn't know what a core looked like, but I could read people, and Ethan Murdock was a good guy.

Still, if he had a core at all, I just needed to know so I could steal it, or use it to trade to save lives. Hopefully when the dust cleared, Mr. Murdock wasn't going to get into trouble.

"You're the artist," he said. "We've got an advertising department if you're interested." He motioned to another of the telescopes, one looking out across St. John's. "Want to see the other ones? That one's probably my favorite."

That telescope in particular was across the room, and I moved to it, wanting to check out behind the walled off section, hoping the core was behind it.

Nothing. More couches. More low lamps. More glass windows. Did he have this core in the sofas?

I checked out the telescope and I got an eyeful of church towers sticking out of the trees in the distance. It was funny to me to see the trees with little crosses sticking up out from among them, like a strange graveyard. Since it was darker now, lights were shining up on the crosses, giving them a weird spectral appearance.

"Ethan," I said carefully. I was taking a chance here, but I had to. "I like this observatory, but I was wondering why the top floor has a security pad."

"It's so no one can break in through the glass and come into the house," he said quietly. "Glass is vulnerable. It's hard to secure. It was easier to simply secure the door to protect the family than it was to somehow secure the glass. Insurance makes me secure everything. They really hate this room. I told them they were being ridiculous. It's the third floor. Who would climb up here just to break into the glass?"

Made sense. That also meant we were chasing a false lead. The core isn't here. Despite what Doyle said, this was just some rich man's home.

But his name was Murdock. Frustration bubbled inside me; we'd lost a whole lot of time, and Alice was playing games, expecting us to access something we couldn't even locate. We needed to do something, to call her and tell her to show us proof that Axel and Marc were missing.

Maybe Avery was right and we needed to call the police in to help.

I pulled away from the telescope, finding Ethan standing close to one of the windows and smiling out into the distance. The lord looking over the land. It was hard not to be jealous of his obliviousness to a dire situation happening around him. I envied his ignorance.

"The church towers are pretty," I said. "It's a nice view, but I guess I can't keep you here. There's a party downstairs." I'd played this game long enough. Time to find Brandon. And I wanted out of this dress.

Ethan smiled politely and then bowed his head a little. "Of course, I should let you go." He gestured to the doorway. "Janet should be downstairs, right? We'll have to go find her."

"I'm sure I'll see her somewhere," I said, waving it off.

"Nonsense!" he said. "I'd love to say hello. I've not seen her in a while, either. Years."

"You're right," I said, inching again toward the door. Maybe he'd follow me downstairs, but after that, I'd split. I needed to find Brandon and get out of here. I was going to kill Doyle if he lied to us.

191

Ethan led the way downstairs. He rambled on about the family I didn't know. Once we got to the lower stairs, he walked right past the guards, which I now thought were just extra attendants looking out for guests and directing them to where they needed to go, simply containing the party to the first floor.

The band seemed a bit louder now, a little more enthusiastic. Ethan talked louder, but I couldn't hear him over the music and through others talking around us. I heard something about Janet, and then shrugged, wondering if he meant he was looking for her and couldn't find her.

He kept talking as I looked for Brandon and an opportunity to leave. Most of it was lost to me, but then I caught "...have you met my new wife, Alice?"

I jolted upright, which made my ankles lock and my heels clack hard against the wood floor. My first thought: coincidence. Had to be.

When I caught Ethan's questioning eyes, and then followed his gesturing hand to the woman who was approaching, I nearly fell over.

Malice eyes, cold blue. Red hair. She wore a white dress, similar to a wedding gown, but simplified and shorter for a reception. A brand new wedding band gleamed on her ring finger.

Alice approached with a cool smile, and anyone else looking at her might simply see a new bride... approaching her husband.

Could it really be the same Alice I saw before? That was just this morning. Threatening my life and Axel's on her wedding day? Maybe I was just going crazy.

But it was her. The lifting corner of her lip told me she recognized me immediately, and found it amusing.

And I was pretending to be a cousin.

"Sweetheart," Ethan said to Alice as she came close.

"Did I ever tell you about my little cousin Angela?"

I tried to smile, biting my tongue. Was I wrong about Ethan? Maybe I'd been in more danger than I realized.

Or maybe Ethan was, and *he* didn't realize.

Alice's face transformed into a mask of warmth that didn't reach her cold eyes. "I have not," she said, very precisely. It made me wonder if English wasn't her first language. "I wasn't aware you had a cousin."

"From my Aunt Janet. Surely I've talked about her."

"Didn't she say she was in Georgia, had to work and couldn't make it? Or did I hear incorrectly?"

I stiffened, easing back a half step. Saying something now to contradict her could be critical. Alice was having fun with me. My mind was in a tizzy, trying to figure out why she was here. She married Ethan. Supposedly, according to Doyle, the signal was from here. She married someone she thought owned the core? Then why try to find someone to gain access to it? And why kill people and threaten lives?

"They must have been able to make it," Ethan said with a happy note, completely missing Alice's attempt to make him suspicious. "And who wouldn't try to attend? I always said I'd be a bachelor forever. Everyone's here witnessing the impossible. You're the one that changed my mind."

"I told you I would, darling," she cooed, all the while keeping her eyes on me. "I always do get what I want."

"So, how long have you known each other?" I asked Ethan. It seemed like a simple enough question, and it was one I was dying to know the answer to.

"Only...what? A couple of months?" Ethan checked in with Alice, who only smiled in reply before Ethan turned back to me. "Sounds ridiculous, but I just love her and we knew. What else can you do?"

"Oh I agree," I said, although alarms were going

through my head. A couple of months and he was already married. She had access to money beyond imagining now. Ethan was clearly very rich. Why was Alice bothering looking for this core? And why threaten Axel and Marc and anyone else to get it? At any rate, I needed to get out of here. I'd have to get Brandon out. We'd get the police called on this property. Maybe stage a robbery, have them investigate Alice...I was making up scenarios in my head, but I couldn't think of a plan B now. Maybe if I got away and snooped around some more, I'd find Axel and Marc locked up in a closet. "I should get going. I need to..."

"Find your boyfriend?" Alice asked. She said it sweetly, with a cocky smile. "I thought I saw you with someone, even if I didn't know who you were. I met him earlier. Corey, right? I think I saw him go outside and get in a car. I hope he didn't leave."

My heart stopped. She thought Brandon was Corey. He wouldn't leave without me. There was the widening of her eyes. The satisfying smirk. It all told me that if Corey... Brandon did leave, it wasn't because he wanted to.

"Boyfriend?" Ethan asked. He turned and then gave me a quick side hug. "Wow. I keep forgetting you're a young lady, not just a little girl any more. I still see you as a six year old and times like when I kept stealing Easter eggs out of your basket."

It was clear he missed the part about my boyfriend supposedly leaving me behind.

"I could still see her as a young girl," Alice said, the ice covered cleverly behind her back-handed compliments. "She does seem so innocent, doesn't she? Naïve and playing little childish games." She turned her attention on her new husband. "Shall we go cut the cake?"

"I think it's about time. And then maybe sneak away for our honeymoon?"

"If you don't get too drunk and pass out first," Alice said. She slipped her arm delicately into his and turned him to walk into the crowd.

Was he drunk? I didn't smell alcohol on him, and I knew the smell well enough. Maybe that's why he mistook me for his cousin so easily.

I didn't trust Alice saying Brandon was gone. I scoured the crowds looking for him. My chest tightened with every step. What an idiot I'd been. I should never have let Brandon separate from me. I made the same mistake with Axel and Marc. This whole thing was a nightmare and I just wanted to wake up already. How could she have married *the* Ethan Murdock that possibly owned this core? How did we not know?

We'd been running to catch up with all this information, though. Alice had always been miles ahead. She was already neck-deep with the guy who we'd just learned about hours ago.

So where was the core? Maybe in an office downtown. Maybe his cell phone was part of...

His cell phone!

I rushed back into the crowd, catching up with Ethan. "Ethan!" I called to him.

He turned. I did my best to look casual, to hide my wild thoughts and last minute plan from Alice. She stood by, an amused quirk to her lips, gazing at me curiously.

Ethan stared, waiting and oblivious.

"I forgot to congratulate you and give you...a hug," I said. Could I do this? Yes. His suit jacket was long. It'd be easy. From the angle, even I could tell he carried a cell phone in his back rear pocket, and a wallet on the other side. The bulges were different. The wallet...would it be useful? I wasn't sure, and it was a risk to take both.

Ethan brightened immensely. Poor guy. I'd never do this in a million years to someone like him. Why did he have to be wrapped up in this? "Of course!" he said. "Come here, cousin."

I approached him, using one hand to wrap around him, squeezing tight around the back, obvious. The other I slipped down, out of Alice's sight. I grabbed the cell first. First a pat low on his back.

Reached in.

Lifted.

I used the shadow of his body and his jacket to hide it from Alice and pulling it around. I hid both items in the folds of the dress and then behind my back in one hand. I turned him toward Alice, egging him on. "Now go," I said. "And have a good honeymoon."

Ethan had turned then, and was facing Alice when I went for the wallet. A small lift, as his pant pockets were loose. And then I had both behind my back. Simple. Alice might have had a husband, but I had his wallet and phone. I called it a small victory.

I could only hope Ethan wouldn't notice until much later, hopefully not until tomorrow. I needed to hurry. I needed to get this phone to someone who could help.

I needed to find Brandon, too.

I came up with a plan. Part of my mistake from the beginning was getting the Academy boys involved, and exposing more of them. I needed to do this my way. It was something unexpected, and Alice wouldn't see it coming. If she thought she had Corey now, she'd try to find a way to get him to work for her.

She didn't know me that well, or she wouldn't have let me get this close to her new husband. She wouldn't be able to know that part of me, because I was just the new girlfriend of Corey's. She would never know I could pick a pocket in a heartbeat, because I'd never been caught. Well, not by anyone outside of the Academy at least.

And if she didn't know I could pull wallets, she didn't

know other things about me. Like that I knew Doyle.

Like I knew a playboy millionaire who could possibly be the only one left that could help save these Academy guys before they were done in.

I needed to do this my way. I had to keep Corey safe before any more people got hurt. Raven needed to stay with Corey to protect him. I had a limited amount of time. I couldn't play fair or safe anymore.

I'd leave now, but I'd be back with someone willing to break the rules and help me get the guys back safe.

♠

HELP FROM UNEXPECTED FRIENDS

I did a wide sweep of the party just in case I'd missed Brandon somewhere, and then left for the rendezvous point down the road, close to the gift shop. I took a side door, and stuck to the shadows, finding a path to the beach, carrying my shoes, the wallet and cell phone. Once I was out of sight, I pulled out the phone bill as well.

At the parking lot was a dark town car similar to the one that had brought us here. The door opened and a man stepped out. He was the same height as North, with dark hair, and at first I wondered if North had come back. As I got closer, I realized he was older, mature with graying sideburns.

He waved shortly to me. I didn't know how he recognized me, but then I thought of the files the Academy had on me and my brother. There were probably a few pictures of us floating around. Still, I kept a distance.

"How'd it go?" he asked. Worry lines creased his forehead. "Is Brandon all right? Is he coming?"

"I don't know," I said, frowning. It was odd trusting this complete stranger. All I had going for me was that Brandon possibly knew him, which meant he was probably with the Academy. How did Brandon and Marc and any of the others trust these people? Did they know all of them? Still, he was the only one left, and if the Academy was going to take action, they needed to do so now.

He seemed to understand my hesitation, especially since I was alone. He held his hands up. "You were with Brandon Henshaw. North Taylor drove you here. We belong to the Academy."

I had to assume Alice still didn't know about the Academy. "Did you hear about Alice?" I asked. "Do you know about her?"

"Yes," he said. "I got a partial report, at least. She's the one who claims she has Axel and Marc?"

"Yes," I said. "And she's here now. She's inside that house we were supposed to scout. She married the man that owns the house. Ethan Murdock, possibly the one who owns the core we're looking for. I was talking to him and she intercepted and now I can't find Brandon at all. He may still be at the house or she may have taken him. She implied she did, but I don't know and I can't confirm."

He frowned. "This isn't good."

"No," I said. "I need you to stay here, and to possibly call in some backup. Someone needs to keep an eye out for Brandon, and someone else should follow Alice. Carefully, though. I don't know how she's managed to get Brandon when he's been careful and knows what she looks like. Obviously, I can't go back." It felt odd giving instructions to an older guy who probably knew more than I did.

He gave no indication he thought it was strange. He only nodded. "What are you going to do?" he asked.

"I've got a cell phone that might be the key to all this," I said. "I should take it to Corey."

"Good idea," he said. "I should probably drive you."

"We don't have time. If you can follow Alice, we might find Axel and the others. She won't recognize you as part of their team, right?"

"She shouldn't," he said. "I'm not exactly connected

to their group." He stepped forward and then closed the door. He went to the trunk and then opened it. "Can you drive?"

I nodded. "Of course." Technically.

"Take the car," he said. He dug into the trunk, putting on a formal jacket. "I'll call for backup and keep an eye on the house. You said she married the man inside?"

"Yes," I said. My heart rose. While I wasn't going to go to Corey, I was glad this guy had jumped up to help. He showed a lot of trust in someone he'd just met two seconds ago. "She was with Ethan, her new husband. Just be very careful. We can't let anyone know you're helping us."

"I'll be careful," he said. He buttoned up the jacket and then smoothed out his hair. He closed the trunk. "Keys are in the ignition," he said. "Drive to the hospital. Don't stop until you get there. Don't worry about Brandon. I've been watching the road. All the cars going by have been identified. Either he's still here, or he can be tracked in whatever car has left. So we'll find him. Hopefully we'll find Axel and Marc, too."

That was a good sign. "Thank you," I said.

"Just stay safe," he said. He moved around the car, and opened the driver's side door for me.

I got in. "What's your name?" I asked.

"Henry Anderson," he said. He reached out, taking my hand. I shook it. He released me, pulled a card from his back pocket and then gave it to me. "If you ever need anything, my team isn't far. Call any of us. Tell them I sent you."

I took the card, checking it. It was plain, with his name on it, and a title: CFO of a non-profit charity. I had a small thought of Brandon and Corey, younger, and donating to charities with stolen money. Like a couple of Robin Hood twins. I wondered if Henry's was one of the charities they'd donated to, unwittingly.

"Thank you," I said. "Be careful. Really."

"I will," he said. He closed my door for me. Before I could turn the car on, he'd already crossed the parking lot, heading back the way I'd come.

I hoped he'd keep his word. Enough of the Academy boys were missing now. Hopefully Henry could help.

I adjusted myself inside the car, and then drove slowly out of the lot, feeling awkward, like I was abandoning Henry for one, Brandon two, and thirdly, I was driving someone else's car.

Ignoring the niggling sensation in the back of my mind, I focused on the road and then on the cell phone I'd claimed. I needed to reach Blake Coaltar. He was probably the only one who could really help me now. I didn't have much of a plan. I just needed another pair of eyes on this. And someone who could convince Doyle to possibly get out here and help me figure out this core.

Should I use the cell phone I had? Why not? At worst, Ethan Murdock might check the records if it was his public phone. And if it was connected to the core, it was supposedly on an underground service. Untraceable. That was why we were trying to break into it, wasn't it?

Ethan was busy with his wedding, anyway.

I didn't know Blake's number though. I also didn't want to drive directly to his house.

As I drove, I had an uncomfortable feeling like I was being followed.

I hated to do it, but I called Avery as I pulled off of Kiawah Island and onto the road that lead to John's Island.

He answered on the third ring. "Taxi."

"Avery? It's Kayli."

He sputtered and then breathed into the phone. "Kayli? You okay?"

"Uh, kind of," I said. "Could you do me a favor?"

"Hang on a second," he said, and then he spoke, but it was muffled and obviously not to me. "Yo. Get out. No, it's close enough. It's a block away. You can walk it. Sorry. Have to go."

He was doing his job in the borrowed car? Guess he had to work after all. It's not like everyone can be Academy guys and just fly off and do whatever.

"Okay," Avery said. "What is it?"

"I didn't mean you should dump your fare," I said.

"My what?" he asked. "Oh. No. We were almost there anyway. Lazy shit can walk. What do you need?"

Rude to customers. Wow. Still, he'd done it to help me out, so I guess I couldn't say anything. "I need you to fetch someone for me and give them a message."

"Are we still messing with kidnappers? Are you sure about this?"

"He's not a kidnapper. I just need to get a message to him."

"You couldn't call him?"

"I don't have his number. I just know where he lives. Can you do it?"

"Sure, okay. Same place? The Aquarium? Or the Sergeant Jasper?"

"No. South of Broad Street."

He whistled into the phone. "You know some fancy people?"

"I need you to hurry."

He shuffled on his end of the phone. "In trouble?"

This was getting to be a routine now. "Maybe."

"Where are you?"

"I'm on John's Island, on my way back from Kiawah. I need a place to talk to him. I don't know if I have anyone following me, so I didn't want to bring them to his house."

"Who's following you?"

"I don't know," I said. I checked the rearview mirrors.

"I'm not sure how to tell."

"The easiest way is to get on a lonely road that doesn't have any off streets," he said. "Try Folly Beach. Pull up to the end of the block on the island, stop there, and turn around. See if anyone rides up or if you can catch them on the way there. If you see anyone, though, you shouldn't stop. We'll have to think of something else. Maybe stop in front of the police and fire station that's right there."

"How do you know this?" I asked.

"Saw it on a cop show once," he said. "You want me to drive your friend out to you?"

I sucked in a breath, turning the wheel, trying to recall the way to Folly Beach. "Maybe...actually, yes. Drive him. I've got a car. I'll meet you at the pier."

"Which house am I going to?" he asked.

I gave him the address. "You want to talk to Blake. Tell him my name. Tell him where I am and that I need him to come with you to get to me, but to be discreet about it."

"Okay, I get you. Blake. You don't want me to tell him Bambi or some other code?"

"You won't have to," I said, hoping. I was gambling as it was. There was a real risk that Blake would possibly slam the door in Avery's face. It was partially why I wasn't going to drive to his house. Avery might throw him off long enough to hear him out and make him realize how serious this was.

I was going to hang up, but Avery was doing his thing, driving, breathing into the phone. "Should I let you go?" I asked.

"Just hang on," he said. "I got you. I mean, just in case he's not sure, I want to keep you on the line."

I grew quiet, occasionally answering him when he asked if I was still there. I drove on toward Folly, and driving the long stretch of two-lane road through the darkness toward the island. Since it was off-season, there shouldn't be a whole lot of activity. I checked my rearview, watching. I was alone save for Avery. Not that Alice really needed me if she thought she had Corey.

I hoped Brandon had escaped and I was wrong about her having kidnapped him.

"Okay, there," Avery said after what seemed like forever. "I'm there. Just knock on the front door?"

"I guess," I said.

Shuffle, shuffle, knock, wait, breathing.

"Can I help you?" A refined Charleston accented male voice made it through the line. My heart rushed and my cheeks heated at the sound. I realized I probably sent Avery to get punched, but hopefully Blake wouldn't lash out at him if he was upset with me.

"You're Blake? You open your own door?"

"Last I checked, it was my door," Blake said. "I reckon you've got the wrong place though. I never ordered a cab."

"Just tell him!" I said, feeling revved up now at hearing Blake's voice. My heart had been racing hard for so long, and the sudden surge made me want to keel over and catch my breath.

"Why are you on the phone?" Blake asked. "Who is that?"

"It's Kayli," he said. "She's on the road right now to Folly Beach. She was kidnapped, but now she's not kidnapped and her friends are kidnapped. They're kidnapping guys now."

There was a shuffle and then Blake's voice. "Kayli?"

"...Yeah?" I said carefully. I swallowed, hoping I was making the right decision. I had flashes of memories sweeping through me of his car sinking into a swamp. And his yacht that had a blown up hole in the side and smashed into an island. And shooting him in the leg. He was my best chance at getting the boys back right now. I didn't have anyone else, not anyone I was willing to risk. Corey couldn't come out of hiding. Then we'd really be in trouble.

I could picture the gold flecks of Blake's eyes burning something fierce. "Did someone kidnap you? Did those criminals get you wrapped up in something else? I told you...I told you..."

"No time," I said. "Are you busy?"

"I'm fixing to lay a hurtin' on your gorgeous ass if you don't stop piddling and tell me what's going on."

Maybe he wasn't that mad at me. "I need you to come talk to me. Let Avery bring you. I've got a car and then we'll let him go. He's already been mixed up in this enough."

"Who's coming for you?"

"I don't know. Two groups of people. Just hurry up before they get here. They might be looking for me now. It's a long story." I was pulling up on Folly Beach and wanted to focus.

There was shuffling on the phone. The guys were talking. Car doors slammed. My heart was in my throat, but at least Blake was on the way.

♠♠♠♠♠♠

I pulled into the empty lot in front of the pier. It was next to a hotel, which was a good idea to run for if someone was following. I pulled around, turned off the lights, waiting. In the meantime, I checked out what Henry Anderson had in his car. An Academy car would have toys, wouldn't it? They were spies after all.

The glove box had binoculars, a medical kit, a brand new cell phone still in the box, a flashlight, a pocketknife and a notepad with a pen. I wish I'd known about the cell phone. I didn't like using Ethan's.

Things got quiet on the phone. "Blake?"

"It's Avery," he said. "Tell this guy I can drive, will you? He took my keys. He's going to wreck the car trying to get it through traffic the way he's driving." He pulled the phone away. "This road. No, wait, stop, if you go that way, there's construction and it'll take longer. There's a back way. Trust me. I drive for a living!"

I took the pocketknife and then got out of the car, popping the trunk. I dug around, looking in the trunk for clothes so I could get out of the dress. Bingo. I hoped Henry didn't mind, but I borrowed a pair of slacks, a belt, and a T-shirt. I grabbed a long-sleeved dress shirt, too, to put on since it was cold. I changed in the parking lot, throwing the dress into the trunk. I had to stab a new hole in the belt to make the pants tight enough to fit around my waist, and then rolled up the lower hem until it was around my ankles. I'd have to make do with the heels since there weren't any shoes in the trunk. I looked ridiculous but I felt better being in pants.

The last thing I needed was for Blake to see me in a dress.

As I was waiting, I checked the contents of Ethan's cell phone, which was filled with text messages: happy wishes on the guy's marriage. He belonged to a local church and had plenty of people who cared about him. It made me wonder about this cell phone and the service it was on. Maybe he kept his secret cell phone somewhere else? Did I steal the wrong one? It seemed silly to own a cell phone service and use a public service. If he had two, wouldn't he still hang onto the second one?

My head was spinning with questions. Sitting in the car, it became difficult to stay awake, so I spent a lot of time walking around outside the car. I was worried about Brandon, and wondered if Axel and Marc were okay.

How could I have lost Brandon again so easily?

Eventually, I heard Avery talking into the cell phone. "We're almost there," he said. "You're still at the pier?"

"Yes," I said. "I'm in the town car."

Avery pulled up, also in a town car, obviously borrowed from North as it appeared to be the same kind of car North had driven earlier. And North was so young. How did he own so many cars? Or was that his job for the Academy? And why were they all town cars?

Blake, wearing jeans, a silver button up shirt and barefoot, hopped out of the driver's side even before the car had fully stopped. Avery yanked the emergency brake, forcing the car to a halt.

Blake marched around the car toward me. "For the love of God," he said. His tousled blond hair was messy and the shadows under his eyes were darker than I'd seen before. His face was thickly unshaven, like it'd been a couple of weeks. It threw me off seeing him like this. Was he sick? I was surprised to see he didn't even have shoes. He'd hopped into the car without even grabbing a pair. The gold flecks of his eyes were there amid the hazel, but even those seemed not right somehow.

"Someone just tell me what the hell is going on?"

"I told you, she was kidnapped," Avery said. "And we should call the police."

"Not you," Blake said. He sliced his hand through the air at him and then pointed at me. He approached me slowly. "No, I want to hear from you. What's this about kidnapping?"

I talked as fast as I could about getting kidnapped with Brandon, my escape, learning about the core, Marc and Axel getting kidnapped and Brandon's escape, and then Alice and the party and Brandon being gone again. I kept the Academy part out of it since Avery was there.

"Good," Blake said. "They get you into this mess,

they should be the ones getting kidnapped. They should be able to get themselves out of it."

"They're going to get killed," I said.

Blake Coaltar's lips thinned and I got the feeling he was holding back saying what he was really thinking. He pressed a fingertip to his forehead. "So a girl named Alice tells you that Axel and Marc are poisoned, that Brandon left, and she wants you to get access to a secret underground cell phone network, of which the supposed owner she just married? Is that the gist?"

"Yup," I said.

"And you've got no proof she actually does have Axel or Marc? Or where Brandon is?"

"...No."

"And you're going on pure faith that if you manage to figure out how to get her access to it, that she's got the ability to deliver them?"

I couldn't answer him. I'd been too afraid of the alternative, knowing Alice was manipulating me.

My brain was tired. I couldn't even remember how long I'd been running. My body ached from the adrenaline rushes and crashes, being so tense for so long. Being kidnapped, having my life threatened... I hadn't had time to even think about my brother, who was still out there somewhere. I'd been trying to make sure the guys were safe, and so far I'd lost three of them. I didn't want to lose more. I was terrified of making a mistake and if one of them ended up dead like the Randall guy...and over something as stupid as his cell phone.

Instead, I stared at Blake, silently begging for his help, because I didn't have a course of action left. I just needed an outside view on how to approach this. Just one direction to go in. *Tell me something so I don't make another mistake.*

I might have pouted a little. It wasn't on purpose. I

was just exhausted.

Blake's face contorted. He pushed his palms into his eyes, and then reached up, tugging at his wild hair. "I've got to be the sorriest..." He sighed and then tossed the keys at Avery. "I guess you want to go now," he said.

Avery caught the keys. "Maybe I should stick around this time," he said. "I could help."

"Thanks, Avery," I said, looking at him as he stood by his car, wearing another Hawaiian shirt, shifting from foot to foot. He was probably worried about getting kidnapped or killed or the police getting called in. "You don't have to. It's probably better if you don't, actually. I may need to call on you again."

He nodded. "Sure. If you need to. I guess that makes sense." He waited another moment, like he was hoping I'd change my mind. When I didn't say anything else, he went around his car toward the driver's side.

"Here," Blake said, stepping forward. He drew his wallet from his back pocket. "Hang on a second. Take this."

Avery started to wave him off. "No, I don't need to be paid."

Blake shook his head and instead handed him a card. "Tomorrow morning, call this number. Tell her I asked you to."

"Why?" Avery asked, taking the card and looking at it. "It's just a phone number. Who am I calling?"

"Just do it," he said. "You'll see."

Avery looked at me. I shrugged. Not my deal. He could call the number if he was curious enough.

Blake and I waited until Avery got into his car and drove off. I stood silently, well after Avery's tail lights had started to fade in the distance, afraid to look at Blake.

Blake, however, wasn't going to give me the luxury of getting out of being yelled at. He grabbed my arm and

209

then pointed out toward the one road that led out of Folly Beach. "Okay, darling," he said, his tone deeper. "Nice trick with calling the taxi to get me out here, but why are we here at Folly and why didn't you come to me yourself? Did you think I'd shoot you or something?"

"Maybe," I said.

Blake's eyes narrowed and then he dropped my arm. "If I wanted to get revenge by shooting you, you'd have a bullet hole way sooner than now." He leaned in closer this time, his nose a breath away from mine. "But I am not your doormat to lay out your problems on and then vanish without a word."

"Huh?" I asked.

"Two weeks," he said. He stayed close to me as the gold in his eyes burned. "Two weeks of no calls, nothing. Sure. I can understand that. After that catastrophe in Florida, you needed the break. But now you call me out of the blue, and is it a thank you? Asking how my day is? How about going to a movie like normal people? No. It's to come save your life, and those guys you hang out with. And it's their mess in the first place. Again."

I cringed, afraid to step back because I thought the car was right behind me. "This wasn't their fault. We all got dragged into it. I didn't mean to..."

"I know you didn't mean to. That's my point. Don't you see?" He gestured again to the road. "You run around with those guys, and they're asking you to do crazy things. Now it isn't just them you could possibly get hurt by, it's some gang, or even two. What happens next time when it's a bomb that goes off downtown? Or an airplane crash with their fingerprints all over it?"

"Or drugs dumping into wells?" I asked him, anger welling up in me. "That first time was with you..."

"And you were out minding your own business before when they got you to chase after me, not even knowing all the information. Don't you see? You're getting your nose into things that have nothing to do with you. Dangerous things."

"Isn't that why you stole the drugs in the first place?" I asked, raising my voice to match his. "Sticking your nose..."

"I'm just yelling to yell," he said. He backed off then, taking a few steps into the parking lot and turning away. "I don't like surprises. And it's been a rough week."

"What have you been up to?" I asked in a quieter tone. "Are you sick? You look..." I didn't want to say it, but he did look awful.

"Nothing," he said. He raised his head, sucked in a breath, held it and then looked at me as he breathed out again. "But if I help you this time, you're coming with me after."

Huh. "Going where?"

"Wherever I want," he said. "Don't you trust me?"

I squinted at him, unsure. As tired as I was, it was easier to just agree. "You think you can help me get Axel, Marc and Brandon back?"

"I know I can," he said. "I'm pretty sure. I just want to get you away from them for a while. Make you see that you're headed to a place you may not want to be. The Academy is deeper than I ever imagined. It's convoluted and whether you meant to be or not, you're in the middle. They took you on a trip to save a kidnapped girl before and you're not even trained." He approached me, slowly this time, talking as he moved, until he was up next to me again. "If you want to do good for other people, there's another way. If that's what drives you. If it's what you want. You don't have to jump in blindly. I can show you. Give me a few weeks. Let me show you what I can do."

Why did it sound reasonable? I studied him for an ulterior motive, of which I was sure there was one. His hazel eyes with the gold flecks shimmered with something alive, and full of promises. I'd believed him before, but I couldn't go on completely blind trust now. "What do you want me to do exactly? Spell it out. I'm not making some weird promise, to find out you want to turn me into one of your sex slaves for a week."

"I'm never so vulgar," he said, looking shocked. "You'd be my *only* sex slave…"

"Nope," I said. I started to turn and he grabbed onto my arm.

"I'm kidding," he said. "You started that. No. What I'm saying is, you're in over your head. You don't even really have to work with me if you don't want to. Just take a damn break that isn't neck deep with these Academy boys. I won't even talk about them. You just need to hang around someone normal for a bit. I won't ever do anything you don't want me to do." He held up two fingers. "Scout's honor."

"Scouts use three fingers."

He flicked up a third finger and grinned. "Sorry," he said. "I won't force you to stay, but stay long enough to complete one of my jobs. If you still aren't happy, you can go back. But it doesn't have to be this way. It doesn't have to be the Academy way. With all the kidnapping and the guns and risking your life."

The deal didn't seem bad, but I knew there was more to it than just promising to work with him for a couple of weeks. I'd seen how he was going to set up one of his jobs, where he was going to poison a well in a foreign town far away. He was trying to save lives in our city, but he was making other people sick in the process.

Most of my concern was for Brandon, Marc, Axel and even Raven and Corey. I would be making a deal that they'd be unhappy about. They'd tell me not to trust him. Just like he was telling me not to trust *them*.

But I was also getting in too deep with Brandon and the others, and headed for full out disaster. I had growing feelings for all of them. I didn't like not being able to choose between them. The longer I held out, the harder it became, and the more I was sure that saying anything at all would destroy the group. Wasn't Blake's offer what was looking for? An opportunity to step back for a little while and consider what I was doing?

The most important part of all was that Blake could very well help me. He had resources of his own, and Alice wasn't aware of him, which gave us an advantage.

Still, in my heart, it felt like I was betraying the boys. Would I rather hurt them by going away for a couple of weeks, or get them killed by Alice by being incompetent? I felt Blake's intentions were honest. From his perspective, it did seem the boys were dragging me down into risky situations.

Blake stood by, looking confident. I squinted at him. "And you won't try anything funny?"

He shook his head. "Nothing. You'll know my every move. And not like last time where I was holding back some little things..."

"Like poisoning a well? And knowing who I was the whole time?"

"You can't blame me for some of that. I probably should have told you the truth about knowing who you were. But you lied to me, too."

I had. Blake and I had gotten off on the wrong foot from the start. I sighed. I didn't have any other option. "Fine," I said. "Two weeks. That's it."

"It'll do," he said. He leaned forward, gave me a peck on the mouth and then smiled. "Seal it with a kiss."

I rolled my eyes. I reached back, wanting to put my hair up in a ponytail or something because it felt messy, but having to settle for combing my fingers through it.

"Just tell me what to do."

"Get in the car, for one. It's chilly out. And why are you wearing that ridiculous outfit? I do like the shoes. Doesn't seem like your style, though."

HUNTING WITH A FOX

Blake drove off the island. It got dark as we pulled away from the island's street lamps. In the car, with the heater on, I could strip off the dress shirt and leave on the T-shirt underneath. "Where are we going?" I asked.

"To see Doyle, first. That's where we'll start."

"I already saw him. He said the core was at the guy's house, only I couldn't find it."

"Doyle's tricky," he said. "And you don't know anything about this core. Doyle will be able to give us more clues. First rule of doing things the smart way: Know what you can do and know what you're doing."

"The guys know things. This was just a surprise. And we were caught off guard. It wasn't any of our business and this Eddie group dragged us in." I was irritated that he was saying the guys were stupid.

"It can happen," he said. "But you don't just go running off after bad guys and secret phone services without knowing what you're handing over and who you're dealing with. Your first mistake was your first move after Brandon was taken. You exposed yourselves. Now it's not just Brandon, but three of them. You shouldn't have been bait."

"I thought they'd kill him," I said. "We were trying to find the core so we could jump them when they showed up."

"And if they had, they wouldn't have just handed him over. They might have shot you, or him, or both. You

215

didn't even know if Brandon was alive at all. If Brandon was already dead, then you were chasing a lost cause."

I bristled, not liking this worst-case scenario where Brandon ends up dead. "Were we supposed to just assume he was dead and stop looking?"

"They were risking your life to do it, and their own lives, too," he said. He combed his hair with his fingers as he drove. "That's something you'll have to learn. Taking a risk is one thing. Suicide missions shouldn't be in the equation. It's common sense. Not looking ahead also meant you were risking Brandon's life; you couldn't have known if trying to save him would have gotten him killed."

I wanted to fight him on this, but I was too tired to play the game of what might have happened. We'd been working with what information we had, even if it wasn't enough.

I fell silent, trying to keep myself from falling asleep, but I think I did sleep for a while. There were stretches of time where I closed my eyes, and then opened them, finding the scenery completely different. Before I could figure out where we were, my eyes would drift closed again.

I jumped at the sound of a car door shutting. I sat up, rubbing my eyes, noticing the outline of Doyle's farmhouse and yard full of satellite dishes.

Part of me was tempted to stay out in the car this time, not wanting to get shot at again. Plus, the car's seat was comfortable and I was really tired.

I drummed up the energy by thinking about the guys: Axel, Brandon, Marc. They were missing. I needed to find them.

There were no outside lights on at the house, and once the car lights went dim, it was shadows and deeper shadows all the way. I kept my hands out and stomped through the grass for anything I couldn't see and might trip or bump into. I tried the cell phone as a light, but it wasn't providing enough. I should have remembered about the flashlight, and was tempted to go back for it, but I didn't want to lose Blake.

I reached out for Blake, wanting to find his back.

The moment I touched him, he shifted and found my hand. He took it in his and held on to it, keeping me beside him. Without a word, he continued through the dark.

I stiffened, but held on, not wanting to get lost. After everything I'd done to him, the surprising warm gesture sent a wave of guilt through me. Despite many things, Blake was here when he had no reason to be, no stake in the game. He was simply here because I had called. It was hard not to be grateful to him.

Blake guided me through the dark front doorway. I paused, waiting for him to find a light.

Instead, he continued through the house. I barely remembered the layout, and kept right behind him. Was he insane? It was one thing to approach Doyle, who had a shotgun, during daylight. What if he thought we were robbing his house? Would he shoot first and ask questions later?

There was smoke in the air, but it was stale. I hadn't checked the time on the way here, but I didn't think it was super late. The house was silent, except for the hum of a refrigerator.

Blake took me through what I'd remembered was the living room, and instead of moving on beyond it to the parlor with the computer and collection of old furniture, he turned down a hallway. From this point on, I was at his mercy. Maybe he'd lock me in a cellar and go after Axel and the others on his own... did Hannahan houses have cellars?

Blake released my hand and whispered, "Keep still.

Don't move."

Why couldn't he have told me to simply wait in the car? I could have slept a little longer instead of standing in the dark in the middle of Doyle's house.

I was left alone in the dark, and waited. The longer I was left waiting though, the more I was anxious and wanted to get moving. Thoughts of ghosts and zombies filled my head. I wasn't scared of the dark, but this was a creepy farmhouse out in the middle of nowhere where I already knew the owner had a shotgun.

Crash.

I jumped and then froze, terrified.

"Fucking Christ, shit!" came a familiar, loud Irish voice.

"What were you thinking letting Kayli go into a place where you know there's an illegal network?"

"Who's Kayli? I don't know..."

Thunk.

There were more noises and grunts. "Doyle," Blake said. "Get up. We've got work to do."

There was more grumbling before a light went on. It was dim, but it managed to show me I was in a hallway, where there was a bathroom with the door open on the right, and a back bedroom on the left, the door open. I tiptoed forward, spotting Blake standing off to the side of the bed. Doyle, wide-eyed with bed-head and wearing only dingy, faded boxers with penguins on them and a lime T-shirt, was standing bent over the side table fiddling with the lamp.

He straightened and pointed at Blake. "You could kill someone doing that. I nearly had a heart attack."

"I just walked into your house without you waking up. If you actually put in a doorbell in this place, I wouldn't have to. You also need an alarm system. Now come on. I need your help."

"It's not my problem," Doyle said.

"It will be when this cell phone network is discovered and the FCC goes looking for secret signals and somewhere in the mix, finds your secret lair. Don't you realize if this gets stolen, they will come looking for you, too?"

"No one knows I'm here," Doyle said. He leaned over, picking up a pair of jeans and stepping into them. "My own mother doesn't even know."

"I'll tell her where you are," Blake said.

Doyle stiffened and stood fully with his pants still only halfway on. He narrowed his bloodshot eyes at Blake. "You wouldn't dare."

"Try me," Blake said. "But I won't if you'll get out here and tell me how to stop this Alice chick."

"Who's Alice?"

♠♠♠♠♠♠

Ten minutes later, I was sitting on one of the overstuffed sofas in the weirdly overcrowded parlor. Doyle, finally dressed, was typing into his computer, Blake stood behind him, looking over his shoulder.

"I can't concentrate with someone looking over me," Doyle said.

"Just tell us what you know," Blake said. "And don't skip the small stuff this time."

"What do you want? Murdock's Core is at that house on Kiawah."

"I was there," I said. I had my feet up on the couch, and yawned, wishing for a blanket. "I've gone through the house. There's no an antenna there, or a big computer. If there is a secret cell phone service, the source isn't there."

"It is," Doyle said. He leaned over until he was looking at me across his wrecked desk. "You checked out every closet? I'm telling you. There's no mistake. The strongest signal is coming from that house."

"What do you mean, strongest signal?" Blake asked.

"I mean a cell phone network isn't going to have just one tower, is it? It'll have a bunch in the area. You can't just have one tower. The signal only goes so far."

"Where are the others?" he asked.

Doyle made a face, and then reached into a desk drawer for a pack of cigarettes. He lit one, and inhaled as he responded. "Scattered all over the city. Duh. I don't know exactly. I wasn't paying attention before. I was trying to keep my nose out of it. I just looked up the core because she asked."

"Is it possible there's just a big tower signal coming from the house, but that's not where the core is? To access it?"

"No," Doyle said. "Trust me, the core is in that house. The service is just transmitted on it, but all the data gets pulled through there. It's like any cell phone service, there's a hub that collects all your data."

"Are they piggybacking on other towers in the area?"

"No. That's how they're not getting caught. They're using completely separate towers and a different frequency that changes randomly to keep separate from what legitimate cell phones are using so there's no interference. It's ingenious, in a way, but still obvious to anyone looking for signals in the air like me. The only thing stopping anyone from pulling data and deciphering it is that blasted security packet."

"And you can't break into that, by chance?" Blake asked.

Doyle made a face. "What do I look like? Someone who cares? No. Well, I could, maybe. But it'd take a while. And it'd be much easier to simply get to the house and check out their core computer."

"Not if they don't have a core computer," I said.

"They have one," Doyle said. "Trust me. I know. I can see it. It's as clear as day."

"There's got to be something else we can do," I said. "I can't just go back there, because Alice is there waiting. If she has Brandon, thinking he's Corey, then she probably has who she needs, and is going to be there trying to work her way in. I just waltzed in and handed her the one person she thinks will give her access."

That hit me hard, and I found it difficult to speak after that. Alice had been a few steps ahead of us from the start, and now I just gave her who she thought would open the doorway she wanted. She had access, because she was marrying the guy she targeted, and now she had a key. It was my fault for letting Brandon get that close.

"But she doesn't have Corey," Blake said. "Right? She has Brandon."

I nodded and swallowed. It might be enough. I breathed in and then tried to focus. "What about these other towers. Could we find one? Is there something we could do? Maybe disrupt the signal a little? Cause a stir?"

The room went silent and Doyle looked at Blake. "She's a bloody genius."

"If we disrupt the signal," Blake said, "by taking out one of the towers, it'll bring someone out to fix the thing. Then we could kidnap that person and ask them questions."

"We're going to kidnap someone that works on this core?" I asked.

Blake smiled like a fox that'd pinned a mouse. "Sometimes you fight fire with fire."

♠

A FALSE LEAD

Blake asked Doyle for a pair of shoes. Doyle tried to trade them to get out of going with us, but Blake made a few more threats and suddenly we were all three in the car. I sat in the back and managed to grab another nap on our way. Doyle sourced a tower we could check out and Blake drove through the night taking Doyle's directions.

I didn't want to sleep through everything, but I was taking what sleep I could, knowing I was going to need to be alert soon enough.

It wasn't really sleep, anyway. It was closing my eyes, and wishing I was back at the Sergeant Jasper, with Corey in his room asleep. Or even with Brandon pretending to be Corey, who I still needed to box in the head and ask him why he was sneaking in and letting me think he was his brother.

I'd even rather be back in the hotel room with Wil, fighting off my father after one of his drunken escapades. I'd face all measure of horrors just to have this terrorizing last couple of days over with.

To my surprise, we ended up on a corner block of residential neighborhood not a couple of miles from Kiawah Island, somewhere amidst the streets of John's Island. Most of the island was asleep, as it was getting on to eleven in the evening by the time we got there.

If Alice's story about the poison was true, then I only had until…maybe ten in the morning? Ten hours until she could give them the antidote, if there was one at all. I didn't want to believe her, but I couldn't risk not believing.

Blake drove Henry Anderson's car, and parked in a lot in front of a grocery store about a block away from where Doyle said the tower was.

"Why don't we just drive there?" I asked, getting out of the car and stretching. My bones ached from tiredness and the chill in the air. We were on the southern end of John's Island, with a lot more trees and a lot of rural sprawl. This particular block was home to two churches, a grocery store, a couple more outlet stores, and one nondescript four-story brick building that looked vacant but happened to have a satellite dish on top. It was supposedly defunct in the 1980s but Doyle said it could be used as a tower, if connected right. The rest of the surrounding buildings were small old homes with broken fences, some in severe need of new paint and repair.

"We should go on foot," Blake said. He stretched and then cracked his neck. "If this is a tower, there might be security. Perhaps cameras or an alarm. We'll have to inspect the building and then find a way up without getting caught."

Doyle emerged from the passenger seat, rumpled and now donning a dark zip-up hoodie. He pressed his palm against his face and opened his eyes wide. "It smells. Doesn't it?" He touched his nose and then pointed out toward the homes across the street. "How do these people live in such a smelly place?"

"It's just outside, Doyle," Blake said, shutting the door to the car and starting to walk off. "This is what outside smells like when you're not smoking your lungs out."

"Hey," Doyle said, catching up with Blake and giving him a slight punch to the shoulder. "Smoking is one of God's greatest gifts to man. How the hell else am I supposed to pass the time here?"

"I don't know," Blake said. "Exercise? Eat some fruit? Try not to kill yourself with carcinogens?"

"Fruit will kill you," he said. He inhaled again and coughed. "Said so on the news. This smell will, too. You know what that is? That's unfiltered smells of the world farting in your face. You need something to cover it up."

"Are you out of cigarettes? Is that why you're still talking?"

"I'm out here where I'm not supposed to be and I don't understand why."

"You're here to make sure the signal goes offline and to help us talk to this guy who shows up. You can tell us if he's lying."

"Like I'm supposed to know?"

I walked behind them, listening to the exchange as they rattled on. It was mostly Doyle complaining about why he was here, and Blake humoring him but not releasing him from going with us.

I wasn't sure if this was the best idea. We weren't targeting Alice or Eddie anymore. We were targeting the people who owned the core. Wouldn't this alert them that someone was onto them and shut it down? And then Alice would kill Axel, Marc and Brandon?

Maybe...or maybe there was someone out there we could talk to that could help us. Maybe Ethan had someone who worked on this core and he'd send him out and we could figure a way around it.

Maybe Blake was right to go to the source, and find a way to communicate without alerting Alice or the others that something was up.

I kept my head down, and had put Mr. Anderson's shirt on in the car to keep myself warm. It wasn't the nicest part of town, either, so I was on the lookout for any local thugs.

Blake and Doyle walked to the brick building and circled it once. The building was plain, brick, with a couple of broken windows, though only one was taped up at all. The church next door was taller.

"Abandoned," Doyle said. He checked his cell phone and read. "It's owned by the same real estate company this Ethan guy works at though."

"We'll have to try our luck and be on the lookout," Blake said. "There could be hobos inside. Or guards planted to keep this core safe."

"You're just full of sunshine and daisy thoughts, aren't you?" Doyle asked.

Blake started to approach the steps and then stopped and looked back at me. An eyebrow lifted. "You okay?"

Something seemed... not right. "Are we sure this thing is here?"

"This neighborhood is where the signal is coming from," Doyle said. "And this is the only place that has any sort of antenna."

"I mean, if you're going to have a multimillion dollar secret phone service, would you set it up on the roof of an abandoned building in this neighborhood?"

Blake looked up the block while Doyle looked the opposite way. The one thing saving this town from looking so plain was the old church, which had old architecture and steeples and a lovely garden with a fountain.

Doyle turned back first. "Who am I to account for the tastes of rich men? I mean, look at Blake? He still eats Pop Tarts like when we were kids."

"Shush your mouth," Blake said, turning to the door and checking on how to open it. "Don't go talking about my Pop Tarts."

I faced Doyle, grinning. "You knew him when you were younger?"

"We grew up together!" he said. "Well, during a few months of the year when my parents dragged me away from Ireland. And then eventually they moved here. We're practically cousins. He got the dumb genes in the family, though. And the ugly ones."

I inserted my arm into Doyle's, and held on to it, trying to drag him up the stairs. "Come tell me about Blake Coaltar and his childhood. And skip the boring stuff."

"What? You mean you just want to hear the dirty bits? No. Nope. I don't even want to think about the time he convinced a bunch of girls in high school to skinny-dip in the school pool and let the whole male swim team watch."

"Don't listen to him," Blake said, bending to look at the lock. "We were young. It was his idea. He started it."

"Oh no," Doyle said. He waved his hand. "No, I couldn't convince girls to do anything. You were the one they listened to. Still do. Like let me tell you about Mrs. Smitherson... Was that her name? Smithtonian? The lady with the red hair and the husband who..."

Blake cleared his throat and stood taller. He pointed at the door. "Can we just hurry along now?"

I was actually grateful for it. As much as I wanted to know about Blake and his past, there were some things I was sure I didn't want to hear about. Especially his playboy teen years. There was a lot I could forgive as boys being boys, of course, but that didn't mean I needed to hear about it.

Although it was interesting to hear that Blake Coaltar grew up like a normal kid. Where did he acquire his enormous wealth? Was it a recent development? I just assumed he'd inherited it.

I checked out the lock Blake was having problems with. "Anyone have a flashlight?" I asked. There was one in the car, along with other tools. I needed to keep some in my pocket. I'd given the phone to Doyle to hang on to for sourcing the signal.

Doyle reached into his pocket, pulling out a lighter.

Blake pushed the light away and then pulled out his cell phone, finding a light app and turned it on. "Let's try not to burn the place down, all right?"

"Like what we used to do with the eggs?" Doyle asked.

I was inspecting the lock but lost focus just enough to look at Doyle. "Eggs?"

Doyle nodded. "Trust me. Don't put a whole carton of eggs into the microwave. That doesn't make hardboiled eggs. He and I learned it the hard way..."

"Guys," Blake said. He put a lot of emphasis into his southern voice. "I don't particularly want to get caught with my pants down here, so if you don't mind..."

"He means get to opening the door before anyone catches us," Doyle said, with a short wave at me.

I rolled my eyes, shaking my head. I checked the lock out again, noticed it was old, and not a deadbolt. "Anyone have a credit card?"

"That trick doesn't work," Doyle said.

"Stick to computers," Blake said. He pulled out a card, started to pass it to me and then right when it touched my palm, he pulled it back, holding it to his chest and then put it back into his wallet. "Hang on, I still use that one."

"I'm not going to break it," I said.

He pulled one out from the back of his wallet. It looked old, with the numbers faded off. I rolled my eyes and then slipped it between the double doors of the building. With a little shake, wedging and a tug of the handle, I had the door open.

The credit card snapped in two as a result. I passed the pieces back. Blake smirked and put them back in his wallet.

I got a draft of old rotten wood, dust, and other disgusting smells all at once. The only light inside was from the church next door's gardens lamps. There was a large open space and then I believe what was meant to be offices in the corners, but the walls had been busted out, and a single staircase rose in the middle. There was trash everywhere. I had a feeling when people couldn't afford to pay their monthly garbage bill, they threw it into this building.

I covered my mouth and nose with my palms. Not that it helped much. I swallowed, trying not to breathe in too much. It was overwhelming.

Doyle made a noise that sounded like he was puking. "Oh my god," he said. "It's disgusting."

"Funny," Blake said. He moved into the building with careful steps, checking the floorboards with his weight. "I thought this would be more like home to you."

"I'd rather go back to Doyle's house right now," I said through my hand.

"See?" Doyle said. "Even the wench knows."

"Don't call her a wench," Blake said.

"I forgot her name."

"It's Kayli," Blake said, and then spoke in exaggeration. "Kaaaay-leeee. Two syllables."

"I'm horrible with names," he said. "I'm still not sure what yours is. You say Blake, but I'm pretty sure it's like Bob. Or Sanchez."

I strolled forward, unsure if I wanted to stick around and listen to the rest of this argument, or conversation, or whatever it was they were doing.

Still, I'd wished I'd begged Doyle for some shoes, too. With the heels, I didn't feel safe walking through trash. I was worried they'd get caught in something. Like an old diaper, which was what this place smelled like. Did hobos use it as a restroom?

I was walking over bags of garbage to get to the stairs when I heard rustling in the corners. I stilled for a moment, afraid to wake a human...or dog or rats... snakes. I hated the thought of snakes more.

Blake was at my back instantly, a hand guiding me forward. "Tiptoe," he whispered at my ear. "Quickly."

I looked back once, spotting Blake with Doyle behind him. Both now looked serious and grim, leading me to believe whoever else was in this building was most definitely human and not someone we wanted to have a conversation with.

The stairs looked hazardous with trash all over them, but the old construction was sound. Sticking to the stairs, I focused on them, rather than looking through the rest of the building.

The further we went in, the more I was convinced this was the wrong place. Rich people would send someone here to put together a sophisticated antenna? It'd be noticed. Even if you didn't have to manage it much, you still had to maintain it. You'd have to keep people out with security measures. There wasn't any way I'd let hobos sleep in the same building as my illegal cell thingie.

While the trash problem lessened as we went up, the cold and the smells were just as bad. I didn't want to voice my opinion when others nearby could be listening in. Even if they were hobos, in the dark we could pretend to be other hobos looking for a spot to sleep and hopefully they wouldn't bother us if we stayed quiet.

We had to walk up and out into the fourth floor to find the way. The stairs to the roof turned out to be an old ladder that was hidden in the ceiling. Blake found it, and had to break the handle to open the door and allow the rusted old ladder to come down. It dropped with a screeching clank. It appeared it'd fall apart the moment anyone stepped on it.

"Ladies first," Doyle whispered.

Uh, no. I nudged Doyle toward it.

He dug in his heels. "No, no," he said, starting to talk a little louder. "I'm not going up there."

"I'll go up first," Blake said. He passed over something small into my palm, and I realized it was the pocketknife. "Hang on to this."

"How did you get that?" I asked. "That was in my pocket."

"I found it in the car floor," he said. "You must have dropped it."

I wasn't sure if that was true, but I'd passed out and forgot about it, so I was glad he was able to grab it, steal it, whatever. I wasn't used to carrying tools.

Blake went up, the ladder creaking and shaking the whole time. Hobos nearby rustled, probably drunk asleep and stirred by the noise. I hoped they weren't angry drunks.

I stepped between the ladder and Doyle. If a hobo approached, I wanted to be able to shimmy up, or at least hide behind Doyle.

"Ugh," Blake said somewhere above our heads.

"What?" Doyle asked. "Is it locked?"

"Spiders," he said. "Come up here."

"No," Doyle said. "I don't do spiders. That's Karen's job."

"Kayli," Blake said. "Her name is Kayli."

"Are you sure?" Doyle asked.

"Sssh!" I hissed at them both.

In a few minutes, Blake had the top opened up. I could see sky and some light and that was about it. Blake disappeared onto the roof.

I caught movement in the corner. There was stirring and something rose up in the darkness. Fear motivated me enough to face spiders and whatever was upstairs simply to avoid the zombie drunken hobo ghost.

Doyle was on my heels. He scampered up, pushing on my ankles. "Hurry or I'll throw you off," he said.

I kicked out below me, hitting him on the arm, but then hurried up.

The fresh air outside was welcome to the musty and rotten odors from below. I didn't want to have to go back through. I thought jumping from the roof was a more viable option this time.

Blake was over by the satellite dish, examining it. As I approached, I caught him scratching his head and checking out the base of it.

"Doyle," he said. He did a come-hither motion and pointed to the base. "Come look at this. Does this look like—"

Doyle shoved him aside before he could finish. He got down on his knees, looking at the wiring and the box that was beside the dish and then angled his head more, nearly putting his ear to the ground to check it out. "What is this?" he asked.

I stood aside quietly, keeping an eye on them and the ladder behind us. I worried one of the hobos would climb it, or put the ladder back and lock us up here.

"You tell me," Blake said. "How do we turn it off?"

"It is off," he said.

"What do you mean?"

Doyle picked up his head and dusted his hands off on his jeans before he raked through his hair. "This isn't it," he said.

I fully turned now, looking at him. Blake stared too. "What do you mean?" Blake asked. "You said this was it."

"So?" Doyle said. "I said the biggest signal was coming from this...general vicinity. It's the most logical place to put it."

"Atop an abandoned building?" I asked. "You thought

the best place to put an antenna that was supposed to be a secret to be on top of a building filled with hobos, with no security and rusted ladders and spiders everywhere?"

"Well, when you put it that way," he said. "But how was I supposed to know about the rustiness of the ladder? But will you look at this dish? It's a perfectly good dish. I'd use it for an underground cell phone service. If I had one. I wouldn't start one though. That's a lot of work. And apparently people named Amanda come after you."

"Alice," I said. "And she's already got to the first one. We need access to another antenna before she figures a way in, and Axel and Marc and Brandon get killed."

"Well, we'll have to find the next one," he said. He stood up and continued to wipe his jeans and look around. "If it isn't here, it's like a false signal or something."

"Or it isn't this building," Blake said. He walked away from us, toward the edge of the roof, looking out toward the church and the churchyard behind it. "You just need something tall, right? Something high enough to send out a signal?"

"Something to bounce signals off of, yes," Doyle said. "And a lot of them."

Blake stared out at the church, and I wasn't connecting it until I caught the cross on top of the steeple, the tallest thing for miles.

That's when it struck me. Brandon had said that an antenna didn't have to be obvious. It could be anything. It was just large metal...with the right sort of signal behind it, anything could act like a cell phone tower.

And then I remembered the large observatory with the telescopes that overlooked a stretch of church towers amid the trees.

"Ethan," I breathed out, stepping up beside Blake and staring off at the church. "The man that started the core. He's a religious man. He's gotten a bunch of emails from church people."

"So no one would think it odd if he happened to come out to church, and did a little fiddling in the steeples," Blake said. He turned to me, smiling big. "That's brilliant. That takes the cake. Using church steeples as antennas system. It's in your face and yet it's hidden."

"Should have figured," Doyle said behind us. "Happens all the time. I mean, churches are evil, aren't they? What with the crosses and the rituals and the singing."

C. L. Stone

A CHURCH STEEPLE AND A PRAYER

*T*here was a debate as to going down the ladder
again or jumping off the side of the roof, when
Blake pointed out there was a fire escape. It was
rusty, and creaky, but we were outside, and it didn't fall
apart on us.

Once we were on the ground, we crossed the street,
heading for the church. The garden had a concrete path
among low hedges and the occasional late blooming rose
bush and a fancy fountain in the center. It was probably
better looking during the day, but for the moment, there
were shadows, and I kept picturing hobos sleeping in the
bushes.

"It's midnight," Doyle said. "Isn't the church
closed?"

I'd been wondering the same thing. "How do we
break into a church?"

"Are you both heathens?" Blake asked. "This is a
church. It's never closed and you don't break into one."

I blinked at him, a little stunned. Churches closed,
didn't they? I mean, no one was here this late. Wouldn't
someone come in and like loot the tithing box? Steal the
gold crosses? Did they even have gold crosses anymore? I
was guessing based on every movie or TV show I'd ever
watched about churches.

While there were lights on, they were minimal,
making the church appear foreboding. It was Catholic,

according to the sign, although I didn't catch the name. The steps up to the front doors were empty, with lights focused on the engraved wooden doors and the shiny brass handles.

I lingered back, intimidated by the building. The grounds had been scary enough. The church itself terrified me. Would a priest see me, know me for what I was, and kick me out? Would I have to go into a confession box? Wasn't I supposed to put holy water on myself at some point?

Blake pulled on the door handle. I held my breath, thinking there was no way this church was open and worried we'd set off some sort of alarm.

But the door opened easily, and with barely a creak.

I swallowed. If it hadn't been open, we'd have had to break into it, but even now, I was expecting fire and brimstone for stepping through the front door.

Nothing happened as I followed the guys inside. The front area, whatever it was called, had a marble floor and high ceilings and lamps that looked like candles. There was a table nearby with pamphlets, one advertising the history of the chapel, and the others about religious services.

I scanned the area, but didn't see anyone. Yet there was a feeling that we weren't completely alone. The place smelled of old wood and an undertone of lemon, like furniture polish.

Blake led the way further in, seeming more comfortable about where we should go. We passed the front entryway and then walked into a chapel. The inside of the church had even higher ceilings, with columns and statues. Stained glass windows were lit up. Every inch of the place was an artistic bible reference in an artifact, name, or picture. I couldn't see the confession boxes at first, but I spotted a couple of dark doors beyond the podium, to the very right of the large room.

I was way too curious and distracted by all the prettiness of the building.

Blake forged ahead, checking out the columns at first and then focused on looking up. I followed his gaze. How were we supposed to get to the steeple in this place? And where was it, exactly?

Doyle's voice echoed in the room still. "Maybe we should have brought a ladder."

"There'll be a stairwell," Blake said. "The steeple should have a bell in it. There would be an access door somewhere."

I scanned the area, seeking out anyone who might be listening. The church was open, so there had to be someone here. Who stayed so late at a church? Priests? How could we explain our need to climb the steeple?

I was walking on my toes as it was. The heels were making clicking sounds if I walked normally. I stood as close as possible to Blake.

Blake quietly reached for my hand, holding it. I allowed it, feeling stronger. I wasn't a shy type of person, but I was completely out of my element here. I didn't do church.

Blake circled around the room, finding a door on the left hand side. He turned to us. "I'll go up with Doyle," Blake said. "We'll just turn it off and we'll wait here in the pews. Someone will have to pass by here to fix it. We can relax until then."

"Right," Doyle said. "And then we flank him? Knock him out with the big cross? By the way, I didn't bring a gun. I left mine back at the house."

"Hopefully it's not a gang of them," Blake said. "If it is, we'll have to settle for staying out of their way and following them. Otherwise, we'll take a chance on just talking to whoever it is. They'll want to know their phone service is being targeted."

"They might turn it off to avoid giving it to anyone else," I said.

"They're not going to turn it off if we explain to them," Blake said. "The man who runs this isn't an idiot. He's not going to scare off his customers by shutting the network off. Not unless he has to." Blake motioned to Doyle to follow him and then directed me to sit in the pews. "We'll be back."

"You're leaving me behind?" I whispered. I did not want to be left alone. It wasn't like I'd be able to blend in.

"It'll be a tight fit up here, and I need you to keep a priest busy if one starts heading this way. We shouldn't be long." He started to turn and then spun around, climbed down the steps and approached me.

I was backing away, wondering if he'd forgotten something and needed to get by me, when he grabbed my shoulders and kissed me roughly on the lips. It was quick but hard and then he released me.

"Don't go anywhere," he said. "And don't get kidnapped."

My heart fluttered. I nodded. Maybe I should have told him no, or backed away, but I was terrified of making another wrong move, and grateful he was taking over the fight. His strength and assurance was giving me the motivation to keep going, and not to simply run off to the hospital and feel the guilt of knowing Axel and Marc and now Brandon were out there somewhere.

It surprised me how much I realized now that I did need someone. I'd realized it before with the boys, and now, with Blake Coaltar, I was feeling it again. There was that doubt if I was making the right decision, and working together with someone made things easier. When I wasn't sure, because it was out of my depth, someone else was there to help.

I hadn't realized how alone I'd been, even while I had Wil and my father around. It hadn't been enough.

Blake disappeared behind a door with Doyle. I was grateful not to be following. Even if the church was open, it was more reasonable for me to be out in the chapel than the non-public areas. It wasn't like they'd let just anyone climb all over their church, right? I wondered if nuns slept here. Would Blake and Doyle spook a nun?

I slinked between the columns and the walls, studying the glass windows and trying to read the words. Some of it was in Latin, but some I struggled to read because of the angle and the fancy fonts, but I admired the artistry. How was it so quiet, but my heart felt like it was alive and thundering so hard?

"Good morning," said a male voice in a whisper, but the voice was deep, so it echoed within the cavernous space. "Early morning, I should say."

I jumped and twisted, spotting an older man with a priest's habit, white collar and rosary, the whole getup. I hadn't realized they still wore all that. His hair was cropped short and he had a thin frame. He stood there smiling, his eyes friendly and curious.

When my heart settled, allowing me to breathe a bit, I pressed a palm to my chest and exhaled. "Uh..."

"Sorry," he said, again in the same soft voice. "I didn't mean to scare you. Did you have any questions? Is there something I could help you with?"

"No," I said quickly. "I mean, I didn't mean to be here if I'm not supposed to..."

He held up a hand and smiled assuredly. "God's children are always welcome here, no matter the hour. Please," he said, and gestured around him, "look around as much as you'd like."

"Oh. Okay," I said, lowering my voice to match his whisper, although I wasn't sure my voice carried the same as his did. My eyes cut from him, to the colored glass above our heads, meaning to turn away and let him resume...whatever it was priests did.

"Do you know this story?" he asked. He sidled up beside me. He pointed to the picture within the glass, of a man carrying a cross who I'd thought to be Jesus. "St. Dismas, the good thief."

I smothered my initial reaction to choke and sputter. "Oh?" I said, my voice weakened, my tired brain going wild. He did know. He knew I was a thief. He knew my background. Doyle was right. Churches were evil. It's not what I really believed, but the coincidence was spooky.

The priest nodded and smiled, directing his gaze to the window, carrying my attention there. "St. Dismas was one of two thieves sacrificed on the cross the same day as our beloved Jesus Christ. It was Dismas who, upon the day of his death, turned to Jesus and asked to be remembered. Jesus promised to be with him in heaven that very day." He paused for a long moment, and then continued, his voice much softer. "I always liked the story. I feel it shows it's never too late for anyone to seek forgiveness and be given a second chance. All it takes is a will, a desire to change."

I swallowed, and hoped he didn't notice. "Personally, I like the one where Jesus feeds a couple thousand people with a fish." I probably got that one wrong. Honestly, it was the only one I could remember.

The priest chuckled, the bass in his voice echoing throughout the chapel. "I have to agree," he said quietly. "That is a good one."

"Have you been here at this church a long time?" I asked. I couldn't think of anything else to say, and at the same time, the priest was looking at me, like he desired to continue the conversation. I felt awkward and small, like a child, even though he was shorter than me and I could probably knock him over with a single punch. He simply carried himself confidently and there was something even greater than that: trust. He simply trusted me to behave and not do him any wrong.

"Oh, a long time," he said. He turned, with his hands clasped behind his back, walking toward the next window. He did this as we talked, pausing briefly before a window and giving me a moment to look, before he continued on. "I am fifty three and I've resided in this church for thirty years. Charleston and even John's Island has changed a lot in that time. I've been given opportunities to go elsewhere, even on missionary work in Africa. I felt compelled to stay in one place."

"Why stay?" I asked. "Why here?"

He shrugged and his fingers moved to the rosary hanging at his waist. He fingered the beads absently. "Some people move about from place to place, learning a little about a lot of different places. I chose to remain, and learn all I can about one. I get to know the people better that way, and how I might help."

If he'd been here a while, there was a chance he knew the Murdock family. Maybe it wasn't appropriate, but I had a gut feeling and I took a chance. "Do you know a Mr... Murdock? Ethan Murdock?"

"Ethan? Of course."

"Does he attend church here?"

The priest laughed, and stopped in front of the altar with the cross and the candles. He turned to me. "Yes, I know Ethan. I've known him since he was young and I first started here. He's a remarkable young man. Full of ambition, like his father. Maybe a little prideful but I don't think a little pride is wrong. Just a smidgen. He's earned it."

"He has?" I asked.

The priest nodded, motioned to the front pew and encouraged me to sit. I did, and he sat next to me, looking up at the front of the chapel as he talked. "Ethan Murdock was younger than you the day he walked in. He'd been raised right, but was a hellion of a teenager, rebelling against his parents. Everyone goes through that phase, but then one day, he seemed to change. He walked in here, giving nearly half of his yearly salary to the church. Each year after that, he's continued to make donations in hefty sums, asking that we use the money to help with children and local families. I think he suspected he'd never have any, or wouldn't settle down, and wanted to be sure to support children that he'd never have."

"So do you see him often now?"

"He attends nearly every church in the area, I hear. He's not a regular to a particular one, but he does come in often."

Because he's got a network of underground cell phone services in your bell towers. I wasn't sure I could admire the man that would use a church for profit. No wonder he made donations. He probably only did it because he felt guilty.

But if he started when he was a teenager, then wouldn't that have been before the cell phone network?

"Does he spend much time here? In weird places? Like in the steeple?"

The priest's smile warmed. "What has you curious about the steeple? Are you an architecture student?"

It was on the tip of my tongue to go with that answer, but then this was a church, and he was a priest... "I...was just..." Coming up with another answer that wasn't an out and out lie was difficult. How could I explain it?

There was an echo of a door further down the chapel closing. My first reaction was to check the door Doyle and

Blake had disappeared behind, to see if they were returning, but the sound was from the wrong direction. I turned, as did the priest.

The priest was closer to the door and blocked my view, but he straightened and smiled. "You can ask him yourself. Seems like God is intervening. Mr. Murdock just walked in."

I stiffened. It was his wedding night, and after midnight. This couldn't be coincidence. Did the priest call Ethan when he'd heard people coming in? Or was there an alarm on the tower up in the steeple? He was here too quickly, it seemed. Doyle and Blake weren't even back yet.

Ethan Murdock, the same man who had shown me his observatory and had been nice to me, taking time out to entertain his fake niece amid the flurry of his own wedding reception, was now walking down the center aisle of the church toward us. He smiled and walked steadily, although there were shadows under his eyes. This was a man who worked hard and enjoyed his work. Driven.

My heart fluttered. I realized the Academy might have followed him from his house to check out what he was up to. By now they ought to know this was Ethan Murdock. Also, if he was here, that meant Alice and her goons might have followed. Eddie might have, too. Worlds were colliding.

He was a walking target and out in the open.

"Dear Ethan," the priest said, standing. He held out his hand toward Ethan's. "Good to see you. You're here at an interesting time."

"Sorry about that," Ethan said. "I couldn't sleep. It was my wedding day tonight. Yesterday, I mean. Is it one yet? So technically it was yesterday."

"I heard," the priest said. "It was downtown, wasn't it? At St. John's? Such a beautiful setting."

"How could I possibly pick among all the lovely churches in the area?" Ethan asked. "Really, I left it up to my wife to choose." He kissed the hand of the priest and then grinned and turned to me, looking both surprised and unsure. "Goodness. I thought you were my dear little cousin for a minute there. You look just like her."

I realized now that perhaps he had been drunk the night before. That and with Mr. Anderson's baggy clothes on and the way I must have looked, it was enough to not realize I was the same person.

"She had some questions for you, I think," the priest said.

"Oh?" asked Ethan.

"Yes," the priest said. "If you'll excuse me, I've got some things to attend to. God's work goes on." He bowed his head and then nodded to each of us. He walked off toward the main doors of the chapel.

Ethan stood, with a dumbfounded grin and innocent eyes. He wore a dark, long coat, and leather shoes. His hair was combed, though he had a little flip in the front, making him appear younger than I'd suspected the night before. "Was there something you needed help with?" he asked.

This was it. My chance to ask him outright. He was in danger without realizing, and he might be the only one who could fix everything. My only problem was that I was a complete stranger. I could be wrong about him and he was a part of this, but somehow I doubted it. He seemed innocent. Convincing him might be tricky, especially if he was masking something that was illegal.

I nodded at him, scrambling for the words to begin. "I know you don't know me," I said quietly. "And you've got no reason to listen to me or believe a word I say but..."

He unbuttoned his coat, his smile fixed. "Whatever it is, you can tell me. I'm not going to bite."

I swallowed, trying again. It was a risk to start talking about it, but I had a gut feeling about Ethan. He was an innocent caught in the middle of this, and his cell phone service was killing people he didn't even know. He had to be made aware. If he had other family members, they were at risk, too. "Your phone service," I said. "The one connected to the church steeples."

Ethan tilted his head, his eyes glinting with surprise. "What?" he asked.

"I know about it," I said. "But more importantly, others do, too. And they're all fighting to get a hold of the technology. They want to break into the core, and access it and..."

"Girl," he said, holding his hand up to stop me. "What are you on about? What phone service?"

I blinked at him. "The...cell phone service. The antenna in the steeples. Murdock's Core."

"I have a core," he said quietly. "But it isn't a cell phone *service*."

I stared at him, his confession making me unsure of my next move. "Some people believe it is," I said. "And they want access to it. There have been deaths, murders..."

His eyes went wide. "What? Who?"

"Randall. Randall Jones. Do you know him?"

Ethan went pale. "Yes," he said. "I'm afraid I do. He was a dear friend of the family. I thought he died in an armed robbery."

I pulled out Mr. Anderson's extra cell phone I'd taken from his car and pointed to it as an example. Blake and Doyle had the other one. "His phone was stolen," I said. "And then he was shot and killed. I've got reason to believe the murderer wanted the cell phone because it was connected to your...your core. Using your service...or at least they thought."

Ethan's eyes lit up with recognition and he took a small step back, putting a palm to his cheek. "Oh dear," he said. "The core."

"The ones who are looking for access suspect rich people use it," I said. "A secret underground cell network that has a security packet. My friend was kidnapped to try to break through the security packet to access the information flowing through it. To try to listen in on phone calls and internet use, I think. Listen for passwords. Use information for blackmail."

He shook his head, standing taller now. "That's ridiculous," he said. "That's not what the core does."

"What does it do?"

"It's just a stingray *finder*. It's in testing stages. It *prevents* hacking. It's not something that runs a network. It just piggybacks on other cell signals, and specific numbers, and follows where it goes. It pinpoints unidentified towers in the area...computers acting as cell phone towers. The police carry some stingrays, the NSA carries them, but criminals do as well. So there are cell phone signals flowing through, but we're not the source. We're just a...protective coating. We redirect your signals to the right towers, block unidentified towers, and add an extra layer of encryption since it's still experimental. And it's only in beta at the moment, since it's not stable. The people using it are just volunteers. The security dog packet was the key to it all, thanks to that clever man who invented it." He squinted at me, absently rubbing at his coat sleeve. "Are you sure they're killing people over it?"

I couldn't believe it. Alice and Eddie and the others were chasing something that wasn't even there. Maybe from the outside, it seemed like a cell phone carrier. An unusual signal, managed by towers, and his friends...all rich people…or in Randall Jones's case, well off enough to be notable. "Did you tell anyone about this?"

"No," he said. "I've been trying to do it in secret. To be completely honest, I'm not entirely sure it's legal. I mean, I wish to use it for good, but I know others might use it to make any cell phone untraceable to NSA stingrays…or anyone else trying to listen in or identify."

I pressed my fingertips to my head, rubbing and trying to figure out who knew the truth, and who was still under the belief this was a secret cell phone service for the rich that could be used to pull data. "Look," I said. "I don't have time to go into details, but I think we should go somewhere else."

Ethan's eyebrows scrunched together. "Where? I came to fix the tower. It informed me there was a power shortage or something."

My heart thundered and my eyes widened. It was too soon for Doyle and Blake to have done anything for Ethan to make it over so quickly.

Which meant someone else had beaten us to it. My eyes flitted to the door and wondered where they were. Was that why they were still gone? Because someone was up there waiting to ambush Ethan, and instead they got two people interfering? If it wasn't Alice, it might be Eddie.

If that might be the case, Blake and Doyle might survive. If it was Alice, then I had to get Ethan out of here before he was trapped, and we had no way to fix this. It would be hard to convince him his new bride wasn't who he thought she was.

"Ethan," I said quietly. "I know you don't have any reason to trust me, but I need you to come with me."

"Where?"

"For the moment, anywhere but here," I said. I checked the church, not knowing the layout. "And we need to go out a door that will be discreet. We'll need to make a run for it."

Ethan's face turned white. "Was someone following me?"

"Several people," I said. "I don't have time to explain. We just need to leave without being seen."

Ethan turned toward the back door and then toward the altar. "There's a small alcove just behind the confession booth," he said, pointing. "And there's a door behind it. A fire escape for the priests in the booth."

Good enough. "Listen," I said, focusing on his face. "I need you to follow me. No matter what happens. We can sort it out later. I just don't want you getting killed."

Ethan pressed his lips together, looking uneasy. "I don't know."

"Please," I said. My body started to shake. I was tired. I was terrified. They were coming to put me in a trunk again, and this time I might not escape. "I know you don't know me, but right now, there's two groups of people chasing you, and people have died. They've got three of my friends, possibly more at this point. People are dying because of your experimental cell thing and it had nothing to do with me or my friends. We've been put in the middle and I just want my friends back. I'm sure you'd love to shake off whoever is chasing you before any more of your friends die for this."

"I hadn't realized they'd died because of it," he said quietly. "It's hard to believe...but then my own cell phone did go missing sometime last night."

I smothered the guilt and tried to go with pleading. "Please? It's just me. You're bigger than I am. You can take me out easily."

He smiled a little. "I should warn my wife."

"She's probably fine. It's you they're targeting. I've got reason to believe they shut off your tower to lure you..."

There was a crash at the door. I heard the priest say a greeting, but he was then cut off. Then there was a thud and a gurgling, pained cry.

I silently swore to kill them all later for harming an old priest. I grabbed Ethan, before he had time to look and ask. They weren't waiting for him to leave. They were coming in after him.

Ethan stumbled behind me and then caught up. He took the lead after we got to the booths. He opened what looked like a simple wood panel, went in, and then pulled me inside.

The moment we entered, he closed the panel and hit a latch inside, which slid a safety bar into place. There were footsteps and some shouting behind us, but Ethan redirected me further into the narrow space.

I put a hand on his shoulder, and he led the way. It was a tight fit and dark. I wasn't sure how he knew where to go.

At the far end, he hit another latch and a door opened up to the outside.

I took a moment outside to get my bearings. We were at the edge of a small graveyard on the far side of the church. Just great. Now we'd get zombies next.

I'd go back for the car, but I didn't have a key, and if Blake and Doyle hadn't been caught, they'd be able to use it to get away. Ethan was the key for us now, and it was most important for me to get him out for now.

"We need to get away from the church," I said.

"Should we take my car?" he asked.

"No," I said. "They'll follow. We need to run somewhere else. Somewhere harder for them to follow. We can worry about a car later."

Ethan pointed, directing to the street just beyond the graveyard. "That way," he said. "It's just a small neighborhood, but I know the area. Plenty of places to—"

There was a crash behind us, and the sound of splintering wood.

"Sounds good to me," I said, and then started to run.

Ethan caught up. I lost one of my shoes in the escape, and then kicked off the other one when running became difficult. I tripped over a headstone, smashing one of my toes.

I felt horrible for leaving the guys now. Tears welled up in my eyes, but I had to swallow and focus on getting away. I could only hope Doyle and Blake could get away.

Ethan stayed in the lead, running. I did my best to keep up. Once we were out of the graveyard and across the street, he passed by two houses, took a left into the side yard of the third. As I followed, he slipped down a narrow alley where there were fences on either side and ducked around the back of a house. On he went, leading me on a maze through the neighborhood.

I got to the point where I was completely lost, thinking we were making a circle. When I couldn't run any more, I reached out for Ethan, grabbing at his sleeve. "Wait!" I said, trying to catch my breath. "Are they still following?"

Ethan paused and then we both listened. We were in the backyard of some house. There was a swing set, with one broken swing and a slide that was crooked. The grass was around my ankles, and I was worried about snakes and spiders, but right then, I'd take on a snake to simply be able to breathe and listen for anyone chasing us.

Moments passed as we stood in the dark, and no one came. Wind swept through the trees around us, slicing through my clothes and freezing me. I wished I had

Brandon's sweatshirt. I wished I was back at the Sergeant Jasper.

Panting, Ethan, stepped closer, checking me out. "Are you okay?"

I nodded. I held on to my ribs, trying to ease a painful stitch, wheezing.

"You sound like you're about to die," he said with a chuckle. "Do you have asthma or something?"

I made a face, although in the dark, he probably didn't see it. "I'm just not much of a runner."

"What's your name?" he asked.

I stood, trying to swallow and not wheeze so much. "Kayli," I said, although it was on the tip of my tongue to lie. "I was simply too worn out and tired to come up with one. Kayli Winchester."

"You do look so familiar," he said. "You look exactly like my niece."

"Angela," I said.

There was an outline of a smile on his face. "You know her?"

"No," I said quietly. "Not exactly. Last night, at your party...you...mistook me for her."

He laughed at first, and then stopped short. "You're serious?"

"It's a long story," I said. "But first, we need to get out of here."

His head shifted from side to side, as if he wasn't quite sure what to make of me. Slowly, he removed his heavy coat and angled to place it on my shoulders. "It's freezing out here," he said.

I was going to deny this, and tell him he was going to get cold, too. Part of me was overheated from running, but my legs were chilled and my arms were icy. It wouldn't be long before I was simply chilled through. I accepted, nodding and put it on. He really was a nice guy. How did he get wrapped up in someone like Alice?

But then, Alice was tricky.

"Where do we go?" he asked. "What next?"

I didn't really have a plan at this point, but I pulled out Mr. Anderson's cell phone and lit it up. There was only one number I actually remembered by heart now.

It took five rings this time, I was sure he was dead asleep. "Kayli?"

"Avery...I know you're asleep but..."

"Where are you?" he asked quickly, and the sound of a crash on the other end. He groaned and then returned. "I'll come get you. Give me a second to put some pants on."

I blew out a breath in relief, grateful.

♠

PHYSICS

*A*very apparently lived on John's Island, not far from where we were, so it only took him about ten minutes to find us after Ethan identified the street and house number of the yard we were standing in. We stayed in the backyard until we caught Avery's taxi sign on top of his car rolling down the street.

"We're probably scaring the neighbors," I said as we walked to the car. "Slinking around at night like this in their yards."

"No worries," Ethan said. "I know most of them. If anyone had looked out, I could have said hello."

"You know people in this neighborhood?" I asked, looking around. It wasn't quite middle class. The people probably owned their own homes, but couldn't afford the upkeep. Homes were run-down in one way or another, with older model cars and secondhand children's toys littering the lawns. Not exactly upper class circles.

"Some might actually work for me," he said. "It can take an army to run an empire, you know. Every person is essential, even if they don't realize it."

"What exactly do you do?" I asked.

Ethan shrugged. "Everything."

Avery was out of his car and holding open the door when we emerged from the backyard. Avery wore only a ribbed tank shirt, jeans and a pair of sandals. His hair was hanging in his face.

Avery stretched. The tattooed words on his chest moving with him. "Where to this time?" He turned to

Ethan. "Who is this?"

Ethan held out his hand in offering. "Ethan Murdock."

Avery looked confused and extended his hand slowly. "Avery." Ethan shook it and then Avery dropped it quickly, looking at me. "Where's the others?"

"Gone." I was trying to figure out where to go from here. I didn't think going to the hospital was a good idea. I couldn't take Ethan to his house. If Blake and Doyle managed to make it out without getting kidnapped or killed, they'd probably head to Blake's house as it was closest. I thought at least I could use it as a starting point to figure out what to do next.

"They took him, too?" Avery asked. "Blake?"

I sighed. "Let's get going. They could be on the way looking for us."

Avery got into the driver's seat. Ethan slid in the back. I raced around to the front passenger seat. Avery pulled the car around and headed out. Moments later, we were heading North toward the Charleston peninsula.

When it started to get warm in the car, I slipped Ethan's coat off my shoulders and passed it back to him. I slumped in my seat, catching my breath and willing my heart to settle. We might have been standing in that yard for a while, but my heart was still racing like we'd been running the whole time. "I don't know how much more of this I can take," I said.

Avery slid a glance at me. "What happened now? What's wrong?"

"Everything," I said. "I'm hungry. I'm tired. I can't sleep, though. My friends keep getting kidnapped over a cell phone service that doesn't even exist." I shoved my hair away from my face. "I mean, how stupid do they have to be to be killing each other and not even know what they're going after?"

Avery frowned. "Hey," he said. "Not our place, you

know? Wasn't any of your business, right? We don't have to figure out why. We just need to stop them. We should call the police. Get some help."

"I can't just stop," I said. "They've got everyone, now."

"We need the police," Avery said. "The FBI should get called in on this. It's gotten way out of hand."

"I agree," Ethan said. "I don't know what's going on, but we can't just run all over the place. The authorities need to be called in. We'll be safe, and they will find your friends."

I shuddered, and slid lower into the seat. Maybe I should, but I wanted to get to a safe spot first and think it over. "I don't know. Eddie said he'd be able to tell if I called the police."

"Eddie wasn't who was killing people, was he?" Avery asked. "And Alice...well..."

"Alice?" Ethan asked.

"Yeah," Avery said. "The bitch that started kidnapping guys, too. It's a long story..."

"Avery..." I said carefully, cutting at my throat with my hand. "Ixnay... uh..."

"I mean, she threatened Kayli here, and then poisoned two of her friends just to get her hands on this core thing, right? Who uses poison as a threat? That's crazy. I don't really believe it. I'm ready to call her bluff."

"Avery," I said louder, cringing, and afraid to look at Ethan, hoping he didn't hear the Alice part correctly.

"Who do you mean, *Alice*?" Ethan asked, bursting my hope. "You can't mean my wife."

"You've got a wife named Alice?" Avery asked. "This is going to be confusing."

I sighed, placing a palm to my forehead. "Ethan, your wife's got my friends. She threatened me and threatened to kill them. She wants the core. She killed off a lot of

Eddie's guys, that's the German gang who wants the core, too."

"Wait a minute," Ethan said. He shifted, and leaned over the back of the passenger seat, looking down at me. "Just one second. You mean to tell me my wife is behind this?"

"You said you'd only known her for a month or two, didn't you?" I asked.

"How did you know?" Ethan asked.

"You told me," I said. "Last night, when you thought I was Angela." I sat up, meeting him at eye level. "I didn't know who you were. I wasn't looking to hurt anyone. I just wanted to figure out where it was and possibly give someone access to it to save a life. You thought I was Angela, and I wasn't supposed to be upstairs, so I just went along with it."

"So you crash my party? My wedding? And now you're accusing Alice of... well, basically you're calling her a killer." He gritted his teeth, his eyes wide. "I don't believe it for a second. Alice has had a hard life, but she couldn't kill anyone."

He said it with such conviction that I thought there was a possibility I had it wrong. She did only imply she might have been responsible for the prior deaths. Despite his attitude about her, Alice flat out said she'd poisoned Axel and wanted access to the core. It was a fact I was trying to leave vague. I knew it would be hard to believe that someone you thought you knew very well turned out to be something else. I had no proof for him now, though.

I pressed a palm to his arm, wanting to draw his attention. "Will you at least believe that there are people out there willing to kill for access to whatever this core is? We need to be careful until we can sort it out." I squeezed his arm, pleading. "Look, I don't want your core. I want nothing to do with it. I just want to find my friends and

C. L. Stone

make sure they're safe. Your life was likely in danger, too. Right now, we need to make sure we're not dismissing any possibility and play it safe until it's sorted. I don't know what else to do."

"Kayli," Ethan said. He stopped, closed his lips and sat back. He was quiet for a long time, studying me and then Avery and then looked out the window. "What do we need to do in order to get this matter over with?"

"Call the police," Avery said.

"Apparently my wife is involved," Ethan said, "and is being accused of murder. I'd like to clear her name before she's escorted to jail when we're supposed to be on our honeymoon."

"We need a way to draw out Eddie and Alice and to get whoever has them to bring Axel and the others out." I had an idea started, but I wasn't sure if it was possible. "I'm thinking of doing a trade."

"How?" Avery asked. "And where am I driving to?"

"Let's go back to Blake's. Do you remember the way?"

"I guess," Avery said. "Why are we going there?"

"We need to stop somewhere," I said. "Just for now. Just until we come up with a plan." I needed clothes, and food and possibly a quiet place to work from until I could prod Ethan for answers that could possibly help us and figure out the next move. I couldn't go to Brandon's shop; I didn't know where it was. And I couldn't go to the Sergeant Jasper. I didn't know where else to go. I didn't think Blake would mind if I invaded his house.

Eventually, Avery found his way to South Battery, and parked out front of Blake Coaltar's three story home. The white house sat quietly under the street lights, the neighbors' homes nearby were just as still. The park across the street was dark and quiet. The smell of the bay was strong. It was such a peaceful, picturesque setting that filled my senses, making me crave sleep.

Ethan and Avery followed behind me to the front door. The stars and moon were now covered with a hazy, low cloud, promising drizzling rain and dampness for a while.

I rushed up the steps, testing the front door: locked. I scanned the front porch, wondering where, and if, he might have left a key in a fake rock or above the framework or hidden in a potted plant.

"He's not home," Avery said behind me. He shuffled in his sandals. "He's been kidnapped, remember?"

"Yeah," I said. I moved around him, back down the steps and wandered around the side of the yard, finding the rear with the yard and the large back porch. I climbed those steps.

"Are you sure we should be here?" Ethan asked. He followed close behind me. "I mean, there could be an alarm system."

"I don't think there is," Avery said, following behind Ethan. "He didn't set one before we left. I'm surprised the front door is even shut. I remember he took off with the door open. I was going to close it when he said to get in the car and hurry."

A neighbor could have shut the door for him if he left in that much of a hurry. I tested the back door, but it was locked, too. I turned to the windows then, and found one near the kitchen where the latch had been left undone. I dug my fingers into the outside screen frame, popping it off and then tried to yank up the window. It started going up and then stopped short, the antique frame catching on the many layers of paint.

Avery came up beside me, putting his palms under the frame of the window and then nodded to me. "One, two..."

"I don't think we should," Ethan said. "This is breaking and entering, isn't it?"

"Three," I said.

Avery lifted at the same time, and after a slow start, it slammed up into the frame above. I think there was a loud *crack*, but I was going to pretend it was old wood, and not glass.

"Kayli," Ethan said. "Are you sure it's okay?"

"He's not home," I said. "And he'd be okay if we used his house for a bit."

"Yeah," Avery said. "He got kidnapped so he'd want us to figure out a way to save him." He turned to me. "Right?"

"I guess." I wasn't totally sure if he'd been kidnapped even. I was hoping that wasn't the case. Maybe he'd gotten away. I felt guilty leaving him behind.

"You guess?" Ethan asked. "Are you even sure?"

I wasn't really sure of anything anymore. All I knew was, Ethan had access to what everyone wanted, and I wanted this to be over once and for all. Even as I worked my way into Blake's house, I was concocting a plan to figure out how I could call everyone out in the open and end it. Maybe Ethan could let them into the observatory under false pretenses and trade for Axel and the others.

It was a dangerous call. I wasn't sure Ethan would agree, and if Alice might somehow manipulate him into not trusting me, get access to the core, and then kill off Axel anyway. By now, she had to know I had Ethan. She could lie and say that *I'd* been lying. "Ethan," I said, starting to climb into the window. "Once you get in here, you need to tell me about—"

I had my foot on the floor one minute, and the next, I was shoved over, and on my back, the wind knocked out of me. For a split second, I wondered if I had passed out and collapsed. But I realized my legs were tangled up and there was a weight pressing me into the wood floor.

A body sat on my legs, a face hovering, looking down

at mine, so close that in the darkness, I couldn't tell who it was.

Hot breath fell on my neck, snapping me into action. My heart pounded as I shoved back with my butt, and then lifted an elbow, making contact.

"*Chto za huy*," a strong, deep voice said in my ear. *Cough. Groan.* "Kayli. Fuck."

I sat up, finding Raven clutching at his lower abdomen. He wore a wrinkled black T-shirt, dark blue jeans, and combat boots. His closely cropped brown hair flattened against his head. The tattoos along his arms and the massive guy that he was made him look scary, especially with his face contorted.

I sucked in a breath, excited and relieved at the same time. I lunged at him, not caring that I'd injured him, and threw my arms around his neck. "Raven! What the hell are you doing here?"

He grunted and wrapped a big arm around my waist, holding me to him. He lowered himself, pressing into me, until I was against the floor. He held me like that for the longest time, simply hugging me against him. "Following my little thief," he said, the thick Russian accent filling in every syllable. "Like I'm supposed to."

"Who is that?" Avery said from somewhere I couldn't see above Raven. "Are we fighting him or are we happy he's here? I can't tell."

"He's fine! He's a good guy. Sort of." I pushed at Raven until he started to sit up. I coughed, still catching my breath, and then rose, scooting out from under him. "Did you come by yourself?" I asked. "Where's—"

"Hey!" said a familiar, cheery voice. A moment later, Corey entered through the doorway. My heart lifted at seeing his face. It felt like a lifetime ago since I'd seen him last. He was so much like his brother, except for his happy eyes and disposition. He wore a Mario Bros. T-

C. L. Stone

shirt, jeans, flip-flops. His hair had that messy, just out of bed look. At first he spotted Raven, and then Ethan and Avery in the doorway, appeared confused, and then walked further into the room until he met my eyes. He smiled big. "There you are."

"You've been following me?" I asked. "For how long?"

Corey shrugged. "Since you took Mr. Anderson's car, and he called it in. Until you ditched it. But then you went into the building and we tried to follow but..."

The noise in the abandoned building. Maybe it wasn't hobos after all. "You didn't tell me?"

"You had people following," Raven said. "We were keeping an eye on them."

"Who?" I asked. "Did you see them? And why did you tackle me?"

"Missed you," Raven said. "I got excited."

I squinted at him. I'd only been gone a couple of days and I get tackled?

Corey helped me up, and the moment I was standing, he gathered me in a hug. "I missed you, too."

"Could we get inside, please?" Ethan asked. "Maybe we should sit down and straighten out this whole mess."

A few minutes later, we were all standing around the kitchen island. I needed food, so I was raiding the freezer, finding a box of frozen chicken sandwiches.

"What are you doing?" Corey asked. "You're stealing his food?"

"He won't care," I said, pretty sure he probably wouldn't even notice. The freezer was filled with Hot Pockets and sandwiches and other frozen delights. It was a mini-grocery store on its own.

Raven opened up one of the pantries, and started to inspect the contents.

"There's Pop Chips in those cabinets somewhere," I

said. "Find me some?"

"Pop Chips?" Corey asked.

Raven opened, and left open, half of the cabinet doors before he came across the chips. He took out two and placed them on the counter. He looked at Corey, and then at Avery and Ethan. "You want chips, too? She'll eat a whole bag. So will I."

I was going to say I couldn't eat a whole bag plus the sandwiches, but then I was hungry. I needed fuel to get my brain working.

"Don't you think we should focus?" Ethan asked. He stood facing the still open window. His eyes went to the door, to the furniture, to us, to the ceiling. He shifted on his feet. "I don't think we should be here any longer than we have to."

"Sure," I said. I studied him. I got that he was uncomfortable being here, but it felt like something else was off about him, too. I started unwrapping sandwiches, at least enough for Raven and myself, and put them in the microwave. "Basically, my idea is to offer up access to your observatory and your core to Eddie and Alice in exchange for Axel and the others. We give them what they want, and then we walk away. Once we're clear, we call in the police. There won't be any harm to anyone, especially if we act quickly."

Ethan stepped forward, pointing at me. "Now wait a second. We can't prove Alice has anything to do with this. What makes you think Alice even has your friend?"

Raven sidestepped in front of me in a protective stance, but I nudged him out of the way. "Because she told me she did," I said. I left the microwave to lean against the kitchen island, staring him in the eyes and hoping he took me seriously. "Yesterday...I think. Maybe. I'm getting my days confused, but..."

"When is the last time you slept?" Corey asked,

squinting at me. He came over, and touched gently at the skin below my eye. He rubbed gently. "You're starting to look like a raccoon."

I slapped at his hand to push it away. "Stop that. We need to get to Axel and Brandon and..."

"Wait a second," he said, his eyes wide. "What do you mean? Where's Brandon?"

Uh oh. Brandon didn't want Corey knowing about him being kidnapped. "Uh..."

"Kidnapped," Avery said. "Bummer, isn't it? Right after he got free the first time, he gets kidnapped again." He bobbed his head and made a sympathetic face.

Corey's eyes widened. "What?"

"Totes," Avery said. "Axel and...uh...Blake, too, right?" Avery looked at me. "There's one more, though. Max?"

"Marc," I said, grimly, looking at the counter. "Marc. And Doyle, I think. Maybe. I'm not sure about Blake and Doyle."

Avery snapped his fingers and then scratched at his head. "Right. Marc. I'm starting to lose track, too. They started out kidnapping girls, and now they're kidnapping guys. So we trade them for this core, yeah? And then the police can sort out the rest."

Corey's mouth was open, his eyebrow arching above one eye. "Hang on a second. So she has Brandon *and* Blake?"

"Yeah," Raven said. "What's this kidnapping?"

I tried to catch them up quickly on what had happened. They probably should have been told what was going on from the start. Maybe Brandon didn't want him chasing after, but I thought Corey was smarter than that.

Raven grunted at the end. "We were supposed to be running around after you so you don't do anything stupid, and trying to identify anyone that might be following

262

you."

"I thought you guys were at the hospital," I said.

"We were," Corey said. "Up until today. Last night when we got a call from Mr. Anderson saying he was going to check up on Brandon inside some house on Kiawah. He said you'd taken his car and were supposed to head to us. Only you never showed up, so we went looking for you. Kevin's back at the hospital in case you showed up. We followed Mr. Anderson's GPS on his cell phone. We were on your tail to Hannahan when you turned around, and then caught up with you at that building before we lost you again. The signal was hard to read after that. But where is Brandon now? With Alice or the other one?"

Did the cell phone not work because it was too close to Ethan's tower? "Last I saw him, he was at Ethan's house. I lost sight of him. Alice told me she had him. Actually, she told me he left me there alone. But she implied she had him, and didn't need me anymore." Sort of. She didn't even imply she had him. It was just girl intuition when someone was lying. But if she thought she had Corey, then it was true she really didn't need me anymore.

Corey's face darkened. Raven's did, too. They shared a look of silent conversation.

"Don't plan anything funny," I said. "I want to go save them, too. That's what we're doing. We can do it with the core." The microwave beeped then and I took out the sandwiches.

"This is ridiculous," Ethan said. "Really. Alice can't be involved. She wouldn't..."

"You told me you've only known her a few months," I said. "And you married her."

"So?" Ethan said.

"Yeah," Raven said, his eyebrow up as he matched

Ethan's expression. "So what's wrong with that? Sounds normal to me. In Russia, you could marry a girl the next day if you wanted. Happens all the time."

I gave Raven the eye, for encouraging Ethan, for one, and for being weird. Russians married their girlfriends after a day? What?

"Exactly," Ethan said. "So I'm not going to help you pin my wife for murder or conspiracy or whatever it is you're planning. There's no proof she's done any wrong."

Corey looked between the two men, looked at me and then gestured for me to be quiet. "How'd you meet her?" he asked Ethan.

Ethan seemed to calm down. "I ran into her at church. My father introduced us. I was working on my system in the steeple and while I was leaving, they were both there."

"Had you ever seen her at that church before?"

"No," Ethan said. "Although she said she'd been attending mass there for a while. She just moved to the neighborhood."

"Kind of random, isn't it?" I asked. "You bumped into her right after you were working on your project?"

Ethan scowled at me. "My father was talking to her first and introduced me. He was there to talk to the bishop in town. I was on a project that has nothing to do with underground networks like you said. I never even told her about the project and she's never asked about it. I do a lot of work around the city and across the country. She's never once asked about my work."

"That's kind of odd," I said. I picked up a sandwich and started to eat. If I was going to argue, I needed to fill my stomach. "If I was with someone, I'd want to know about what they did for work. Especially if it was important to you."

Raven reached over, grabbing one of the sandwiches and started eating with me. Avery shimmied over and took one from the plate.

Ethan frowned, and mumbled something. "That doesn't mean anything. I liked that she wasn't interested in my work."

Corey quietly lifted his cell phone out of his pocket. He turned it on and then thumbed through the screen. After a moment of searching, he lifted it to show Ethan. "Is this her?" he asked.

Ethan studied the phone. "Yeah," he said. "Her hair's different, but that's her. Is that an old picture?"

"That's a security picture taken at an airport three months ago," Corey said. "But the passport used to enter the country wasn't for an Alice. It's for an Anja."

So Corey's search for Alice's face was working! I tried not to look impressed and happy we were on to something. Ethan wasn't going to like this.

Ethan's lips parted, and again he studied the image. "There's got to be a mix up," he said.

"No mix up," Corey said. "She flew in three months ago. From Germany."

It was my turn to stare. I dropped the second sandwich I'd started on. "Hold up," I said, leaning against the counter. "Are you serious? Show me the picture."

Corey turned the phone around, showing me the image. It was Alice, with the same cold eyes and the satisfied smirk that made me want to stab her in the face.

"She's never been to Germany," Ethan said slowly. "I don't think so at least. She's been here for the last six months or so. And before that she said she lived up north, somewhere near the Canadian border."

"She doesn't have a driver's license," Corey said.

"Yes, she does," he said. "We just got married. She needed to show one to get the marriage license."

"Did you see the marriage license?" Corey asked. "The national database didn't show her having a driver's license. It managed to get her passport picture, though, and then we discovered when she entered the country. It's the only time she's used the passport."

Ethan fumbled for a moment. "Well, I...I don't remember now about seeing the license. It's probably at the house. We'll have to get it turned in to get the certificate."

"We should check," Corey said. When Ethan opened his mouth to protest, Corey lifted his hand. "If you want to verify, one way or another, and clear her name, it'll be better if we do it now, so we're all in agreement when the police are called in. This could be mistaken identity, but if that's true, then we need to get to the bottom of it before she's pinned for murder."

Ethan nodded abruptly. "That's all I ask."

"So," I said. "If we're okay with getting Axel and the others back in the meantime, I've got a plan."

"I have one, too," Corey said quietly, and turned toward the door. Raven did as well, and started walking away.

I dashed around the kitchen island, blocking the doorway. "Where are you going?"

"Out of the way, Kayli," Corey said grimly.

"No," I said. "You can't just go after them."

"I can," he said. "This was my fault. I was the one that left my name in a security packet. They were looking for me, weren't they?"

I nodded slowly. "But it doesn't mean you run in and get yourself killed. If you go now, they won't need Axel or Marc. They'll kill them and use Brandon over your head to do what they want. Right now, they think Brandon is you. It's the only advantage we have."

"What advantage is that, exactly?" Corey asked. "So he gets killed in the middle of this and I don't? How is that an advantage?"

I wasn't sure, exactly, either. I was going on what Brandon had said. Keep Corey safe and out of the picture. Limited liabilities.

"Let me go," Corey said. "I'll get them access to this...core."

"There's no access to get, "I said. "It's not a real phone service."

Corey blinked. "What is it? All the communication I read said it was."

"She's right," Ethan said, stepping up beside us. "There's no underground cell phone service. It's a stingray interference experiment. It's not even fully functioning. It's to identify false tower signals. The Guard Dog security packet encrypts the signals so they bounce, or it basically double coats a phone signal in security code so it isn't worth it for the bad guys to actually spend the time to decode. They might as well go after some easier signal."

Corey's jaw slackened and he stared at him. "So you weren't creating the signals. You were borrowing them for testing your security features. Can the NSA listen in on it? Would it be illegal if the FCC and NSA couldn't crack your code if something was masked in it?"

He nodded. "Maybe...I'm not sure. It'd be up to them to say something within the signal was illegal information and they would have to get a warrant for me to pull down the security encryption. But then, it wasn't like anyone had access; it was in a closed beta test and only open to select people who agreed to be part of my experiment. They never knew which phone calls were encrypted and which weren't. It would just randomly pick up a phone call signal from their line, and trace where it bounced off from, from different towers."

"It's why Randall Jones died," I said. "I think... someone killed him to steal his cell phone, thinking this was that secret underground service."

Corey scratched at his eyebrow. "It doesn't matter now what it really is. It matters what this Eddie, and possibly Alice, think it is, and that they might be holding people against their will to gain access. We need to get the guys back before they discover it isn't what they thought it was and kill everyone just to cover their tracks."

"Here's a plan," I said. "I say we go back to the house on Kiawah. We contact Eddie and tell him we've got access, and we all agree to trade him access to the room and drop the code in exchange for the others being released. They get what they think they want, then we walk away." I turned to Avery. "Then it's your job."

"Name it," Avery said, looking grim. "We need to stop these guys."

"You said you knew a cop?" I asked. "Someone you'd trust?"

"I thought we weren't calling any cops," Ethan said. "I don't want to drag Alice..."

"I just want a cop on board at the right time," I said. "If we dangle access to the core out, the ones who want it will come get it. They can fight over it. We back off, they think they get what they want, and the cops can roll in and bust anyone who was really involved."

Ethan started to talk, but I held up a hand to stop him. "And if Alice doesn't come bulldozing in for your core, and we get the guys back without her around, and if she's truly innocent, she won't have anything to worry about. I won't even mention her threatening me if it turns out I'm wrong about her."

Ethan started to shake his head, but then his shoulders relaxed. "It seems reasonable," he said in a low tone.

I got the impression he really didn't like this plan and was just agreeing with me, but there wasn't much else we could do.

Corey nodded slowly. "How do we make this trade,

though? How do we get them to come to us? We don't have a phone number, do we?"

"I'll have to do it," I said. "I can go to the house with Ethan, and Ethan can turn off the security packet thing. We just need you to maybe figure out a way to make it look like they're getting what they want. By giving them access to a signal they can listen in on?" I looked at Corey, asking quietly if that would work.

"No," Raven said. "We're not targets. We don't make ourselves into targets. If we are there, there's nothing to stop them from shooting us all for knowing about it."

"We just need to get them out long enough that they start fighting each other rather than us. They want this core thing. They can fight over it while we get away."

Corey shifted on his feet. "We could rig something up so it just *looks* like we're giving them access." He looked at Ethan. "If I can get there before they do, do you think we can fake a cell phone tower signal? Maybe draw in some normal cell phone data from nearby towers?"

"I could show them the cell phone signals I've been working with," he said, putting a finger to his chin. "But I'd need to contact my people to let them know to use their cell phones."

"Or," Corey said, "we could load more numbers into your system. Then it'll look like more than just a couple of friends. It'd be an actual underground cell service."

Suddenly, the floor shook. Glass shattered somewhere, it sounded like it was coming from the front of the house.

Raven ran to the kitchen door, opening it with his back, and peering out. "There's three people at the front door trying to bust it in." He closed off the kitchen door, hitting a latch on the lock. He lifted part of his shirt, revealing a belt across his waist, and lifted a gun from a back holster. He pointed the nose at the ground and steadied himself with his back against the doorframe. "Get down. Kayli, behind the counter. Corey..."

At first, I stared at the gun. I hadn't noticed it before.

Without a word, Corey went to the windows and started shutting the blinds. Raven went to the table, and started pushing it in front of the door, blocking off access. Avery and Ethan moved to the counter, getting behind it.

"You're barricading us in," I said. "Let's sneak out the back. Or tell them we're going to give them access to the core if they'll just..."

"They've got guns," Raven said. "I saw them. They're not here to talk to us. They're here to kill us."

"Then we need to get out of here," I said. "Not lock ourselves in."

"I don't know how many there are," he hissed. "They could be coming around the back, too. Kayli, down. Now."

Corey peered out the window. "I don't see anyone."

Raven scanned the windows, as if he wasn't sure, but then looked at Corey. Together, they nodded at the same time. "Take them out," he told Corey.

I scanned the kitchen, not wanting Raven to play the hero and stay behind to ward them off. I spotted the microwave and got an idea. "Corey, go back out through the window. Go through the backyard and make a run for it. Take Ethan and Avery. We'll meet you at the lake."

"What are you going to do?" Corey asked.

I looked at Raven. "I heard a rumor about what happens when you put whole raw eggs in the microwave."

Raven's eyes lit up and his chest puffed out. "My little thief thinks the way I think. This is fate."

Corey eyeballed each of us in turn and then groaned. "I know that face. We can't..."

Raven moved over, shoving Corey in the shoulder toward the window. "Out. Now."

Corey looked at me, pleading, but I shrugged. We'd

provide the distraction as they ran off. We had to let Eddie's people—or Alice's—know we wanted to negotiate, but at the Murdock house.

Corey went to the window. Ethan and Avery followed. Corey surveyed the backyard, and then went out first. Ethan and Avery crawled out behind him.

Another crack in the house, and a slam of wood against thicker wood, like the front door bursting open. Raven kept his back to the doorframe of the kitchen and pointed to direct me. "Go to the fridge, and dig out as many cartons of eggs as you can. Don't take the eggs out, just leave them in."

"Is this how you blew up his yacht?" I asked, doing as he told me and finding five cartons stacked neatly in the fridge, all ready for blowing up.

"No," he said. He pointed to the microwave. "It's time to play Texas and load the microwave."

I thought about what he said. "Tetris? The game?"

"Same."

I was getting the gist that when he said "Same", what he really meant was, 'that was what I meant'.

I opened the microwave, and started stacking the cartons inside. The fifth one was a tight squeeze. Why did Blake have so many eggs? But then, his fridge and cabinets were overstuffed with food, more than he could eat. I assumed that's how the rich worked. Overabundance.

There were footsteps in the hall outside. "What do you want?" Raven asked loudly.

There was a voice shouting, muffled through the wall, but then the crack of a gun sounded.

I ducked beside the kitchen island.

Raven was steady. "They aren't here to negotiate," he said.

"Tell them we've got Ethan Murdock," I said.

Raven unlocked the door and then opened it just wide enough to point his gun out, aiming up. He shot a couple of bullets, a warning to get their attention. "We've got Ethan Murdock," Raven said. "Do you want him?"

"Give him to us," someone shouted. I wasn't sure who it was but the accent wasn't as heavy as Eddie's.

Raven pointed the gun toward them. "Back up, or I shoot him, and then I shoot you."

"You shoot him, we'll shoot you all!"

"Back up!" Raven yelled. "There's five of us with guns in here."

I grimaced at his lie, and then looked around for a weapon, considering the kitchen knives in the wood block. Not much use in a gunfight, though.

"Send Ethan out and we'll walk away," said the voice.

Raven backed his head up, pointing to the microwave and then held up five fingers. I took it to mean five minutes.

I swallowed, wondering how quickly the explosion would happen. I hit five minutes. As soon as the microwave kicked on, I headed toward the window, crouching and trying to be out of the way in case it was an instant explosion.

Raven yelled at the guys while motioning to me to get out. "We'll leave him here and then we're going to his house," Raven said. "I'll count to ten. I'm going to back away and put Murdock in the middle. Come in then."

"We'll count," they said. "One..." There was a long pause, and then murmurs as it sounded like they were conversing about the situation.

Raven backed up quickly and shoved me out the window. I fell out onto my back on the porch, got up and continued to duck as I moved away from the window, waiting for Raven.

It was way too long before Raven eventually joined

me.

"What did you do?" I asked as he scrambled over to me. "You were right behind me."

"Forgot to set the oven," he said. He grabbed at my arm, urging me along.

"You mean the microwave?"

"No," he said, shoving me. "Run."

How far would a microwave blow up? Wouldn't the door just blow off? It would sound enough like an explosion so we could make a getaway before they realized we'd escaped.

I didn't have time to ask. Raven was shoving me away. I ran with him off the back porch and then through the yard, heading toward a low wall that met with the neighbor's back yard. We hopped it together.

The moment we were on the other side, Raven was on top of me, holding me down into the grass. I cursed at him to get off of me.

At that moment, a series of shouts, followed by an explosion...followed by a louder, thundering explosion. With heat...

I shoved Raven off enough so I could look over the wall. He got up beside me, keeping a hand on my back.

The whole outside wall of Blake's house was a mess of shattered glass and wood, blown out from the explosion. The house itself was on fire.

"Raven!" I cried. "What did you do?"

"I set the oven," he said. "The stove, I mean. He has a gas stove."

Had a gas stove. From the looks of it, there wasn't much left of the kitchen. "Did...did we kill..."

"No," he said. He reached for me and then grabbed my hand, pulling me into him. "No, no, Little Thief. We're not murderers. Not unless they got in the way of the blast like idiots."

That wasn't comforting. "How did you...why..."

"Physics," he said.

I stared at him. "What?"

"It's a matter of physics. I'm a professional Russian," he said.

I still didn't understand. Maybe it was lost in the translation. The fire from the hole in the house lit up the area. Neighbors' lights started turning on.

We needed to get going. "Let's get out of here."

He lifted me and pushed me to start running. "They'll be after us. Or the police will be here in a minute. Get to the road. Walk fast but don't run. Look normal."

Easier said...

♠

THE CHASE

*A*s we walked through the night, cutting through side streets in the neighborhood, sirens filled the air. We didn't pass any cruisers on our way, and I only hoped Corey and the others made it out without getting picked up by police.

We hurried, but no one appeared to be chasing us. Either they ran off after the blast, or...I didn't want to assume they might be dead. Raven didn't seem worried about it. I tried not to be. Hopefully they got the message that we'd be heading to Murdock's house. We just needed to get there before they did.

It had to be two in the morning now. My heart was beating fast, but my body was tired and I felt sluggish. Raven eventually put an arm around me, and I leaned into him as I walked.

I was really feeling down. Was I getting sick? I tested for a fever, but it was hard to tell.

When Raven and I got to Colonial Lake near the apartments, I scanned the park. The cement surrounding the small lake was clear of people. Did Corey get lost? Avery wouldn't have gotten lost. He knew the way. Or did he only know it by car?

"Please tell me they didn't get picked up by someone else?" I turned to Raven. I didn't expect him to be psychic and know, but I'd already lost a lot of people and I was ready to sit down and get taken away, too, giving up the chase, if everyone I cared about was going to get carted off not matter what I did.

Raven looked over the area and shook his head. "I've got a feeling Corey might have went to go save his brother."

My jaw popped open. I grabbed Raven's arm and shook it. "He'd do that?"

"He won't want to wait," Raven said. "Not for Brandon. Now when it's his life. He thinks too much like me."

I didn't want to believe him. Corey wouldn't just run off...

Suddenly, a person appeared from a sidewalk and ran across the street toward us. Raven got in my way, covering me.

As the person got close, I recognized the shape. "Corey?"

He jogged faster. When he got to us, he bent over, holding his chest and breathing heavy. "We lost Ethan."

"What?" I asked. "Why? We need him."

"He said he was going to find his wife. I couldn't stop him. Avery went with him." He looked at me. "He said you should call him for updates. He'd stay with him."

I nodded. The traitor. He was going to tip off Alice. He knew the plan. Hopefully Avery could keep him safe...Avery the stoned taxi cab driver was in way deep now.

"Then we need to get to the house before anyone else," Corey said. "Before they ruin the plan."

I raced beside him toward the Sergeant Jasper that was near the lake. Every bone in my body wanted to simply take the elevator upstairs and pass out and let Raven and the others take care of it. It wasn't that I didn't care. I was dizzy, and it was late and my body was refusing to cooperate. I breathed in some cool air, hoping for some energy. With the cloud cover it was damp and dreary. I craved warmth.

Raven and Corey cut through the middle of the building, only to spill out on the other side to the parking lot. Corey scanned the area, and pointed to a black SUV. I scurried after them.

Raven went to the driver's seat. "You've got a key?" I asked.

He grunted. I think it meant yes.

Corey got in the front passenger. I hopped in the back.

I collapsed into the seat, laying on my side. Raven turned the car on, and then the SUV lunged as he pulled around and raced out of the lot.

I closed my eyes, and tried to ignore the sounds of cars honking and screeching of tires. Russian driving.

♠♠♠♠♠♠

Eventually, I had to sit up, because Raven's driving was even scarier when I couldn't see what was happening. He slowed down enough to almost a stop at the entrance of Kiawah.

He rolled down the window. "Let us in," he said.

The guard was a woman. "Where are you two headed?" she asked with a small smile, looking wary. She glanced at me in the back, and then a small look of surprise. "I mean three?"

I felt around my head, and found a rat's nest of hair. "I was at...the gift shop earlier, got a flat and left my car here," I said carefully. "I wanted to pick it up before it got towed. He's here to help me fix it."

The woman lifted a brow, weighing out my story

and then eyeballed Raven, who appeared to be biting his tongue. Corey smiled pleasantly, nodding. He was probably the most normal looking one.

"I'll give you twenty minutes," she said. The guard pushed a button, and the gate lifted. I managed a quick wave in thanks as Raven continued on.

"We should stop," I said. "We shouldn't drive in. If Alice is at the house, she'll spot us."

"We don't have time to pussyleg," Raven said, and I assumed he meant pussyfoot, but he moved on before I could correct him. "And that guard lady is a snitch."

"She gave us twenty," Corey said. "But I'm willing to bet she'll forget about us when she gets other people driving in later, like Eddie's men."

"We need a plan," I said. "We don't have Ethan to let us into his house. And we need to scout it before just barging in."

"We don't have time for plans," Raven said. "We already had one."

"Raven!" I grabbed his shoulder and squeezed hard. "I don't want to kill Brandon if he's stuck there with Alice. We don't need to barge in and get shot at, either."

He revved the engine, lunging the SUV forward and I leaned into his seat, but then it slowed and he did a small turn. He slid the car into a parking spot near the closed gift shop.

"How far is the house from here?" he asked.

I pointed in the direction. "I know which one. If we walk from the beach..."

"We'll be spotted quickly," he said. "But we don't have a choice. They'll be expecting people coming in cars, they'll be keeping an eye on the road. We'll have to take the beach."

"I'll know when we get close," I said. "We can circle the house, maybe peek in a few windows and see who might be home."

Corey groaned and opened his door. "I'm going to get shot at today. I can tell."

Raven climbed out. When we were standing at the edge of the beach together, he pointed at us to get our attention. "Don't plan anything. Our only goal is to get our team out. Nothing heroic beyond that. Get them out and run. No trying to get revenge, okay?"

I pouted. "If they aren't hurt," I said. "But no promises if they've even got a little bruise."

He smiled, and it lit up his dark eyes. He pressed his hand to the top of my head, and scratched at my scalp with his rough fingers. "My little thief is back."

I moved toward the beach, ready to get going. "What do you mean, back?"

"You've been...dead," he said, doing a short jog to catch up with me. "The last few weeks. Ever since Florida."

"I wasn't dead," I said. I was walking on the sand now, and had to focus on it to make sure I didn't trip on a dune. "I was working with you. Remember? On those houses?"

"He's right," Corey said, walking up beside me. "You've been out of it. You wouldn't smile. You'd barely eat, you know?"

Raven put an arm around my neck. "Now you're ready to kick someone's ass. I've missed you."

Maybe I hadn't been myself, but was he really only happy with me when I was scared out of my skin, and running on the edge?

Raven was warm, though, and since he was close, I was using him as support. My head felt light, and I was starting to get dizzy every so often. I needed coffee and food; more than the few bites of sandwich I'd grabbed back at Blake's. I needed to sleep. I couldn't stop, though. Not yet.

We walked quietly toward the house. In the length of time it took us to get to the corner of the Murdock property, I had a thousand scenarios going through my head. An army of Germans. Alice on the lawn with a bazooka. Aliens hovering over the house to collect it and move into outer space.

The yard and house were oddly quiet. The doors were shut. Windows shuttered. There was no hint there had been a party there earlier. No cars in the driveway.

"I expected World War III by now," I said as we peeked around. I hoped no one could see us standing on the neighbor's lawn, but really, there didn't seem to be any activity. It was the middle of the night, and the neighboring homes were still.

Raven studied the house and then pointed up. "What's that? That's the roof with all the glass?"

"It's an observatory," I said. "I thought that core was in there. I guess it is. I don't know how it works though."

"You said the church steeples were used as antennae?" Corey asked.

"Yeah."

Raven laughed. "So couldn't the obituary be used as an antennae?"

I was going to correct his term, but then I looked up at the observatory, with the metal beams that held up the glass between each pane. "Raven," I said. "You're smarter than the average bear."

"What? What bear? Like my tattoo bear?"

"Never mind," I said. It was brilliant. There wasn't

an antennae here, because the entire third floor was the antennae. Looking up at it now, with the metal beams, it was obvious. He did have it under security. Ethan just didn't realize anyone cared about his project. "It's too quiet, though. We don't know if anyone is inside. What should we do?"

"I should get inside," Corey said. "I need to look at his work, at the core. We'll need time to prepare for this trade."

Raven slunk along the edge of the property, and to the outside wall that was the garage. He went to the window and checked inside. "One car," he said. "It's covered in a sheet."

"Is no one home?" I asked. "Not even Alice?"

Raven shrugged. "Let's go in," he said, and then started around the wall. "I hate waiting."

Ditto.

I caught up with Raven. He darted across the lawn, around the pool, and toward the back door. Corey stayed behind us, watching our backs.

Raven tried the handle to the door. Locked.

He inspected the door, and then pulled a wallet from his pocket. From it, he pulled out what looked like a credit card.

"That won't work on this door," I whispered. "There's a deadbolt."

"It's not the deadbolt that's locked," he said. Then he showed me the card, which had tools buried into the plastic. "And we've got a bump key."

I remembered Axel once telling me about bump keys. "What about the security panel? The alarm is probably on."

"I'll take care of that," Corey said.

"I know the code," I said.

281

Corey smirked. "Well then what were you worried about? The box should be near the door. Find it and enter the code."

Was that how security panels worked? The one upstairs for the observatory was on the outside. I wondered if the codes were different for the bottom floor.

Raven unfolded the plastic card to reveal a long metal piece. He inserted one end of the key into the door, and then used his knee to pound against it while twisting the handle at the same time.

The door opened with a shudder and then quieted.

I cringed at the noise and then checked over Raven's shoulder. If someone was downstairs, they would have certainly heard that.

Raven walked in slowly ahead of me. He put his bump key away, but then his fists clenched, unclenched, clenched. He was ready to throw a punch if someone got in our way. I spotted his gun in the holster at his back. Did he have any bullets left?

Corey found the panel on the wall in an alcove. I pressed in the security code, and held my breath.

It beeped, and then quieted. We all exhaled in relief.

We walked through a small rear entertainment room and then an adjoining kitchen. I'm not a quiet person, and Raven is a bear on hard floors. Everything seemed to creak underfoot. Someone should have heard us.

"Is anyone even home?" I asked.

"Let's check this obituary," Raven said.

"Observatory," I said.

"What's observatory?"

I looked at Corey for help. I wasn't even sure. As far as I knew, it was a fancy room. I found it amusing, though, to be teaching Raven English. Corey shrugged and I continued. "The third floor," I said. "It's called an observatory. I guess you observe things from it. Like it has telescopes you can check out from up there."

"Oh," Raven said. He angled his head into the hallway, checking it out, and then eased into it, inspecting around the corners. "Like stars and shit?"

"Like things on the ground, too. Like spy on your neighbors." I followed him out, and tensed, anxious about the quiet around us. Wouldn't Alice be protective of something she wanted access to?

"Oh," he said. He did the Russian version of tiptoeing, sliding his feet across the floor. "We have an observe-rotary."

Corey laughed. "Who does?"

"You mean the top of the Sergeant Jasper?" I asked. I started to mimic him, but then picked my feet up and walked on my toes. And when no one came around the corner or jumped us, I simply walked.

"Shhh," Raven said. "No I meant Corey. He's got one in his computer."

Did he consider Corey's ability to spy on those around him the observatory? Teaching English was harder than I thought. I shared a glance with Corey.

Corey sighed. "No one is here."

Raven nodded. "Doesn't mean no one is on the way. They could be here any minute."

"Let's go upstairs," I said.

Raven followed me as I led him up to the second floor. Corey took up the rear again. We stopped on the second story landing, listening.

When no one rushed at us or shot at us, and the floor seemed quiet, we took our time, checking out what was behind every door.

When Raven opened up the second floor office, he

started to go inside.

"Someone in there?" I asked.

"No, but it has a computer."

"It's nothing," I said. "I already checked it."

Corey came out from checking the master bedroom.

"Corey," Raven said. He inspected the office again. There wasn't a closet door inside, so no one was hiding anywhere. He pointed inside and then went in. "Come in here."

Corey went in after him. "There was nothing," I said, following. "Just a regular computer."

"Let's get some info on Ethan," Corey said. "And who exactly his friends are. And maybe there's info on Alice...or Anja."

That seemed like a good idea. "There wasn't a computer upstairs, either," I said. "I was up there the other night. Could he run it from this computer?"

"Maybe," Corey said. He turned the computer on, checking history, opening up email screens, and searching through files.

I felt another wave of dizziness and entered the room to sit on a chair to stabilize myself.

Raven was watching Corey work and then came over to me. He nudged me with his boot. "What's wrong?" he asked. "Sick?"

I shook my head. "Tired."

"Sleep," he said.

I sat up, frowning and shaking my head to wake myself more. "No," I said. "We'll need to get this done first."

"You should probably head back to the hospital," Corey said, focused on his computer. "If you're that tired, it's not going to get better. You won't be able to run."

"I don't want her driving alone," Raven said. "And I can't leave you here alone. No one does things alone right now. I'm in charge now."

Corey's lips lifted in a small smile. "You're carrying her if she passes out."

"*Khorosho*."

I wasn't sure if I should be insulted, but I was too tired to care. I continued to sit, but made myself sit up, and occasionally pinched myself to stay awake. It was hard not to lean back and simply sleep while Corey worked.

Fortunately, it didn't take Corey long to figure out what he wanted. "No locked files," Corey said. "Ethan didn't have much to hide in here. Church emails, like on his phone. The only thing interesting are his conversations with his father."

I recalled the photos in the hallway of the older gentleman surrounded by kids. "He's the one that introduced him to Anja. How did he meet her?"

"I don't know," Corey said. "But according to some of these news reports he's saved, it was about Ethan dispelling rumors about the company. Fraud and there was a questionable branch they started in Africa that seemed to contract in arms deals. Fingers were pointed at his dad, and but it was Ethan telling everyone it was a lie. No investigation ever put together enough evidence to convict."

Interesting. "I don't...Ethan didn't lie to us about this core, did he?" I asked. "If there's rumors, something's going on, right?"

"Rumors could be false," Raven said. "Or rumors are smoke and there's a fire. Sometimes bigger than the rumor."

"That's not the impression I got," Corey said.

"Ethan seemed genuine. His ideas were honest and he appeared to care about Anja...Alice a great deal." He stood, turning off the monitor. "But we should check out this core. Let's find out what he's up to."

When we cleared the second floor, we continued up along the second staircase. The wall panel was the only light in front of us on the third floor and I couldn't find a switch. I went to the panel, remembered the numbers and then started to type it in.

Raven materialized beside me and slapped my hand. "Don't."

"Stop it," I said, slapping his hand back. "It's the same as the one for downstairs."

"It's not the number that's the problem," he said. He pointed to the panel. It was different from the one downstairs, but I followed his direction, checking it out.

There was a small camera lens inside the unit.

"Did the downstairs one have that?" I asked.

"No," Corey said. He came up, tucking me behind him and inspected the panel. "Looks like... too small for an iris scanner. Looks like facial recognition."

Huh. Extra security for the upstairs room. And this panel was on the inside. The core had to be up here, and it was designed to keep people out. Ethan had lied to his niece. It was hard to believe we could be wrong about him. "How do we get in?" I asked.

"Give me a minute," Corey said. "Don't touch anything. I'll be back."

I glanced at Raven. He frowned and then started to follow him down the stairs. He stopped at the landing, a guard between Corey and me. He was keeping an eye on both of us.

Corey was back in a few minutes, carrying a freshly printed sheet of paper. He showed it to me, a picture of

Ethan.

"The flaw about facial recognition cameras," he said, holding it up to the lens and motioning me to put in the code. I started typing it in. "They can't tell the difference between a picture and the real thing."

That was clever. I wouldn't have known. Maybe that's what kept everyone out.

It still made my heart skip a beat when the unit beeped after I finished. When it did, though, the panel read: Alarm Off.

Raven blew out a breath on my neck. "You're lucky. If it were Russian alarm, it would explode if you got the wrong number."

That sounded like Russian gloating. "No, it wouldn't," I said.

"Tell me I'm wrong," he said, his chest puffing out. "Look me in the face and say it."

I rolled my eyes and then opened the door.

The observatory was in the same shape it was in before. I found a switch, flicked it, and the low-level lamps lit up. Raven closed the door behind us, and then used the panel nearby. "I'm setting the alarm, since you're a know-it-all and know the pass code. Anyone coming in now will set it off."

I did a circle in the large room, checking the furniture, with the slight hope that someone else was here. Brandon. Anyone. "There's no point, really," I said. "If they aren't here, we'll have to figure out where they went."

"We're chasing tails," he said. "Let's make them chase us."

Corey looked around the room, checking out the furniture. He went to the window, touching the metal bar framework. "I don't see a network base. How does it even work?"

"That's what confused me," I said. "But it's got to be up here somewhere. He had facial recognition to keep people out. That's got to mean something."

Raven clomped across the room in his boots, looking out through the windows, surveying. He checked out one of the smaller telescopes and swung it to look down the road. "Let's turn off the... thing. The core? Right?" he stood, and then looked at Corey. "If we take out the power, it'll shut it off."

"There might be a generator somewhere," Corey said. He got down on his hands and knees. He smoothed his hands across the floor, and traced the grooves. "And we want to bribe them with access. We have nothing to negotiate with if we shut it down."

I knelt beside Corey, "What are we looking for?"

"It might be in a crevice somewhere," he said. "Look for a panel. The floor, the wall."

There wasn't much wall. I lifted one of the carpets. Raven started shoving furniture around.

Corey circled the room. He groaned. "We're running out of time," he said. "It's got to be here somewhere."

"We're out of time," Raven said. He was by one of the windows near the front of the house. "Someone just drove up."

Corey and I raced to the window.

While it was still dark, the front drive was lit up by garden lights, and the front porch light was on.

A car was parked in the drive with its headlights on. There was movement from what I could see inside the windshield, but whoever it was remained in the car.

Corey went back into the room, and started pacing. "We need more time. They can't come up here yet.

I met Raven's stare. Raven focused on me for the longest time. His mouth set, his eyes wide and wild. It struck me, looking at him, realizing he was feeling the same as I was. His friends were out there somewhere, and we didn't have answers or a means to free them yet. We didn't have the ability to check on them. We only had access to this room right now.

"I don't want Alice to kill them," I said quietly.

His head reeled back for a moment, and then he shook it. He stepped forward, coming at me with those intense eyes. The closer he got, the bigger he seemed to me. He wasn't as tall as someone like Corey, but he didn't have to be. He had mass on him that was unbelievable and made me feel small next to him.

He cupped my cheeks in his wide palms and forced me to look at him. His eyes held steady with mine. "No one will kill us," he said. "Family first. That's what they taught me."

It took me a moment to remember this was something to do with the Academy. "Isn't that an... a rule or something?"

"The first one," he said. "And the most important. You and I aren't going to get killed. We'll save our family. Are you with us? Will you be with me?"

I wasn't entirely sure what he was asking. Did he mean my being part of the group? I nodded, my cheeks brushing against his palms. Maybe I hadn't really heard all he was saying. I was feeling dizzy again.

"Say it," he said, his voice deeper.

I wasn't sure what this had to do with Axel not getting killed. "Yeah," I said. "I mean, being with the group and all."

He smirked then leaned in and kissed my forehead quietly.

I closed my eyes. It was a split second of warmth from him, after a lot of running around. He'd kissed me before, but this was something different. We were in this together. This meant something much more.

"My little thief," he said quietly. He pulled his head back gazed at me steadily. "Let's pull the trigger together. Let's shut down their core. We make them come to us. I'll call in the A...our team, tell them to meet us here. We'll take them all down together."

He wanted to call in the Academy. "And Axel? And Marc? And the others?"

He brushed his fingers against my cheek. "They would want us to push the button."

"We don't need to shut it off," Corey said. He was still looking at the wood paneling on the floor. "Just help me find the thing. We still have time. I just need to look at it."

I stepped away from him and looked outside. Whoever was out there was waiting, possibly for backup. If it was Eddie, he might be waiting for more of his team to show up. If it was Alice... I didn't know what to expect. "We need a backup plan. We should maybe call Kevin. Let him know to be on the way, and what we're doing."

Raven pulled out his phone, and then held it up. He started to type into it, and then sent the message. He waited, but then looked confused. "I'm not getting a signal."

"We're inside a big cell tower thing," I said. "Or one that messes with signals. I think it can interfere with your cell phone if you're too close."

"We'll have to find another way," Raven said, looking around. He motioned to a side table near a couch that had a wired landline phone beside it. "Call Kevin."

I went to it, and pressed in the number he relayed to me. Raven kept an eye on the car. Corey searched the room. I waited through three rings before Kevin picked up."

"Yo," he said. "This is Kevin."

"It's Kayli."

"Hey!" he said, sounding surprised. "Where are you? Did the guys find you?"

"Sort of," I said. "We need you to come to Ethan Murdock's house."

"Why?" he said, his voice deep.

I glanced at Raven, who was splitting his attention between the car outside and me on the phone. When he caught my eye, his eyebrows went up, asking me quietly what I wanted.

"We're going to get the bad guys to come here and negotiate for Brandon's and the other's lives."

"What?" Kevin asked loudly into the phone. "What the hell is going on? Where's Raven?"

"We're at Ethan's house," I said. "Raven's right here."

"Give the phone to him."

I cringed. He wasn't happy. I held out the phone.

Raven motioned I should take his place at the window. We traded spots and Raven took up the phone. "Kev," he said. "No. No. No. Come here. Bring some people. Big people. But don't run in."

"Found it!" Corey exclaimed. He dug his fingernails into a wood beam, scraping at it. "It is in the floor. I just need to figure out how to open it. There's probably a switch somewhere."

"No," Raven said into the phone. "That's just Corey."

There was movement outside and I watched another car pull up. This one was a ritzy long limo. It stopped, the driver jumping out quickly after it parked behind the first car. He raced over to the back seat and opened the door.

Out stepped Alice. She wore a slim-fitting suit, and her hair was tied up in a bun on her head.

"Alice is here," I said.

"Shit," Raven said, he tried to walk across the room and then couldn't drag the phone that far. He talked into it. "Just shut up and get here. Bring a gun. Or two." He threw the phone down until it cracked on the floor. He jogged over to the window. "You go help Corey. "I'll keep an eye on her."

I ran over to Corey, who was wedging the wood between the floor and his discovered panel. "It's stuck. I don't know if it rolls down and to the side, or if it comes up."

"If you had a secret computer in the floor," I said, "behind a security panel, where would you hide the button?"

Corey stopped his scratching and thought about it, glancing around the room. "It'd probably be another security panel. Something you could enter a code into? Or another face scanner?"

"She's coming in," Raven said. "I can't see who she's got with her, but the people in the first car are staying put. She's got two guys coming through the front."

"We'll have to be quiet," I said. "We're on the third floor."

Corey got up, and went to the security panel near the door. "This might be it," he said. "It's in the same panel."

"We don't have time to guess," I said. I thought about it and went back to the phone.

Kevin had hung up. I dialed Avery's number from memory this time. I sat on the sofa as another wave of dizziness hit me. I bit back the sensation. Just a little longer...

Two rings and the phone clicked. "Tell me this is Kayli," Avery said on the line.

"How'd you know?"

"You're the only one who calls," he said.

Was his giving out business cards not working for him as a taxi driver? "Where are you guys?" I asked. "Is Ethan with you?"

"Yeah. We went to go check on the priest that married them to talk about the wedding license, but he's not home. He wanted to ask him about Alice's license. He tried calling her but she's not answering. Where are you?"

"At Ethan's house with Raven and Corey," I said. "We're upstairs. Alice is downstairs. She's with two guys. Bodyguards maybe."

Avery relayed the information to Ethan. Ethan said something back but it was muffled. "Okay, okay," Avery said. "We'll go there. Settle down. No need to bark."

"We need to know how to access the computer to the core," I said. "We need to make it look like we have something to negotiate with."

Avery didn't say anything for a minute, but then relayed, "She says Alice is helping them get to the bottom of it with Eddie." I almost corrected him, but then realized Avery was telling him exactly what he needed to hear to cooperate. "But they don't know how to access the computer. The one upstairs?"

There was more muffled conversation. I waited, listening for noises downstairs. I couldn't hear anything. Corey waited by the door, his ear pressed to it. Raven kept an eye on the car. My heart was in my throat, sending waves of dizziness through my tired brain.

"He says you use the security panel by the door," Avery said. "It comes up through the floor. Use code: 979627. It'll check for his face, though. Maybe you should wait."

C. L. Stone

"We've got that covered," I said and I relayed the information to Corey.

Corey picked up the paper with Ethan's face, and then entered in the digits. "Got it," he said.

The floor that Corey had picked out as the computer started to shift. From it arose a framework, servers that connected to each other, and wires running from each side back into the floor. With it came a small desk, and on it were two monitors.

"We got it," I said into the phone.

"Shit!" Raven said. "Eddie just pulled up. He's got three guys with them. They're surrounding the first car…One of them has Brandon."

Corey and I looked at each other. How? Brandon was with Alice. I groaned. If Corey needed more time, we had to give that to him. "Raven," I said, pulling the phone away from my ear. "Let's let them in. We'll go deal with them."

"No," Raven said. His fists clenched and he held them up like a boxer. He took a few swings toward the glass without striking at it. "Let's knock them out and take him."

"They aren't going to shoot Brandon if he can pretend to work on this core for a short time…" I gulped. We really had run out of time. "Corey needs more time to set it up. We'll stall them. Brandon won't work without leverage…And I guess I'm it."

"That's not an option," Avery said into the phone. "Kayli, don't you dare."

I dropped the phone further to smother out Avery's shouting. I focused on Raven, whose wild eyes were firing bullets down at the German team below. I dropped the phone to check out what was going on. Two of the goons had guns pointed in the first car that had stopped. The other people were trying to wrestle Brandon up the steps as he struggled against his bindings. Who was in the car?

Alice was inside, too. Eddie was going to run into her. There might be a firefight. Brandon would be in the middle of it.

"Raven," I said carefully, feeling his intensity. I reached for his arm, holding it firmly. "Listen, I need you to stay with Corey. Go help him and maybe call Kevin and update him."

"Why? I can't hold my gun steady if I'm not using two hands."

"Don't shoot them," I said. "If I give myself up, I think I can get Brandon to at least pretend to be hacking at this core. Or there might be another way. We might still get out of this." What I was having problems with was how Eddie got Brandon. Did he escape Alice only to run into Eddie?

Raven shook his head. "I'll be bait."

"I'm bait," I told him. "You're going to hide and shoot them if they try to kill us. You're the one with the gun."

Raven grumbled, long and loud, uttering words in Russian. "I don't like your plan," Raven said.

"You don't like planning, anyway."

He sighed looking down at the commotion going on. Brandon was still resisting. "That's going to be a lot of bodies to cart off. I should probably get a boat."

"No bodies!" I cried. I went and picked up the phone. "Avery?"

"I got you," he said. "What are you doing?"

"I'm handing you over to Raven."

"Uh oh."

"Raven will fill you in." I nodded to Raven and passed the phone over.

Raven gripped it in a fist. Then he grabbed me by my shirt, pulled me in and kissed my mouth. It was a short, but hard kiss, and he nipped my lip quickly at the end. He pulled back and stared at me. "Don't... die."

"Oh-kay," I said, exaggerating the word to match his tone, but I understood. I didn't want anyone to die either.

I looked over at Corey, who was by the computer. He touched the monitor which popped up with another password field.

I stopped by him just long enough to give him a quick hug and a kiss on the cheek. "You don't die, either."

Corey chuckled. "You're the one going down to the firing squad," he said. He reached into his pocket, pulling out a thick plastic Taser. "Take this with you, but don't let them see it. And be careful. I really don't like your plan, either."

Neither did I.

♠

SNEAKY

I had to use the security code and picture to get back out. Eddie and his team were making a racket downstairs. I slunk down the first flight of steps, using their noise to cover my footsteps. I stuck the Taser into my pocket. I couldn't use it to take out everyone, so I'd have to use it sparingly.

On the second floor landing, I snuck over into the hallway to hide myself from view. I didn't want to just run in.

I had gotten out of sight when I heard more voices, this time it was Alice.

"It's like the party hasn't ended," she said. "It was quite the wedding, wasn't it?"

"Do we really want to talk about that?" a voice said, that sounded like Eddie. "It was disgusting."

Alice spoke. "The champagne wasn't bad."

"It was French," Eddie said. "Should have picked a Cordon Rouge. Something from home."

Eddie didn't talk to Alice like he was afraid of her. He was here for the party?

I crouched down, crawling toward the stairwell, wanting to see what was going on.

I got a partial view of the room. Alice was confronting Eddie ahead of the two guys that must have followed her inside. One had a head full of white hair, no jacket, the other had dark hair, the clothes were more formal and stiff.

Another big man was nearby, holding onto Brandon. I imagined that was Mack Truck. Eddie and the other guy that had come in with him, I couldn't see.

Brandon was sweating, with duct tape over his mouth and his hands bound behind his back. He glared at Alice and at the others in the room around him.

"That's enough of that," the old man with Alice said. "Shouldn't we get down to business? We don't have much time."

"Don't we need your son?" Eddie asked. "To get inside the third floor?"

"Don't I look enough like my son?" the old man said.

My heart dropped. Ethan's father. He was working with Alice? It was hard to tell. Eddie didn't sound nervous and afraid of her, either.

Alice took Mr. Murdock's arm. Mr. Murdock, wore leather shoes, and expensive clothes. His lips were heavily lined as he frowned, his eyes beady. He was an old man who gave off the look of someone about to croak, but stood tall and those eyes could kill you if you stepped on his lawn.

"It may not be good enough," Alice said. "But if it isn't, your son is on the way. He sent me a text not too long ago."

I bit back a curse. We should have detoured Ethan. I considered going back and having Raven make a call to get them to hold back. Maybe they'd get delayed and we'd have more time.

"We don't want to involve him," Mr. Murdock said.

"What's one more body?" Eddie asked. "We've got three here to deal with after everything is over."

My heart sunk. This wasn't good. Three. Axel and Marc and Brandon. If Brandon was in here, where were the other two?

"What about the two outside?" Mr. Murdock asked. "The set in the car?"

"They wanted a piece of the action," Alice said. "One claimed he could give us access to the core if this one won't participate. They called to negotiate."

Who was in the car?

Brandon said something, unintelligible. Mack Truck shook him and jabbed him in the stomach.

"Nothing from the peanut gallery," Eddie said. He sighed. "We might need them. He's not willing, not even with his friends at risk."

"Let's get him and his buddies upstairs," Mr. Murdock said. "He may change his mind if we put a couple of holes in his friends while he's right there next to the computer."

Brandon shouted something through his taped mouth. I could almost hear the cursing flying, matching my own thoughts.

I weighed my options. They had Axel and Marc here, possibly in the trunks. Either Alice was negotiating with Eddie, or they were on the same team. Either way, this wasn't good. Mr. Murdock was involved, too.

Ethan had spent years defending his father from rumors. I got the feeling maybe Raven was right, and the rumors were true. And now he was duping his own son for a project he was working on.

Poor Ethan.

What could I do? I needed to distract them from going upstairs. The alarm might stall them a little, but if Mr. Murdock was able to dupe the face scanner... did he know about the computer in the floor? Could he access that, too?

I needed another set of hands. I wanted to get outside and see who was helping them, and at the same time, stall them from going upstairs to give Corey and Raven a chance to finish up what Corey needed to do.

Dizziness threatened to make me fall over. I clutched the wall. I needed to hurry before I couldn't stay awake any more.

♠

ONE DOWN, MORE TO GO

I retreated, taking the back staircase, and ended up in the kitchen. I glanced at the microwave. If I blew up this one, they might shoot first and ask questions later. Hopefully, I wouldn't be in the room, but I wasn't sure it was enough. I couldn't risk blowing up the entire thing like at Blake's house, and then have the police come in. I'd need just enough time to distract them downstairs so I could get outside and maybe free Axel and Marc.

Near the kitchen, on the other side of the hallway, was an entertainment room with a large television. I spotted a remote on a side table near the sofa. Two distractions. That might work. I needed one more, but I thought I could get Brandon to help me.

I started by sneaking over to grab the remote. In the kitchen, I took out just three eggs and put them in the microwave. Now I just needed my extra set of eyes and hands.

I crept as quietly as I could through the house while Alice and Eddie were still discussing things with Mr. Murdock downstairs.

I didn't want to get caught, but I needed Brandon's attention without the guards becoming aware so I could let him know help was here and that he had to distract them for as long as possible.

I found a door that led to the garage, and then came up with my plan. With my foot on the rear stairwell, I aimed the remote toward the widescreen television in the back room and hit the power button, and then pressed the volume up, hoping something interesting was on.

I got the news. The voice of the anchor reporting the weather got very loud really quickly. Good enough.

I shuffled up the stairs when I heard Eddie and someone else asking what the noise was about.

At the top of the stairs, Mack Truck was still holding onto Brandon, this time closer to the front door, like he was ready to take Brandon away if needed. Eddie, Alice's guard, Alice and Mr. Murdock were out of sight. I didn't know about the third guy with Eddie, but I assumed he was standing nearby still.

I angled myself on the steps to be in for Brandon's line of sight, but just out of view for Mack. I waved, and used the light in the remote that lit up to try to get his attention.

He blinked and his eyes drifted up. I smashed buttons on the remote, blinking at him again and again.

Finally he picked up his head, looking up at me.

I grinned, waved.

He started to shake his head, but dropped it quickly, checking himself. Slowly, his eyes went up but he kept his head even. He wasn't going to alert the guards that I was there. His eyes were dark now, cursing at me for risking my neck.

I pointed up. I made a C with my hand, and then a bird with both hands and pointed upstairs.

He gave me a microscopic nod.

I did my best to hand gesture. Pointing at my wrist to indicate time. I pointed at him and then at his goon and the ones in the living room and pointed to the ground floor. *Keep them downstairs.*

He paused as he looked at me, and then looked down. I wasn't sure if he understood that time.

Then suddenly Brandon dropped. He became a dead weight against Mack Truck. Mack Truck moved to catch him, but Brandon fell to the floor, almost face down. Pretending to have fainted?

Mack Truck shouted. Someone nearby, the third to Eddie's party, joined in. The TV was still running loud, and then cut off. They must have finally found the power buttons. More footsteps in the hallway. They were responding to Mack Truck.

At least Brandon would keep them busy. Hopefully he didn't get shot.

I raced back down the rear steps, stopping to scan the kitchen. It was empty. The TV was off. They were all probably back in the foyer.

Still, I snuck to the microwave. I hit the five minute button and then went for the hallway. The microwave hummed. How much time did it need before it blew?

For the fun of it, as I stood in the garage, I leaned over and I powered up the TV again. This time the sound was loud instantly.

I ducked into the garage and closed the door. Hopefully Brandon used this chaos to keep them contained. Time for round two.

♠

HELP

I slunk my way to the front of the garage doors, where there were windows, and peered out.

There were two men standing by the first car that had driven up. They had guns out, but were talking to each other. In the car, there were two more guys sitting in the driver and passenger seats.

Behind them were Blake and Doyle. Doyle looked like he was asleep with his head back against the seat. Blake had his arm up against the window of the car, his head on his palm. He was watching the guards, waiting.

My heart lifted but then dropped. There were more guys out here than I had thought. Axel and Marc… maybe they were in the trunks. I just needed a way to get rid of those guards…And for my eyes to stop crossing. I squeezed them tight, willing myself to stay moving and awake.

There were two garage doors, and then the car inside that was covered with a tarp. There were two buttons on the wall as well. Door openers.

I took the Taser out. I wasn't sure this would even knock them out completely, or just stun them for a minute. I also couldn't hit more than one guy.

I went back to the window. The men were still talking amongst themselves.

Blake, however, lifted his head, squinting at me. At least he was paying attention. His eyes were wide, questioning me from a distance.

Charades again. I sucked at this game. I checked out the men who were talking. I could lure one into the garage. I showed Blake my Taser, pointed to the guards, and held up one finger.

The guards were facing Blake, and while he could watch me, he couldn't signal back without drawing attention. He did, however, wake up Doyle. He said something to him. Doyle rolled his head, said something and then sat up, rubbing his eyes.

I moved back to the buttons, hovered my hand over them both and, aimed my body to be ready to run behind the car.

Smack.

Run for my life.

I ducked behind the car, and crab-walked the long way around toward the bumper and squatted.

Both doors opened with a loud hum. The men outside of the car turned toward it, looking confused.

Blake rolled down his window. "Hey," he said. "What's going on? Are we going in?"

One of the guys said something to the other. They split up. One went into the garage, the other moved toward Blake. The two additional men inside the car talked to the guard. There was a short conversation, and they got out, signaling to Blake and Doyle to get out of the car; they were all heading inside.

My heart was beating hard and fast. I might just have made this worse, but if Ethan and Avery were on the way, as were the Academy backup, then having people outside with guns when they showed up wasn't a good idea. My blood was pumping. I breathed, trying to steady myself.

The one that entered the garage did it slowly, with his gun out. He checked out around the corners. He took his time, covering his back.

Doyle and Blake were inside with more guards. I was on my own now. Taking one down was a start. At least then I'd have a gun.

I checked out the Taser, and was excited to find it was the kind that spat out barbs.

I snuck around the car, waited until the guy was on the steps, looking at the garage door buttons, and then aimed for his back.

I fired.

The barbs flew, connecting at the back. I wasn't too far from him, so it hit and latched onto him.

The man jerked, fell back, and landed on the ground. He dropped his gun. Because he fell on his back, and the current was still working on him, he was basically stuck with the Taser barbs in him.

I didn't really feel sorry for him.

I stepped around the car, still holding onto the Taser button so electricity was flowing through. I needed him down as long as possible.

I picked up the gun, a .45. I checked for the safety and then aimed it at the guy that was still down on the ground, his legs twitching. He moved slowly, still alive, but seemed to be having a hard time working his muscles.

I checked the garage, found duct tape on the wall and went for it.

Releasing the Taser's button and putting the black box on the ground, I moved to hover over the guard. I checked his pockets, finding a knife in a holster, some magazines with bullets inside, his wallet and cell phone, and a radio. I put those aside, out of his reach.

I taped his mouth first, and then taped up his wrists and ankles. And then I got tired and taped him to the ground around his back, thighs and biceps, using long strips. He might get up eventually, but it would take a lot of work. I found another tarp and draped it over him.

Totally obvious but at least the man was down and couldn't call for help.

I went to the door of the garage. No one came back outside. I wasn't sure if anyone was watching. Maybe Raven upstairs. I'd kept the gun, the knife and the man's radio. The others I tossed into the garbage can inside the garage. I'd almost kept the wallet. Old habits. Felt like a waste to throw it.

I held onto the radio in my pocket and carried the gun with me. The car was still, the second car was empty with everyone inside the house. I crossed my fingers that I could get at least Axel and Marc out. After that point, it would be a matter of getting everyone else out.

I slunk over to the car, opening the passenger door on the far side. I popped the trunk. I waited for a minute, just in case someone like Eddie noticed. When no one came rushing out with guns, I scurried over.

Axel and Marc were inside, tied up with black sacks over their heads. They were in the same clothes as the other day, only now their clothes were dirty. They were sweaty, and Marc's arms were bruised.

"Axel," I said. They were still. I was worried they were dead. Maybe we were too late for a cure.

Axel shot up. Marc did, too, mumbling something through the bindings.

I got Marc first, removing the hood and starting on his arms, using the knife to cut through. Marc sucked down air the moment I released the hood. He coughed hard, spitting and coughing again, I thought he was going to be sick.

"Did she poison you?" I asked. "Are you guys okay?"

"She said she did," Marc said. He wiped at his mouth and then stood up. His mismatched eyes looked watery. His nose had been bleeding at one point but now was just caked with dried blood. "I feel fine. Outside of the beating."

Axel mumbled something, nodding his head and showing me his bindings. I used the knife to cut him free.

The moment Axel's head was free, he was coughing, too. His long dark hair was mashed up against his sweaty face. I raked it away from his mouth and nose so he could breathe. "Thallium," Axel said first thing after his initial coughing spasm. He broke into another round soon after. He spoke between coughs as I cut through his arm bindings. "It's thallium. She's poisoned all of us."

"How?" Marc asked. "I don't feel bad. Just beaten up."

"We won't feel it," Axel said. He started to get up, and I assisted him until he was on the ground outside the trunk. "It takes days to go through your system before you'll react. I heard her talking about it when she thought we'd passed out. Everyone involved has been injected."

"Who?" I asked.

He spat and then looked up at me, his dark eyes thundering. "Everyone," he said. "Anyone who's been caught by them. Including you."

My stomach turned. I'd been tired, but I didn't feel sick... Or didn't think so for sure until now. Suddenly my stomach cramped and my tired body shook. I willed myself to forget it for now. "For how long?"

"Since you were picked up with Brandon. Eddie and his gang carried a vial, and injected you with it. Unless we get everyone to a hospital, we could die in a few days. That was her goal. Even if she faked letting us go, she would have killed us days later and it would look like we were all sick from something else." He fished in the trunk, pulled out a pair of glasses and put them on his face, blinking. His hair fell in front, giving him a wild look.

Fierce like a storm. "Where's Brandon? What's going on?"

I caught them up quickly on Corey's plan, about Raven with a gun watching him. "Brandon's still downstairs, creating a distraction to give them time, but Doyle and Blake just got escorted inside by three armed gunman."

"They killed Randall," Axel said. "But they'll have a hard time getting rid of all these bodies. Poison would be the perfect solution for them. Given at varying times. We wouldn't notice until it was too late and they'd gotten away. It's untraceable. The only ones who aren't affected are anyone she hasn't been able to capture."

"Raven and Corey," I said.

"And Kevin," Marc said. He was sitting on the ground, sucking in air and holding his guts. "I feel like shit."

They were both rolling around on the ground, pretty beaten up. There was no way they could help me with people on the inside.

"Ethan Murdock is on the way," I said. "And Avery. Kevin is heading in with Academy people. They should be almost here."

"We'll have to head in ourselves," Axel said. "We have to stop it before it becomes a hostage situation."

"You can't go in like that," I said.

Marc grabbed Axel's arm. "We need people to come out, not go in. We need a plan to get them to let hostages go."

"They were going to let them go if they got what they wanted, right?" I asked.

"Maybe," Axel said. "They aren't beyond shooting anyone." He spat again and shook his head, pressing a palm to his neck. "You said Raven's inside?"

"Yeah," I said. "Corey's working on the core. It should be done soon. We just need them to think they've gotten what they want. We need to stop Brandon from getting shot before then."

"Then you'll have to listen carefully," Axel said. He swallowed, coughed and then swallowed again. "Because I have to teach you how to manipulate terrorists in two minutes."

♠

SICK

*A*xel was hanging back behind the car and waiting for Avery and Ethan to show up with their part in the plan. Marc was covering us from the back. The goal was simple: One by one if needed, get anyone captured safely outside without alerting the guards.

Easier said than done. I was about to go back inside and direct the plan from the inside. Get anyone not captured, like Raven and Corey, on the same page.

I fought off a wave of dizziness. I had the knife. Marc had the gun, and Axel went for the cell phone in the trash to contact Kevin.

I was in the garage when the radio I'd been holding went off. I turned down the volume and listened. It was in German, unhelpful. It wouldn't be long before they came to look for their buddy. Axel was in no condition to take him out. And Marc couldn't shoot anyone without people hearing it and coming to see what was going on.

I peeked in through the door inside the garage. No one appeared to be in the hallway or the kitchen. There was talking inside, but further away and I couldn't hear.

There was a smell coming from the kitchen. Eggy. I guessed the exploding microwave thing worked. It meant they were on guard now. I'd have to be careful.

I went for the back stairs, stopped halfway up, and listened closely.

"Your guards are idiots," Blake said. "She used a Taser and got one outside. He's sick behind the garage puking his guts out. That's why he's not answering."

I cringed. He was telling them I was here? Now they'd be on the lookout.

A male voice cut in, speaking German. It echoed on my radio and I turned the volume down to a whisper.

"You know," Doyle's voice came through. "I could go check on him. I need a smoke anyway."

"No one is going anywhere," Mr. Murdock said. "Everyone gets to go upstairs. We'll handle this quietly. We just need to make those adjustments to this core. Everyone gets to walk away after. No fuss."

"That sounds like a reasonable solution," Alice said. "We won't need to worry about the annoying bug if everyone is upstairs and we've cut her off."

I gulped. I needed to get upstairs before they did. I'd be trapping myself in with the rest of them, and there weren't that many places to hide. I wasn't sure how I'd get out of there with everyone if they locked us all in upstairs.

I scurried up while they were still talking. I used the printout of Ethan's face and then pressed the code.

I got behind the door, locking it again. Maybe it'd delay them for a minute.

I checked the room. Raven and Corey were missing. The computer was back in the floor. Had they left?

I heard a cough somewhere in the room. I couldn't source it, but then I heard voices behind me on the stairwell.

"He's not getting up," Eddie was saying.

"Punch him again. He'll get up." That was Mr. Murdock.

I ground my teeth. I'd shoot them both in the face.

"Hey there," Blake called. "Someone need some help? Is that a control pad? Do you guys know the password? Let me take this one. No, he's fine. Look, he'll walk. Doyle, help me."

Eddie spoke. "Alice, they're your people. They're getting your cut, not mine."

Maybe they weren't working as closely together as I thought.

I found a couch to hide behind, close to the door. I wanted to be able to have access. I wasn't sure how else to get them to escape, but I got a good view of the room from behind the sofa next to one of the windows.

Mr. Murdock spoke. "Let's just get everyone inside."

"We need the passcode," Alice said. "Won't you be a dear and type it in quickly for us?" She pointed to the third floor. "Before your son gets here."

"My son is a moron," Mr. Murdock said, disgust thick in his tone. "He's an ungrateful bastard who doesn't get how the world works. You have to kick a few balls to get ahead."

"Let's get this over with," Eddie said.

"We're going to trust these guys?" Mr. Murdock asked, walking up the steps.

"This one," Alice said, "is about to beat your little security dog into submission. So type in the password and we can get going."

"Where to?" Mr. Murdock asked. "Back to the cabin? Where I can shit in a pot and eat nothing but frozen dinners? I didn't work this hard to go back to living like a Neanderthal." He coughed, though underneath, it sounded like swearing and muttering. There was a small noise as each time he hit a number on the security pad.

The alarm beeped and then quieted.

The door opened, and I pulled back, waiting. From under the sofa, I spotted feet coming inside. Lots of them. This was going to be harder than I thought. I wedged myself further into the corner, just so I could look between the sofa arm and a side table.

Mr. Murdock stood by the security panel. He typed in another passcode and then the computer lifted from the floor again. "You shouldn't need me now."

"We should stay for a minute," Alice said. "Just in case anything else comes up. I've got a plan, and we don't need anyone leaving early."

"If I wanted to watch a moron type at a computer for an hour, I'd have watched my kids with their games and their Facebooks." He looked at Brandon, who was being dragged in by Mack Truck and then pushed down on one of the sofas, sitting in it and folding his arms. "Just get it over with already. I want to get out of here."

Brandon glared at everyone. His face had more cuts. I wondered if his poison would work faster if he was beaten like that. He was slightly shaking his head. I realized he didn't know what was going on but he was still trying to resist. Then I spotted his eyes going up, down, left... He was looking for Raven and the others without making it obvious. It probably looked like Blake and Doyle had teamed up with the bad guys as well. Hopefully he knew better.

I stared hard at him, looking calm.

Slowly, as Brandon scanned the room, he passed me once, and then his eyes came back. He squinted. Slowly, I smiled, and then winked.

Brandon frowned at me and I could tell he didn't like me being up here.

While Doyle looked over the two monitors, Blake and the others watched over him. I wasn't really sure what to do at this point. There were five guards now with guns, including Mack Truck; way too many to mess with. I didn't know if Eddie had a gun, but he wore a jacket, which could have concealed one in a back holster. From what I could tell, Mr. Murdock's pocket had a wallet on one side, a cell phone in the other. Alice had a cell phone in her right front pocket. No purse. Unless she kept a gun between her breasts, she was unarmed.

Only Raven had a gun up here, and since he'd used up bullets at Blake's house, I wasn't sure if he had many left, if any at all. Hopefully he brought more, but one gun wasn't going to take many of them out if they started firing, even if he was Russian.

But it wouldn't really work if they left before we came up here.

I scanned the room, and then I noticed Brandon was still staring at me from across the room. Then he dragged his eyes up toward the ceiling. I followed his gaze.

Raven was above the group, in the ceiling, hanging from a couple of exposed metal beams above us. They were so high up, I wasn't sure how he'd gotten up there. He caught my eyes instantly, giving me a thumbs up, ready to go.

Corey wasn't with him, though. I checked the room again for him. I glanced once more up at Raven. He quietly pointed to Brandon and then held up ten fingers, mouthed the word 'minutes', and then nine fingers, eight fingers: a countdown.

I nodded. We needed ten minutes for something to happen.

I checked around, and noticed the phone was missing. While I couldn't see him, I thought Corey must be behind that sofa, using the phone as a communication line.

"Can I sit?" Blake asked. "Is that allowed?"

"Everyone can sit," Alice said. "No pressure here. If everyone does what they're supposed to, no one needs to be harmed."

Eddie snorted. He must have known about the poison. Bastard.

Blake started toward the sofa that I suspected Corey was behind. Brandon coughed through his taped-up mouth, looked right at Blake and shook his head just the slightest bit.

Blake got the gist, and rerouted to the other side, closer to where I was.

A gunman followed him; his own a personal guard. He stood in front of Blake, his gun drawn.

Mack Truck moved next to Brandon. Brandon grunted, sitting back, breathing deeply through his nose.

I gulped quietly as Mack Truck took his gun out and watched over him.

It felt like the execution line. Wasn't exactly how I thought it would work out.

Up in the rafters, Raven looked unhappy.

I looked at Blake, who was staring out the windows. "Nice view," he said. "Makes me want to sit here quietly and watch the sunrise."

I looked at Brandon who nodded curtly; he agreed with this.

I nodded from behind the couch. For now, lay low and wait. Seemed everyone on our team was aware who was in the room now. We'd have to trust each other to get out of this.

Brandon closed his eyes. He did nothing. I wondered if he had passed out sitting up. I was peeling my eyes open every couple of seconds. I was fighting sleep, too.

He'd fought to slow them down when I asked, getting beaten in the process. I could have kissed him then for being one of the bravest guys I'd ever known.

Doyle stared at the two monitors. He tapped at the screen. "A pop-up keyboard? What is this shit? The man can't afford a proper keyboard?"

"This new technology is a bitch," Mr. Murdock said. "Just do your job."

Doyle groaned, but focused on the screen. He stabbed at it with his fingers as he worked. "I need a cigarette."

"Please hurry," Alice said. "And no smoking."

"It's not like this is rocket science. That shit is easy to read. This is code. It's going to take a minute."

"Will it take a shorter or longer amount of time with a bullet in your leg?" Eddie asked.

"Longer," Doyle said, although he was still reading the screen. "Because I'd be in pain, and I don't like that."

"What if we shot your friend?" Eddie asked, motioning to Blake. "Would that motivate you?"

"Shoot him," Doyle said. "I don't like his hair. It's too shiny."

Blake groaned softly.

Doyle continued to study the computer and occasionally made comments, usually complaining that the code was crap.

I glanced up at Raven, who was hanging up there. He was pretty exposed. With everyone lounging around, one of the guards might spot him.

Suddenly, there was a sound downstairs.

"Hello?" someone called. "Honey? Alice? You home?

Ethan. My eyes widened, I looked up at Raven.

He gave me a thumbs up.

There was a thunder of footsteps on the stairs. Mr. Murdock went to the panel, putting the computer back into the floor. Mack Truck and the other goon repositioned themselves, guns drawn but behind the wall in the middle, on the other side of the door. The dragged Brandon with them.

"Everyone else stay calm," Alice said. "Hide your guns and try to smile. I'll take care of him."

The other guards that were exposed put their guns at their sides, sitting down on the sofas.

C. L. Stone

In came Ethan Murdock, followed closed by a dressed-up man behind him, and on Ethan's other side so I couldn't see who he was.

Ethan spotted his father, Alice, and then Eddie. He looked at everyone on the sofa. "Who's here? Leftovers from the party?" He turned to his dad and beamed. "Dad! You made it. I thought you were in Brazil."

"Change of plans," Mr. Murdock said. "The wedding and all. I came up to check out the observatory. I wouldn't have decorated it this way, but there's no accounting for taste."

Doyle on the couch still, picked up his head. "Are there leftovers from this party? I don't suppose I could get a whiskey. You know, something expensive and obviously disgusting but gets you drunk faster."

"Is this your relative?" Ethan asked. He turned to Alice. "Alice. Sweetie. Are you okay? Did they wake you? I thought I left you sleeping."

I cringed, and made a face. I wasn't sure if this was a good idea.

"Ethan," Mr. Murdock said, standing. He held out his hands. "He's got a good idea. I need a drink, too."

Ethan shrugged, but his eyes were on his wife. "Do you want to join us? We could all go downstairs."

Raven caught my attention by waving and then made a motion with his hand, pointing to the guy that had come in with Ethan.

I couldn't see without leaning over more. I waited until I was sure no one was paying attention and then leaned further.

His hair was slicked back, and his face was freshly shaven, but once I saw his face, I realized it was Avery. He wore a dark suit coat and slacks like the others.

Alice and Eddie looked at him, but since he came in with Ethan, I supposed they couldn't very well ask who he was when they had several of their own goons in the room. They seemed to dismiss him, maybe assuming he was a friend of Ethan's, another party guest.

My head snapped up to Raven. Avery. What about him?

Raven looked confused, shook his head and gave me a thumbs up.

I couldn't focus on him for too long since I was afraid one of the others would catch me. I sank back and when I was hidden, I looked up again. Raven was giving Avery another thumbs up. Then he pointed to me, to Alice and then to me again. He gave me a thumbs down. He did it again.

I was getting frustrated. I didn't know what he meant.

Avery wasn't moving or talking. He stood beside Ethan, still, like an assistant or driver. He was waiting for something to happen.

I groaned inwardly. I was going to have to tackle someone. I was so tired. My head was spinning. Why couldn't Blake do it?

Blake, however, had his sights on Eddie and then the guard.

As quiet as a spider, Raven made his way across the rafters to hover right over where Mack Truck was.

"Do you still want to see the sunrise?" Ethan asked his father, and then looked at Alice. "Should we make some coffee for our guests? The sun coming up over the ocean is beautiful. We should grab some breakfast downstairs and bring it up here."

The guard next to Blake started to shift.

"Easy," Blake whispered. "Everyone just hold back."

The man next to him muttered something in German.

Mr. Murdock sliced his hand through the air. "Enough." He grabbed his son's shoulder and directed him to the stairs. "Why don't you and I go downstairs and grab this coffee. We'll come back up in a minute."

"Sure," Ethan said. He looked at Alice. "Alice? Want to come along?"

He was trying to get his dad and Alice downstairs. Either there was a trap set for them, or Ethan was trying to get Alice out before something big happened. I had a sinking feeling maybe he still believed his wife was innocent.

Alice held up her hand. "I'll stay up here and keep our guests company." She winked and smiled at him.

"It might take more than two of us to carry it all upstairs."

Alice turned to the guard that was near Blake. The guard stood, keeping his gun behind his back. "He'll help," Alice said. "Won't you, Cousin Jim?"

The corner of Ethan's mouth dipped but he recovered it quickly.

But if Axel and Marc were downstairs... maybe the plan could be to get people downstairs one at a time, even if it were the guards or Alice. If we couldn't get hostages out, we could at least reduce the number of bad guys in the room.

Alice did approach Ethan and gave him a kiss. Then she hugged Mr. Murdock. "It's great to have a sweet father-in-law."

Alice's movements seemed stiff while Mr. Murdock grunted.

And then I caught Alice's hand as she slipped something into his pocket. She patted at it once and then released him.

It had looked like a prescription bottle. The poison. She passed it to Mr. Murdock, either to hang on to, or Ethan was about to get a dose.

Once Ethan had started to head down the stairs with Mr. Murdock and the extra guard, Alice closed the door. She pushed a series of buttons on the panel and the desk started to rise again. She turned to Eddie. "He doesn't suspect."

"Not yet," Eddie said. "But we should hurry."

"His father will keep him contained," Alice said. "But you're right. If we get this done now, we can go downstairs." She turned to Brandon and Doyle, but addressed everyone. "Keep calm, gentlemen. We'll get out of this unscathed yet. Just deliver what you promised."

Ethan hadn't seemed bothered with Eddie being there. He might have been around before now. As a friend of Alice's no doubt. That meant they'd been working together for a while. And with Alice marrying Ethan, she had a chance to take her time with getting into the core

So why did the game change? Why suddenly kidnap everyone? My head felt hot and I was sucking in air slowly, fighting my need to simply ay on the floor and sleep. Plain and simple, Alice and Eddie had manipulated us. Hate burned in my heart at being duped. I was angry for Ethan, who seemed innocent, for falling into their little trap.

I looked up, seeking out Avery, but he was gone. Had he left with Ethan?

Eddie came over to Doyle. "Are you done yet?"

Doyle shrugged. "I got distracted. Hard to focus with everyone coming and going."

"Look," Eddie said. "Just get rid of the security packet. That's all we need."

"I know," Doyle said. He tapped at the monitor. "It's a real pain in the ass. Tell me about it. I'm looking at it right now. It's not like pushing a button. You have to pull the code from the core without it flipping out and shutting down. It's like brain surgery...hence why I was asking for the whiskey."

I was watching, waiting, when I spotted Avery slinking along the far side, going around the center walls that hid the stairwell. Avery low, ducked behind a couch.

I kept an eye on him. He was circling behind Mack Truck and one of the other goons. There were still plenty of people with guns up here, even if two people were downstairs now, hopefully getting taken out by Axel or Marc.

What now?

Raven signaled to me. Giving me a thumb's up. We were good to go. I didn't know what he wanted at first, but he then pointed to Doyle and gave me another thumbs up and then a slice across the throat. He wanted Doyle to stop.

Blake was alone on the couch right now. I reached up quietly, and eased my hand on the back of his neck. I wrote my name on his skin.

Blake stayed perfectly still. If he knew I was behind him, he wasn't going to give my position away.

I released him. While Alice and Eddie were busy, I inched up as close as I dared to the back of his head and whispered.

"Tell Doyle to fail. Now."

Blake coughed, looking at Doyle.

Doyle ignored him, looking at the screen.

Alice and Eddie were talking quietly to each other. I sank back as Mack Truck started to circle the room, moving closer to Blake, gun raised. They stayed out of line of sight of the door though. Apparently they were expecting Ethan to possibly come back and wanted to hide again just in case.

Raven above kept quiet and moved, staying above wherever Mack Truck was.

Blake coughed again.

Doyle slid a look to him. "Do you need a drop? Because I don't have one."

Blake made a face and then winked. I only caught his cheeks bunching, but I took a guess he was signaling to him what we needed.

Doyle straightened up, tapped several keys, hit the enter key and stood. "Okay," he said to the group. "I'm done. This is stupid."

Eddie and Alice turned. Mack stayed where he was with the gun pointed down, but clearly keeping an eye on Blake now. The other men came around, two with Alice and Eddie, and the other keeping by where they'd stashed Brandon on the other side.

Avery slipped, silently behind where Doyle had been sitting, staying close.

Alice and Eddie came over to Doyle to look at what he was doing.

Doyle showed them a moving screen with lots of code in it. "That's what you wanted, isn't it? Well, guess what? Unless we've got a magic lamp, there's a brick wall."

Eddie stared at it and then spoke to Alice. "You mean the security packet can't be dropped?"

"You want it to keep operating while dropping the encryption?" Doyle asked. "Check this shit out. It's designed to stop working if the signals can't be protected. It's a safety feature built in. The moment I take this out, it'll stop the service."

Alice leaned in, studying the code. "Yes," she said. She made a kissing face with her mouth. "But look at the volume of calls coming through. Sweet husband, you have been busy. I never knew how many you really sold your service to."

"What is it?" Eddie asked. "It's the data?"

C. L. Stone

"Yes," Alice said. She pointed at the screen. "See that? Lots of it. This is better than I thought." She stood up. "At least we know it is there." She turned to Doyle. "So you're saying you can't do the rest?"

"I could puke on it and short it all out," Doyle said. "Because it'll be about as effective as anyone reaching in and trying to take out that encryption. Might as well pull the plug."

"Not yet," Alice said. She turned to Brandon. "I bet Corey could help us. Sorry, gentlemen. I'm afraid your services aren't required after all."

Blake stood up. Mack Truck pointed his gun at him, but Blake waved him off. "Hang on a second. We got you this far."

"But you didn't deliver what you promised," Alice said. She looked once at the guards with guns. "Take them downstairs, put them in a room on the second floor without being seen by anyone on the first floor. Keep them contained."

The two gunmen escorted Blake and Doyle to the door. Eddie, Alice, Mack Truck and one more goon were left. They were outnumbered, but with the guns, we couldn't exactly jump them. At least they were splitting up. I wasn't sure if Axel and Marc could take on two men with guns in their condition, but hopefully they had backup on the way, if not here already.

Brandon was alone now as a hostage. He glared at them, hate raging from his eyes.

"Well," Alice said. "We've got a conundrum, don't we?"

"Let's bring one of his friends upstairs," Eddie said. "We could shoot him once every time he stops working. I'll start with the foot and work up."

Alice looked at Brandon for the longest time and then shook her head. "No," she said. "That won't work. He thinks we won't keep our promise about letting them go if they only behaved. So we'll have to find him a little more motivation."

"Maybe I should start shooting *him* in the foot," Eddie said.

"He doesn't really need his foot to work, I suppose," Alice said. She sighed. "I'm afraid it's come to this. Use one of the sofa pillows, will you? It'll keep it quiet and then you can use it to keep the blood contained."

Brandon started to shout, squirming, yelling and cursing at them, even with his mouth taped.

I saw a hand wave and then looked up. Raven was pointing at me, and then at Alice. I was supposed to distract her somehow?

And then suddenly across the room, Corey snuck around the corner by the door, and opened it, darting past it as people turned around. "Wait," he said, standing to look like he'd just walked in.

Damn it. I bit back the urge to yell at him. Raven looked upset. I was supposed to be the one to stand, not Corey. I'd been too late. Corey couldn't help but get up and protect his brother.

Guns moved from Brandon to Corey. Corey lifted his hands up in the air. His cerulean eyes fixed on his brother, though he spoke to the others. "Let him go. I'm the one you want."

♠

STRUGGLE

*A*lice and Eddie did a circle around Corey.

"It's his brother," Eddie said. "It's a trick. We checked. We've got Corey. He's got the same cuts I gave him the first time we nabbed him from his room."

"I'm Corey," Corey said. "You've got Brandon. I've been trying to track you all for days."

"How do we know you're him?" Alice asked. "Prove it?"

"How do you think I found you?" Corey asked. He motioned to Eddie. "I remember you. From the park. I was there with my girlfriend."

"No," Eddie said. He pointed to Brandon. "He was the one I grabbed from the bedroom with the girl. I put a tracker on him and he still had one on when we caught him again. This is Corey."

"I followed the encrypted cell phone signal," Corey said. "I traced it here. Who else could do that? You didn't give me much information to go on. Just a name: Randall Jones."

Alice stood still for a minute, considering. She tapped a finger against her cheek, and then pointed to Corey. "If you say you're Corey, you can help us with our little problem, can't you?"

"Let my brother go and I'll help," he said.

Alice smiled coyly. "Such a hero," she said. "But I think it'd be better if we kept your brother here, for now. It seems he's having trouble walking on his own."

"I can make it harder on him," Eddie said. One of the goons raised his gun toward Brandon's leg.

Corey's eyes widened and he held his hands out. "Hang on. I'm not going to help if you shoot him."

Out of the corner of my eye, I could see Raven moving above. He quietly shifted, positioning himself above Eddie and Mack Truck.

Avery had stilled behind the couch that Brandon was still sitting on.

"What should we do?" Eddie asked Alice.

"Hmm," Alice said. "I think we should let this new Corey take a stab at it. I'll watch him and make sure he doesn't do anything funny."

Corey moved to the core computer. He looked over the information flowing in front of him. "I'm still catching up," he said. "But I'm guessing you want the security removed?"

"Without turning off the core and alerting users that the system is down," Alice said. "We want them to continue using their cell phones."

I checked in with Raven. He held a fist out and then spread out his fingers and lowered them. Lay low. The game plan had changed. We're giving them what they want.

I was bitter at the idea of letting them escape.

A wave of dizziness took over me. I clamped a palm over my forehead. Just a little longer.

Corey looked over the screens. "What's to say you won't shoot us both when I'm done?"

"I have no desire to deal with blood and dead bodies," Alice said. She looked at Eddie. "But he will if he has to." She turned back to Corey, her lips puckered and then she spoke. "Give us access to the core, and we all walk away. Ethan gets his home back. I will quietly disappear. Eddie will go home. Everyone will forget about us, or we'll come after you. Our access to the phone system will go unnoticed. No one else has to get hurt for this."

"Ethan will notice," Corey said.

"It's why I'm his wife," Alice said and smiled. "I'll keep him busy long enough."

"I'd just like a little assurance," Corey said. "Randall Jones died."

"An accident," Eddie said. "He fought us off, or tried. Doesn't have to happen again."

Corey lifted a brow. He smoothed out this Mario Bros. T-shirt and sighed. "Guess I'm not going to be given a choice. But I feel uncomfortable with my brother up here and a gun pointed at him."

The gunman moved his weapon, pointing it at Corey instead.

I glanced up at Raven, who was mouthing curses.

We needed a way to motivate Alice and Eddie to walk out of here without killing anyone. Just giving them what they wanted didn't guarantee that.

I looked at Raven for help, but he was focused on the gunman trained on Corey. He had his own gun out, aiming down.

This was going to turn into a blood bath quickly, if Raven lost his patience and temper. Maybe he was good with a gun, but he was still outnumbered and none of the rest of us had weapons.

Axel had said the goal was to give them exactly what they wanted, and to walk away. We could case them later when we got everyone cleared of harm. What we needed was for Alice and her team to actually leave the premises without any hostages.

I studied Alice, who was looking at the screen and then at Corey. She curled her fingers at him. "Come sit next to me," she said. She sat near the computer. The goon guarding Brandon pulled him down onto the floor. Alice patted the spot near her. "We'll do this together."

Corey eyeballed his brother and then settled near the computer, checking out the screens. He pressed at the monitor. "The encryption is pretty integrated."

"Can it be taken out?" Alice asked.

Corey tilted his head, thinking. "Maybe. It'll take a few minutes to see."

Alice held something in her hands, I saw a glint of something glass. She must have had more of that poison. She was going to give it to Corey somehow.

Avery moved then, quietly. He was right next to Alice.

He held something, a similar looking bottle. He was going to try to swap it out?

Avery the magician.

He needed a distraction though.

I was on the farthest side of the room. I considered what I had. The radio...

I pulled it from my pocket and fiddled with the buttons, but keeping the frequency. I pressed the call button, and rubbed my finger quietly over the mouthpiece.

A radio in the room went off. It crackled with noise.

Eddie pulled it from his pocket, adjusting the volume. He pushed the button and spoke into it. "Who's that? Check in."

When he released the button, he got more of the same crackling. I held the button down. If I kept the line busy, it meant they couldn't communicate with people downstairs.

"Fuck this core," Eddie said. "It's messing with our signal or something."

"Or something happened downstairs," Alice said. She placed her poison on the sofa next to her to pat Corey. "Don't pay any attention."

There was a quick movement. Avery reached over the arm, replacing the poison.

I turned off the signal, and then pushed the button, sliding my finger across, trying to make different noises.

"Someone should go check on them," Eddie said.

"No one moves," Alice said. "We're going to get out of here soon."

It wasn't much, but at least Alice didn't have her poison. I was wondering if she even carried the cure.

She looked back at Corey, who was typing at the monitor. "Is it working yet?"

"I'm not taking out the code," Corey said. "If you want him to be able to continue using it and not notice it's been altered, you'll need the security packet to stay in place."

"Maybe you aren't as smart as I thought you were," Alice said. "I thought I made it clear that we want access to the data."

"I'm not taking out the packet," Corey said. "I'm changing it. It still secures the line, but it reroutes information to a single phone." He looked up. "Tell me where you want the information sent to."

Alice squinted at him. She looked at Eddie and then back at Corey. "What do you mean?"

"You'll be part of the data collection," Corey said. "You'll get part of the information."

"We don't want *part*," Eddie said. "She wants all of it."

Corey shook his head. "How were you going to access the data, even if I simply left the encryption open? It only flows through here."

"That's why I married Ethan," she said. "To stay here and collect data in pieces while I could, learning passcodes and secrets as I wished."

"Look," Corey said. He pointed at the screen. "You won't have to do that. If I make a cell phone able to pick up chunks of data, you'll be able collect some on the go. You don't have to stay. To users, it'll look like the service stalled a minute, but it'll pick back up. They'll just have to hit refresh."

"And Ethan won't notice?" she asked.

"Nope," Corey said. He gave off a smile, a little crooked. He was forcing it. "You could walk away. Pick up the cell phone data from anywhere. You'll just have to remember to clear your memory every once in a while. It won't be everything, but it's sacrificing all data for mobility."

Eddie coughed and then shook his head. He nudged Alice's arm. "That's not what you wanted," he said. "You can stay here and collect the data from the source. What's to say he won't just make it not work once we're gone?"

Alice considered this, staring at Corey, as if weighing out his proposition. "We don't need all of the data here," she said. "A little at a time to make use of...And all directed to a singular cell phone."

"Just tell me the number where to send the data," Corey said. "The security dog packet will remove the encryption just before the last tower, and the final destination of the receiving call. That means you pick it up after the encryption.

"Let's see if it can do what we want first," Alice said. "Show me."

Eddie frowned, grumbled, and walked over to the window, looking out.

Corey was giving them a chance to walk away. My heart was in my throat. The dizziness was trying to take over. I glanced at Brandon, still on the ground. He had his eyes closed, unmoving.

Corey looked down at his brother. He nudged him with a foot. Brandon wasn't moving. "What did you do to him?" Corey asked.

"He's tired," Alice said. "Been up for days. Don't mind him."

Possibly poisoned. I had a suspicion…did the poison work faster the more stress you were under?

My heart was thudding. Was I being poisoned slowly now, too? Being exhausted, my body wouldn't be able to fight it much.

Corey frowned and then focused on the screen. "I need the number. Who will be getting the data?"

"I should," Eddie said.

"Nonsense," Alice said, and she smiled sweetly, looking at Eddie. "I should. I'm the only one who could possibly use it."

"I don't trust you," Eddie said. "I'll give you the data a little at a time. When you get something good from it, I'll give you more."

Alice's lips twitched. I gathered she didn't like being told what to do. "Okay," she said.

Eddie gave Corey the number. He typed it in.

Moments later, Eddie's cell phone started buzzing to life. He pulled it from his back pocket.

I got an eyeful of the gun he had in a holster behind him. So he did have a weapon.

Eddie checked his phone, scowling. "What's this?"

Corey stood. This caused a reaction from the guard to aim his gun closer in warning. Corey held up his hands. "I'll just take a look," he said. "To make sure it's working."

The guard looked at Alice, who nodded. The guard lowered his gun.

Corey leaned over, looking at Eddie's screen. "Yeah," he said, and pointed to the phone. "See? You're getting in text messages like they're being delivered to you. Open up your browser."

Eddie did. "It's moving on its own."

"Every window you open, it'll show you someone else's use of it. What you're seeing is a live stream of someone else's cell phone's signals being sent out. Flashes of websites from across the network. Except now…" He pointed lower on the screen. "The encrypted data isn't there."

"I can see a password," Eddie said. He showed it to Alice. "Someone's bank account."

Alice smiled. "Surprisingly useful."

"The information will be random," Corey said, "but you'll be able to get it from anywhere in the city. You'll just have to be within range of one of Ethan's active towers."

"So we can't go overseas?" Eddie asked. "Back home?"

Corey shook his head. "You'll lose contact with the right towers. It won't work."

"We can't go far," Alice said. "But we don't have to stay here."

"But again," Eddie said, putting the cell phone in his pocket, "you should stay. Don't arouse suspicion."

"You know, Eddie," Alice said, rising slowly. "I'm getting tired of you believing you're smarter than I am."

Eddie backed up a step, scowling. "Don't get stupid," he said. "We're almost out of here."

"I've got what I came for," she said. "Mr. Murdock and I can leave now."

"I've got what you want," Eddie said. "This is my protection. You weaseled your way in far enough. If you want a piece of this, you'll have to leave my men alone and we'll split this evenly. I don't trust you to simply walk away—"

Alice snapped her fingers. Mack Truck and the other goon moved instantly, pointing guns at Corey, and at Eddie.

Eddie started to reach for his gun, but Mack Truck stepped up, loaded a bullet into the chamber by cocking his gun, and aimed square at Eddie's chest. He said something in German I couldn't understand, but the threat was obvious.

Eddie slowly put his hands in the air, and then barked something back at Mack Truck, also in German. Mack took out Eddie's gun from his back holster, and tossed it onto another couch nearby.

Well, that was one guy down. I checked with Raven. He showed me a fist, and hand down. *Wait.*

I groaned internally. I was so tired of waiting. Waves of dizziness was washing over me now. I wasn't going to survive much more of this. I pinched myself to keep awake and to focus.

"What do you expect me to do?" Eddie said to Alice. "You expect me to sit here and let you walk out?"

"Yes," Alice said. "Although not without motivation. Your friend is going to sit here with you for a while." She winked at Mack Truck.

Eddie glared at Mack Truck. I wasn't sure if Mack Truck was a traitor, or if he'd always been on Alice's team and worked with Eddie to see through their plans.

"Where are you going to go?" Eddie asked.

"I'm going to go for a drive with my friend, Brandon," she said and gestured to Brandon lying on the floor at her feet.

Corey stood then, but a goon pointed a gun at his face. He ignored it and glared at her. "You said you wouldn't hurt him."

"I don't plan on it," she said. She nodded to a second goon, who lifted Brandon up by the arm, and draped him over his shoulder.

Corey flexed his hands and then made fists. "Stop," Corey said. "Don't take him."

"Be a good boy," Alice said, stepping back toward Eddie. She went into his pocket, pulling out the phone. She put it in her own pocket and then moved toward the door. "But I didn't trust you to let the information continue while I was away. So I'm taking a little...insurance."

"I'll find you," Corey said.

"Don't," Alice said. She smirked. "I'll have your brother. If the data stream stops, or if someone comes looking for your brother, he'll die. When I am satisfied, I'll let him go. And you'll have no other choice but to believe me. After today, you won't see me again.'

Corey moved toward her, but the guard put his gun at his chest, threatening. Corey stopped, baring his teeth.

My heart was going wild. Another wave of dizziness. The room spun.

Raven was above Mack Truck, and was signaling to me. My eyes crossed. I wasn't able to see exactly what he wanted. I was fighting the dizziness and nausea. A hot flush broke out over my body and I felt a bead of sweat slide down my back.

The poison must have been working faster. And with me being so tired, I wasn't going to last long at all.

Alice headed for the door. "Everyone stays here for a whole day," she told Mack Truck. "Let them enjoy the view, then at sunset, walk out and lock them in. I'll keep Ethan busy for a while so he won't come up."

Mack nodded.

Alice opened the door, holding it for the gunman that had Brandon as he walked through. Alice kept her eyes on everyone, taking the second goon's gun to aim. Mack backed away from Eddie, and guided Corey and Eddie into the same corner to keep them together.

Last chance. I checked on Raven, who was following Mack.

Avery appeared then, close to where the door was on my side, covered by the wall.

Avery pointed to me, pointed to Alice. He pointed to himself, and the gunman. He started to count down from five on his hand. Four. Three.

I started to sneak out from behind the couch. Take out Alice. No problem.

Before Avery could count to one, there was a shout from the first guard, followed by a quick thumping and crash on the stairs.

Brandon!

I had no time to think about it. I launched myself at Alice, aiming my feet at her knees and then grabbed for the bun on her head.

She screamed, and bent backward, reaching around, trying to grab for me.

I caught Avery sailing past me, using his arm and ramming the door into the second guard.

Mack tried to turn, but suddenly Raven flew down on top of him, and as soon as he landed, he was tossing Mack's gun away and punching. Eddie joined in. Corey was after Avery, trying to help him.

It was all I caught before Alice reached back, using a flat palm against the side of my head. A wave of dizziness took over me. I wasn't going to last.

Then I remembered Brandon and being the dead weight on Mack Truck. Drop dead fainting was something I could do right now.

I grabbed Alice by her shoulders. I hung on tight and then dropped to the floor

Alice fell on top of me, knocking my head hard into the hardwood floor.

Colors flooded over my eyes.

And then went black.

♠

PROMISES

I woke up with a headache from hell, my throat parched.

Wherever I was, it smelled like bleach and medicine.

I turned on my side, and the bed creaked. The thin blanket wasn't enough for the cool air sweeping over me. The light was too bright. I pulled my pillow, a flat one, over my face.

This was the worst motel ever. I quietly reminded myself to ask for another pillow and a blanket from the maids.

"Kayli," said a deep voice. "You awake?"

That wasn't Wil. I opened my eyes, and peeked out from the shadow of the pillow.

Brandon sat in a bed next to me.

My eyes widened and I stat up, feeling a tug at my hand. I looked down and saw the IV needle poked into my vein and taped down to my skin. A fluid bag hung nearby.

I'd been dreaming I was back in the motel. I looked around the hospital room now. The wide windows were filled with sunshine for an early morning.

Brandon was in a green hospital gown. His muscular legs and arms were bare. His left eye was swollen shut and he had more cuts and bruises along his body. "You okay?" he asked.

I swallowed, nodding. "I passed out?" I asked.

He nodded. "Corey carried you out. Raven got me."

"Alice…" I said, everything coming back to me in a rush.

Brandon frowned. "Axel was outside just as Kevin and some Academy members arrived, she managed to get out of the chaos and run off. They're looking for her now."

My mouth dropped open. "How? And what about Eddie and Mr. Murdock."

"Mr. Murdock slipped Ethan something to make him sleep. But then he spotted Marc coming in, and he bolted as his guard held back and tried to ward us off. The only ones we managed to keep contained were Eddie and the others. We don't even have a right to hold them, only give them up to the police to deal with, and Ethan woke up eventually to press charges against them. Mr. Murdock and Alice are long gone by now."

I groaned. I supposed I should be happy that Brandon was okay. "Everyone's good?"

"So far it seems like it," Brandon said.

I fell back in the bed, overwhelmed and suddenly feeling sick. "Did we get cured yet?"

Brandon smirked. "We're stuck here until we're cleared." He lifted his hand, showing me the needle in his hand. "We're getting the antidote now. And possibly for a couple of weeks."

I closed my eyes. It felt like hours before I opened them. "How long was I out?" I asked.

"Four days," Brandon said.

My eyes widened, and I looked at him, thinking he had to be joking. His face was stern.

"So the bad guys got away," I said.

"Sometimes it happens like that," Brandon said. "But now the police are looking for them. We're out."

"And her phone she got was fake?"

Brandon nodded and smiled, showing me the cut on his lip near the corner that was starting to heal. "My brother's a genius. Who would have thought of that? He didn't just give them what they asked for. He changed the game to motivate them to fight over who got the phone, and then how to proceed. If you ever have to go up into a den of thieves, throw in one gold coin and stand back."

My head spun at the overload of information. I coughed to clear my throat but it wasn't helping making it feel better. "I feel like…"

"Shit?" Brandon asked. "Yeah. Me, too."

Things got quiet for a moment. I had my eyes closed. I think I might have passed out for a couple of minutes. When I opened my eyes again, Brandon had moved to sit on my bed. He had his hand on my stomach.

It was uncomfortable, considering I was nauseated, whether from the poison or the cure, I didn't know. I reached up, intending to grab his hand and move it off of me.

Once I touched him, he gripped my hand and held it. He looked down at me. "Kayli," he said in a gruff voice.

Awkward. I wasn't thinking clearly. I sucked in a breath, wanting to tell him he should go to sleep. If needed, I'd go back to sleep and put off talking to him. The job was done. We'd be here for days. He'd want to talk relationships. I wasn't in the mood.

I pressed a palm to my head, finding it was bandaged. Must have cut it when I hit the floor after tackling Alice. "So everyone's alive, at least," I said.

"On our team, yeah," Brandon said. "Eddie's group is in jail."

"Are we going to get questioned?" I asked. I figured if the police had gotten called in, and I was taken to the hospital, there would be a lot of questions. I squirmed. Cops.

"Nope." Brandon released me and rubbed his face. "No cops. Not for us."

"How did that happen?"

Brandon shrugged. "They're not going to ask about us. We weren't there. Corey stayed behind, as did Axel to testify."

My eyes widened. "What?" Where are they?"

"Axel's getting treatment, too. Marc is with him. Raven and Corey are taking care of things at the apartment. Kevin's running errands for us now." Brandon stood up, stretching and twisting.

I caught an eyeful of muscled butt cheek, and then forced myself to look up.

"Anyway," he said. "Corey isn't in trouble. Ethan turned off his machine once everyone cleared out. We've got some people stationed there to watch out for him until Alice and Mr. Murdock have been captured." He thought some more. "Oh yeah, and Avery. Smart guy, but he seemed to disappear after. We'll have to thank him somehow for helping out.

That was good. Avery did deserve a big reward or something. Maybe they could fix up his car nice for his job. He deserved more. I sighed, falling back on the bed. I turned on my side, trying to make the nausea subside.

Brandon got in beside me, his stomach to my back. He wrapped his arm around my waist.

I closed my eyes. I wasn't going to complain; he was warm. "Brandon," I said. "You were in the bed with me the first night we got captured."

"Yeah," he said behind me. His breath fell on my neck.

"But I was in Corey's bed."

Brandon fell quiet.

"I thought…you were Corey."

"Do you snuggle up to Corey?" he asked.

341

"Were you pretending to be him?"

He made a noise. "I thought you knew it was me."

I turned onto my other side. I had to be careful with stretching out the IV line.

Brandon's cerulean eyes were shining as he peered down at my face. His cheeks were tinged with red.

I kept my hand under my cheek, fighting off going to sleep again to get to the bottom of this. I wasn't sure if I was mad. Maybe because I was tired. I just wanted to know. "You thought I'd know it was you if you crawled into bed next to me?"

"I thought you could tell the difference," he said. "I figured you'd know it was me if I...If I snuggled into you."

I was quiet for a long time, considering. "I didn't know," I said. "That late at night, Corey sometimes just kind of snuggles up close to be comfortable. I didn't think anything of it."

Brandon's side of his mouth lifted. "I'm not jealous," he said. "I told you he's gay."

"I know," I said. "So it wasn't going to go anywhere."

He nodded.

We fell into silence. I was looking at his chest, and then my eyes closed. I was drifting. I thought about Ethan, wondering if he could get an annulment. I wondered when Alice...*Anja*, would be caught. I wondered where Marc was so I could get him to make some food. I thought my stomach might settle down if I at least had some bread or crackers. Or a milkshake and fries.

Brandon leaned in closer. His lips brushed my cheek. "You know now I can't leave you," he whispered.

I mumbled something, trying to tell him to shut up and let me sleep, but I found it hard to focus long enough to utter a syllable. Whatever was in the IV, it was making me really sleepy.

"I need you near me," Brandon said. "I'll never sleep unless you're there. My luck, I'll lose you again."

There was a long pause. I felt his breath on my face, warm.

I couldn't argue with him, really. I was thinking the same thing. I needed to hold onto him, or he might get zapped and we both end up in a trunk again.

I wanted Marc nearby, too. And Axel. Corey and Raven should be here. It didn't feel right without them.

My heart dropped at that thought. Like a heavy weight, sinking me down further.

I was in too deep. Blake was right. I needed to leave sometime before it was too late and I destroyed the group.

*T*here was a knock at the door. Brandon turned, sitting back on the bed and scooting over to Kayli's feet. He smoothed out his hospital gown, covering his privates with the blanket over his waist. Laying next to Kayli had gotten him a little excited. He couldn't help it. "Come in."

Dr. Roberts opened the door. Brandon hadn't seen him in a while. His white hair was combed to one side. His aged face lit up at once. "Good. You're up. Has she woken yet?"

Brandon nodded. "I talked with her for a bit. She's still pretty out of it. She was mumbling for a while."

"That's a good sign if she's waking up." He closed the door behind himself and walked in. "If she wasn't vomiting or convulsing when she woke up, it means the worst of this poison is out of her system. How are you feeling?"

"Fine," Brandon said. He swallowed, feeling uncomfortable in his stomach. The only way he got around the nausea was when he was asleep, and he didn't feel like sleeping right now. He pointed to his own IV fluid bag hanging from a pole. "Does this stuff make you feel sick still, though? My stomach hurts."

"It'll be normal to experience some nausea and light-headedness for a few days," Dr. Roberts said. He adjusted his doctor's coat, unbuttoning it down the center and then pulled a seat up close to the bed. "Funny enough, the cure for thallium is a component that contains cyanide. Of course, not enough to be lethal, but still might make you feel funny."

Brandon checked on Kayli. She was pretty passed out. Her face was relaxed, a look that didn't often appear on her unless she was sleeping. She had scars, cuts and scrapes all over her. She was thinner, too. Running around without eating much for a few days made her look like death was hanging overhead.

Brandon kept a hand on her ankle, but she was dead to the world. That was good; she didn't need to hear this conversation, one he had been expecting. "So when can we leave?" Brandon asked. "Just a few days, right?"

"Sure," Dr. Roberts said. He'd carried in a file. He put it in his lap and then propped his chin up in his hand. "But while we're here, I think it's time we had a talk."

Brandon said nothing, simply waiting out Dr. Roberts. He knew what it would be about. Dr. Roberts wanted a few details of the last few days. He'd given a report, but Brandon had been ill, and sometimes when you're sick, you miss giving important clues that could help an investigation. Luckily it was Dr. Roberts and not a police officer.

Dr. Roberts motioned to Kayli but spoke to Brandon. "She's been hanging around a lot. Are we making friends?"

His eyes widened in surprise and instinctively he turned and looked at Kayli again, to see if she was awake. He wasn't sure if he should talk about her while she was right there. He shrugged. "I know she got involved, but she was with me when I was kidnapped and—"

"The moment she got out," Dr. Roberts said, "she should have been here at the hospital."

"Don't look at me," Brandon said. "I was kidnapped and in the back of a car. I agree she should have come straight here."

"And the moment you were un-kidnapped," Dr. Roberts said, "you were with her." Dr. Roberts lifted his

345

head and then grabbed the file. He held it up to show Brandon the thickness. "Now I've got a lot of people asking me who this girl is and why was she involved."

"Shouldn't we talk about this somewhere else?" Brandon asked. He stood, motioning to the door.

Dr. Roberts held up a hand. "Sit," he said. "I just want to hear from someone who will give me an honest answer."

"Who hasn't given you an honest answer?" Brandon asked. He moved, sitting on the other bed, hoping not to disturb Kayli by sitting next to her again.

"All your friends say she's *their* girlfriend," Dr. Roberts said. "I think they feel if they tell me she's just a friend that I'm going to insist she find another place to live. I've sworn that isn't the case, but they seem insistent."

This wasn't the conversation Brandon wanted to have right now. What did it matter to him who she was with? But then, the Academy wanted to be aware of the activities of anyone they associated with. Brandon suspected they didn't really care *who* she was with, only that they got a straight answer.

The others claimed her as their girlfriend? He wasn't sure how to respond. Technically... no. It's not like he'd asked her for a commitment. He was fond of her, but he couldn't call her a girlfriend at this point.

Before Brandon could figure out a response, Dr. Roberts continued, "And then I've got another young man in my lobby right now, claiming he wants to see Miss Winchester. I told him I couldn't allow for him to come in until she was awake."

Brandon nearly jumped to his feet again. *Young man?* "Who?" he asked, panic taking over. "Is it Wil?" If it was, he was ready to race downstairs and drag that brother of hers up here. She'd be thrilled. They could finally put the whole mess behind them and start new.

Dr. Roberts opened his mouth and then stopped, frowning and looking sympathetic. "Sorry," he said. "I didn't mean to get your hopes up. It's Blake Coaltar." He paused, giving Brandon a stern look. "The same man we had targeted months ago, and seems to keep popping up on our radar."

Disappointment flooded through Brandon. "I didn't call him," he said. "Sometime while I was kidnapped, she got in touch with him."

"And he's claiming she now works for him," Dr. Roberts said. "Newly hired."

Brandon's head reeled back. "Can't be," he said. "When?"

"I don't know, but he's demanding to see his employee. Someone has to deal with him."

"You want me to?"

"No," Dr. Roberts said. He pointed to Kayli sleeping. "She has to.'

Brandon tilted his head. That didn't seem likely right now. "What do you mean?"

"Blake keeps getting roped into your assignments, and now this kidnapping. She's the one calling him." Dr. Roberts patted the file. "It's in here that she's getting involved with him. If you're going to keep hosting her at your apartment, she needs to either let go of Mr. Coaltar or you need to keep her at distance. We don't want this new guy getting too much information. We strongly advise against contact."

Brandon shook his head. "We can't let her go now. We promised to hang onto her while we searched for her brother. He's missing."

"What does it matter where she stays if she's looking for her brother?" he asked. "Rent her another apartment. On the other side of town."

Brandon frowned, looking at the floor. This sounded more like an Academy request, one that he might not be able to avoid. "So either she gets rid of Blake or she has to move."

"You've got it," Dr. Roberts said. "There's a rumor going around that his friend Doyle has been getting access to Academy intel, and they're examining our little organization. I have a feeling she might be feeding them information."

Brandon stood up this time, fists clenched. "That's not possible."

"We wish to eliminate the possibility. She's on our closed adoption list, and she's learned way too much for someone your team hasn't yet established trust with." Dr. Roberts stood, carrying his file, and headed toward the door. "Think about it, Brandon. If she's leaking information, there's no way she'll be invited into the Academy, and there's a good chance her adoption will come under investigation, and she'll be redirected to another team that can keep an eye on her better."

Shit. That wasn't good. The Academy, if it wanted to and thought it was necessary, would remove a person from any group. Leaking secret information was bad for the Academy. Lives were at stake. Reputations were important to them. Exposure risked them all.

It also meant if their team was exposed in some way as being part of some secret group, the Academy would remove the team. Brandon, Marc and the others would have to forfeit their own positions within the Academy in order to save the entire group from becoming discovered. Limited liabilities. They might be under protection of the

Academy forever, but they wouldn't be able to take up an assignment for a while.

"Won't happen again," Brandon said. "I'll keep an eye on her. I'll make sure Blake stays out of contact."

"We may take your team off of accepting assignments for another month. Not just for recovery time, but to allow you to focus on her brother and straighten out your situation before we risk exposing anyone further."

Brandon's head lowered and he stared at the ground. He wished Axel was here, or Marc. But they might not be able to do anything about it. The decision had already been made.

He had to get Kayli to understand. Was she really giving up Academy secrets to Blake? He avoided looking at her now. Didn't she understand what she was doing? They'd told her it was a secret. He wanted to believe she'd only turned to Blake for help.

She needed training, then. She needed to know who was acceptable to turn to for help.

Dr. Roberts opened the door and stepped out. He stopped, popped in his head again and said, "By the way, when you've got time, you should really go see Mr. Henry Anderson."

Brandon lifted his head. He recalled the older man from another team, who'd helped them out at Ethan Murdock's party. "Henry? Why?"

"I've got a feeling you might want some help with Miss Winchester. If you're going to keep her under a closed adoption, you'll need to know how to handle her since she's been so deeply involved."

Brandon nodded quietly, consenting.

Dr. Roberts closed the door.

Brandon looked over at Kayli. She slept on. He was surprised she managed to stay asleep.

Brandon yawned, and rubbed gently at his severely bruised ribs. Every muscle in him hurt.

But he couldn't sleep. He needed to talk to Axel and the others. The Academy might remove Kayli from the group, or if the team refused to let her go, they could remove the group from the Academy altogether. They couldn't risk that. He had to get them to agree to stand together to keep her.

He couldn't let her go. He'd told her that already and he'd been dead serious. He kept his promises. He'd make sure Kayli was safe, that Wil was safe.

He had his own growing need now, too. He had to keep an eye on Kayli. Alice and Mr. Murdock were still out there somewhere. If they weren't caught, who knew when they might look for revenge, or try for something else.

Kayli had turned to Blake for help, though. That was a problem. She didn't understand why that would be dangerous. He didn't know what she saw in him. Sure, Blake had helped them out. Twice.

Didn't matter. He was dangerous. His very existence right now threatened Kayli and their team with the Academy.

And the last person he'd lose Kayli to would be Blake Coaltar.

THANK YOU!

Thank you for purchasing this book!
For new release and exclusive Academy and
C. L. Stone information sign up here:
http://eepurl.com/zuIDj

If you enjoyed reading *The Academy - Fake*, let me know.
Review it: at your favorite retailer and/or Goodreads

Connect with C. L. Stone online
Twitter: https://twitter.com/CLStoneX
Facebook: https://www.facebook.com/clstonex

Books by C. L. Stone

The Academy Ghost Bird Series:
Introductions
First Days
Friends vs. Family
Forgiveness and Permission
Drop of Doubt
Push and Shove
House of Korba
The Other Side of Envy (April 2015)

The Academy Scarab Beetle Series
Thief
Liar
Fake
Accessory (Summer 2015)

Other Books:
Spice God
Smoking Gun

BONUS!

Turn the page for an exclusive sneak peek at ACCESSORY, the next book in The Scarab Beetle Series

The Academy

The Scarab Beetle Series

Accessory

Book Four

♠

Coming Summer 2015

Written by C. L. Stone

Published by

Arcato Publishing

♠

HARD ROAD

*A*fter a battle with a poison and taking a couple of days off to recover, I'd spent an entire day with Corey playing video games. Eventually, Corey needed to go with Brandon to some secret Academy meeting, and I was left with Raven for the evening. I told them I didn't need a babysitter, but as usual, no one listened.

I was in the middle of gorging on McDonald's chicken nuggets with Raven when Marc rushed in, finding us at the coffee table with piles of food and the TV on an episode of Sponge Bob: one of the few shows Raven could understand without asking me a jack ton of questions about what words meant.

Marc was breathless, as if he'd taken the stairs instead of the elevator. "I think I've got a lead on Wil," he said.

I abandoned the food and the television was immediately forgotten, but I couldn't wrestle any other information out of Marc, no matter how much I begged or threatened.

But at least we got moving; he rushed us out and into the black SUV in the parking lot. It was dark, around nine, and chilly.

We were quiet until Marc pulled the truck onto the I-26 ramp. I'd been trying to simply wrap my head around what we were doing. Marc may have found Wil. We were supposed to keep our distance, but he was taking me to see him.

"Where is he?" I asked, unable to keep silent a second longer. Since it was late on a Friday night, he obviously wasn't at school.

"We're headed his way," Marc said. He pointed out toward the horizon. "If we hurry, we might catch him. I don't know how long he'll stay, so I thought you could at least get a visual."

Marc obviously wasn't going to give up more details, so I fell quiet, like if I spoke, Wil might hear us coming for him and leave before I got a chance to see him. My excitement rose as the miles passed.

My heart swelled for Marc, too, for continuing to hunt for Wil, even while I had almost given up. I didn't want to admit it to any of them, but I felt if Wil really wanted to talk to me, he would have found me by now. Maybe he was in danger and avoiding me, but how much danger could he be in to not even let me know he was safe? No, I was starting to believe maybe I'd done something wrong. Maybe he thought I was neglectful or didn't care.

I wouldn't admit it to the guys, but I was afraid to face him and find out.

I felt in my pocket for a ponytail holder and combed my hair back with my hands until I could put it up. I'd left the apartment in my own old jeans, a new pair of boots Corey had bought for me, one of Brandon's T-shirts, and a jacket stolen from Marc's closet when it had started getting cold out. I carried a cell phone now, too. It was something they all insisted on and Corey had programmed each of their numbers in, plus a few extra from Academy members around the area, just in case.

Marc was in a leather jacket, black boots and jeans. His longer hair on top had grown down over his blue-green eyes, the mismatched colors contrasted with his dark lashes and hair. His hands twisted at the wheel as he drove. Lines etched into his face told me I wasn't the only one anxious about getting there in time.

Raven was complacent. Sitting calmly with his dark eyes and short cropped hair, he was the epitome of patience as he stared fixedly out the front windshield. Wearing a thick, long-sleeved black sweatshirt, jeans and boots, he almost hid all the tattoos. The only thing left to show his rebellious nature was the lip ring he'd put back in. He fiddled with it with his tongue; I could see it poke out further every once in a while.

Every bit of him was Russian: looks, voice, and attitude.

"Where is Wil?" I asked, breaking the silence again. "Should we be interfering? I mean, that Mr. Blackbourne had said..."

"I just want you to see him," Marc said. He slid a glance over at me. "Could you confirm it's him?"

I sat up quickly, swallowing against my heart in my throat, suddenly thinking the worst. "Did you find a body?"

Marc's expression moved from shocked to confused. "No," he said quickly. "I just want to make sure I'm following the right guy. You don't have to approach him now, but we should follow him where we can. See what he's up to."

"He's not a troublemaker," I said, defensive. "He's a good guy."

"I believe you," Marc said. He smiled. "Don't worry, I

3

just want to make sure. If all he's doing is trying to live on his own and take care of himself, then maybe we can approach him about college. We can even do it in a way to make it look like you weren't helping."

"I don't feel like I am," I said.

"Little Thief," Raven said, reaching an arm around and squeezing my shoulder once tightly. I leaned into his side, feeling the muscle of his chest and stomach against my arm. It was a small amount of support and I welcomed his comfort. "There are many reasons to leave a home. Don't assume bad when it could be something else, even stupidity."

"He's not stupid."

Raven blew out a slow breath that caught wisps of my hair, pressing the strands back against my forehead. "We all do stupid things sometimes."

I started to wrestle myself away from him but he pulled me back in. "No, listen. We all think we can do things alone. It's not how it works. We need other people."

"Right," Marc said. "It's unlikely he is in trouble to a degree that it is threatening his life, but just in case, we don't want to start running around without checking first. If we follow him around, we can see who is influencing him. Or maybe he's just hanging out with friends. We'll figure out the truth."

"But he's just a kid," I said, still feeling strongly that Wil wasn't a bad guy. "He wouldn't be doing something stupid. He wouldn't get into trouble with the police. Where are we going?"

"There's a shelter," he said.

"Shelter?"

"A place where runaways are taken if they get picked up. Or beaten and abused kids who need a place to stay go while the system figures out where to put them next. There's a couple of them in town."

"But how did you find out he was there?"

"A boy with his description was caught by the police recently and taken there. He used another name, but I thought he might have lied."

"Why would he?" I asked.

"If you are going to run away from home, you usually come up with a name. If he gave them a false one, it would take the police several days to identify who he is."

"So we are going to the shelter," I said, putting the pieces together. "Just in case."

"We want to get to him before he finds an opportunity to run off again."

"But once he's in the system, won't they hold on to him? We tried to leave my dad once but the police picked us up and brought us back. They said if we tried again we'd go to juvenile court."

"They were scaring you," Raven said. "They don't have time to chase runaways all over. They have too much to do. So they warn you to scare you into staying."

Marc twisted his hands at the wheel again, and then sped up well over the speed limit. "But if he got picked up and didn't talk to the police and lied about his name, they'd put him in a shelter until they can figure out where to put him. That is, he'll be there until he can find a way to leave."

"He can leave?"

"You can't keep a kid still if he really wants to leave."

"How do you know all this?"

Marc pursed his lips, turning to look out the side window. The intersection he stopped at was dark and he looked like he wasn't sure which way to go. He made a left, heading along a street that looked run down, with trees on either side and potholes in the asphalt. "Because I ran away a lot as a kid. I've been through the system. Several times."

He did seem to know where we were going. I swallowed, checking outside to see where we were headed.

The potholes were plentiful. The truck careened forward and I grabbed onto both Marc and Raven before smacking my head into the dashboard. The lane was small, like it only fit one car at a time, so there was no way to avoid the bumpy ride.

A house sat at the end of the lane, surrounded by thick trees. It was wide, one story and brick with a circular gravel driveway. Marc stopped the truck close to the entrance and shut off the engine. The house had shuttered windows, bushes pruned until they were almost sticks and a few dried leaves still attached. "This looks like someone's home," I said. For some reason, a local government run shelter felt like it should be more institutional looking. I wasn't sure what I'd been expecting at the word *shelter*, but this wasn't anywhere close to what I would have dreamed up.

"Yup," Marc said. He opened the door, hopping out and reaching a hand out for me. "Raven, stay here. No offense but one look at you and they're going to have their guard up."

"Just hurry," he said. He slid over, taking up position behind the wheel.

Gravel crunched under my feet as we headed for the front door. The place gave off a forgotten feel. *Don't look at us. Nothing to see here.*

We stood on the tiny concrete porch. Marc pushed the doorbell.

"Let me talk to her," he said.

"To who?"

The door rattled as locks were being undone then cracked open just enough to reveal a shadowy figure behind a still-linked chain. She was older, with wrinkles around her eyes and mouth. Her blond hair was pulled back sharply and her eyes were critical.

"Who are you?" she asked in a tense voice.

"Mary," he said. "It's Marc."

She tilted her head to the side, like she was trying to get a better angle. "Marc Weiland? What are you doing here?"

"Sorry to just show up like this," he said quietly. "We're looking for someone."

"Hang on." She shut the door and released the chain and opened it again, stepping back to give us room. She reached over and flicked a switch.

Harsh florescent lights shone in the nearly empty hallway. The tiles were utility, like what you'd expect in a hospital or a school. Walls were bare except for a security keypad beside the door. There was a single bench, a door to the right and the end of the hall extended to the right and left, not revealing anything else about the interior. It was surreal that, like the outside, while poorly illuminated, it looked like a regular, everyday house and the first step inside had the feeling of an institution.

Mary's wrinkles extended to her neck and her hands

were bony. She had a small frame, and wore jeans and a light sweater. She turned to Marc after she shut the door. "Who in heaven's name..." She trailed off, as if losing her train of thought.

"Did anyone new show up here in the last few days?" Marc asked. "A guy, almost seventeen, glasses?"

"We've had an influx of kids," she said. "Some left and others..."

"Do you still take Polaroids of the intakes?" he asked.

"I've got a digital camera now," she said. "Come on."

They headed to the office. I lingered in the foyer for a moment. Somehow I felt like if I stared hard enough through the walls, I would see the rest of this house. I wanted to, because if Wil was here, I wanted to get to him quickly. I couldn't imagine being brought to a place like this. Mary seemed nice, but it still felt like a cold institution. Did anyone actually live here?

As if in answer to my curiosity, a young girl popped her head out from around the hall corner. She was a little black girl with apple cheeks and rows of short braids along her head. Her eyes were big and she stared at me.

I did a short two finger wave.

She continued to stare.

"You lost?" I asked quietly.

Her stare continued, and I got the feeling she wasn't curious about me as much as she was looking for Mary and she supposed to be poking her head down here.

I pointed to the door where Mary was. "She's in there. You want me to get her for you?"

Still the stare continued. She wasn't going to tell me to do anything.

"Kayli," Marc reappeared in the doorway. He gestured

to come in.

I pointed toward the girl. "I think Mary is being requested elsewhere," I said.

Marc peered down the hallway at the little girl. He squinted at her and then leaned back into the office. "Mary, you've got a straggler."

Mary emerged, and the little girl pulled back, disappearing behind the corner. Mary shook her head. "Go ahead into the office," she said, encouraging me. "I left the pictures on the desk. I'll see what she needs." She walked down the hallway, disappearing after the girl. There were murmurs, mostly Mary, and it sounded like she was disciplining the young girl to be patient and wait and not to go down the hall unless it was an emergency.

I joined Marc inside the small office. It, too, was very sparsely furnished. A simple desk sat in the middle of the room, with a single computer on it. There was a file cabinet, and a chair in front of the desk. The walls were dingy and bare.

The desk contained a tablet. Marc was swiping through a photo album on the illuminated screen. He curled his fingers at me. "Come take a look."

I hovered over his shoulder, looking through the array of pictures, some girls, but mostly boys. One I recognized as the girl from down the hallway.

None looked like Wil.

Disappointed, I nudged Marc aside, going through each picture one by one. There weren't many. Some were marked as having been taken in, but then left. One looked sort of like Wil, but his hair was too long, and the glasses weren't his. Plus, the jawline wasn't right.

"No," I said, pointing to the look-a-like. "I can see

why you'd think this one might be him but..."

"What about him?" he asked, pointing to another boy, who had a similar haircut and glasses but didn't resemble Wil anywhere else.

I shook my head, feeling some relief. Part of it was I couldn't imagine Wil living in a place like this. No that it might have been horrible, but that it didn't seem all that comfortable from my perspective.

The other part was that I didn't have to confront him yet. I preferred the idea of him approaching me when he was ready. It was torture to think of what I'd say to him if I did run into him again.

I was going to explain to Marc that I appreciated his help, when a phone rang. I looked at Marc expectantly.

Marc took his phone out, looked at it and then shook his head. "Not mine. Must be yours."

I blinked, surprised. I wasn't used to having one. I took it out, noticed an unknown number, but answered it just in case. "Hello?"

"Kayli-Bayli!" cried a shrill voice, male. Sort of. "God, tell me you've got a nice club or casino in this town."

I had a flash of a memory: a dark-skinned, bubble-butt crossdresser in yellow spandex and a blue halter. "Future?"

"Did you forget your old friend already?" she asked. "Look, I've got a favor to ask you."

I looked at Marc, who shrugged. I wasn't sure if he could hear, but I must have looked confused. "How did you know this number?"

"I asked your boyfriend," she said, and left it at that, leaving me to wonder who she meant. "I need you to meet me at the pier. The one off of...where are we?" she asked to someone on her end. There was a voice, but I couldn't understand what was being said. She came back. "Palm Island?"

"Isle of Palms?" I asked. "You're in town?"

"Sure," she said. "There's a pier here, and you have to come see this boat. It's striking. I'd almost give up my boobs for one of these. Maybe if I show my boobs to enough guys I could afford it."

I checked the window; it was dark outside and the wind was sweeping through the nearby trees. "You want me to go right now?"

"It won't take five minutes. After everything I did in Florida to help you out, could you come hang out with me for a bit?"

"What's going on?" I asked.

"You'll see," she said and then hung up.

I made a face as I put the phone down.

"Something bad?" Marc asked.

I shrugged and then put the phone away. "Future is calling in a favor. She's in town."

Marc stared blankly at me for a minute, and then his eyes widened and his mouth popped open as he seemed to remember who I was talking about. "Oh my god. She's back? Tell me we don't have to. What favor? What..." He pressed a palm to his cheek, rubbing. "Wow."

I was feeling the same way. I couldn't guess the sort of favor Future would ask, but I had a feeling it was going to be something beyond my wildest imagination.

ABOUT C. L. STONE

Certification

- Marvelour of Wonder

- Active Participant of Scary Situations

- Official Member of F.A.M.E.

Experience

Spent an extraordinary number of years with absolutely no control over the capping of imagination, fun, and curiosity. Willingly takes part in impossible problems only to come up with the most ludicrous solution. Due to unfortunate circumstances, will no longer experience feeling on a small spot on my left calf.

Skills

Secret Keeper | Occasion Riser | Barefoot Walker Strange Acceptance | Magic Maker | Restless Reckless | Gravity Defiant | Fairy Tale Reader | Story Maker-Upper | Amusingly Baffled | Comprehensive Curiousness | Usually Unbelievable

Made in the USA
Charleston, SC
27 March 2015